About the Authors

Maureen Child is the author of more than 130 romance novels and novellas that routinely appear on bestseller lists and have won numerous awards, including the National Reader's Choice Award. A seven-time nominee for the prestigious RITA® award from Romance Writers of America, one of her books was made into a CBS-TV movie called The Soul Collecter. Maureen recently moved from California to the mountains of Utah and is trying to get used to snow.

Sophie Pembroke has been dreaming, reading and writing romance ever since she read her first Mills & Boon novel as a teen, so getting to write romance fiction for a living is a dream come true! Born in Abu Dhabi, Sophie grew up in Wales and now lives in Herfordshire with her scientist husband, her incredibly imaginative daughter and her adventurous, adorable little boy. In Sophie's world, happy is for ever after, everything stops for tea and there's always time for one more page.

Nikki Logan lives amongst a string of wetlands in Australia with her partner and a menagerie of animals. Her stories are full of romance in descriptive, natural environments. She believes the richness and danger of wild places perfectly mirror the passion and risk of falling in love. Nikki authored her first romance on a sabbatical from work. Determined to be published by forty, her first book hit shelves in February 2010, her fortieth year, and she hasn't looked back since.

Scandalous Secrets

Scandalous Secrets:
Scandalous Reputation

MAUREEN CHILD

SOPHIE PEMBROKE

NIKKI LOGAN

MILLS & BOON

First Published in Great Britain 2020
By Mills & Boon, an imprint of HarperCollins*Publishers*
1 London Bridge Street, London, SE1 9GF

SCANDALOUS SECRETS: SCANDALOUS REPUTATION
© 2020 Harlequin Books S.A.

To Kiss a King © 2012 Maureen Child
A Groom Worth Waiting For © 2014 Sophie Pembroke
Rapunzel in New York © 2011 Nikki Logan

ISBN: 978-0-263-28207-8

MIX
Paper from
responsible sources
FSC
www.fsc.org
FSC™ C007454

This book is produced from independently certified FSC™ paper to ensure responsible forest management.

For more information visit: www.harpercollins.co.uk/green

Printed and bound in Spain
by CPI, Barcelona

TO KISS A KING

MAUREEN CHILD

To Susan Mallery, a great writer and an
even better friend. For all of the shared dreams,
all of the good laughs and all those yet to come.
Thanks, Susan.

One

Garrett King was in Hell.

Dozens of screaming, laughing children raced past him and he winced as their voices hit decibels only dogs should have been able to hear. Happiest Place on Earth? He didn't think so.

How he had let himself be talked into this, he had no idea.

"Getting soft," he muttered darkly and leaned one hand on the hot metal balustrade in front of him only to wrench his hand back instantly. He glanced at his palm, sighed and reached for a napkin out of his cousin's bag to wipe the sticky cotton candy off his skin.

"You could be at the office," he told himself sternly, wadding up the napkin and tossing it into a trash can. "You could be checking invoices, keeping tabs on the new client. But no, you had to say yes to your cousin instead."

Jackson King had pulled out all the stops getting Garrett to go along with this little family adventure. Jackson's wife, Casey, was apparently "worried" because Garrett was alone too much. Nice woman Casey, he told himself. But did no one ever consider that maybe a man was alone because he *wanted* to be?

But he still could have begged off if it had been just Casey and Jackson doing the asking. But Garrett's cousin had cheated.

He had had his daughters ask "Uncle" Garrett to go with them and frankly, when faced with three of the cutest kids in the world, it would have been impossible to say no. And Jackson knew it, the clever bastard.

"Hey, cuz!" Jackson's shout sounded out and Garrett turned to give him a hard look.

Jackson only laughed. "Casey, honey," he said, turning to his stunning wife, "did you see that? I don't think Garrett's having any fun."

"About that," Garrett cut in, lifting his voice to be heard over the raucous noise rising from the crowd, "I was thinking I'd just head out now. Leave you guys to some family fun."

"You *are* family, Garrett," Casey pointed out.

Before he could speak, Garrett felt a tug at his pants leg. He looked down into Mia's upturned face. "Uncle Garrett, we're going on the fast mountain ride. You wanna come?"

At five, Mia King was already a heartbreaker. From her King blue eyes to the missing front tooth to the dimple in her cheek, she was absolutely adorable. And not being a dummy, she knew how to work it already, too.

"Uh…" Garrett glanced behind Mia to her younger sisters Molly and Mara. Molly was three and Mara was just beginning to toddle. The three of them were unstoppable, Garrett told himself wryly.

There was just no way he was getting out of this day

early. One girl pouting was hard to resist. Three were too much for any man to stand against.

"How about I stand here and watch your stuff while you guys go on the ride?"

Jackson snorted a laugh that Garrett ignored. For God's sake, he owned the most respected security company in the country and here he was haggling with a five-year-old.

Garrett and Jackson had been good friends for years. Most of the King cousins were close, but he and Jackson had worked closely together over the years. Garrett's security company and Jackson's company, King Jets, fed off each other. With Garrett's high-priced clients renting Jackson's luxury jets, both companies were thriving for the loosely defined partnership.

Jackson's wife, Casey, on the other hand, was one of those happily married women who saw every determined bachelor as a personal challenge.

"You going on the Matterhorn with us?" Jackson asked, plucking Mara from his wife's arms. The chubby toddler slapped at his cheeks gleefully and Garrett watched with some amusement as Jackson practically melted. The man was a sap when it came to his family. Funny, because in business, Jackson King was a cutthroat kind of guy that nobody wanted to cross.

"Nope," Garrett told him and lifted the baby out of his cousin's arms. With the crazed population explosion in the King family, Garrett was getting used to dealing with kids. Comfortably settling the tiny girl on his hip, he said, "I'll wait here with Mara and the rest of your—" he paused to glance down at the stroller and the bags already piled high on it "—stuff."

"You could ride with me," Mia insisted, turning those big blue eyes on him.

"Oh, she's good," Jackson whispered on a laugh.

Garrett went down on one knee and looked her in the eye. "How about I stay here with your sister and you tell me all about the ride when you get off?"

She scowled a little, clearly unused to losing, then grinned. "Okay."

Casey took both of the girls' hands, smiled at Garrett and headed for the line.

"I didn't ask you to come along so you could just stand around, you know," Jackson said.

"Yeah. Why did you ask me along? Better yet, why'd I say yes?"

Jackson laughed, looked over his shoulder at his wife and then said, "One word. Casey. She thinks you're lonely. And if you think I'm going to listen to her worry about you all by myself, you're nuts."

Mara slapped Garrett's face. He swiveled his head to smile at the baby. "Your daddy's scared of your mommy."

"Damn straight," Jackson admitted with a laugh. He headed off after the rest of his family and called back, "If she gets cranky, there's a bottle in the diaper bag."

"I think I can handle a baby," he shouted back, but Jackson was already swallowed by the crowd.

"It's just you and me, kid," Garrett told the girl who laughed delightedly and squirmed as if she wanted to be turned loose to run. "Oh, no, you don't. I put you down, you disappear and your mommy kills me."

"Down." Mara looked mutinous.

"No."

She scowled again then tried a coy smile.

"Man," Garrett said with a smile. "Are women *born* knowing how to do that?"

Bright, cheerful calliope music erupted from somewhere nearby and the smell of popcorn floated on the breeze. A dog wearing a top hat was waltzing with Cinderella to the cheers of the crowd. And Garrett was holding a baby and feeling as out of place as—hell, he couldn't even think of anything as out of place as he felt at the moment.

This was not his world, he thought, jiggling Mara when she started fussing. Give Garrett King a dangerous situation, a shooter going after a high-profile target, a kidnapping, even a jewelry heist, and he was in his element.

This happy, shiny stuff? Not so much.

Owning and operating the biggest, most successful security company in the country was bound to color your outlook on the world. Their clients ranged from royalty to wealthy industrialists, computer billionaires and politicians. Because of their own immense wealth, the King brothers knew how to blend in when arranging security. Because of their expertise, their reputation kept growing. Their firm was the most sought-after of its kind on the planet. The King twins flew all over the world to meet the demands of their clients. And he and his twin, Griffin, were good with that. Not everyone could be relaxed and optimistic. There had to be people like he and Griff around to take care of the dirty jobs.

That was his comfort zone, he told himself as he watched Jackson and his family near the front of the line. Casey was holding Molly and Jackson had Mia up on his shoulders. They looked...perfect. And Garrett was glad for his cousin, really. In fact, he was happy for all of the Kings who had recently jumped off a cliff into the uncharted waters of marriage and family. But he wouldn't be joining them.

Guys like him didn't do happy endings.

"That's okay, though," he whispered, planting a kiss on Mara's forehead. "I'll settle for spending time with you guys. How's that?"

She burbled something he took as agreement then fixed her gaze on a bright pink balloon. "Boon!"

Garrett was just going to buy it for her when he noticed the woman.

Alexis Morgan Wells was having a *wonderful* day. Disneyland was everything she had hoped it would be. She loved everything about it. The music, the laughter. The cartoon characters wandering around interacting with the crowd. She loved the gardens, the topiary statues; she even loved the smell of the place. It was like childhood and dreams and magic all at once.

The music from the last ride she'd been on was still dancing through her mind—she had a feeling it would be for hours—when she noticed the man coming up to her. Her good mood quickly drained away as the same man who had followed her on to It's a Small World hurried to catch up. He'd had the seat behind her in the boat and had come close to ruining the whole experience for her as he insisted on trying to talk to her.

Just as he was now.

"Come on, babe. I'm not a crazy person or anything. I just want to buy you lunch. Is that so bad?"

She half turned and gave him a patient, if tight, smile. "I've already told you I'm not interested, so please go away."

Instead of being rebuffed, his eyes lit up. "You're British, aren't you? The accent's cool."

"Oh, for heaven's sake."

She was really going to have to work on that, she told herself sternly. If she wasn't paying close attention, her clipped accent immediately branded her as "different." Though it would take a much better ear than that of the man currently bothering her, to recognize that her accent wasn't British, but Cadrian.

But if she worked at it, she could manage an American accent—since her mother had been born in California. Thinking about her mom brought a quick zip of guilt shooting through her, but Alex tamped it down. She'd deal with it later. She was absolutely sure her mother would understand why Alex had had to leave—she was just in no hurry to hear how much worry she'd caused by taking off.

After all, Alex was a bright, capable adult and if she wanted a vacation, why should she have to jump through hoops to take one? There, she was feeling better already. Until she picked up on the fact that her would-be admirer was still talking. Honestly, she was trying to stay under the radar and this man was drawing way too much attention to her.

Trying to ignore him, Alex quickened her steps, moving in and out of the ever-shifting crowd with the grace earned from years of dance lessons. She wore a long, tunic-style white blouse, blue jeans and blue platform heels, and, at the moment, she was wishing she'd worn sneakers. Then she could have sprinted for some distance.

The minute that thought entered her mind, she dismissed it, though. Running through a crowd like a lunatic would only draw the notice she was trying to avoid.

"C'mon, babe, it's *lunch*. What could it hurt?"

"I don't eat," she told him, "I'm an oxygenarian."

He blinked at her. "What?"

"Nothing," she muttered, hurrying again. Stop talking to him, she told herself. Ignore him and he'll go away.

She headed for the landmark right ahead of her. The snow-topped mountain in the middle of Anaheim, California. This particular mountain was probably one of the best known peaks in the world. Alex smiled just looking at it. She lifted her gaze and watched as toboggans filled with screaming, laughing people jolted around curves and splashed through lagoons, sending waves of water into the air. The line for the mountain was a long one and as her gaze moved over the people there, she saw *him*. He was watching her. A big man with black hair, a stern jaw and a plump baby on his hip.

In one quick instant, she felt a jolt of something like "recognition." As if something inside her, *knew* him. Had been searching for him. Unfortunately, judging by the black-haired little girl he was holding, some other woman had found him first.

"Quit walking so fast, will ya?" the annoying guy behind her whined.

Alex fixed her gaze on the sharp-eyed man and felt his stare hit her as powerfully as a touch. Then his eyes shifted from her to the man behind her and back again. He seemed to understand the situation instantly.

"There you are, honey!" he called out, smiling directly at Alex. "What took you so long?"

Smiling broadly, she accepted the help he was offering and ran to him. He greeted her with a grin then dropped one arm around her shoulders, pulling her in close to his side. Only then did he shift his gaze to the disappointed man.

"There a problem here?" Her Knight in Shining Denim demanded.

"No," the guy muttered, shaking his head. "No problem. Later."

And he was gone.

Alex watched him go with a sigh of relief. Not that he had ever scared her or anything, but she hadn't wanted to waste her first day in Disneyland being irritated. The big man beside her still had his arm around her and Alex liked it. He was big and strong and it was hard not to appreciate a guy who had seen you needed help and offered it without a qualm.

"Boon!"

The little girl's voice shattered the moment and with that reminder that her hero was probably someone else's husband, Alex slipped out from under his arm. Glancing up at the little girl, she smiled. "You're a beauty, aren't you? Your daddy must be very proud."

"Oh, he is," the man beside her said, his voice so deep it seemed to sink right inside her. "And he's got two more just like her."

"Really." She wasn't sure why the news that he was the father of three was so disappointing, but there it was.

"Yeah. My cousin and his wife have the other two on the ride right now. I'm just watching this one for them."

"Oh." She smiled, pleasure rushing through her. "Then you're not her father?"

He smiled, too, as if he knew exactly what she was thinking. "Not a chance. I wouldn't do that to some poor, unsuspecting kid."

Alex looked into his eyes and enjoyed the sparkle she found there. He was relishing this little flirtation as much as she was. "Oh, I don't know. A hero might make a very good father."

"Hero? I'm hardly that."

"You were for me a minute ago," she said. "I couldn't seem to convince that man to leave me alone, so I really appreciate your help."

"You're welcome. But you could have gone to a security guard and had the guy thrown out. Probably should have."

No, going to a security guard would have involved making statements, filling out paperwork and then her identity would be revealed and the lovely day she'd planned would have been ruined.

She shook her head, pushed her long blond hair back from her face and turned to sweep her gaze across the manicured flower gardens, the happy kids and the brilliant blue sky overhead. "No, he wasn't dangerous. Just irritating."

He laughed and she liked the sound of it.

"Boon, Gar," the little girl said in a voice filled with the kind of determination only a single-minded toddler could manage.

"Right. Balloon." He lifted one hand to the balloon seller, and the guy stepped right up, gently tying the string of a bright pink balloon to the baby's wrist. While Garrett paid the man, the baby waved her arm, squealing with delight as the balloon danced and jumped to her whim.

"So, I think introductions are in order," he said. "This demanding female is Mara and I'm Garrett."

"Alexis, but call me Alex," she said, holding her right hand out to him.

He took her hand in his and the instant her skin brushed along his, Alex felt ripples of something really intriguing washing throughout her body. Then he let her go and the delightful heat dissipated.

"So, Alex, how's your day going?"

She laughed a little. "Until that one little moment, it was going great. I love it here. It's my first time, and I've heard so much about this place…"

"Ah," he said nodding, "that explains it."

She tensed. "Explains what?"

"If it's your first time here, you're having so much fun that all of these crowds don't bother you."

"Oh, no. I think it's wonderful. Everyone seems so nice, well, except for—"

"That one little moment?" he asked, repeating her words to her.

"Yes, exactly." Alex smiled again and reluctantly took a step back. As lovely as this was, talking to a handsome man who had no idea who she was, it would be better for her if she ended it now and went on her way. "Thank you again for the rescue, but I should really be going…"

He tipped his head to one side and looked at her. "Meeting someone?"

"No, but—"

"Then what's your hurry?"

Her heartbeat sped up at the invitation in his eyes. He didn't want her to leave. And how nice that was. He actually liked her.

The darling little girl was still playing with her balloon, paying no attention at all to the two adults with her.

Alex looked up into Garrett's pale blue eyes and did some fast thinking. She had to keep a low profile, true. But that didn't mean she had to be a hermit during her… vacation, did it? And what kind of holiday would it be if there were no "romance" included?

"What do you say," he added, "hang with us today. Rescue me from a day filled with too many kids?"

"*You* need rescuing?"

She saw the teasing glint in his eyes and responded to it with a smile.

"Trust me. My cousin's girls all have my number. If you're not there to protect me, who knows what might happen?"

Tempting, she thought. So very tempting. She'd only been in America for three days and already she was feeling a little isolated. Being on her own was liberating, but, as it turned out, *lonely*. And it wasn't as if she could call the few friends she had in the States—the moment she did, word would get back to her family and, just like that, her bid for freedom would end.

What could it hurt to spend the day with a man who made her toes curl and the family he clearly loved? She took a breath and made the leap. "All right, thank you. I would love to rescue you."

"Excellent. My cousin and his family should be back any minute now. So while we wait, why don't you tell me where you're from. I can't quite place your accent. It's British, but...not."

She jolted a little and fought to keep him from seeing it. "You've a good ear."

"So I've been told. But that's not really an answer, is it?"

No, it wasn't, and how astute of him to notice. She'd been trained in how to answer questions without really answering them from the time she was a child. Her father would have been proud. *Never answer a question directly, Alexis. Always be vague. Watch what you say, Alexis. You've a responsibility to your family. Your heritage. Your people...*

"Hey. Alex."

At the sound of his concerned voice, she shook her head, coming out of her thoughts with relief. That was the second time Garrett had rescued her today. She didn't want to think about her duties. Her role in history. She didn't want to be anything but Alex.

So instead of being evasive again, she said, "Why don't you try to figure out where I'm from and I'll let you know when you've got it right?"

One dark eyebrow lifted. "Oh, you're challenging the wrong guy. But you're on. Five bucks says I've got it by the end of the day."

Oh, she hoped not. If he did, that would ruin everything. But she braved it out and asked, "Five dollars? Not much of a wager."

He gave her a slow grin that sent new flashes of heat dancing through her system. "I'm open to negotiation."

She actually *felt* her blood sizzle and hum.

"No, no. That's all right." She backed up quickly. Maybe she wasn't as prepared for that zing of romance as she had thought. Or maybe Garrett the Gorgeous was just too much for her to handle. Either way, she was nervous enough to try to cool things down between them just a little. "Five dollars will do. It's a bargain."

"Agreed," he said, one corner of his mouth lifting tantalizingly. "But just so you know, you should never bet with me, Alex. I always win."

"Confident, aren't you?"

"You have no idea."

A thrill of something hot and delicious swept through her veins. Nerves or not, she really enjoyed what he was doing to her. What was it about him that affected her so?

"That was fun, Uncle Garrett!"

A tiny whirlwind rushed up to them and threw both arms around Garrett's knees. The girl gave him a wide smile then shifted suspicious eyes to Alex. "Who are you?"

"This is Alex," Garrett told her. "Alex, meet Mia."

She smiled at the child and couldn't help noticing that the little girl held on to Garrett's legs just a little more tightly.

"Mia, don't run from me in these crowds," a deep male voice shouted.

Alex turned to watch an impossibly attractive couple approach, the man holding on to a smaller version of the still-wary Mia.

"Alex," Garrett said briskly, "this is my cousin Jackson and his wife, Casey, and that pretty girl with them is Molly."

"It's lovely to meet you all."

Jackson gave her a quick up and down, then winked at his wife. "Wow, leave Garrett alone for a few minutes and he finds the most beautiful woman in the whole place—"

His wife nudged him with an elbow.

"—not counting you of course, sweetie. You're the most beautiful woman in the *world*."

"Nice recovery," Casey told him with a laugh and a smile for Alex.

"Always were a smooth one, Jackson," Garrett mused.

"It's why she loves me," his cousin answered, dropping a kiss on his wife's head.

Alex smiled at all of them. It was lovely to see the open affection in this family, though she felt a sharp pang of envy slice at her, as well. To get some time for herself she'd had to run from her own family. She missed them, even her dictatorial father, and being around these people only brought up their loss more sharply.

"It's nice to meet you, Alex," Casey said, extending her right hand in welcome.

"Thank you. I must admit I'm a little overwhelmed by everything. This is my first trip to Disneyland and—"

"Your *first* time?" Mia interrupted. "But you're *old*."

"Mia!" Casey was horrified.

Garrett and Jackson laughed and Alex joined them. Bending down slightly, she met Mia's gaze and said, "It's horrible I know. But I live very far away from here, so this is the first chance I've ever had to visit."

"Oh." Nodding her head, Mia thought about it for a minute then looked at her mother. "I think we should take Alex to the ghost ride."

"Mia, that's *your* favorite ride," her father said.

"But she would like it, wouldn't you, Alex?" She turned her eyes up and gave her a pleading look.

"You know," Alex said, "I was just wishing I knew how to find the ghost ride."

"I'll show you!" Mia took her hand and started walking, fully expecting her family to follow.

"Guess you'll be spending the day with us for sure, now," Garrett teased.

"Looks that way." She grinned, delighted with this turn of events. She was in a place she'd heard about her whole life and she wasn't alone. There were children to enjoy and people to talk to and it was very near to perfect.

Then she looked up at Garrett's blue eyes and told herself maybe it was closer to perfect than she knew.

"And after the ghost ride, we can ride the jungle boats and then the pirate one." Mia was talking a mile a minute.

"Molly, honey, don't pick up the bug," Jackson said patiently.

"Bug?" Casey repeated, horrified.

Still holding Mara, Garrett came up beside Alex and said softly, "I promise, after the ghost ride, I'll ride herd on my family and you can do what you want to do."

The funny thing was, he didn't know it, but she was already doing what she had always wanted to do.

She *wanted* to be accepted. To spend a day with nothing more to worry about than enjoying herself. And mostly, she wanted to meet people and have them like her because she was Alex Wells.

Not because she was Her Royal Highness Princess Alexis Morgan Wells of Cadria.

Two

She was driving Garrett just a little crazy.

And not only because she was beautiful and funny and smart. But because he'd never seen a woman let go and really enjoy herself so much. Most of the women who came and went from his life were more interested in how their hair looked. Or in being sophisticated enough that a ride on spinning teacups would never have entered their heads.

But Alex was different. She had the girls eating out of her hand, and, without even trying, she was reaching Garrett in ways that he never would have expected. He couldn't take his eyes off her.

That wide smile was inviting, sexy—and familiar, somehow.

He knew he'd seen her before somewhere, but damned if he could remember where. And that bothered him, too. Because a woman like Alex wasn't easily forgotten.

At lunch, she had bitten into a burger with a sigh of pleasure so rich that all he could think of was cool sheets and hot sex. She sat astride a carousel horse and he imagined her straddling him. She licked at an ice cream cone and he—

Garrett shook his head and mentally pulled back fast from that particular image. As it was, he was having a hard time walking. A few more thoughts like that one and he'd be paralyzed.

Alex loved everything about Disneyland. He saw it in her eyes because she didn't hide a thing. Another way she was different from the women he knew. They were all about artful lies, strategic moves and studied flirtation.

Alex was just…herself.

"You'll like this, Alex," said Mia, who had appointed herself Alex's personal tour guide. "The pirate ships shoot cannons and there's a fire and singing, too. And it's dark inside."

"Okay, kiddo," Jackson told his daughter, interrupting her flood of information, "how about we give Alex a little rest?" He grinned at her and Garrett as he steered his family into the front row of the boat.

Garrett took the hint gratefully and pulled Alexis into the last row. A bit of separation for the duration of the ride would give them a little time to themselves.

"She's wonderful," Alex murmured. "So bright. So talkative."

"Oh, she is that," Garrett said with a laugh. "Mia has an opinion on everything and doesn't hesitate to share it. Her kindergarten teacher calls her 'precocious.' I call her a busybody."

She laughed again and Garrett found himself smiling in response. There was no cautious titter. No careful chuckle. When Alex laughed, she threw her soul into it and everything about her lit up. Oh, he was getting in way too deep. This was ridiculous. Not only did he not even know her last name, but he hadn't been able to pin down what country she was from, either.

Not for lack of trying, though.

The sense of familiarity he had for her was irritating as hell. There was something there. Something just out of reach, that would tell him how he knew her. Who she was. And yet, he couldn't quite grab hold of it.

The ride jolted into motion and Alex leaned forward, eager to see everything. He liked that about her, too. Her curiosity. Her appreciation for whatever was happening. It wasn't something enough people did, living in the moment. For most, it was all about "tomorrow." What they would do when they had the time or the money or the energy.

He'd seen it all too often. People who had everything in the world and didn't seem to notice because they were always looking forward to the next thing.

"Wonderful," she whispered. Their boat rocked lazily on its tracks, water slapping at its hull. She looked behind them at the people awaiting the next boat then shifted her gaze to his.

Overhead, a night sky was filled with stars and animatronic fireflies blinked on and off. A sultry, hot breeze wafted past them. Even in the darkness, he saw delight shining in her eyes and the curve of her mouth was something he just didn't want to resist any longer.

Leaning forward, he caught her by the back of the neck and pulled her toward him. Then he slanted his mouth over hers for a taste of the mouth that had been driving him nuts for hours.

She was worth the wait.

After a second's surprise, she recovered and kissed him

back. Her mouth moved against his with a soft, languid touch that stirred fires back into life and made him wish they were all alone in the dark—rather than surrounded by singing pirates and chattering tourists.

She sighed and leaned into him and that fired him up so fast, it took his breath away. But who needed breathing anyway? She lifted one hand to his cheek and when she pulled back, breaking the kiss, her fingertips stroked his jaw. She drew a breath and let it go again with a smile. Leaning into him, she whispered, "That was lovely."

He took her hand in his and kissed the center of her palm. "It was way better than lovely."

A kid squealed, a pirate's gun erupted too close to the boat and Alex jolted in surprise. Then she laughed with delight and eased back against him, pillowing her head on his shoulder. He pulled her in more closely to him and, instead of watching the ride, indulged himself by watching her reactions to their surroundings instead.

Her eyes never stopped shifting. Her smile never faltered. She took it all in, as if she were soaking up experiences like a sponge. And in that moment, Garrett was pitifully glad Jackson had talked him into going to Disneyland.

"I'm having such a nice day," she whispered in a voice pitched low enough that Garrett almost missed it.

"*Nice?* That's it?"

She tipped her head back and smiled up at him. "*Very* nice."

"Oh, well then, that's better." He snorted and shook his head. Nothing a man liked better than hearing the woman he was fantasizing about telling him she was having a "nice" time.

"Oh, look! The dog has the jail cell keys!" She was off again, losing herself in the moment and Garrett was charmed. The pirates were singing, water lapped at the sides of their boat and up ahead of them he could hear Mia singing along. He smiled to himself and realized that astonishing as it was, he, too, was having a *very* nice day.

After the ride, they walked into twilight. Sunset stained the sky with the last shreds of color before night crept in. The girls were worn-out. Molly was dragging, Mara was asleep on Casey's shoulder and Mia was so far beyond tired, her smile was fixed more in a grimace. But before they could go home, they had to make their traditional last stop.

"You'll like the castle, Alex," Mia said through a yawn. "Me and Molly are gonna be princesses someday and we're gonna have a castle like this one and we'll have puppies, too…"

"Again with the dog," Jackson said with a sigh at what was apparently a very familiar topic.

Alex chuckled and slipped her hand into Garrett's. His fingers closed over hers as he cut a glance her way. In the soft light, her eyes shone with the same excitement he'd seen earlier. She wasn't tired out by all the kids and the crowds. She was thriving on this.

Her mouth curved slightly and another ping of recognition hit him. Frowning to himself, Garrett tried to pin down where he'd seen her before. He knew he'd never actually *met* her before today. He wouldn't have forgotten that. But she was so damned familiar…

The castle shone with a pink tinge and as they approached, lights carefully hidden behind rocks and in the shrubbery blinked on to make it seem even more of a fairy-tale palace.

Garrett shook his head and smiled as Mia cooed in delight. Swans were floating gracefully in the lake. A cool wind rustled the trees and lifted the scent of the neatly trimmed rosebushes into the air.

"Can I have a princess hat?" Mia asked.

"Sure you can, sweetie," Jackson said, scooping his oldest into his arms for a fast hug.

Garrett watched the byplay and, for the first time, felt a twinge of regret. Not that it would last long, but for the moment, he could admit that the thought of having kids like Mia and her sisters wasn't an entirely hideous idea. For other people, of course. Not for him.

"Alex, look!" Mia grabbed Alex's hand and half dragged her up to the stone balustrade overlooking the lake. The two of them stood together, watching the swans, the pink castle in the background and Garrett stopped dead. And stared.

In one blinding instant, he knew why she looked so familiar.

Several years ago, he'd done some work for her father.

Her father, the King of Cadria.

Which meant that Alex the delicious, Alex the sexiest woman he'd ever known, was actually the Crown Princess Alexis.

And he'd kissed her.

Damn.

He scrubbed one hand across the back of his neck, took a deep breath and held it. This changed things. Radically.

"Do you want to live in a castle, Alex?" Mia asked.

Garrett listened for her answer.

Alex ran one hand over Mia's long black hair and said, "I think a castle might get lonely. They're awfully big, you know. And drafty, as well."

Garrett watched her face as she described what he knew was her home. Funny, he'd never imagined that a princess might not like her life. After all, in the grand scheme, being royalty had to be better than a lot of other alternatives.

"But I could have lots of puppies," Mia said thoughtfully.

"Yes, but you'd never see them because princesses can't play with puppies. They have more important things to do. They have to say all the right things, do all the right things. There's not a lot of time for playing."

Mia frowned at that.

So did Garrett. Was that how she really felt about her life? Was that why she was here, trying to be incognito? To escape her world? And what would she do if she knew he had figured out her real identity? Would she bolt?

Alex smiled and said, "I think you might not like a real castle as much as you do this one."

Nodding, the little girl murmured, "Maybe I'll just be a pretend princess."

"Excellent idea," Alex told her with another smile. Then she turned her head to look at Garrett and their gazes collided.

He felt the slam of attraction hit him like a fist to the chest. He was in deep trouble here. A princess, for God's sake? He'd kissed a *princess?* He took a good long look at her, from her platform heels to the blue jeans and the pair of sunglasses perched on top of her head.

She had worked very hard to disguise herself, he thought, and wondered why. As a princess, she could have had a guided tour through the park, swept through all of the lines and been treated like—well, royalty. Instead, she had spent her day wandering through Disneyland just like any other tourist.

Alone.

That word shouted through his mind and instantly, his professional side sat up and took notice. Letting go, for the moment, of the fact that she'd lied about who she was—where was her security detail? Where were her bodyguards? The entourage? Didn't she know how dangerous it was for someone like her to be unprotected? The world was a dangerous place and helping out the wackos by giving them a clear shot at you didn't seem like a good plan to him.

So just what was she up to?

As if reading his troubled thoughts from the emotions in his eyes, Alex's smile faded slightly. Garrett noticed and immediately put his game face on. She was keeping her identity a secret for a reason. Until he found out what that was, he'd play along.

And until he knew everything that was happening, he'd make damn sure she was safe.

In the huge parking lot, they all said goodbye and Jackson and Cascy herded their girls off toward their car. The parking lot lights above them flickered weirdly as tourists streamed past like zombies in search of the best way home.

Garrett turned to look at Alex again. "Where's your car?"

"Oh, I don't have one," she said quickly. "I never learned to drive, so I took a cab here from the hotel."

A cab, he thought grimly. On her own. She was asking for disaster. It was a freaking miracle she'd made it here without somebody recognizing her and tipping off the press. "Where are you staying?"

"In Huntington Beach."

Not too far, he thought, but far enough that he didn't want her repeating the "grab a cab" thing. His gaze scanning the crowded lot and the people passing by them, he said, "I'll give you a ride back to your hotel."

"Oh, you don't have to do that," she argued automatically.

He wondered if it was sheer politeness or a reaction to his change in attitude. The closeness, the heat that had been between them earlier and definitely cooled. But how could it not? She was a runaway princess, and he was the guy who knew better than to give in to his urges, now that he knew the truth.

She was a *princess* for God's sake. Didn't matter that his bank account was probably close to hers. There was wealth and then there was *royalty*. The two didn't necessarily mix.

"Yeah," he told her, "I really do."

"I can take care of myself," she said.

"I'm sure you can. But why wait for a cab when I'm here and ready?"

No way was he going to let her out of his sight until he knew she was safe. She was too high-profile. Princess Alexis's pretty face had adorned more magazine covers than he could count. Reporters and photographers usually followed after her like rats after the Pied Piper. Her luck was bound to run out soon and once it did, she'd have people crowding all around her. And not all of them would be trustworthy.

Nope. He'd be with her until he got her back to her hotel, at least. Then he'd figure out what to do next.

"Well, all right then," she said with a smile. "Thank you."

The traffic gods were smiling on them and it didn't take more than twenty minutes before he was steering his BMW up to the waterfront hotel. He left his keys with the valet, took Alex's arm and escorted her into the hotel. His gaze never quit moving, checking out the area, the people, the situation. The hotel lobby was elegant and mostly empty. Live trees stood in huge, terra cotta pots on the inside of the double doors. A marble floor gleamed under pearly lights and tasteful paintings hung on cream-colored walls.

A couple of desk clerks were busily inputting things into computers. A guest stood at the concierge, asking questions, and an elevator hushed open to allow an elderly couple to exit. It all looked fine to his studied eyes, but as he knew all too well, things could change in an instant. An ordinary moment could become the stuff of nightmares in a heartbeat.

Alex was blissfully unaware of his tension, though, and kept up a steady stream of comments as they walked toward the bank of elevators. "It's this one," she said and used her key card to activate it.

While they waited, he took another quick look around and noted that no one had paid the slightest attention to them. Good. Seemed that her identity was still a secret. Somehow that made him feel a bit better about his own failure to recognize her.

But in his own defense, you didn't normally see a princess in blue jeans taking a cab to Disneyland.

She was staying in the penthouse suite, of course, and he was glad to see that there was a special elevator for that floor that required a key card. At least she had semiprotection. Not from the hotel staff of course, and he knew how easily bribed a staff member could be. For the right price, some people would sell off their souls.

When the elevator opened, they stepped into a marble-floored entryway with a locked door opposite them. He waited for her to open the door then before she could say anything, he stepped inside, to assure himself that all was as it should be. His practiced gaze swept over the interior of the plushly decorated suite. Midnight-blue couches and chairs made up conversation areas. An unlit fireplace took up most of one wall and the sliding glass doors along a wall of windows afforded an amazing view of the ocean. Starlight filled the dark sky and the moon shone down on the water with a sparkling silver light.

He stalked across the suite to the bedroom, gave it and the master bath a quick, thorough look then moved back into the living room. He checked the balcony then swept his gaze around the room. No sign of anything and just the stillness in the room told him that there hadn't been any intruders.

"What're you doing?" she asked, tossing the key card onto the nearest table.

"Just making sure you're okay." He brushed it off as if it were nothing more than any other guy would have done. But she was no dummy and her blue eyes narrowed slightly in suspicion.

Her nose was sunburned, her hair was a wild tangle and she looked, he thought, absolutely edible. His body stirred in reaction and he told himself to get a grip. There wouldn't be any more kisses. No more fantasies. Not now that he knew who she was.

Alex was strictly off-limits. Oh, he wanted her. Bad. But damned if he was going to start an international incident or something. He'd met her father. He knew the king was not the kind of man to take it lightly if some commoner was sniffing around the royal princess. And Garrett didn't need the extra hassle anyway. Yeah, she was gorgeous. And hot. And funny and smart. But that crown of hers was just getting in the way. And beside all that was the fact that she was here. Alone. Unprotected. Garrett was hardwired to think more of her safety than of his own wants. And mixing the two never worked well.

"Well, I appreciate it," she said softly, "but I'm really

fine. The hotel is a good one and they have excellent security."

Uh-huh. He wasn't so sure of that, but he'd be doing some checking into the situation, that was for damn sure. True, it was a five-star hotel and that usually meant guests were safe. But as he had found out the hard way, mistakes happened.

"Thank you again."

Alex walked toward him and everything in him wanted to reach out, grab her and pull her in close. He could still taste her, damn it, and he knew he wouldn't be forgetting anytime soon just how good she felt, pressed up against him. His body was hard and aching like a bad tooth, which didn't do much for his attitude.

"I had a wonderful day." Her smile widened and she threw her arms out. "Actually, it was perfect. Just as I'd always imagined my first day at Disneyland would be."

That statement caught him off guard and he laughed. "You imagined a five-year-old talking your ears off?"

"I imagined a day spent with friends and finding someone who—" She broke off there, letting the rest of what she might have said die unuttered.

Just as well, Garrett told himself. He might be a professional security expert, but he was also a guy. And knowing that she felt the same pulse of desire he did was almost more than he could take.

Hell, if he didn't get out of there soon, he might forget all about his principles and better judgment.

"Guess I'd better go," he said, stepping past her for the open doorway while he could still manage it.

"Oh. Are you sure?" She waved one hand at the wet bar across the room. "Maybe one drink first? Or I could call room service…"

She wasn't making this easy, he told himself. Need

grabbed him at the base of the throat and squeezed. It would be so easy to stay here. To kiss her again and take his time about it. To feel her body respond to his and to forget all about who she was. Who he was. And why this was a really bad idea.

"I don't think so," he said, "but thanks. Another time."

"Of course." Disappointment clouded her features briefly. And after a day of watching her smile and enjoy herself, damned if he could stand her feeling badly.

"How about breakfast?" He heard himself say it and couldn't call the words back.

That smile of hers appeared again and his heart thudded painfully in his chest. Garrett King, master of bad mistakes.

"I'd like that."

"I'll see you then," he said and stepped out of the penthouse, closing the door quietly behind him.

In the elevator, he stood perfectly still and let the annoying Muzak fill his mind and, temporarily at least, drive out his churning thoughts. But it couldn't last. He had to think about this. Figure out how to handle this situation.

Yes, he wanted Alex.

But his own code of behavior demanded that he protect—not bed—the princess.

He watched the numbers over the elevator doors flash and as they hit the first floor and those doors sighed open, he told himself that maybe he could do both.

The question was, should he?

Three

"Did you and Mickey have a good time?"

"Funny." Garrett dropped into his favorite, bloodred leather chair and propped his feet up on the matching hassock. Clutching his cell phone in one hand and a cold bottle of beer in the other, he listened to his twin's laughter.

"Sorry, man," Griff finally said, "but made me laugh all day thinking about you hauling your ass around the happiest place on Earth. All day. Still can't believe you let Jackson con you into going."

"Wasn't Jackson," Garrett told him. "It was Casey."

"Ah. Well then, that's different." Griffin sighed. "What is it about women? How do they get us to do things we would never ordinarily do?"

"Beats the hell outta me," Garrett said. In his mind, he was seeing Alex again as he said goodbye. Her eyes shining, her delectable mouth curved…

"So was it hideous?"

"What?"

"I swear, when I went to Knott's Berry Farm with them last summer, Mia about wore me into the ground. That kid is like the Tiny Terminator."

"Good description," Garrett agreed with a laugh. "And she was pumped today. Only time she sat down was when we were on a ride."

Sympathy in his tone, Griffin said, "Man, that sounds miserable."

"Would have been."

"Yeah…?"

Garrett took a breath, considered what he was about to do, then went with his gut. He was willing to keep Alex's secret, for the time being anyway, but not from Griffin. Not only were they twins, but they were partners in the security firm they had built together.

"So, talk. Explain what saved you from misery."

"Right to the point, as always," Garrett murmured. His gaze swept the room. His condo wasn't big, but it suited him. He'd tried living in hotels for a while like his cousin Rafe had done for years until meeting his wife, Katie. But hotels got damned impersonal and on the rare occasions when Garrett *wasn't* traveling all over the damn globe, he had wanted a place that was *his*. Something familiar to come home to.

He wasn't around enough to justify a house, and he didn't like the idea of leaving it empty for weeks at a stretch, either. But this condo had been just right. A home that he could walk away from knowing the home owner's association was looking after the property.

It was decorated for comfort, and the minute he walked in, he always felt whatever problems he was thinking about slide away. Maybe it was the view of the ocean.

Maybe it was the knowledge that this was his space, one that no one could take from him. Either way, over the past couple of years, it really had become *home*.

The study where he sat now was a man's room, from the dark paneling to the leather furniture to the stone hearth on the far wall. There were miles of bookshelves stuffed with novels, the classics and several gifts presented to him by grateful clients.

And beyond the glass doors, there was a small balcony where he could stand and watch the water. Just like the view from Alex's hotel room. Amazing how quickly his mind could turn and focus back on her.

"Hello? Garrett? You still there?"

"Yes, I'm here."

"Then talk. No more stalling. What's going on?"

"I met a woman today."

"Well, shout hallelujah and alert the media!" Griffin hooted a laugh that had Garrett wrenching the phone away from his ear. "'Bout time you got lucky. I've been telling you for months you needed to loosen up some. What's she like?"

"Believe me when I say she defies description."

"Right. You met a goddess at Disneyland."

"Not exactly."

"What's that mean?"

"She's a princess."

"Oh, no," Griffin groaned dramatically. "You didn't hook up with some snotty society type, did you? Because that's just wrong."

Frowning, Garrett said, "No, she's a *princess*."

"Now I'm confused. Are we talking a real princess? Crown? Throne?"

"Yep."

"What the—"

"Remember that job we did for the King of Cadria a few years ago?"

Silence, while his brother thought about it, then, "Yeah. I remember. They were doing some big show of the crown jewels and we set up the security for the event. Good job."

"Yeah. Remember the daughter?"

"Hah. Of course I remember her. Never met her face-to-face, but I saw her around the palace from a distance once or twice. Man she was—" Another long pause. "Are you kidding me?"

Garrett had gotten a few of those long-distance glances, too. He remembered not paying much attention to her, either. When he was on a job, his concentration was laser-like. Nothing but security concerns had registered for him and once that had been accomplished, he and his brother had left Cadria.

Since the small island nation was just off the coast of England, he and Griffin had flown to Ireland to visit their cousin Jefferson and his family. And never once had Garrett given the crown princess another thought.

Until today.

"Nope. Not kidding. Princess Alexis was at Disneyland today."

"I didn't see anything about it on the news."

"You won't, either." Garrett took a swig of his beer and hoped the icy brew would cool him off. His body was still thrumming, his groin hot and hard, and he had a feeling it was only going to get worse for him, the longer he spent in her company. "She's hiding out or some damn thing. Told us her name was Alex, that's all."

"What about her security?"

"Doesn't have any that I could see."

Griffin inhaled sharply. "That's not good, bro."

"No kidding?" Garrett shook his head as Griffin's concern flashed his own worries into higher gear. Alex was all alone in a hotel room and *Garrett* was the only one who knew where she was. He couldn't imagine her family allowing her to be unprotected, so that told him she had slipped away from her guards. Which left her vulnerable. Hell, anything could happen to her.

"What're you gonna do about it?"

He checked the time on the grandfather clock on the far wall. "I'm going to wait another hour or so, then I'm calling her father."

Griffin laughed. "Yeah, cuz it's that easy to just pick up a phone and call the palace. Hello, King? This is King."

Garrett rolled his eyes at his brother's lame joke. They'd heard plenty just like that one while they were doing the job for Alex's father. Kings working for kings and all that.

"Why am I talking to you again?"

"Because I'm your twin. The one that got all the brains."

"Must explain why I got all the looks," Garrett muttered with a smile.

"In your dreams."

It was an old game. Since they were identical, neither of them had anything to lose by the insults. Griffin was the one person in his life Garrett could always count on. There were four other King brothers in their branch of the family, and they were all close. But being twins had set Garrett and Griffin apart from the rest of their brothers. Growing up, they'd been a team, standing against their older brothers' teasing. They'd played ball together, learned how to drive together and dated cheerleaders together. They were still looking out for each other.

To Kings, nothing was more important than family. Family came first. Always.

Griffin finally stopped laughing and asked, "Seriously, what are you going to do?"

"Just what I said. I'm going to call her father. He gave us a private number, remember?"

"Oh, right."

Nodding, Garrett said, "First, I want to find out if the king knows where she is."

"You think she ran away?"

"I think she's going to a lot of trouble to avoid having people recognize her, so yeah." He remembered the blue jeans, the simple white shirt, the platform heels and her wild tangle of hair. Nope. Not how anyone would expect a princess to look. "Wouldn't be surprised to find out no one but us knows where she is. Anyway, I'll let the king know she's okay and find out how he wants me to handle this."

"And how do *you* want to handle it?" Griffin asked.

Garrett didn't say a word, which pretty much answered Griffin's question more eloquently than words could have. What could he possibly have said anyway? That he didn't want to handle the situation—he wanted to handle *Alex?* Yeah, that'd be good.

"She must be something else."

"Y'know? She really is," he said tightly. "And she's going to stay safe."

Memories flew around him like a cloud of mosquitoes. Nagging. Irritating. He couldn't stop them. Never had been able to make them fade. And that was as it should be, he told himself. He'd made a mistake and someone had died. He should never be allowed to forget.

"Garrett," Griffin said quietly, "you've got to let the past go."

He winced and took another drink of his beer. As twins, they had always been finely attuned to each other. Not exactly reading each other's minds or anything—thank God for small favors. But there was usually an undercurrent that each of them could pick up on. Clearly, Griffin's twin radar was on alert.

"Who's talking about the past?" Bristling, Garrett pushed haunting memories aside and told himself that Alex's situation had nothing to do with what had happened so long ago. And he would do whatever he could to see that it stayed that way.

"Fine. Be stubborn. Keep torturing yourself for something that you did. Not. Do."

"I'm done talking about it," Garrett told his brother.

"Whatever. Always were a hard head."

"Hello, pot? This is kettle. You're black."

"Hey," Griffin complained, "I'm the funny one, remember?"

"What was I thinking?" Garrett smiled to himself and sipped at his beer.

"Look, just keep me posted on this. Let me know what her father has to say and if you need backup, *call*."

"I will," he promised, even though he knew he wouldn't be calling. He didn't want backup with Alex. He wanted to watch over her himself. He trusted his brother with his life. But he would trust *no one* with Alex's. The only way to make sure she stayed safe was to take care of her himself.

Alex couldn't sleep.

Every time she closed her eyes, her mind dredged up images snatched from her memories of the day. Mostly, of course, images of Garrett—laughing, teasing his nieces, carrying a sleeping baby…and images of him as he leaned in to kiss her.

Oh, that kiss had been…well, way too short, but aside

from that, wonderful. She could still hear the water slosh-
ing against the boat, the singing from the pirates and feel
the hot wind buffeting their faces. Still feel his mouth
moving over hers.

It had been, she told herself with a small smile, *magic*.

She picked up her hot tea off the room service cart and
stepped onto the balcony of her suite. A summer wind
welcomed her with the cool kiss of the sea. She stared up
at the night sky then shifted her gaze to the ocean where
the moon's light danced across the surface of the water,
leaving a silvery trail, as if marking a path to be followed.
In the middle of the night, everything was quiet, as if the
whole world was dreaming.

And if she could sleep, Alex knew her dreams would
be filled with Garrett.

She took a sip of the tea and sighed in satisfaction.

Alexis knew she should feel guilty for having left
Cadria the way she had, but she just couldn't manage it.
Maybe it was because of the years she had spent doing all
the "right" things. She had been a dutiful daughter, a helpful sister, a perfect princess. She was always in the right
place at the right time saying the right things.

She loved her father, but the man was practically me-
dieval. If it weren't for her mother's restraining influence,
King Gregory of Cadria would probably have had his only
daughter fitted for a chastity belt and tucked away in a
tower. Until he picked out the right husband for her, of
course.

Alex had had to fight for every scrap of independence
she had found over the past few years. She hadn't wanted
to be seen only at state occasions. Or to christen a new
ship or open a new park. She wanted more. She wanted
her life to mean something.

And if that meant a twenty-eight-year-old woman had to run away from home—then so be it.

She only hoped her father would eventually forgive her. Maybe he would understand one day just how important her independence was to her.

Nothing had ever been *hers*. The palace deemed what she should do and when she should do it.

Even her work with single mothers in need, in the capital city of Cadria, had been co-opted by the palace press. They made her out to be a saint. To be the gently bred woman reaching out to the less fortunate. Which just infuriated her and embarrassed the women she was trying to help.

Her entire life had been built around a sense of duty and privilege, and it was choking her.

Shaking her head, she tried to push that thought aside because she knew very well how pitiful that sounded. Poor little rich girl, such a trying life. But being a princess was every bit as suffocating as she had tried to tell little Mia earlier.

Mia.

Alexis smiled to herself in spite of her rushing thoughts. That little girl and her family had given Alex one of the best days of her life. Back at the palace, she had felt as though her life was slipping away from her, disappearing into the day-to-day repetitiveness of the familiar. The safe.

There were no surprises in her world. No days of pure enjoyment. No rush of attraction or sizzle of sexual heat. Though she had longed for all of those for most of her life.

She had grown up on tales of magic. Romance. Her mom had always insisted that there was something special about Disneyland. That the joy that infused the place somehow made it more enchanted than anywhere else.

Alex's mother had been nineteen and working in one

of the gift shops on Main Street when she met the future King of Cadria. Of course, Mom hadn't known then that the handsome young man flirting with her was a prince. She had simply fallen for his kind eyes and quiet smile. He kept his title a secret until Alex's mother was in love—and that, Alexis had always believed, was the secret. Find a man who didn't know who she was. Someone who would want her for herself, not for who her father was.

Today, she thought, she might have found him. And in the same spot where her own mother had found the magic that changed her life.

"I can't feel guilty because it was worth it," she murmured a moment later, not caring that she was talking to herself. One of the downsides of being by yourself was that you had no one to talk things over with. But the upside was, if she talked to herself instead, there was no one to notice or care.

Her mind drifted back to thoughts of her family and she winced a little as she realized that they were probably worried about her. No doubt her father was half crazed, her mother was working to calm him down and her older brothers were torn between exasperation and pride at what she'd managed to do.

She would call them in a day or two and let them know she was safe. But until then, she was simply going to *be*. For the first time in her life, she was just like any other woman. There was no one to dress her, advise her, hand her the day's agenda. Her time was her own and she had no one to answer to.

Freedom was a heady sensation.

Still, she couldn't believe she had actually gotten away with it. Ditching her personal guards—who she really hoped didn't get into too much trouble with her father— disguising herself, buying an airplane ticket and slipping out of Cadria unnoticed. Her father was no doubt furious, but truth to tell, all of this was really his fault. If he hadn't started making noises about Alex "settling down," finding an "appropriate" husband and taking up her royal duties, then maybe she wouldn't have run.

Not that her father was an ogre, she assured herself. He was really a nice man, but, in spite of the fact that he had married an American woman who had a mind of her own and a spine of steel, he couldn't see that his daughter needed to find her own way.

Which meant that today, she was going to make the most of what she might have found with Garrett—she frowned. God, she didn't even know his last name.

She laughed and shook her head. Names didn't matter. All that mattered was that the stories her mother had told her were true.

"Mom, you were *right,*" she said, cradling her cup between her palms, allowing the heat to seep into her. "Disneyland is a special place filled with magic. And I think I found some for myself."

He had already been cleared for the penthouse elevator, so when Garrett arrived early in the morning, he went right up. The hum of the machinery was a white noise that almost drowned out the quiet strains of the Muzak pumping down on him from overhead speakers.

His eyes felt gritty from lack of sleep, but his body was wired. He was alert. Tense. And, he silently admitted, eager to see Alex again.

Stupid, he knew, but there it was. He had no business allowing desire to blind him. She was a princess, for God's sake and he was now, officially, her bodyguard.

Garrett caught his own reflection in the mirrored wall opposite him and scowled. He should have seen it coming, what had happened when he finally got through to the King of Cadria. The fact that he had been surprised only underlined exactly how off course his brain was.

In the seconds it took for the elevator to make its climb, he relived that conversation.

"She's in California?"

The king's thundering shout probably could have been heard even without the telephone.

Well, Garrett told himself, that answered his first question. He had been right. The king had had no idea where Alex was.

"Is she safe?"

"Yes," Garrett said quickly as his measure of the king went up a notch or two. Sure he was pissed, but he was also more concerned about his daughter's safety than anything else. "She's safe, but she's on her own. I'm not comfortable with that."

"Nor am I, Mr. King."

"Garrett, please."

"Garrett, then." He muttered to someone in the room with him, "Yes, yes, I will ask, give me a moment, Teresa," he paused, then said, "Pardon me. My wife is very concerned for Alexis, as are we all."

"I understand." In fact Garrett was willing to bet that "very concerned" was a major understatement.

"So, Garrett. My wife wished to know how you found Alexis."

"Interestingly enough, I was with my family at Disneyland," he said, still amused by it all. Imagine stumbling across a runaway princess in the heart of an amusement park. "We met outside one of the rides."

No point telling the king that Garrett had come to Alex's rescue, not knowing who she was. No point in mention-

ing the kiss he had stolen in the darkness of a pirate ride, either.

"I knew it!" The king shouted then spoke to his wife in the room with him. "Teresa, this is your fault, filling our daughter's head with romantic nonsense until she—"

Listening in on a royal argument just underscored what Garrett had learned long ago. People were people. Didn't matter if they wore a king's crown or a baseball cap. They laughed, they fought, they cried—all of them. And it sounded to Garrett that the King of Cadria, like any other man, didn't have a clue how to deal with women.

The king's voice broke off and a moment later a soft, feminine voice spoke up. The queen, Garrett guessed, and smiled as he realized that she clearly didn't let her husband's blustering bother her.

"Hello, Garrett?"

"Yes, ma'am."

"Is Alexis well?"

"Yes, ma'am, as I told your husband, she was fine when I took her back to her hotel last night."

"Oh, that's such good news, thank you. You say you met her at Disneyland?"

"Yes, ma'am."

More to herself than to him, the queen murmured, "She always dreamed of visiting the park. I should have guessed she would go there, but—"

A princess dreaming about Disneyland. Well, other young girls dreamed of being a princess, so he supposed it made sense. Garrett heard the worry in the queen's voice and he wondered if Alex was even the slightest bit concerned about what her family was going through.

"Thank you again for looking out for my daughter," the queen said, "and now, my husband wants to speak to you again."

Garrett smiled to himself imagining the phone shuffle going on in a palace a few thousand miles away. When the king came back on the line, his tone was quieter.

"Yes, my dear, you're right. Of course. Garrett?"

"I'm here, sir."

"I would like to hire you to protect our daughter."

Instantly, Garrett did a quick mental step backward. This wasn't what he'd had in mind. He didn't want to guard her body. He just wanted her. Not the best basis for a protection detail.

"I don't think that's a good idea—"

"We will pay whatever you ask, but frankly my wife feels that Alexis needs this time to herself so I can't very well drag her back home, much as I would prefer it. At the same time, I'm unwilling to risk her safety."

Good point, Garrett couldn't help but admit. Whether she thought so or not, there was potential danger all around Alexis. Which is why he had placed this call in the first place. He thought she should be protected—just not by him. "I agree that the princess needs a bodyguard, but..."

"Excellent." The king interrupted him neatly. "You will keep us informed of what she's doing, where she's going?"

Instantly, Garrett bristled. That wasn't protection; that was being an informant. Not once in all the years he and his twin had run their agency had they resorted to snapping pictures of cheating spouses and damned if he was going to start down that road now.

"I'm not interested in being a spy, your majesty."

A dismissive chuckle sounded. "A spy. This isn't the situation at all. I'm asking that you protect my daughter—for a handsome fee—and along the way that you merely observe and report. What, Teresa?" Garrett heard furious whispers during the long pause and finally the king came back on the line. "Fine, it is spying. Very well. Observe and not report?"

He still didn't like it. Then the king spoke again.

"Garrett, my daughter wants her holiday, but she's managed to lose every guard I've ever assigned her. We would appreciate it very much if you would watch over Alexis."

Which was why he had finally agreed to this.

Garrett came back out of his memories with a thoughtful frown at his image. He had the distinct feeling that this was not going to end well.

But what the hell else was he supposed to do? Tell a man, a king, that he *wouldn't* protect his daughter? And still, he would have refused outright if the king had insisted on the spying.

But damned if he could think of a way to get out of guarding her. The king didn't want Alex's presence announced to the world, for obvious reasons, and since Garrett had already met her, and was a trained security specialist besides, how could he *not* take the assignment?

If he had said no and something happened to Alexis, he'd never be able to live with himself. His frown deepened as he silently admitted that the truth was, he already had one dead girl haunting him—he wouldn't survive another.

Four

At the knock on her door, Alex opened it and smiled up at Garrett.

The slam of what she had felt around him the day before came back harder and faster than ever. He was so tall. Broad shoulders, narrow hips. He wore black jeans, a dark green pullover shirt—open at the collar, with short sleeves that displayed tanned, muscular forearms. His boots were scuffed and well worn, just adding to the whole "danger" mystique. His features were stark, but somehow beautiful. His eyes shone like a summer sky and the mouth she had thought about way too often was quirked in a half smile.

"I'm impressed."

"You are?" she asked. "With what?"

"You're ready to go," he said, sweeping his gaze up and down her before meeting her gaze again. "Not going to have me sit in the living room while you finish your hair or put on makeup or decide what to wear?"

Her eyebrows lifted. He had no way of knowing of course, but she had been raised to be punctual. The King of Cadria never kept people waiting and he expected the same of his family.

"Well," she said, "that was completely sexist. Good morning to you, too."

He grinned, obviously unapologetic. "Wasn't meant to be sexist, merely grateful," he said, stepping past her into the living room of her suite. "I hate waiting around while a woman drags her feet just so she can make an entrance." He gave her a long, slow look, then said, "Although, you would have been worth the wait."

She flushed with pleasure. A simple compliment simply given, and it meant so much more than the flowery stuff she was used to hearing. As for "entrances," she got way too many of those when she was at home. People standing when she entered a room, crowds thronging for a chance at a handshake or a photo. A band striking up when she was escorted into a formal affair.

And none of those experiences gave her the same sort of pleasure she found in seeing Garrett's reaction to her. Alex threw her hair back over her shoulder and tugged at the hem of her short-sleeved, off-the-shoulder, dark red shirt. She had paired the top with white slacks and red, sky-high heels that gave her an extra three inches in height. Yet still she wasn't at eye level with Garrett.

And the gleam in his eyes sent pinpricks of expectation dancing along her skin. Funny, she'd been awake half the night, but Alex had never felt more alert. More…alive. She should have done this years ago, she thought. Striking out on her own. Going incognito, meeting people who had no idea who she was. But then, even as those thoughts raced through her mind, she had to admit, if only to herself, that the real reason she was feeling so wired wasn't her little holiday. It was Garrett.

She'd never known a man like him. Gorgeous, yes. But there was more to him than the kind of face that should be on the pages of a magazine. There was his laughter, his kindness to his little cousins—and the fact that he'd ridden to her rescue.

And the fact that the black jeans he wore looked amazing on him didn't hurt anything, either.

Alex watched him now as he scanned the perimeter of the room as if looking for people hiding behind the couches and chairs. Frowning slightly, she realized that she'd seen a similar concentrated, laserlike focus before. From the palace guards and her own personal protection detail. He had the air of a man on a mission. As if it were his *job* to keep her safe. Doubt wormed its way through her mind.

Was it possible this had all been a setup? Had her father somehow discovered her whereabouts and sent Garrett to watch over her?

Then she silently laughed and shook her head at the thought. Garrett had been at Disneyland with his family. Their meeting was accidental. Serendipity. She was reading too much into this, letting her imagination spiral out of control. Alex was projecting her concerns onto Garrett's presence with absolutely no reason at all to do so. The man was simply looking around the penthouse suite.

She was so used to staying in hotels like this one she tended to forget that not everyone in the world was blasé about a penthouse. Inwardly smiling at the wild turns paranoia could take, she ordered herself to calm down and patiently waited for Garrett's curiosity to be satiated.

Finally, he turned to look at her, his features unreadable. "So. Breakfast?"

"Yes, thanks. I'm starving."

He gave her that grin that seemed designed to melt her knees and leave her sprawling on the rug. Really, the man had a presence that was nearly overpowering.

"Another thing I like about you, Alex. You admit when you're hungry."

She shook off the sexual hunger clawing at her and smiled back at him. "Let me guess, most women you know don't eat?"

He shrugged as if the women in his life meant nothing and she really hoped that was the case.

"Let's just say the ones I've known consider splitting an M&M a hearty dessert."

She laughed at the image. "I know some women like that, too," she said, snatching up her red leather bag off the closest chair. "I've never understood it. Me, I love to eat."

"Good to know," he said, one corner of his mouth lifting.

And there went the swirl of something hot and delicious in the pit of her stomach. How was she supposed to keep a lid on her imagination if every look and smile he gave her set off incendiary devices inside her?

This holiday was becoming more interesting every minute. When he took her hand and drew her from the penthouse, Alex savored the heat of his skin against hers and told herself to stop overthinking everything and just enjoy every moment she was with him.

They had breakfast down the coast in Laguna Beach, at a small café on Pacific Coast Highway. On one side of the patio dining area, the busy street was clogged with cars and the sidewalks bustled with pedestrian traffic. On the other side, the Pacific Ocean stretched out to the horizon. Seagulls wheeled and dipped in the air currents, surfers rode waves in to shore and pleasure boats bobbed lazily on the water. And Alex was only vaguely aware of any of it. How could she be distracted by her surroundings when she could hardly take her eyes off Garrett? His thick, black hair lifted in a capricious breeze and she nearly sighed when he reached up to push his hair off his forehead. The man was completely edible, she thought, and wondered vaguely what he might look like in a suit. Probably just as gorgeous, she decided silently, but she preferred him like this. There were too many suits in her world.

This man was nothing like the other men in her life. Which was only one of the reasons he so intrigued her.

But Garrett seemed…different this morning. Less relaxed, somehow, although that was probably perfectly natural. People were bound to be more casual and laid-back at an amusement park than they were in everyday situations. The interesting part was she liked him even more now.

There was something about his air of casual danger that appealed to her. Not that she was afraid of him in any way, but the sense of tightly reined authority bristling off him said clearly that he was in charge and no one with him had to worry about a thing.

She laughed to herself. Funny, but the very thing she found so intriguing about him was what drove her the craziest about her father.

"Want to share the joke?" he asked, that deep voice of his rumbling along every single one of her nerve endings.

"No," she said abruptly. "Not really."

"Okay, but when a woman is chuckling to herself, a man always assumes she's laughing at *him*."

"Oh, I doubt that." Alex reached for her coffee cup and took a sip. When she set it down again, she added, "I can't imagine too many women laugh at you."

Amusement sparkled in his eyes. "Never more than once."

Now she did laugh and he gave her a reluctant smile.

"Not intimidated by me at all, are you?" he asked.

"Should I be?"

"Most people are."

"I'm not most people."

"Yeah," he said wryly, "I'm getting that." He leaned back in his chair and asked, "So what next, Alex? Anything else on your 'must see' list besides Disneyland?"

She grinned. It was wonderful. Being here. Alone. With him. No palace guards in attendance. No assistants or ministers or parents or brothers hovering nearby. She felt freer than she ever had and she didn't want to waste a moment of it. Already, her excitement had a bittersweet tinge to it because Alex knew this time away from home couldn't last.

All too soon, she would have to go back to Cadria. Duty was far too ingrained in her to allow for a permanent vacation. Another week was probably all she could manage before she would have to return and be Princess Alexis again. At the thought, she almost heard the palace doors close behind her. Almost sensed the weight of her crown pressing against her forehead. *Poor little rich girl,* she thought wryly and briefly remembered Garrett's tiny cousin wistfully dreaming of being a princess.

If only the little girl could realize that what she already had was worth so much more. A ripple of regret washed through Alex as she turned her gaze on the busy street.

She wondered how many of the people laughing, talking, planning a lazy day at the beach were like her—on holiday and already dreading the return to their real world.

"Alex?"

She turned her head to look at him and found his gaze locked on her. "Sorry. Must have been daydreaming."

"Didn't look like much of a daydream. What's got you frowning?"

He was far too perceptive, she thought and warned herself to guard her emotions more closely. "Just thinking that I don't want my holiday to end."

"Everything ends," he said quietly. "The trick is not to worry about the ending so much that you don't enjoy what you've got while you've got it."

Nodding, she said, "You're absolutely right."

"I usually am," he teased. "Ask anybody."

"You're insufferable, aren't you?"

"Among many other things," he told her, and she felt a tug of something inside her when his mouth curved just the slightest bit.

Then he turned his back on the busy street and looked out at the water. She followed his gaze, and nearly sighed at the perfection of the view. Tiny, quick-footed birds dashed in and out of the incoming tide. Lovers walked along the shore and children built castles in the sand.

Castles.

She sighed a little at the reminder of her daydream, of the world waiting for her return.

"So no big plans for today then?" he asked.

"No," she said with a suddenly determined sigh, "just to see as much as I can. To enjoy the day."

"Sounds like a good idea to me. How about we explore the town a little then take a drive along the coast?"

Relief sparkled inside her. She had been sure he'd have to leave. Go to work. Do whatever he normally did when not spending time with a runaway princess. "Really? That sounds wonderful. If you're sure you don't have to be somewhere…"

"I'm all yours," he said, spreading his arms as if offering himself to her.

And ooh, the lovely sizzle that thought caused. "You don't have to be at work?"

"Nope. I'm taking a few days off."

"Well, then, lucky me."

The waitress approached with the check, Garrett pulled a few bills from his wallet and handed them to her.

"Hmm, that reminds me," Alex said when the woman was gone again. "You owe me five dollars."

His eyebrows lifted. "For what?"

She folded her arms on the table. "We had a wager yesterday and you never did guess where I'm from."

He nodded, gaze locked on hers, and warmth dazzled her system. Honestly, if he were to reach out and touch her while staring at her as he was, Alex was sure she'd simply go up in flames.

"So we did," he said and reached into his wallet again.

"You don't have to actually pay me," she said, reaching out to stop him. Her hand touched his and just as she'd suspected, heat surged through her like an out of control wildfire. She pulled her hand back quickly, but still the heat lingered. "I just wanted you to admit you lost. You did buy breakfast after all."

"I always pay my debts," he said and pulled out a five. Before he could hand it over, though, Alex dug into her purse for a pen and gave it to him. "What's this for?"

"Sign it," she said with a shrug and a smile. "That way I'll always remember winning my first wager."

He snorted an unexpected laugh. "That was your first bet?"

No one but her brothers—and they didn't count—ever made bets with a princess. It would be considered tacky. A tiny sigh escaped her before she could stop it. How much

she had missed just because of how things might "look."
"You're my first—outside my family of course. And I did pretty well, I think, don't you? I did earn five dollars."

"So you did," he said, clearly amused. "Okay then…" He took her pen, scrawled a message, signed it and handed both the pen and the money to her.

Alex looked down and read, "Payment in full to Alex from Garrett." She lifted her gaze, cocked her head and said, "I still don't know your last name."

He nodded. "Don't know yours, either."

"Seems odd, don't you think?" Her gaze dropped to his signature. It was bold, strong and she had no doubt that a handwriting analyst would say that Garrett was confident, powerful and even a little arrogant.

"I'll tell you my name if you tell me yours," he taunted.

Her gaze snapped to his. Tell him her last name? She considered it for a second or two. Wells was common enough; maybe he wouldn't think anything of it. But then again, if he put her first name with her last, it might ring a familiar bell that she'd rather remain silent.

She was having too much fun as "just Alex" to want to give it up this early in her holiday. So why risk it? Why insist on last names when it didn't really matter anyway? After all, when her holiday was over, they'd never see each other again. Wasn't it better for both of them to keep things light? Superficial?

He was still watching her. Waiting. She couldn't read his expression and she really wished she could. Alex would have loved to know what he was thinking about this…whatever it was between them. If he was as intrigued, as filled with a heightened sense of anticipation as she was.

"So?" he asked, a half smile curving his mouth as he waited for her decision.

"First names only," she said with an emphatic nod. "It's more fun that way, don't you agree?"

"I think," Garrett said as he stood up and held one hand out to her, "the fun hasn't even started yet."

"Is that a promise?" she asked, slipping her hand into his and relishing the rush of heat and lust that immediately swamped her.

"It is," he said, "and I always keep my promises."

Garrett looked down at their joined hands then lifted his gaze to hers as the buzz between them sizzled and snapped like sparks lifting off a bonfire. "Fun. Coming right up."

They spent a couple of hours in Laguna, wandering down the sidewalks, drifting in and out of the eclectic mix of shops lining Pacific Coast Highway. There were art galleries, handmade ice cream parlors, jewelry stores and psychics. There were street performers, entertaining for the change dropped into open guitar cases and there were tree-shaded benches where elderly couples sat and watched the summer world roll by.

Alex was amazing. She never got tired, never got bored and absolutely everything caught her attention. She talked to everyone, too. It was as if she was trying to suck up as much life as possible. And he knew why. Soon she'd be going back behind palace walls and the freedom she was feeling at the moment would disappear.

Hard to blame her for wanting to escape. Who the hell didn't occasionally think about simply dropping off the radar and getting lost for a while? He'd done it himself after—Garrett shut that thought down fast. He didn't want to relive the past. Had no interest in wallowing in the pain and guilt that had ridden him so hard for so long. There was nothing to be gained by remembering. He'd learned his lesson, he assured himself, and that was why he was sticking to Alex like glue.

It had nothing to do with how she looked in those mile-high heels. Or the brilliance of her smile or the damn sparkle in her eyes.

He could tell himself whatever he wanted to, he thought, but even *he* didn't believe the lies.

"You're frowning," she said, snapping him out of his thoughts. He was pitifully grateful for the distraction.

"What?"

"Frowning," she repeated. "You. Do I look that hideous?"

He shook his head at the ridiculousness of the question, but dutifully looked at the drawing the caricature artist was doing of Alex. The guy had an easel set up under one of the trees along the highway and boxes of colored pastels sat at his elbow. Garrett watched him drawing and approved of the quick, sure strokes he made.

Alex was coming alive on the page, her smile wider, her eyes bigger and brighter and her long blond hair swirling in an unseen wind.

"So?" she asked.

"It looks great," he muttered, not really caring for how the artist had defined Alex's breasts and provided ample cleavage in the drawing.

"Thanks, man," the guy said, layering in a deeper blue to Alex's eyes. "I love faces. They fascinate me. Like you," he said to Alex, "your face is familiar, somehow. Like I've seen you before. But with that accent no way you're from around here."

Garrett's gaze snapped to her in time to see her face pale a bit and her eyes take on a wary sheen.

"I'm sure I've just got one of 'those' faces," she said, trying to make light of the guy's statement. "You know they say we all have a double out there, wandering the world."

"Yeah," the artist murmured, not really listening. "But you're different. You're..."

"You done?" Garrett asked abruptly.

"Huh?" The guy glanced up at him and whatever he saw in Garrett's eyes convinced him that he was indeed finished. "Sure. Let me just sign it."

A fast scrawl with a black chalk and he was tearing the page off the easel and handing it to Alex. She looked at it and grinned, obviously pleased with the results. In fact, she was so entranced by the drawing, she didn't notice the artist's eyes suddenly widen and his mouth drop open in shock.

Apparently, Garrett thought grimly, he'd finally remembered where he had seen Alex before. Moving fast, Garrett caught the other man's eye and gave him a warning glare that carried threats of retribution if he so much as said a single word.

His meaning got across with no problem. The tall, thin man with the straggly beard closed his mouth, wiped one hand across the back of his neck and nodded in silent agreement.

Garrett pulled out his wallet and handed over a wad of cash. Way more than the price of the drawing, this was also shut-the-hell-up-and-forget-you-ever-saw-her money. When the guy whistled low and long, Garrett knew the bribe was successful.

"Thank you!" Alex said and finally looked at the artist. "It's wonderful. I know just where I'll hang it when I get home."

"Yeah?" The artist grinned, obviously loving the idea that one of his drawings would soon be hanging in a castle.

"Well, cool. Glad you like it, Pr—" He stopped, shot a look at Garrett and finished up lamely, *"Miss."*

Alex missed the man's slipup. She reached into her purse. "How much do I owe you?"

"It's taken care of," Garrett said, stepping up beside her and dropping one arm around her shoulders. He shot another warning look at the artist. "Isn't it?"

"You bet," the guy said, nodding so hard Garrett half expected the man's head to fly off his neck. "All square. We're good. Thanks again."

Garrett steered her away from the artist, and got her walking toward where he'd parked his car. Best to get out of here before the guy forgot just how threatening Garrett could be and started bragging about how he had drawn the portrait of a princess.

"You didn't have to buy this for me, Garrett," she said, with a quick glance up at him. "I appreciate it, but it wasn't necessary."

"I know that. I wanted to."

"Well, I love it." She turned her head to study the portrait. "Whenever I look at it, I'll think of today and what a lovely time I had. I'll remember the ocean, the ice cream, the tide pools, the shops…"

She came to a stop and the people on the sidewalk moved past them like water rushing around a rock in a fast moving stream. She looked at him, reached up and cupped his cheek in her palm. He felt her touch all the way to his bones.

Her blue eyes shone with the glitter of promises when she said, "And I'll remember *you* most of all."

He knew with a soul-deep certainty that he'd never forget her, either.

Five

Decker King looked more like a beach bum than a successful businessman. And that was just how he liked it.

Garrett only shook his head while Decker flirted like crazy with Alex. Decker wore board shorts, flip flops and a T-shirt that read, Do it With a King.

And in smaller letters, King's Kustom Krafts.

The man might be annoying, but his company built the best luxury pleasure crafts in the world. His specialty was the classic, 1940s style wooden powerboats. Decker had customers all over the world sitting on waiting lists for one of his launches.

"You sure you want Garrett to take you out?" Decker was saying, giving Alex a smile meant to seduce.

"Yeah," Garrett interrupted. "She's sure."

Decker glanced at him and smirked. "Okay, then. My personal boat is moored at the dock out back." He tossed the keys to Garrett. "Don't scratch it."

"Thank you, Decker," Alex said with a smile as Garrett grabbed her hand and headed for the dock.

"My pleasure, Alex," he called back as she was hustled away. "Anytime you get tired of my dull cousin, just call me!"

"I don't think you're dull," Alex said on a laugh, her hand tightening around his.

"Decker thinks anyone with a regular job is dull. He's talented but he's also a flake."

"But he runs this business…"

"Yeah, like I said, talented. He's like a savant."

Alex laughed again as they stepped out into the sunlight, leaving the airy boat-building warehouse behind. "Oh, come on. He's very sweet."

"All women like Decker." Garrett looked down at her and smiled. "None of the cousins have figured out why, yet."

"None of you? How many cousins do you have?"

"I can't count that high," he said with a half laugh. "We're all over California. Like a biblical plague."

She laughed and Garrett let the sound ripple over him like sunlight on the water.

"Must be nice, having that much family."

"It can be," he admitted. "It can also be a pain in the ass from time to time."

They stopped at the end of the dock, and Garrett helped her into the sleek boat waiting for them. He untied the rope, tossed it aside then jumped in beside her. The wood planks of the hull gleamed a dark red-brown from layers of varnish and careful polishing. The red leather bench seats were soft and the engine, when Garrett fired it up, sounded like the purr of a mighty beast.

Alex laughed in delight and Garrett couldn't help grin-

ning in response. In a few minutes, he was out of the
harbor and headed for open water.

"I love this boat," she shouted over the engine noise.
"It's like the ones in that Indiana Jones movie!"

"I love that you know that!" He grinned and gunned the
engine harder, bringing the bow up to slap at the water as
they careened across the surface.

When they were far enough out that Garrett was convinced that Alex was perfectly safe, he eased back on the
throttle. The roar of the engine became a vibrating purr
as the sleek powerboat shifted from a wild run into a lazy
prowl.

Garrett slanted a look at her. "So, action movie fan are
you?"

"Oh, yes." She turned her face up to the sun, closed her
eyes and smiled. "It's having three brothers, I think. They
had no time for comedies or romance, so movie night at
our house meant explosions and gunfire."

"Sounds like my house," he said, remembering the
many nights he and his brothers had spent reveling in
movie violence. Garrett and Griffin especially had enjoyed the cops and robbers movies. The good guys track-
ing down the bad guys and saving the day in the end.
Maybe that was why he and his twin had both ended up
in the security business.

"You have brothers?"

"Four—one of them is my twin."

"A twin! I always thought it would be wonderful to be
a twin. Was it?"

"Wonderful?" He shook his head. "Never really thought
about it, I guess. But yeah, I suppose so. Especially when
we were kids. There was always someone there to listen.
To play with and, later, to raise hell with."

Being a twin was such a part of who and what he was

that he'd never really considered what it must look like from the outside. Griffin and he had done so much together, always right there, covering each other's backs that Garrett couldn't imagine *not* being a twin.

"Did you? Raise a lot of hell?"

"Our share," he mused, lost briefly in memories of parties, football games and women. "When we were kids, being identical was just fun. Swapping classes, tricking teachers. As we got older, the fun got a little more…creative."

"Identical?" She took a long look at him. "You're exactly alike?"

He shook his head and gave her a half smile. "Nah. I'm the good-looking one."

She laughed as he'd hoped she would.

"Must have been nice," she said, "raising a little hell once in a while. Having someone to have fun with."

"No hell-raising in your house?" he asked, though he couldn't imagine her and her brothers throwing any wild parties when the king and queen were out of town.

"Not that you'd notice," she said simply, then changed the subject. "Decker seemed very nice." She ran her fingertips across the small brass plaque on the gleaming teak dashboard. *King's Kustom Krafts.*

"Decker King is his name?"

"Yeah." He hadn't even considered that she would learn Decker's last name. And what kind of thing was that for a man like him to admit? Hell, he made his living by always thinking three steps ahead. By knowing what he was going to do long before he actually did it. By being able to guess at what might happen so that his clients were always safe. But around Alex, his brain wasn't really functioning. Nope, it was a completely different part of his body that was in charge now.

And it was damned humbling to admit he couldn't seem to get his blood flowing in the direction of his mind.

"Yeah. Decker's okay."

"He builds lovely boats."

"He really does," Garrett said, relaxing again when she didn't comment on Decker's last name. "So, you've heard about my family, tell me about these brothers of yours."

She looked at him and he read the wary suspicion in her eyes. "Why?"

"Curiosity." He shrugged and shifted his gaze to the sea. No other boats around. But for the surfers closer to shore, they were completely alone. Just the way he preferred it. Giving her a quick glance he saw her gaze was still fixed on him as if she were trying to make up her mind how much to say.

Finally, though, she sighed and nodded. "I've already told you I've got three brothers. They're all older than me. And very bossy." She turned her face into the wind and her long blond hair streamed out behind her. "In fact, they're much like my father in that regard. Always trying to order me about."

"Maybe they're just looking out for you," he said, mentally pitying the brothers Alex no doubt drove nuts. After all, the king himself had told Garrett that Alex managed to lose whatever bodyguards were assigned to her. He could only imagine that she made the lives of her brothers even crazier.

"Maybe they should realize I can look after myself." She shook her head and folded her arms over her chest in such a classic posture of self-protection that Garrett almost smiled.

But damned if he didn't feel bad for her in a way, too. He hated the idea of someone else running his life. Why should she be any different? Still, every instinct he possessed had him siding with her brothers and her father. Wasn't he here, protecting her, because he hadn't been able to stand the idea of her being on her own and vulnerable?

"Guys don't think like that," he told her. "It's got nothing to do with how capable they think you are. Men look out for our families. At least the decent guys do."

"And making us crazy while you do it?"

"Bonus," he said, grinning.

Her tense posture eased as she gave him a reluctant smile. "You're impossible."

"Among many other things," he agreed. Then, since he had her talking, he asked more questions. Maybe he could get her to admit who she was. Bring the truth out herself. *And then what?* Was he going to confess that he already knew? That her father was now *paying* him to spend time with her? Yeah, that'd go over well. How the hell had he gotten himself into this hole anyway?

Disgusted, he blew out a breath and asked, "So, you've got bossy brothers. What about your parents? What're they like?"

She frowned briefly and shifted her gaze back to the choppy sea, focusing on the foam of the whitecaps as if searching for the words she needed. Finally, on a sigh, she said, "They're lovely people, really. And I love them terribly. But they're too entrenched in the past to see that their way isn't the only way."

"Sound like normal parents to me," he mused. "At least, sounds like my dad. He was always telling us how things had been in his day, giving us advice on what we should do, who we should be."

She tucked her hair behind her ears and, instantly, it blew free again. Garrett was glad. He was getting very fond of that wild, tangled mane of curls.

"My parents don't understand that I want to do something different than what they've planned for me."

He imagined exactly what the royal couple had in mind for their only daughter and he couldn't picture it having anything to do with boat trips, ice cream and Disneyland. He knew enough about the life Alex lived to know that she would be in a constant bubble of scrutiny. How she dressed, what she said and who she said it to would be put under a microscope. Reporters would follow her everywhere and her slightest slip would be front page news. Her parents no doubt wanted her safely tucked behind palace walls. And damned if he could blame them for it.

"Give me an example," he said, steering the boat along the coastline. More surfers were gathered at the breakers and, on shore, towels were scattered across the sand like brightly colored jewels dropped by a careless hand.

"All right," she said and straightened her shoulders as if preparing to defend her position. Her voice was stronger, colored with the determination she felt to run her own life. "At home, I volunteer with a program for single mothers."

Her expression shifted, brightening, a smile curving her mouth. Enthusiasm lit up her eyes until they shone like a sunlit lake. When she started talking, he could hear pride in her voice along with a passion that stirred something inside him.

"Many of the women in the program simply need a little help in finding work or day care for their children," she said. "There are widows or divorcées who are trying to get on their feet again." Her eyes softened as she added, "But there are others. Girls who left school to have their babies and now don't have the tools they'll need to support themselves. Young women who've been abused or abandoned and have nowhere to turn.

"At the center, we offer parenting classes, continuing

education courses and a safe day care for the kids. These young women arrive, worried about the future and when they leave, they're ready to take on the world. It's amazing, really."

She turned on the bench seat, tucked one leg beneath her and rested one arm along the back of the seat. Facing him, she looked him in the eye and said, "The program has grown so much in the past couple of years. We've accomplished so many things and dozens of women are now able to care for their children and themselves. A few of our graduates have even taken jobs in the program to give back what they've received."

"It sounds great."

She smiled to herself and he saw the well-earned pride she felt. "It is, and it feels *good* to do something to actually help, you know? To step outside myself and really make a difference."

"Sounds like you're doing a good thing," Garrett said quietly.

"Thank you." She shrugged, but her smile only brightened. "I really feel as though I'm doing something important. These women have taught me so much, Garrett. They're scared and alone. But so brave, too. And being involved with the program is something I've come to love. On my own."

She sighed then and beneath the pride in her voice was a wistfulness that tore at him. "But my parents, sadly, don't see it that way. They're happy for me to volunteer—organizing fundraisers and writing checks. But they don't approve of me donating my time. They want me in the family business and don't want me, as they call it, 'splitting my focus.'"

"They're wrong," he said and cut back enough on the throttle so that they were more drifting now than actually motoring across the water. "You are making a difference. My mom could have used a program like that."

"Your mother?"

Garrett gave her a small smile. "Oh, my mom was one of the most stubborn people on the face of the planet. When she got pregnant with my brother Nathan, she didn't tell our father."

"Why ever not?"

"Always told us later that she wanted to be sure he loved *her*." He smiled to himself, remembering the woman who had been the heart of their family. "She was alone and pregnant. No job skills. She supported herself working at In and Out Burgers. Then, a week before Nathan was born, my father showed up."

"Was he angry?"

"You could say that." Garrett laughed. "Mom insisted later that when he walked into the burger joint and shouted her name, there was steam coming out of his ears."

Alex laughed at the image.

"Dad demanded that she leave with him and get married. Mom told him to either buy a burger or get out of line and go away."

"What did he do?"

"What any man in my family would do," Garrett mused, thinking about the story he and his brothers had heard countless times growing up. "He demanded to see the owner and when the guy showed up, Dad bought the place."

"He bought the *restaurant?*"

"Yep." Grinning now, Garrett finished by saying, "He wrote the guy a check on the spot and the first thing he did as new owner? He fired my mother. Then he picked her up, carried her, kicking and screaming the whole way, to the closest courthouse and married her."

He was still smiling to himself when Alex sighed, "Your father's quite the romantic."

"More like hardheaded and single-minded," Garrett told her with a rueful shake of his head. "The men in our family know what they want, go after it and don't let anything get in their way. Well, except for my uncle Ben. He didn't marry *any* of the mothers of his kids."

"Any?" she asked. "There were a lot of them?"

"Oh, yeah," Garrett said. "That branch of the family still isn't sure they've met all of the half brothers that might be out there."

"I don't even know what to say to that," she admitted.

"No one does."

"Still, passion is hard to ignore," she told him, then asked, "are your parents still that way together?"

"They were," he said softly. "They did everything together. Even dying. We lost them about five years ago in a car accident. Drunk driver took them out when they were driving through the south of France."

"Garrett, I'm so sorry." She laid one hand on his arm and the touch of her fingers sent heat surging through him as surely as if he'd been struck by lightning.

He covered her hand with his and something…indefinable passed between them. Something that had him backing off, fast. He let her go and eased out from under her touch. "Thanks, but after the shock passed, all of us agreed that it was good that they had died together. Neither of them would have been really happy without the other."

"At least you have some wonderful memories. And your family."

"Yeah, I do. But you're lucky to still have your parents in your life. Even if they do make you nuts."

"I know," she said with a determined nod. "I just wish I could make them understand that—" She broke off and laughed. "Never mind. I'm wasting a lovely day with complaints. So I'm finished now."

Whatever he might have said went unspoken when he heard the approach of another boat. Garrett turned to look and saw a speedboat seemingly headed right for them. As casually as he could manage, he steered their boat in the opposite direction and stepped on the gas, putting some distance between them.

"What's wrong?"

He glowered briefly because he hadn't thought she was paying close attention to what he was doing. "Nothing's wrong. Just keeping my distance from that boat."

She looked over her shoulder at the boat that was fading into the distance. "Why? What're you worried about?"

"Everything," he admitted, swinging the little boat around to head back toward shore.

"Well, don't," she said and reached out to lay one hand on his forearm again. The heat from before had hardly faded when a new blast of blistering warmth shot through him. Instantly, his groin tightened and he was forced to grind his teeth together and clench his hands around the wheel to keep from shutting the damn engine off and grabbing her.

Seriously, he hadn't been this tempted by a woman in years.

Maybe never.

Shaking his head at the thought, he said, "Don't what?"

"Don't *worry*, Garrett." She released him and even with the heat of the sun pouring down on them, his skin felt suddenly cool now at the loss of her touch. "I'm taking a holiday from worry and so should you."

That wasn't going to happen. Garrett made his living worrying about possibilities. About danger around every corner. Possible assassins everywhere. Not an easy thing to turn off, and he wasn't sure he would even if he could.

"And what do you usually worry about?" he asked.

"Everything," she said, throwing his own word back at him. "But as I said, I'm taking a holiday. And so are you."

Then she laughed and tipped her face up to the sky. Closing her eyes, she sighed and said, "This is wonderful. The sea, the sun, this lovely boat and—"

"And—?"

She looked over at him. "You."

He nearly groaned. Her blue eyes were wide, her lush mouth curved and that off-the-shoulder blouse of hers was displaying *way* too much off-the-shoulder for his sanity's sake. Now it had dipped low over her left shoulder, baring enough of her chest that he could only think about getting the damn fabric down another two or three inches.

For God's sake, she was killing him without even trying. Garrett was forced to remind himself that he was on a job here. He was working for her father. It was his job to *guard* her luscious body, not *revel* in it.

Besides, if she knew the truth, knew who he was and that her father was paying him to spend time with her… hell, she'd probably toss his ass off the boat and then drive it over him just for good measure.

Knowing that didn't change a damn thing, though. He still wanted her. Bad.

"Alex…"

"I've been thinking." She slid closer. Their thighs were brushing now and he felt the heat of her through the layers of fabric separating them.

He almost didn't ask, but he had to. "About what?"

"That kiss."

Briefly, he closed his eyes. Throttling back, he cut the engine and the sudden silence was overwhelming. All they heard was the slap of water against the hull, the sigh of the wind across the ocean and the screech of seagulls wheeling in air currents overhead.

That kiss.

Oh, he'd been thinking about it, too. About what he would have done if they'd been alone in the dark and not surrounded by laughing kids and harassed parents. In fact, he'd already invested far too much time indulging his fantasies concerning Alex. So much so that if she moved another inch closer…pressed her body even tighter to his…

"Garrett?"

He turned his head to look at her and knew instantly that had been a mistake. Desire glittered like hard diamonds in her eyes. He recognized it, because the same thing was happening to him. He felt it. His whole damn body was on fire, and he couldn't seem to fight it. More, he didn't want to.

He hadn't asked for this. Hadn't expected it. Didn't need it, God knew. But the plain truth was he wanted Alex so badly he could hardly breathe.

The worst part?

He couldn't have her.

He was working for her father. She was a princess. He was responsible for her safety. In the real world, a holiday romance was right up his alley. No strings. No questions. No complications. But *this* woman was nothing *but* complications. If he started something with Alex, regret would be waiting in the wings.

All good reasons for avoiding this situation. For brushing her off and steering this damn boat back to Decker's yard as fast as possible. For dropping her at her hotel and keeping an eye on her from a distance.

And not one of those reasons meant a damn thing in the face of the clawing need shredding his insides.

"Not a good idea, Alex," he managed to say.

"Why ever not?" She smiled and the brilliance of it was blinding. She leaned in closer and he could smell the soft, flowery scent of her shampoo.

Her question reverberated in his mind. *Why not?* He couldn't give her any of the reasons he had for keeping his hands to himself. So what the hell was he supposed to say?

That he was actually a monk? That he didn't find her the least bit attractive? She wouldn't buy either of those.

"It's a beautiful day," she said, pressing her body along his on the bench seat. "We're both on holiday—" She stopped suddenly and looked at him. "Unless you're involved with someone already and—"

"No." One word, forced through clenched teeth. He took a breath. "If I were, I wouldn't be here with you."

"Good. Then Garrett…kiss me again."

He ground his teeth in a last ditch effort to hang on to his rampaging desires, or at least his professionalism. Then her scent came to him again on a soft wind and he knew he was lost. Maybe he'd *been* lost since the moment he met her.

Alex the princess might be easy enough to ignore, but Alex the woman was an entirely different story.

He grabbed her, pulled her onto his lap as he moved out from under the steering wheel and looked down into her eyes. "This isn't a good idea."

"I think it's a brilliant idea," she countered with a smile, then lifted her face to his.

Her eyes were bright, her mouth so close he could almost taste it and her hair flew about them like a blond cloud, drawing him in. He didn't need any more encouragement. Right or wrong, this was inevitable.

He took what she offered, what he needed more than

he'd like to admit. He'd curse himself later for surrendering. For now, there was Alex, a soft sea breeze and the gentle lap of water against the hull of the boat. They were alone and damned if he'd waste another minute.

Six

His mouth came down on hers and the first taste of her sent Garrett over the edge. The kiss they'd shared at Disneyland had haunted him until he had damn near convinced himself that no kiss could be as good as he remembered it.

He was wrong.

It was better.

He knew the contours of her mouth now, how her body folded into him, the sigh of her breath on his cheek. She wrapped her arms around his neck and pressed herself more tightly to him. Her hands swept up into his hair, and each touch of her fingers was like lightning through his bloodstream.

He parted her lips with his tongue and she met him eagerly, stroking, tasting, exploring. Mouths fused, breaths mingling, hearts hammering in time, they came together with a desperate need that charged the air around them.

Garrett set his hands at her hips and lifted her up, shifting her around until she was straddling him, her pelvis pressed to his hard, aching groin. It wasn't enough, but it was a start. She groaned into his mouth as his hips arched up against her.

Alex moved with him, rocking her body against his, as demanding as he felt. She slanted her head, giving as well as taking, tangling her tongue with his, losing herself in the heat that seemed to be searing both of them.

His hands swept up, beneath the hem of that red shirt that had been making him crazy all morning. He skimmed his fingers across her skin until he could cup her lace-covered breasts in his palms. Then he swept his thumb back and forth across her erect nipples until she was twisting and writhing against him, grinding her hips against his.

Her kiss grew hungrier, more desperate.

He knew the feeling.

Her moans enflamed him. Her touch, the scrape of her short, neat fingernails over the back of his neck, felt like accelerant thrown onto a bonfire. He was being engulfed and he welcomed it.

It was as if everything in his life had come down to this moment with her. As if his hands had always ached for the touch of her. His body hard and ready, all he wanted was to peel her out of her white slacks and panties and bury himself inside her.

The ocean air slid around them like a cool caress, keeping the heat at bay and adding new sensations to the mix. Hair rippled, clothing was tugged as if even nature wanted them together in the most basic way.

"You're killin' me," he muttered, tearing his mouth from hers long enough to drag in a deep breath of the salt-stained air.

"No," she said with a sigh and a grin as she licked her lips. "Not interested in killing you at all, Garrett."

He returned that smile, and slowly lifted the hem of her shirt, baring her abdomen and more to his gaze. When her lace-covered breasts were revealed, he reached behind her, unhooked her bra with a flick of his fingers then lifted the lacy cups for his first good look at her breasts.

Round and full, with dark pink, pebbled nipples, they made his mouth water. He lifted his gaze to hers and saw passion glazing her eyes. She licked her bottom lip, drew a shallow breath and leaned into him.

"Taste me," she whispered.

And it would have taken a stronger man than Garrett to turn down that offer. He bent his head and took first one nipple, then the other into his mouth. Moving back and forth between them, he licked and nibbled at her sensitive skin until she was a jangle of need, practically vibrating against him.

Finally, he suckled at her left breast while tugging at the nipple of her right with his fingers. His tongue traced damp circles around her areola and his mouth worked at her, sucking and pulling, drawing as much of her as he could into him.

"Garrett, yes," she whispered, holding his head to her, as if afraid he might stop.

But he had no intention of stopping. Now that they had crossed the barrier keeping them apart, nothing would keep him from having her completely.

"That feels so good." She was breathless, her body moving of its own accord, looking for the release she needed.

And as she moved on him, his groin tightened to the point of real pain and he wouldn't change anything. He dropped one hand to the juncture of her thighs and through the material of her white slacks, he felt her heat. Felt the dampness gathering there at her core.

He rubbed her, pressing hard against the nub of sensation he knew would be aching as he ached. She groaned again, louder this time, and moved restlessly on him. Dropping her hands to the snap and zipper, she undid them, giving him a view of the pale, ivory lace panties she wore before going up on her knees on the bench seat.

Garrett released her nipple, looked up into her eyes and lost himself in their passion-filled depths. He lifted one hand and deliberately, slowly dipped his fingers beneath the elastic band of her panties. She took a breath, let her head fall back and tensed, waiting for his first touch.

She looked like a pagan goddess.

Breasts bared to the sun, face lifted to the sky, hair flying in the wind and her center, open and waiting. He was rocked right down to his soul. She was magnificent. And the need clamoring inside him whipped into a churning frenzy.

He cupped her heat with his palm and was rewarded by a soft sigh of pleasure that slid from her elegant throat. Garrett's hand moved lower, his fingers reaching. She moved with him, giving him easier access. Her hands dropped to his shoulders to steady herself and when his thumb stroked over that one bud of passion, she jolted and gasped in a breath.

"Garrett…Garrett…" It was both plea and temptation.

He watched her, gaze fixed on her expressive face as he dipped first one finger, then two, inside her damp heat. He worked her body, making her rock and twist as she climbed that ladder of need to the climax that was waiting for her. His thumb moved over that nub again and again until she was practically whimpering. Her fingers dug into his shoulders, her sighs came fast and furious.

He stroked her, inside and out, until her body was bowed with building tension, until she was so blindly wrapped up in her own need, he, too, felt the gathering storm. When the first shocking jolt of release hit her, Garrett steadied her with one hand while with the other he pushed her higher, and higher, demanding more, always more.

"I can't," she whispered brokenly. "No more…"

"There's always more," he promised and then delivered—another orgasm, crashing down on her right after the first.

She wobbled on unsteady knees and finally dropped to his lap. Only then did she open her eyes and look into his. Only then did she lean forward and kiss him with a long, slow passion that left him as breathless as she felt.

Never before had he taken so much pleasure from his partner's climax. Never before had he been willing to put his own needs on hold for the simple joy of watching a woman shatter in his arms.

Dragging his hand free of her body, he reached up and smoothed her tangled hair back from her face. Then he cupped her cheek and drew her in close. He kissed her then, relishing the slow slide of her tongue against his.

Alex's mind splintered under the assault of too many sensations at once. His hands, his mouth, his breath. He was everything. The center of the universe, and she was left spinning wildly in his orbit. This moment, this touch, this kiss, was everything.

And in the aftermath of two amazing orgasms, it was all she could do to breathe.

She had thought she knew what it was to kiss Garrett. Truthfully, though, she'd had no idea. This was so much *more* than she had experienced before, there was no way she could have been prepared for what she would feel when it was more than a kiss. When his touch lit up her insides like the firework-lit skies over the palace on Cadria's Coronation Day.

Alex stared into his blue eyes, suddenly as dark and mysteriously hypnotic as the deepest seas, and tried to gather up the frayed threads of her mind. A useless endeavor.

Her brain had simply shut down. Her body was in charge now and all she knew was that she needed him. Needed to feel his skin against hers. Though she was still trembling with the reaction of her last orgasm, she wanted more. She wanted his body locked inside hers.

She traced her fingertips across his cheek, smiled and whispered, "That was amazing. But we're not finished... are we?"

"Not by a long shot," he told her before he gave her a quick, hard kiss that promised so much more.

"Thank heaven," she answered and dropped her hands to the hem of his shirt. As she went to tug it up, though, a deep, throaty noise intruded. A noise that was getting closer. They both turned to see the speedboat, racing toward them again.

Instantly, Alex pulled her shirt down, fastened her bra and quickly did up her pants. The other boat was too far away still for anyone to get a glimpse of bare skin, but the intimacy of the moment had been shattered anyway, and she didn't want to risk a stranger getting a peek at her.

Garrett's gaze narrowed on the approaching craft and his mouth firmed into a grim line. In seconds, he went from ravaging lover to alert protector. He lifted her off his lap, slid behind the wheel of the boat and fired up the engine. The throaty roar pulsed out around them and still, the racing boat's motor screamed loud enough that Alex wanted to cover her ears.

They watched as the speedboat came closer, its hull bouncing and crashing over the surface of the water. A huge spray of water fantailed in its wake as the driver swung in their direction.

"What's he doing?" Alex shouted.

"I don't know," Garrett called out, focus locked on the fast-approaching watercraft.

The boat was close enough now that Alex could see a couple up near the front of the boat and a child standing alone in the back. She whipped her head around, but saw no one else nearby. Just the far away surfers and the jet boat coming ever closer.

"Guy's an idiot," Garrett told her as the boat swung into a sharp turn. "If he doesn't throttle back, someone's going to—"

Before he could finish the sentence, the child flew off the back of the boat, hit the water hard and promptly sank. The boat kept going, the two other people on board apparently unaware they had lost the child.

"Oh, my God!" Alex stood up, frantically waving both arms at the driver to get his attention, but she went unnoticed. "The boy! He hasn't surfaced!"

Garrett shut off the engine, yanked his shirt over his head and tossed it to the deck then shouted, "Stay on the boat!" before he dove into the water.

His body knifed below the surface so cleanly he hardly made a splash. Terrified, Alex watched as he swam with swift, sure strokes, tanned arms flashing in and out of the water as he headed for the spot where the boy had gone under.

Alex's stomach jumped with nerves. With outright fear. She threw a glance at the jet boat, still flying across the water then looked back to where Garrett was swimming purposefully toward the child in trouble. She felt helpless. Useless. She had to *do* something.

Sliding behind the wheel, she fired up the engine and carefully eased the throttle forward, inching the boat closer to Garrett. She'd never driven a boat before and the power at her hands terrified her. One wrong move and she could endanger both Garrett and the child. Too much gas, she could run over them—if she didn't hit them outright. And there was the damage the propellers below the surface could do.

Tension gripping her, Alex's hands fisted on the steering wheel as she fought her own fears and her sense of dread for both the boy and Garrett. She kept her gaze locked on Garrett's sleek figure slicing through the water. Where was the boy? Why hadn't he come up? How could Garrett find him?

Fear ratcheted up another notch or two inside her as she inched ever closer. She risked another glance around; she was still alone out here. The jet boat hadn't returned.

"Do you see him?" she shouted.

Garrett shook his head, water spraying from the ends of his hair just before he suddenly dived deep, disappearing beneath the water entirely.

Alex cut the engine and stood up, watching the ever-churning water, hoping, waiting. What felt like *hours* ticked past.

"Come on, Garrett," she chanted, studying the water, looking for any sign of him. "Come back up. Come on!"

How could he hold his breath that long? What should she do? If she jumped in as well, would she make it that much more dangerous? One more person flailing about? She wasn't a strong swimmer anyway.

She heard a roar of sound and turned her head to see the jet boat hurtling toward them. If they didn't slow down…

"Stop!" Waving her arms and jumping up and down like a crazy woman, Alex screamed and shouted to get their attention. Idiots. Complete idiots. Didn't they realize that they could run over both Garrett and the child they must have finally realized was missing?

The boat slowed and when the engine cut off, the silence was deafening.

"Tommy!" The woman yelled as the man on board dived off the stern of his boat. Hanging over the railing, the woman was oblivious to Alex's presence, her focus concentrated solely on the dark water and what might be happening below.

Alex felt the same.

She didn't know how long Garrett had been underwater. She'd lost track of time. Couldn't think. Could hardly breathe. Dimly, she was aware that prayers were whipping through her mind at a furious rate and she hoped that someone upstairs was listening.

Apparently, they were. *"There!"*

Alex pointed at the shadow of movement in the dark water as it headed toward the surface. The woman on the boat behind her was still screaming and wailing. Alex hardly heard her.

Garrett shot out of the water, shaking his hair back from his face. In his arms, a boy of no more than five or six lay limply, eyes closed. A moment later, the man from the jet boat popped up beside Garrett and tried to take the boy.

Garrett ignored him and swam toward the jet boat. Alex followed his progress, her gaze locked on him and on the pale, young face he towed toward safety.

"Oh, God. Oh, God." The woman was babbling now,

tears streaming down her face, voice breaking on every word. "Is he breathing? Is he breathing?"

Garrett laid the boy on the cut out steps at the back of the boat and tipped the child's head back. While Alex watched, Garrett blew into the boy's mouth once. Twice. The waiting was the worst part. The quiet, but for the water continually slapping the hull and the now quiet weeping from the woman who had to be the boy's mother.

Again, Garrett breathed air into the boy's lungs and this time, there was a reaction.

Coughing, sputtering, retching what seemed a gallon of sea water, the little boy arched up off the deck of the boat, opened his eyes and cried, "Mommy!"

Instantly, the woman was on her knees, gathering her son to her chest. Rocking him, holding him, murmuring words only he could hear between the sobs racking her.

Tears streaked down Alex's cheeks, too, as she watched the man in the water grab Garrett and give him a hard hug. "Thanks, man. Seriously, thank you. I don't know what— If you hadn't been here—"

Garrett's gaze drifted to Alex and she felt his fury and relief as surely as she felt her own. But mixed in with those churning emotions, pride in what Garrett had done swelled inside her. He'd saved that child. If not for him, the boy would never have been recovered. His parents might have spent hours looking, wondering exactly where the boy had fallen in, having no idea where to search for him.

"Glad I could help," Garrett said tightly. "Next time slow down. And give that kid a life vest when you're on a damn boat."

"Right. Right." The man swiped one hand across his face, looked up at his family and Alex saw him pale at the realization of what might have happened.

"Yeah," he said. "I will. I swear it."

"Thank you," the woman said, lifting her head long enough to look first at Garrett and then at Alex. "Thank you so much. I don't know what else to say—"

She broke off, her gaze narrowing as she stared at Alex, a question in her eyes. "Aren't you…"

A knot of panic exploded in Alex's stomach. Would this woman recognize her? Say something?

"You'd better get him to a doctor," Garrett blurted. "Have him checked out."

"Yes," the woman said, tearing her gaze away from Alex long enough to nod, then stare down at her son again. "Good idea. Mike?"

"Coming," the man said, pushing himself out of the water and onto the boat. "Thanks again. It's not enough but it's all I can say."

Relieved that not only the boy was safe, but her secret as well, Alex watched Garrett swim toward her. She paid no attention when the speedboat owners fired up their powerful engine and took off—at a slower pace than they had been going previously. She was just glad to see them gone. Of course she was happy the child had survived. Happy that Garrett had been able to save him. But she was also grateful that her identity was still a secret. What were the odds, she wondered, of being in the middle of an ocean with a child near drowning and that boy's mother recognizing her?

She shoved those thoughts away as Garrett braced his hands on the edge of the boat and hoisted himself inside. Then he just sat there, holding his head in his hands. Alex sat down beside him, uncaring about the water sluicing off his clothes, soaking into hers.

Alex wrapped her arms around him and leaned her head on his shoulder.

"You were wonderful," she said softly.

"I was lucky," he corrected, lifting his head to look at her. "Saw a flash of the kid's white T-shirt and made a blind grab for him."

"You saved him," Alex said, cupping his cheek in her palm. "You were wonderful, Garrett."

A slow smile curved his mouth. "If you say so."

She smiled too. "I do."

"I learned a long time ago—never argue with a beautiful woman." He caught her hand in his, squeezed it briefly then leaned in to give her a fast kiss. "But, I think our boating trip is over."

Her heart tumbled in her chest. She didn't want the day to end. It had been filled with emotional ups and downs and moments of sheer terror. A boy's life had been saved and her own life had taken a wild turn in a direction she hadn't expected.

Alex looked at Garrett and couldn't even imagine *not* being with him. She'd known him only two days and he had touched her more deeply than anyone she had ever known. He was strong and capable and funny. He kissed her and her body exploded with need. He caressed her and the world fell away. She had never felt more alive than she did when she was with Garrett.

So no, she didn't want this day to end because every day that passed put her one day closer to leaving—and never seeing him again.

"Hey," he asked, brow furrowing, "what is it? What's wrong?"

"Nothing," she said. "It's nothing. I just…didn't want today to be over, I suppose."

He brushed a kiss across her mouth and eased back. "Day's not over, Alex. Just the boat ride."

"Really?"

"Really. Dress codes in five-star restaurants are a

lot looser in California than anywhere else, but…" He slapped one hand against his jeans and looked ruefully at his sodden boots. "I think they'll draw the line at soaking wet. I need to change clothes before I take you to dinner."

What he was saying made sense, but the look in his eyes told a different story. It was as if in saving the child, he'd closed a part of himself off from her, and Alex wanted to know why. He was pulling back, even sitting here beside him. She could feel a wall going up between them and wasn't sure what to do about it.

So for now, she let it go and gave him the answer she knew he was expecting.

"In that case," she told him, "we'd better get going."

Seven

The King Security company building was quiet. Halls were dark, phones silent and Garrett appreciated the peace. The light on his desk shone like a beam of sunlight in the darkness as he added his signature to a stack of papers Griffin had already signed in his absence.

The puddle of light from his desk lamp was bright and golden and threw the rest of the room into deep shadow. But Garrett didn't need light to find his way around. This place had pretty much been his life for the past ten years. He and Griffin had adjoining offices with a shared bathroom complete with shower separating them. There were plenty of times they had to leave fast for a job and having a shower and a change of clothes around came in damn handy.

There were bookcases on two of the walls and floor-to-ceiling windows overlooking the ocean on another. Family photographs and paintings hung on the remaining wall, and plush leather furniture completed the room. There was a fireplace, wet bar and a long couch comfortable enough to have served as Garrett's bed more than once.

This was the company he and Griffin had built with a lot of hard work, tenacity and the strength of their reputation. He was proud of it and until recently, hadn't so much as taken a day off. Garrett King lived and breathed the job. At least he *had*, until Alex came into his life.

And just like that, she was at the forefront of his thoughts again.

Instantly, his mind turned back to the afternoon on Decker's boat. His body reached for the sense memory of Alex trembling against him, but his brain went somewhere else. To the child falling into the water and nearly drowning. To Garrett's split-second decision to leave Alex alone and unprotected while he saved the child.

He couldn't have done it differently and he knew that, but still the decision haunted him. She had been alone. What if it had all been a setup? Some cleverly disguised assassination or kidnapping attempt on a crown princess? Sure, chances were slim, but they were *there*. The boy could have been a champion swimmer, doing exactly what he had been paid to do.

Absurd? he asked himself. Maybe. Paranoid? Absolutely. But stranger things had happened, and he'd been around to see a lot of them. Gritting his teeth, Garrett silently fumed at his complete lack of professionalism. He'd saved the boy but risked Alex and that was not acceptable.

He could still feel the slide of her skin beneath his fingers. Hear her whispered cries and the catch in her breath as her climax took her. His body went hard and tight as stone and he told himself the pain was only what he deserved.

Never should have let any of it happen, he told himself.

Hell, he knew better. Years ago, he'd learned the hard way that putting your own wants before the job was a dangerous practice that could end up costing lives.

Garrett threw the pen and swiped one arm across his desk, sending the stack of papers flying like a swarm of paper airplanes. Releasing his temper hadn't helped, though, and he pushed back from his desk, swiping one hand across his face. His eyeballs felt like sand-crusted rocks. He couldn't sleep for dreams of Alex.

That was why he was here, in the middle of the night. He had hoped that focusing his mind on work would keep thoughts of Alex at bay. So far he'd been there for two hours and it wasn't working.

Instead his brain insisted on replaying that scene in the boat over and over again. Those few, stolen, amazing moments that even now, he couldn't really regret. How the hell could he?

He had tried to tell himself that Alex was no different than any other celebrity or royal needing protection. That being with her didn't really mean a damn thing. But then she would laugh and his calm reason flew out the window.

The woman had a hell of a laugh.

It was just part of what he'd noticed about Alex at Disneyland. What set her apart from every other female Garrett had ever known.

She threw herself into life—she held nothing back. Even there in his arms, she had been open and vulnerable, offering him everything. It was damn sexy to watch, and every minute with her was a kind of enjoyable misery. His body was so tight and hard, he could hardly walk. He felt like a damn teenager again. No woman had ever affected him like this. Which was a big problem. She wasn't his. Not even temporarily.

She was a damn princess, and he was lying to her every

minute he was around her. She thought she was free and on her own, and he was being paid by her father to look out for her.

How much deeper was this hole he was in going to get?

Shaking his head, Garrett bent to scoop up the fallen papers and shuffle them back into some kind of order. Griffin had been right when he had ragged on Garrett for being practically monklike for months. Garrett had long ago burned out on women who were more interested in what being seen with a King could do for them than they were in him. And frankly, the women he knew were all the damn same. They all talked about the same things, thought the same way and, in general, bored the hell out of him.

Not Alex.

Nothing about her was ordinary. Or boring.

He never should have called the king. Never should have agreed to this bodyguard gig. Hell, he never should have gone to Disneyland.

Yeah, he told himself wryly. It was all Jackson's fault. If he'd never gone with his cousin and his family, if he'd never met Alex at all…he didn't like the thought of that, either.

"Son of a bitch." He tossed the papers to his desktop and glared at them hard enough to start a fire.

"Problem?"

Garrett snapped a look at the open doorway where his twin stood, one shoulder braced against the doorjamb. The shadows were so thick, he couldn't see Griffin's face, but the voice was unmistakable.

"What're you doing here in the middle of the night?" Garrett leaned back in his black leather chair and folded his hands atop his flat abdomen.

"Funny," Griffin said, pushing away from the doorway

to wander into his brother's office, "I was going to ask you the same thing." He dropped into one of the visitor's chairs opposite Garrett. "Was headed home from Amber's place and imagine my surprise when I spotted a single light on in the office. I figured it was either you or a really stupid burglar."

Garrett looked at his twin. His tuxedo was wrinkled, the collar of his shirt opened halfway down his chest and the undone bow tie was hanging down on both sides of his neck. Apparently at least *one* of them had had a good night.

"How is Amber?"

Griffin snorted and shoved one hand through his hair. "Still talking about getting that modeling job in Paris. I heard all about her packing tips, what she'll be wearing in the runway show and what kind of exfoliant will leave her skin—and I quote here—'shimmery.'"

He had to laugh. Shaking his head, he studied his brother and asked, "Why do you insist on dating women who don't have two active brain cells?"

"There are…compensations," Griffin said with a grin. "Besides, you date women who can walk and talk at the same time and you don't look happy."

"Yeah, well." What the hell could he say? He wasn't happy. Things with Alex were more complicated than ever.

He was tangled up in knots of hunger and frustration. Torn by his sense of duty and responsibility. For two days, he'd fought his every urge and instinct. All he wanted to do was get Alex naked and have her to himself for a few hours. Or weeks.

Instead, he'd made damn sure that the scene in the boat or anything remotely like it, hadn't happened again. For those few moments with Alex, Garrett had allowed himself to forget who and what she was. To put aside the reality of the situation. He'd indulged himself—putting her in a potentially dangerous situation—and now he was paying for it.

Every cell in his body was aching for her. He closed his eyes to sleep and he saw her. He caught her scent in his car, on his clothes. He was being haunted, damn it, and there didn't seem to be a thing he could do about it.

Disgusted, he said, "I'm happy."

"Yeah, I'm convinced." Griffin scowled at him.

He was really not in the mood to listen to his twin. He didn't want to hear about how he should let go of the past. Stop blaming himself for what had happened so long ago. He didn't want to talk. Period.

"Go away," he said, snatching up his pen again and refocusing on the papers in an attempt to get Griffin moving. Of course, it didn't work.

"Princess giving you problems?"

Garrett's gaze snapped to his twin's.

"Whoa. Quite the reaction." Griffin's eyebrows lifted. "So she's getting to you, huh?"

He dropped the pen, scraped both hands across his face and then shoved them through his hair. When that didn't ease his tension, he pushed out of his chair and stalked to the window overlooking the ocean. The moon was out, shining down on the water, making its surface look diamond studded. It was a scene that had soothed him many times over the years. Now, all it did was remind him of Alex. Of being on that boat in the sunshine. Of holding her while she—

"She's not getting to me. Everything's fine. Leave it alone, Griff."

"I don't think so." His twin stood up and walked to join him at the window. "What's going on, Garrett?"

"Nothing. Absolutely *nothing*. That's the problem."

Griffin studied him for a long minute or two and even in the shadowy light, Garrett saw amusement flicker in his twin's eyes. "You've got it bad, don't you?"

"You don't know what you're talking about."

"Right. Everything's great with you. That's why you're here. In the middle of the night, sitting alone in the dark."

"My desk light's on."

"Not the point."

"What *is* the point, Griffin?"

His twin gave him a half smile. "The point is, the mighty Garrett King is falling for a princess."

"You're out of your mind."

"Sure I am."

"She's a job. Her father hired us, remember?"

"Uh-huh."

"She's a princess. And God knows I'm no prince."

"Rich as one," Griffin pointed out helpfully.

"It's not enough and you know it." He shook his head. "Royalty hangs with royalty. Period."

"Not lately." When Garrett glared at him, Griffin shrugged. "I'm just sayin'…

He shifted his gaze away from his twin and stared unseeing at the ocean. Alex's face swam into his mind and as much as he tried to ignore it, she wouldn't go away. He was getting in too deep here and he knew it. But damned if he could see a way out.

"She's a job," he repeated, and which of them he was trying harder to convince, Garrett wasn't sure.

"Sure she is." Griffin slapped him on the shoulder. "Look, making yourself nuts over this just isn't worth it, Garrett. Why not just tell her the truth? Tell her who you are, that you're working for her father."

He'd thought about it. But confessing all wouldn't solve

anything. He'd still want her. And he still wouldn't be able to have her. And as a bonus, she'd be hurt.

"Can't do that."

"Fine, then let me take over," Griffin said.

Garrett just stared at him. "What?"

"Wouldn't be the first time we twin-switched somebody."

"You can't be serious," Garrett said with a snort of laughter.

"Why not? If she's just a job, I'll show up as you, spend some time with her…"

"Stay the hell away from her, Griffin."

His twin grinned. "So I'm right. She *does* mean something to you."

Blowing out a breath, Garrett frowned and turned his face back to the window. His own reflection stared back at him.

"Yeah, guess she does," he murmured, talking to his brother but somehow hoping to reassure the man in the glass as well. "Damned if I know what, though. But in another week or so she'll be gone. Problem solved."

"You think so?"

"I know it." All he had to do was find a way to keep his hands off her. Then she'd be back behind palace doors and his life would go back to normal. If the man in the glass didn't look reassured at all, Garrett ignored it.

Glancing at his twin, he deliberately changed the subject. "As long as you're here, bring me up to speed on what's going on with the business."

"Garrett…"

"Drop it, Griff," he said tightly. "Just, drop it."

"The most stubborn son of a—fine. Okay then, we've got a new client." Griffin moved back to the chair and sat down, stretching out his legs and crossing them at the ankle. "He's opening a luxury resort in Georgia and apparently he's having trouble with some local protestors."

"What're they protesting?"

Griffin snorted. "He's building a golf course and apparently threatening the home ground of the three-legged-gnat-catcher-water-beast-frog or some damn thing. Anyway, to protect the insects, they're threatening our client, and he wants to hire us to protect his family."

"It's a weird world, brother," Garrett muttered. "Protect the gnats by killing people."

"You got that right. Still, upside is, the weirdness is good for business. Anyway…"

Garrett nodded and listened while his brother outlined his plans for their latest client. This was better. Work. Something definable. Something he could count on. All he had to do was keep his focus centered. Remember who he was and why it was so important to keep a hard demarcation line between him and Alex.

He took a seat behind his desk, picked up the pen and began making notes. King Security was his reality.

Not a runaway princess looking for a white knight.

Three days.

It had been three days since they were together on that boat. Three days since Garrett had touched her in any but the most impersonal way. Three days that Alex had spent in a constant state of turmoil, waiting for it all to happen again and then being crushed when *nothing* happened.

Which was making her insane.

"Honestly," she demanded out loud of the empty room, "what is he waiting for?"

She knew he wanted her as much as she did him. When they were together, she felt the tension rippling off him in waves. So *why* was he working so hard at keeping her at arm's length? And why was she allowing it? For heaven's sake, this wasn't the nineteenth century. If she wanted him, she should go after him. No subtlety. No more waiting. He was determined to ignore what was between them, and she was just as determined that he be unable to.

Time was running out for her, Alex thought grimly. Soon enough, she would be on a plane headed back to Cadria and all of this would be nothing but a memory. And damn it, if memories were all that was going to be left of her, then she wanted as many of them as she could make.

With that thought firmly in mind, she checked her mirror and gave herself an objective once-over. Garrett had had some business to take care of that morning and so she'd had a couple of hours to herself and hadn't wasted them. A cab had taken her to the nearest mall where she had shopped until her feet gave out.

It had been good, walking through the Bella Terra mall, just another woman shopping. The freedom she felt was still thrilling, and she didn't know how she would get used to being under the palace microscope once her bit of freedom had ended. Being just one of a crowd was so liberating. She'd laughed with salesgirls, had a hamburger in the food court and then spent a lovely hour in a bookstore.

In fact, it would have been a perfect morning but for the fact that she'd had the oddest sensation that she was being watched. Ridiculous really and probably her own nerves rattling around inside her. No one here knew who she was so why would anyone be interested in what she was doing? She simply wasn't totally accustomed to being alone, that was all. Since leaving her guards behind her, she had been with Garrett almost every moment. Of course she would feel a touch uncomfortable. But it meant nothing.

Brushing off those thoughts, she returned to studying her reflection with a critical eye.

Hair good, makeup perfect and the slinky black dress she'd purchased just that morning clung to her like a second skin. The neckline was deep, displaying cleavage that should surely catch Garrett's eye. And the hemline was just barely legal. Paired with a pair of four-inch black heels, she looked, if she had to say so herself, hot.

Which was her intention, after all.

Her insides swirled with anticipation as she imagined the look on Garrett's face when he saw her. "Let him try to ignore me *now*."

A smile curved her mouth as she let her mind wander to all sorts of interesting places. Damp heat settled at her core and a throbbing ache beat in time with her pulse. She needed him as she had never needed anyone before. And tonight, she was going to make sure he knew it.

An extremely vivid memory rose up in her mind. In a flash, she recalled just how it felt to have Garrett kissing her, touching her. Showering her body with the kinds of sensations she'd never known before. And she wanted it again, blast it.

"What's missing in this holiday romance," she told her reflection sternly, "is *romance*."

Her time here was almost over. She couldn't very well put off her return indefinitely. First of all, she wouldn't do that to her family. But secondly, even if she *tried,* her father would never stand for it. If she didn't go home soon, the king would have an army of investigators out searching for her and they *would* find her. Her father was nothing if not thorough.

Now that she considered it actually, she was a little surprised her father hadn't already sent a herd of search dogs after her. It wasn't like him to let her minirebellion stand.

Frowning at the girl in the mirror, Alex shifted her gaze to the telephone on the bedside table. Guilt gnawed at her as she thought about calling home. At least letting her mother know that she was safe. The problem was, reaching her mother wouldn't be easy. The queen didn't have an email account. And she refused to get a cell phone, despite the palace and the king's insistence, so Alex would have to go through the palace phone system. Then she would have to talk to who knew how many ladies-in-waiting, assistants and secretaries before finally reaching her mother.

And during that interminable wait, everyone she talked to could spill the beans to her father the king, and Alex was in no mood to hear another lecture on the evils of selfishness.

"No," she said, staring at the phone, "I'm sorry, Mother, but I'll be home soon enough."

Just thinking about home had Alex imagining the castle walls closing in around her. She took a deep breath and reminded herself that she was still free. Still on her own. She still had time to enjoy life in the real world. To enjoy her time with Garrett.

Garrett.

She frowned again and turned to the laptop computer sitting on the desk near the terrace. She still didn't know Garrett's last name. They'd never discussed it again after that first time when they had decided to keep their identities a mystery. But...she did know his *cousin's* last name.

Garrett had kept her so busy the past couple of days, she'd hardly had a moment to think about the possibilities that knowledge provided. Every day had been so filled with activities and rushing about that when he brought her back to the hotel at night, she was so exhausted she usually just fell into bed.

But tonight...

She chewed at her bottom lip and wondered. What if there was a reason Garrett hadn't made any further moves?

Maybe he had lied when he said he wasn't involved with someone. Maybe he had a *wife*. That thought jolted and rocked through her on an equal tide of disappointment and righteous indignation.

For the first time, she considered the fact that she actually had a *reason* for keeping her last name a secret. Perhaps Garrett did, too.

"Right, then," she told herself. "Time to find out more about Garrett."

Decision made, she walked quickly to the computer, booted it up and took a chance. She entered the name Garrett King in the search engine and hit Enter.

In seconds, her world tilted and her stomach dropped. The first listing read *King Security, Garrett and Griffin King*.

King Security?

She couldn't believe it. Mouth dry, heart pounding, she clicked on the link and watched as their website opened up. She clicked on the About Us tab and there he was.

Her Garrett.

Garrett King.

Security expert.

"Bloody hell."

Garrett waited outside the penthouse door. He shot his cuffs, smoothed the lapels of his tailored, navy blue suit and wondered what the hell was taking Alex so long. Damn, hadn't taken him much time to get used to her being painfully punctual. Now that she was taking a few seconds to open the door, he was both bothered and worried.

Was she safe?

He knocked again and the door flew open. Alex was there and she looked…amazing.

The misery of the past couple of days gathered into a twist of knots in his gut. Just looking at her was pure, unadulterated torture. How the hell was he supposed to not touch her?

Garrett took a breath and reminded himself *again* of just what had happened the last time he'd allowed his dick to make his decisions for him. He had thrown professionalism aside in favor of his own wants and someone else had paid the price.

He'd be damned before he'd do the same damn thing again and have Alex paying for it.

When she just stared at him, he finally said, "You're so beautiful, you're dangerous."

She inclined her head in what he could only call a "regal" gesture. "Thank you." Grabbing her black bag from a nearby table, she hooked her arm through his and stepped out of the suite. "Shall we go?"

"Sure." Frowning to himself, Garrett felt the first stirrings of unease creep through him.

If he were out in the field, he'd be checking for snipers or some other bad guy sneaking up on him. It was just a feeling, but it had never let him down before.

Something was wrong.

Damian's was the hottest new restaurant on the coast. Designed to mimic the lush, noir atmosphere of the forties, the restaurant boasted a view of the ocean, a teakwood dance floor, linen-draped tables dusted with candlelight and the best seafood in California.

The place had struck a solid chord with the public—older people loved coming here to remember their youth and the younger crowd seemed to enjoy the romance and elegance of another era. It was easier to get a private audience with the pope than it was to land a reservation at

Damian's. Not a problem for Garrett, of course. It paid to be related to the owner.

A singer on stage, backed by a small orchestra working to evoke the feel of the big band era crooned about apple trees and lost loves. Dancers swayed to the music, bathed in spotlights that continually swept the floor.

Garrett wasn't surprised this place was a rousing success. Damian King was known for running restaurants that became legendary. At the moment, Damian was in Scotland, brokering a deal for a new "ghost" theme club to be opened in Edinburgh.

Jefferson King was happily living in Ireland. Garrett's brother Nash called London home and now Damian was in Scotland. He smiled to himself as he realized the Kings of California were slowly but surely starting to take over the world.

"It's lovely," Alex said and he turned to look at her.

Those were the first words she'd spoken to him since they'd left her hotel. She'd been polite, cool and completely shut off from him. The complete opposite of the Alex he had come to know over the last several days. There was no joy in her eyes, no easy smile and her spine was so straight, her shoulders so squared, it was as if she were tied to her chair.

"Yeah," he said warily. "Damian did a nice job of it. But then he always does."

"This isn't his only restaurant?"

"No, he's got a string of 'em up and down California."

"Interesting."

Okay, this was not right. She couldn't have made it plainer that something was chewing at her insides. He studied her and tried to figure out what the hell was going on. It was his *business,* after all, to be able to read people.

But for the first time since he'd known Alex, he didn't have a clue what was going on in her mind.

Her eyes were cool, dispassionate. Her luscious mouth was curved in a half smile that didn't reach her eyes. She was the epitome of the kind of sophisticated, aloof woman he usually avoided. Who was she and what had she done with Alex?

"Your cousin. That would be Damian *King?*"

"Yeah."

She nodded again, letting her gaze slide from his briefly. When she looked back at him again it was as if she was looking at a stranger.

That eerie-ass feeling he'd had earlier rose up inside him again. This whole night had been off from the jump. Something was up with Alex, and she wasn't even trying to hide it. He watched her. Waited. And had the distinct sensation that he wasn't going to like what was coming. She stroked her fingertips along the stem of the crystal water glass, and he was damn near hypnotized by the action.

A waitress approached and Garrett waved her away. Whatever was coming, he didn't want an audience for it. Keeping his gaze locked on the woman opposite him, he asked, "What's going on, Alex?"

"I was just wondering," she said, icicles dripping from her tone, "how many lies you've told me since the day we met."

A sinking sensation opened up in the pit of his stomach. A dark, yawning emptiness that spread throughout his system as the seconds ticked past.

"How long have you known?" she demanded quietly, her blue gaze frosty as it locked with his. "How long have you known who I am, Mr. *King?*"

The proverbial crap was about to hit the fan. He

shouldn't have been surprised. Alex was a smart woman. Sooner or later she was going to figure things out. Put two and two together and, any way you added it up, he was going to look like an ass.

No wonder everything had felt off to him tonight, Garrett thought grimly.

The woman sitting opposite him wasn't the Alex he knew.

This was Princess Alexis.

Eight

He didn't say anything.

Alex watched him, saw the flicker of an emotion dart across his eyes, but it came and went so quickly she couldn't identify it. Why wasn't he talking? Explaining? Because there was nothing he could say? Because if he tried to explain, it would only result in *more* lies?

The anger that had filled her since she had found his website spiked and roiled inside her. It had cost her every ounce of her self-control to keep what she was feeling locked within. She'd waited, half hoping that he would tell her the truth spontaneously. But then, why would he, when he was such a consummate liar?

King Security.

Alex felt like an idiot.

She'd believed everything.

Had *trusted* him, when all along, it had been nothing more than a game. He'd pretended to *like* her. Pretended to be attracted to her. When all along, he had known that she was a princess. God, she was a fool.

Garrett and his company had actually *been* to the palace. Had done work for her father. She hadn't recognized him because when he was in Cadria to provide security for the crown jewel celebration, Alex had avoided the whole situation. At the time, she and her father had been feuding over her involvement with the women's shelter. She'd been so furious with her father that she'd refused to have anything to do with the palace goings-on. Including, it seemed, meeting the security man brought in for the occasion.

If she had, she would have noticed Garrett. Looking at him even now, she could admit that he was most definitely a hard man to ignore. And if she'd met him then, she would have recognized him at Disneyland.

None of this would have happened. Her heart wouldn't be bruised, her feelings wouldn't be battered and she wouldn't now be wrapped in what felt like an icy blanket from head to toe.

She never would have found something with him that she could convince herself was real. She never would have believed that she, too, had discovered the same kind of magic her mother had found at the famous amusement park.

Instead she was left feeling the fool and staring into the eyes of a man she had thought she knew.

"How long?" she demanded, keeping her voice low enough that no one but him could hear her.

The strains of the music rose up and swelled around them, and the irony of the slow, romantic sound wasn't lost on her. She had hoped for so much from tonight. She'd wanted to seduce Garrett. Now all she could hope for was that she wouldn't get angry enough to cry.

She *hated* crying when she was furious.

Tilting her head to one side, she watched him. "Did you know at Disneyland?"

"Not right away," he admitted, and the iron bands around her chest tightened another inch or so until every breath was a minor victory.

That statement told her that at least part of what she had thought of as a magical day had been colored with lies.

Betrayal slapped at her. Was it before he'd kissed her in the dark during the pirate ride? While they laughed with his nieces on the carousel?

She looked into his blue eyes and searched for the man who had been with her on his cousin's boat a few days ago. The man who had touched her, shown her just how amazing two people could be together. But Alex didn't see him. Instead, she saw a cool-eyed professional, already pulling back from her. A part of her wondered how he could turn his emotions on and off so easily. Because right at that moment, she'd like nothing better than to be able to do the same.

"I didn't know you at first," he was saying. "Not until you and Molly were standing at the castle, talking about being a princess."

She nodded, swallowed hard and said, "So that's why you insisted on taking me home that night."

"Partly," he admitted.

She laughed shortly, the sound scraping against her throat. "Partly. It wasn't about me that night, Garrett. Not *me,* Alex. It was about protecting a princess. And you've been with me every day since for the same reason, haven't you?"

Scraping one hand across the back of his neck, he said, "I called your father that first night."

"Oh, God…" Just when she thought the icy cold enveloping her couldn't get worse…it did.

"I told him where you were. That you were alone and that I was…concerned."

"You had no right."

"I had a responsibility."

"To *whom?*" she demanded.

"To myself," he snapped. "I couldn't walk away leaving you unprotected once I knew who you really were."

"No one asked for your help."

"Your father did."

She shook her head, not wanting to hear any more. But she knew that was a futile hope.

"That's wonderful. Really. Your responsibility. Your decision. Your phone call." She narrowed her gaze on him. "But *my* life. This was never about you, Garrett. This was about me. What I wanted. And it never mattered, did it? Not to you. Not to anyone."

"Alex—"

She looked around the restaurant as if searching for an exit. But all she saw were couples sitting at tables, laughing, talking, easy with each other. They were enjoying the restaurant, the music, the romance of the place, and Alex suddenly envied them all so much it choked her.

"I never intended to hurt you."

"How nice for you then," she said, looking back at him. "Because you haven't hurt me. You've enraged me."

"Now who's lying?"

That snapped her mouth shut and all she could do was glare at him. Yes, she was lying because she *was* hurt. Devastated, in fact, but damned if she would show him how much his lies had cut at her.

"There's more," he said.

"Of course there is."

"Like I said before, your father hired me to protect you."

His words sunk into her consciousness like a rock tossed to the bottom of a lake. The sense of betrayal she had felt before was *nothing* compared to this. Her mouth opened and closed a few times as she struggled to speak past the hard knot of something bitter lodged in her throat. Finally, though, she managed to blurt, "Yes, he's *paying* you to spend time with me."

Garrett huffed out a breath and glanced to each side of him before he spoke again and a small part of Alex's brain chided her for dismissing just how careful he was. For thinking that he was simply a cautious man. She remembered thinking not long after they met that he was acting a lot like one of the palace guards. Foolish of her not to realize just what that actually might mean.

Then she pushed those thoughts aside and concentrated solely on what he was saying.

"Your father hired me as a personal bodyguard. We were both worried about what might happen if you were on your own."

"Yes," she said tightly, amazed that she could form thoughts, let alone *words*. "Can't have Alex out and about behaving like an actual person. No, no. Can't have *that*."

"Damn it, Alex, you're deliberately misunderstanding."

"I don't think so," she snapped. "And you know? Maybe you and my father were right. Maybe poor Alex doesn't have a brain in her head. After all, she was foolish enough to think a handsome man wanted to know her better when, in reality, he was on her father's payroll." Her fingers clenched into useless fists. She wanted to throw something. To surrender to the temper frothing and boiling inside her. Unfortunately, her breeding and training had been too thorough. Duty and dignity ran through her veins along with the blood.

Circumspection was another watchword of the royal family and she was too steeped in its tradition to give rein to what she was feeling now. Still, she couldn't continue sitting across from him as if this were a date. She couldn't look at him now without feeling like a complete idiot. She couldn't watch his eyes, cool and dark, without remembering the heat and passion that had flared there so briefly.

At that thought, she gaped at him, horrified. "What about the boat? What happened there? Are you getting a bonus?"

"What?"

She leaned in toward him, pushing the flickering candle to one side. "Was that on the agenda? Show the princess a good time? Or did you just want bragging rights? Want to be able to tell your friends how you got a princess naked? Is that it?"

He leaned in, too, and the flare of the candle flame threw dancing patterns across his features. His eyes were more shadowed, his cheekbones more pronounced. "You know damn well that's not true."

"Do I?" she countered. "Do I really? I know! I should trust you on this because you've been so honest with me from the first, I suppose."

"You kept secrets, too," he argued.

That stopped her for a second. But only a second. "I did, but I wasn't *spying* on you."

"I'm not a damn spy!" His voice pitched a little too loud just as the song ended and several people turned to look. He glared them away before staring back at her. "I told your father I wouldn't be an informer, and I haven't been."

"Again," she said coolly, "with your sterling reputation, I should just take your word?"

His mouth worked furiously as though he were fighting an inner battle to keep his temper in check and angry words from spilling free. Well, she knew just how he felt.

Finally, he managed to say, "You're angry, I get it."

"Oh, I'm well beyond angry, Mr. King," she snapped and stood up. "Fury is a good word and still it doesn't capture exactly what I'm feeling. But thankfully, neither of us has to suffer the other's presence any further."

"Where do you think you're going?" he asked, standing up to look down at her.

Her body lit up inside and Alex silently cursed her response to him. What was it about this man that he could get to her even when she was more furious than she had ever been in her *life?* That simply wasn't right. "Anywhere but here. This *is* a free country, isn't it?"

"Alex, don't do anything foolish just because you're mad."

"I'll do what I please, Garrett King, and I'll thank you to stay away from me." She turned to go, but he caught her arm and held on to her.

She glared down at his hand and then lifted her gaze to his. "You know, when we first met, I thought you were a hero. Now I know you're the villain in the piece."

The muscle in his jaw twitched, and she knew he was grinding his teeth into powder. Good to know that she wasn't the only one feeling as if the top of her head was about to blow off.

"I'm not a hero. Never claimed to be. But I'm not a damn villain, either, Alex. I'm just a man."

"Doing his *job,*" she finished for him and jerked her arm free of his grasp. "Yes, I know."

Head up, chin lifted in a defiant tilt, she headed for the bar. He was just a step or two behind her. "What're you doing?"

"I think I need a drink."

"Don't be an idiot. Come back to the table. We'll talk about this."

"Now I'm an idiot, am I?"

"I didn't *say* that," he muttered.

"Well, you're right on one score. I have *been* an idiot. But not any longer." She hissed in a breath. "I don't want to talk to you, Garrett. Go away."

"Not a chance," he whispered, close to her ear.

His deep voice rumbled along her spine and lifted goose bumps across her flesh. She so wanted to be unaffected by him. But it looked as though *that* wasn't going to happen anytime soon.

The worst part of all of this? Beyond the humiliation of her father going behind her back and the man she was... involved with selling her out to the palace?

She still wanted Garrett.

Mingled in with the anger and the hurt were the underlying threads of desire that still had her wrapped up in knots. How could she still want him, knowing what she did now?

Alex stalked into the bar and gave a quick glance around. There were a dozen or so tall tables with singles and couples gathered at them. A long, gleaming bar snaked around the room in a semicircle. Three bartenders in World War II military uniforms hurried back and forth filling drink orders. Mirrors behind the bar reflected the candlelight and the stony face of the man standing behind her.

The face that had haunted her dreams from the day they met. Their gazes locked in the mirror and Alex felt a jolt of something hot and wicked sizzle through her system in spite of everything.

Deliberately, she tore her gaze from his and walked to

the bar, sliding onto one of the black leather stools. She crossed her legs, laid her bag on the bar top and ordered a gin and tonic.

In the bar mirror, she watched Garrett take a seat a few stools down from her. Not far enough, she thought, but better than nothing. She was only surprised that he was giving her this small amount of space.

"Hello, gorgeous." A deep voice spoke up from just behind her and Alex lifted her gaze to the mirror.

A tall, blond man wearing a black suit and a wide smile stood watching her. "You are way too beautiful to be alone," he said and sat down without waiting for an invitation.

"Thank you, that's very kind." She saw Garrett's reaction from the corner of her eye and seeing him fume made her smile a welcome at the man beside her.

"An accent, too?" He slapped one hand to his heart in a dramatic gesture that had Alex smiling. "You're going to fuel my dreams for weeks."

"That's a lovely thing to say," she told him, though truthfully she thought he was a little on the ridiculous side. With his glib lines, and over-the-top reactions, he was nothing like Garrett with his quiet, deadly, sexy air. Ordinarily, in fact, she wouldn't have been the slightest bit interested in the blond. Still, she caught a glimpse of Garrett's face in the mirror and noted the abject fury on his features. So she leaned toward her new admirer and asked, "What's your name, love?"

"I'm Derek. Who're you?"

"Alexis," she said, "but you can call me Alex."

"You're no 'Alex,' babe," he said with a wink. "So Alexis it is."

In the other room, the music started up again and Derek stood, holding out one hand. "Dance?"

From the corner of her eye, Alex saw Garrett stand up as if he was going to try to stop her. So she quickly took Derek's hand and let him lead her to the floor.

Damn woman.

She was doing this on purpose. Letting that slick guy give her a lame line and then sweep her off to the dance floor. Well, fine, if that's what she wanted, she could have the plastic blond guy. But she wouldn't be alone with him. Garrett was still working for her father and damned if he was going to leave a woman like Alex to the likes of *that* guy.

He followed them into the other room and stood to one side as the blond pulled Alex into his arms and started moving to the music. Alex looked like a vision. That wild mane of blond hair, those heels that made her legs look ten miles long and where the hell had she gotten that dress, anyway? Didn't she know he could practically see her *ass*?

Alex laughed at something Blondie had to say and Garrett's teeth crushed together. He'd known from the start that his lies would eventually catch up with him. Maybe, he told himself, he should have listened to Griffin and confessed the truth to Alex himself. Then at least he would have had the chance to smooth things over with the telling.

But how much smoothing could he have done, realistically? She would still have been hurt. Still have been pissed. And he'd *still* end up standing here watching as some other guy made moves on her.

Moves, he told himself, that she wasn't deflecting.

Irritated beyond belief, Garrett stood like a statue, arms crossed over his chest, feet braced wide apart in a fighting stance. His gaze never left the couple as he watched Blondie ooze his way across the dance floor. Surely, Alex wasn't buying this guy's lines? Any minute now in fact, she'd probably step out of the dance and walk away.

Any minute.

Walking.

Damn it, Alex.

The music slid around the room and the singer's voice wrapped them all in a sensual web. His arms ached to hold her. His hands warmed at the thought of touching her again and his mouth craved the taste of her.

His eyes narrowed as Blondie steered Alex off the dance floor and out onto the dark balcony overlooking the ocean. While the music played and couples danced, Garrett moved through the crowd with a quiet intensity. Focused on his target, he was aware of his surroundings in a heightened way, but all he could think about was reaching Alex.

He stepped onto the polished wood balcony and heard the rush of the sea pushing into shore. Moonlight washed the whole scene in a silvery glow and the wind sweeping across the ocean was nearly icy. Voices came to him and he turned his head in response. That's when he spotted them, at the end of the deck, in a puddle of darkness that lay between the more-decorative-than-useful balcony lights.

Alex was facing the water, and Blondie was plastered up behind her, as close as he could get. Garrett's mind splintered a little and he actually *saw* red around the edges of his vision.

Then his eyes nearly popped from his head in an onslaught of pure fury. Blondie had one hand on Alex's ass and was giving it a rub—and Alex wasn't even trying to stop him.

What the hell?

It only took a few, long strides to carry him to Alex's

side, where he dropped one hand on Blondie's shoulder and squeezed. Blondie looked up, annoyed at the interruption, but annoyance faded fast when he got a good look at Garrett's expression.

"Dude, we're having some private time here."

"Dude," Garrett corrected through gritted teeth. "You're done. Take off."

Alex whipped her windblown hair out of her face and glared at him. "Go away, Garrett."

Astonished, the handsome guy stared at her. "You know this guy?"

"Yes, but pay no attention to him," Alex said.

Garrett's hand on Blondie's shoulder tightened as he silently convinced the other man it would be a much better idea to disappear. Fast.

Message received.

"Yeah, right. Okay. Outta here." He hunched away from Garrett's grip, gave Alex a wistful look and shrugged. "Sorry, babe. I don't do violence. I think *he* does."

"Damn straight," Garrett assured him.

"Oh, for—" Alex set her hands at her hips and glared at Garrett as Blondie hurried back to the restaurant, in search of easier prey. "What do you think you're doing?"

"Hah!" Garrett backed her up against the railing, looming over her as he planted his hands at either side of her. His grip on the cold, damp, iron railing tightened as he looked down into her eyes. "What am I doing? I'm keeping you from getting mauled in public."

"We were hardly in public and what if I *liked* being mauled?" she snapped, her eyes flashing with the kind of heat that any sane man would accept as a warning.

Garrett, though, had passed "sane" a couple of exits back. He was too close to her, bodies aligned, that damn dress of hers displaying way too much beautiful, smooth skin. Heat seared his insides and his dick went to stone. Just the scent of her was enough to drive him insane. He fought for clarity. Fought for control.

"Damn it, Alex. I get that you're pissed at me. And fine. I can deal with it."

"Oh, how very gracious of you."

"But," he continued, leaning close enough that her breasts were pillowed against his chest. That she could feel his erection pressing into her abdomen. Her eyes widened and her lips parted on a sigh. "I'm not going to stand around and watch you make a mistake."

"Another one, you mean?"

In the background, the music was soft, tempting; the singer's voice a lure, drawing them into a world where it was just the two of them, locked together. He felt every inch of her luscious body aligned along his. And in a heartbeat, control and focus went out the window, and Garrett found he couldn't even give a good damn.

"You didn't want that guy's hands on you, Alex."

She let her head fall back. Her eyes met his and a long sigh slid from her throat. "Is that right? And how do you know that?"

"Because you want *my* hands on you," he muttered, his gaze raking over her features before settling on her eyes. "You want *me* touching you and no one else."

She opened her mouth to say something, but Garrett didn't let her speak. Instead, he cupped her face in his hands, leaned down and took her mouth with his.

Pissed or not, Alex wanted him, too. He felt it in her instant surrender. She wrapped her arms around his neck, held his head to her and gave him everything she had. Their tongues entwined, caressing, stroking. The cool air swept past them, and danced across their heated skin.

She shivered, and he wrapped his arms around her,

holding her closer, tighter, until he felt her frenzied heartbeat racing in time with his own. Every inch of his skin hummed with anticipation.

He knew they had been headed for this moment since the day they had met. It didn't matter that he had fought it. This was inevitable. Pulling his head back, he looked down into her glassy eyes and whispered, "Your hotel's only a few minutes from here."

Dragging in a breath, she shivered again and leaned into him. "Then why are we still standing here?"

A fierce grin split his face briefly. Then he took her hand and headed around the edge of the balcony toward the front of the place. Now he was glad he hadn't bothered with valet parking. He didn't have the patience to hang around while some kid ran to bring him his car.

No more waiting.

That first taste of her pushed him over the edge. Touching her wouldn't be enough this time.

This time, he had to have it all.

Nine

It was minutes that felt like hours.

Desire pumping in the air around them, making each heartbeat sound like a gong in their heads, the drive to Alex's hotel was bristling with sexual heat. Somehow, Garrett got the car parked, and Alex through the lobby into the private elevator. Somehow, they managed to walk through the door of the penthouse and slam it closed behind them.

And then all bets were off.

Hunger was king here and neither of them had the strength or the will to fight it any longer.

Garrett tore off his jacket and tossed it aside. Alex's hands fumbled at the buttons on his shirt while he ripped his tie off and discarded it, as well. The moment his shirt was undone, her hands moved over his chest and every one of her fingers felt as if it were imprinting itself on his skin. Heat sizzled back and forth between them, leaving each of them struggling for air. Sighs and groans were the only sounds as they kissed again, hungrily, frantically.

He stabbed his fingers through her wild mane of hair and let the silkiness slide across his skin like cool water. She opened her mouth under his, offering him everything and he took it. Garrett was through pretending that their relationship was strictly business.

At least for this one night, he wanted everything that he had been dreaming of, thinking of, for the past several days. He couldn't touch her enough. Couldn't kiss her enough. He wanted more. Wanted all. Had to have her.

"Now, Alex," he muttered, tearing his mouth from hers to drag his lips and tongue and teeth along the elegant sweep of her neck.

She sighed and tipped her head to one side, as she held his head to her throat. "Yes, Garrett. Yes, please, *now*."

He unzipped the back of her dress and pushed the slender straps down her arms, letting it fall to the floor at her feet. She stepped out of the puddle of fabric and kicked it to one side.

"You're amazing," he whispered, gaze moving over her as she stood there, naked but for those high heels she loved and a tiny scrap of black lace panties. She looked like every man's fantasy and she was his. All his.

Garrett caught her, pulled her in close, then bent his head to take first one then the other erect, pink nipple into his mouth. Her fingers threaded through his hair and pressed his head to her breasts as if afraid he would stop.

He had no intention of stopping.

The taste of her filled him. Her scent surrounded him. A haze settled over his mind, shutting out everything but the present. All there was in the world was this woman.

His hands moved over her skin, up and down her back, around and across her abdomen to the tiny scrap of black lace she wore. His fingers gave a sharp tug and she was naked, open for his touch.

Still suckling at her, he dropped one hand to the juncture of her thighs and sighed against her when she parted her legs for him. He stroked that single bud of pleasure until she was whimpering and rocking against his hand. Her hips twisted and moved in time with his touch, and he smiled against her breast as he felt her climax build.

Lifting his head, he stared at her as his fingers worked her body into a frenzy. She licked her lips, tossed her hair back and took breath after greedy breath.

Her gaze locked with his and her voice was soft as she said, "I want you inside me this time, Garrett. I need to feel you inside me."

He wouldn't have thought he could get any harder. But he did. Reluctantly, he let her go just long enough to strip out of his clothes. He paused only long enough to take a condom from his wallet and sheathe himself. When she made to kick off her high heels, though, he shook his head. "Leave 'em on."

She gave him a slow, wide smile, then dropped her gaze to take in all of him. Her eyes widened and when she looked up at him again, she was even more eager for him. "Now, Garrett. Be with me. Be *in* me."

They were still in the damn living room of the suite and Garrett knew that they'd never make it to the bedroom. Neither of them was willing to wait that long.

He swept her close to him and when his erection pushed at her, she moaned and moved into him, feeding the fires that were already swallowing him. "That's it. Right here, right now. We'll do it slow next time."

"Next time," she agreed.

He carried her a few short steps to the couch, set her on the high back and stepped in between her thighs. She opened herself wider for him and when he entered her, Alex groaned aloud.

Garrett gritted his teeth to keep from shouting as his body invaded hers in one hard thrust. Her damp heat enveloped him, a tight glove, squeezing. When he was seated to the hilt, Alex held him even closer. She moved on the precarious edge of the couch as much as she could. Now she did kick off those heels so she could lock her legs around his hips and hold on as he set a fast, dizzying pace that pushed them both as high as they could go.

They raced to the edge together. Gazes locked, bodies joined, two halves of the same whole. Again and again, his hips pistoned against her and she took everything he had, urging him on.

As the first crash of her orgasm slammed into her, she called out his name and Garrett felt her body spasm around his. He watched her shatter, felt the strength of her climax shaking her. And Garrett realized he'd never known this before. Never been this connected to any woman before. He watched her pleasure and felt it as his own.

He heard her sighs and wanted to capture them forever. Heard his name on her lips and felt both humbled and victorious. Possession raged through him and his only thought as his own release finally claimed him was: *mine*.

Seconds ticked past, became minutes, and those could have been hours for all Alex knew. Or cared.

With Garrett's body still locked with hers, she had everything she had been craving for days. The incredible feel of him deep inside her. The dazzling orgasm that was so much better than anything she had ever felt before. The sweet sensation of his arms wrapped around her. It was all…perfect.

As if she really had found the magic she had been looking for when she first began this holiday.

But even as that thought flitted through her mind, she

knew it wasn't true. Despite what she was feeling, she knew now that Garrett didn't share it.

Want wasn't romance.

Desire wasn't love.

Love? Now where had that thought come from? She stiffened in his arms as the word circled round and round in her mind. She didn't want to believe it, but how could she not? What she felt for Garrett was so far beyond what she had ever known with anyone else.

What else could it be, but love?

Which put her in a very uncomfortable position.

She was in love with a man who was only with her because he had been hired by her father.

"Alex…" Garrett's voice thundered down around her, sounding like a summer storm, and she knew that their moment was over.

She looked up at him, watching his face as he spoke again.

"I'm sorry."

She blinked. "You're *sorry?*"

He pulled away from her and she instantly missed the feeling of his body pressed into hers. And she wanted to kick herself for it. How could she possibly love such a Neanderthal?

"It shouldn't have happened," he muttered, raking one hand through his hair and stepping back so she could slide off the back of the couch. "I let myself be distracted and allowed you to do the same."

"Allowed?" she echoed. "You *allowed* me?"

He didn't pick up on the temper in her voice, or if he did, he wasn't paying attention. His mistake.

"I take full responsibility for this, and I want you to know, it won't happen again."

"You…you…" She opened and closed her mouth several times, but nothing came out. Well, who knew that "stunned speechless" could actually happen? Her bare toes curled into the rug beneath her feet as if she needed all the help she could get just to keep her balance.

"I know what you're going to say," he told her, with a small, brief smile. "And you don't have to. I know you regret this as much as I do."

Oh, she wanted to do something to wipe that "understanding" expression off his face. But once again, her breeding rang true and she settled for quietly seething instead. When she could speak again, she did so quietly. "So you're writing my dialogue for me as well, are you?"

"What?"

Fury flashed inside her like an electrical storm. She actually *felt* bolts of white-hot anger stabbing through her system, and it was all she could do to keep from screaming. Looking up at him, Alex shook her head and said, "You pompous, arrogant, dim-witted, ego-maniacal... *twit!*"

He scowled at her. "What the hell?"

"Oh," she said, eyes widely innocent. "Weren't expecting that, were you?"

"What are you so pissed about *now?*"

"The very fact that you could even ask me that proves your twit-dom!"

"That's not even a word."

"It is now," she told him, stalking a few paces away because she was simply so furious she couldn't stand still. She should have been embarrassed, or, at the very least, uncomfortable, walking about her suite stark naked. But truthfully, she was too angry to care.

"I'm trying to do the right thing," he said, each word grinding out of his throat.

"For the both of us, it seems," she snapped. Her gaze

fixed on him, she said, "Did it even occur to you that what I might regret most is your ridiculous attitude?"

"Ridiculous? I'm taking responsibility for this mess. How is that ridiculous?"

"How is this a *mess?*" she countered.

"You know damn well how," he muttered. "Because I'm here to protect you."

"But not from pompous asses, apparently," she said.

"Okay, that's enough."

"Have you decided that, as well?" she asked, a sugary sweet tone to her voice.

"What the hell, Alex? We both know this shouldn't have happened."

"So sayeth the almighty arbiter of everything sexual."

"You're starting to piss me off."

"Well, join the bloody club!" Walking back to him, she stopped within a foot of his gorgeous body, tipped her head back and glared into those eyes that only moments ago had been glazed with passion. Now there were ice chips in those depths and damned if she didn't find them just as attractive. "I'm not a naive young virgin out for her first romp in the hay, you know. You're not the first man in my bed. You're simply the first to regret it the moment it was over. Well, thank you very much for that, Garrett King.

"Now, why don't you take your sense of responsibility and leave?"

"I'm not going anywhere until we settle this."

"Then I hope you packed a lunch," she quipped, "because I don't see that happening anytime soon."

"Maybe if you'd be reasonable…"

She sucked in a gulp of air and gave him a shove. He didn't budge an inch. Like shoving a bloody wall. "Reasonable? You think I'm *not* being reasonable? It's only my exceptional breeding and the training of my mother, not to mention countless governesses, that's keeping me from punching you in the nose!"

He laughed at the very idea, which infuriated her enough to curl her hand into a fist and take a wild swing at him, just as her brothers had taught her to. Garrett, though, was too fast for her and caught her hand in his before she could make contact.

"Nice 'breeding,'" he said with a half smile.

"You're insufferable."

"You've said that before."

"Then clearly I'm an astute human being."

He sighed. "Alex, look me in the eye and tell me you think this was a good thing. I'm not looking for a relationship. This is going nowhere."

His words slapped her, but she wouldn't let him see it. She wouldn't be the needy one while he tried to make light of something that had shaken her to her very foundations. So she took a page from his book...she lied. "What makes you think I'm looking for a future with you? Are you really that egotistical? Do you think one night in bed with you is enough to make a woman immediately start craving white picket fences? Start scribbling her name next to yours surrounded by lacy hearts?

"I'm a *princess,* Garrett. I may have run off for a holiday but I know what my duties are. I know what my life will be. God knows, it was planned for me practically from the moment I drew my first breath! And nowhere in that plan does it say *fall in love with a Neanderthal, move to California and remain barefoot and pregnant.*"

Her breath was coming fast, in and out of her lungs. Her heartbeat was racing and her blood was pumping. Being this close to him was feeding more than her anger. In spite of everything, she wanted him.

He was stupid and clueless and impossibly arrogant—
and, he was the most intriguing man she had ever known.
Even the fact that he had lied to her from the beginning
wasn't enough to cool off the fires licking at her insides.
And Alex had the distinct feeling that thirty years from
now, when he was nothing more than a hazy memory, she
would *still* want him.

"Neanderthal?"

Her fury abated for the moment, she only asked, "How
would you describe yourself at this moment?"

"Confused, angry—" he paused, tucked his fingers beneath her chin and lifted her face, her eyes, up to his "—and
more turned on than I was before."

He felt it, too. That soul-deep stirring. He didn't want
it, either, but it seemed as though neither of them had a
choice when it came to what lay sizzling between them.
Arguments didn't matter. Differences didn't matter.

All that mattered was the next touch. The next kiss.

"Oh," she admitted on a sigh, "me, too."

He kissed her and the rest of the world fell away. Alex
let go of her anger and gave herself up to the wonder of
what he could make her feel.

His arms came around her as his mouth took hers. He
carried her into the bedroom and laid her down atop the
silk duvet. The slide of the cool fabric against her skin was
just another sensation to pile onto the rest.

Sliding his hands up and down her body, Alex arched
into him, allowing her mind to drift free so that she could
concentrate solely on the moment. Every stroke was a
benediction. Every caress a promise of more to come.

Her body felt alive in a way it never had before. His
touch was magic…kindling sparks of flame at every spot
he touched. He leaned over her, kissing her, then sliding

along her body, nibbling his way down. Then he stopped, pulled back and slid off the bed.

"Where are you going?"

"Right back," he swore, his eyes fixed on hers.

True to his word, he was gone only moments and she saw that he had another condom with him, sheathing himself as he came closer.

A smile tugged at the corner of her mouth. "You always carry those in your wallet?"

"I have since I met you," he admitted, kneeling back on the bed, dropping his head for a quick kiss. "Just in case."

"Always prepared?" she asked.

"Babe, those are the Boy Scouts. And trust me when I say I'm no Boy Scout."

"No," she whispered as he moved down the length of her body again, letting his mouth and tongue blaze the trail, "you're really not."

Alex sighed deeply and stared up at the ceiling. Moonlight poured through the windows, along with a chill ocean breeze that ruffled the white sheers and sent them into a sensual dance that mimicked her own movements beneath Garrett's talented hands.

"You're torturing me," she whispered and arched into him as his lips crossed over her abdomen.

"That's the plan," Garrett assured her.

"You're an evil man," she said on a sigh. "Don't stop."

"Not a chance," he promised.

Then he moved, shifting down to kneel between her thighs and Alex looked at him. Slowly he scooped his hands beneath her bottom and lifted her from the bed. Everything in her tensed in expectation. Her gaze locked with his as he lowered his mouth to her center and—

She groaned at the first sweep of his tongue across a bud of flesh so sensitive it felt as if it had a life of its own.

Electric-like jolts of sensation shot through her, coiling the tension within her even tighter. Alex moved into him, loving the feel of his mouth on her.

Reaching down, she pushed her fingers through his hair as he pushed her higher and faster than she had gone before. This intimacy was so overwhelming; her system was flooded with emotions tangling together. She felt so much, wanted so much, *needed* so much.

It was close. She felt it. The orgasm hovering just out of reach was almost on her and she wanted him inside her when it hit. "Garrett, please."

Instantly, he pulled away from her, sat back on his thighs and lifted her onto his lap. Alex went up onto her knees and slowly, deliberately, lowered herself onto him. It was delicious. The tantalizingly slow slide of his hard thickness pushing into her depths. She gloried in every inch of him. She let her head fall back as she wrapped her arms around his neck and swiveled her hips against him, taking him even higher and deeper than she had before.

Until she was sure he was touching the tip of her heart.

"You feel so good," he whispered, kissing the base of her throat, locking his lips against her pulse point. His breath hot against her skin, he whispered words she couldn't hear—could only *feel*.

And then she moved on him and his hands settled at her hips, guiding her motions, helping her set a rhythm they both kept time with. Again and again, she rocked her body onto his, and, over and over, they tore apart and came together. They moved as one. Breathed as one.

And at last, they shattered as one.

Ten

In the dark, when it was quiet, reality crashed down on top of them again, and Alex was the first to feel its sharp tugs at the edges of her heart.

Grabbing up her short, blue silk robe, she slipped it on, then crossed her bedroom, opened the French doors leading to the balcony that wrapped around the entire penthouse suite and stepped outside. The stone floor was cool and damp beneath her feet and the wind off the ocean lifted her hair and teased her heated skin.

Staring out at the moonlit sea, Alex tried to get a handle on the rampaging emotions crashing through her. Her mind was alive with careening thoughts that rushed up to be noticed then were swallowed and replaced by the next one. In fact, the only thing she was truly sure of was that she did love Garrett King. Infuriating as he was, she loved him.

They'd known each other such a short time, it was hard

to believe. But the simple fact was, as her mother had always told her, love didn't come with a timetable. It was either there or it wasn't and no amount of waiting would change that.

Her heart ached and her mind whirled. There was misery along this road and she knew it. Garrett had made no secret of the fact that he wasn't interested in a relationship. And even if he were, their lives were so different. They didn't even live on the same *continent!* What possible chance was there for anything more than what they had already shared?

Taking hold of the iron railing in front of her, she squeezed tightly in response to the tension within.

A moment later, Garrett joined her, and her heart sped into a gallop. She glanced at him. He was wearing the slacks he'd abandoned what felt like hours ago, but he was barefoot and shirtless and his broad, sculpted chest seemed to be begging for her touch. She gripped the handrails to keep from giving in to that urge.

"Alex, we really need to talk."

"That never bodes well," she replied, deliberately turning her gaze on the ever-shifting surface of the water below.

He stood beside her. Close, but not touching and still, she felt the heat from his body sliding into hers.

"It's too late to do a damn thing about it, but none of that should have happened, Alex."

She stiffened. He still regretted being with her. How would he react, she wondered, if he knew she loved him? She glanced over the railing to the sand ten stories below. He'd probably jump.

"No doubt you're right."

"Huh." She felt more than saw him turn his gaze on her. "You surprise me. I expected a different reaction."

Alex steeled herself then turned to look up into his eyes. "What were you thinking? Keening? Gnashing of teeth?" She gave him a smile that felt stiff and wooden. "Sorry to disappoint."

"Not disappointed. Just surprised."

"Well, you shouldn't be," she said, silently congratulating herself on how calm and cool she sounded. Honestly, if she weren't a princess, she should think of going on the stage. "You'd already made yourself quite clear on the subject, and, as I've mentioned, I'm not an idiot, Garrett. I know that we don't suit. I know we mean nothing to each other and that this isn't going anywhere...."

Those words ripped a new hole in the fabric of her heart, but better *she* say them than him.

"I didn't say you mean nothing to me, Alex," he said, laying his hands on her shoulders and turning her so that she faced him.

God, she didn't want to look into his eyes. Didn't want to feel the heat of him spearing through her body. Didn't want to think about the pain she would feel when she was gone and back in the palace.

The only way to get through any of it was to pretend none of it mattered.

So she gave him that forced smile again and hoped he wouldn't notice. "Ah, yes, I forgot," she quipped. "I do mean something to you after all. Quite a hefty paycheck, I'm guessing."

"I didn't say that, either," he ground out.

"You haven't said much, Garrett," she told him. "What else am I to think?"

"That you're an amazing, smart, funny, incredibly sexy *princess*."

"It always comes back to that, doesn't it?" she mused, stepping out of his grip and turning to face the sea again.

"If I'd known how you would focus on that, I would have worn my crown while we were in bed together."

"I don't give a damn for your crown, Alex," he snapped, voice near growling now. "In fact this would all be a hell of a lot easier if you *weren't* a princess. You think your father would be thrilled to know that I'm here with you?"

"What's my father got to do with any of this?"

Clearly exasperated, he snapped, "I've done security work for royalty all over the globe. You know what's the *one* thing they all have in common? They don't get involved with non-royals. Hell, I've got more money than a lot of them, but I'm still a 'commoner.' You think your father feels any different?"

"Probably not."

"Exactly." Garrett shook his head. "It all comes down to that, Princess."

"Story of my life," she murmured, sliding a glance at him.

"What's that supposed to mean?"

"Please," she scoffed. "Do you think you're the only man who has run screaming into the night trying to escape the glare of the palace? You're not." Shaking her head she added, "And for all of those that run away, dozens more run *toward* the crown. None of them see me, Alex. They see the princess. Some hate the very idea of royalty and others covet it. People on the outside look at the royal family and think, *Isn't it wonderful? All the pomp and pageantry. How nice to shop wherever you like and not worry about the price.*

"Well," she continued, "there's *always* a price, Garrett. It's just one that most people never see. It's a lack of privacy. A lack of freedom and imagination. It's being locked into centuries of tradition whether you like it or not, and it's duty."

Her gaze narrowed, her breath coming fast and furious, she hurried on before he could say a word. She looked up into his eyes and watched them flash with emotion, but she didn't let that stop her.

"You think I don't understand your 'duty' to protect me? Trust me when I say that's the one thing I am all too aware of. Duty is the first thing I was taught. Duty to my country, to the citizens of Cadria and to my king. My family has ruled for centuries. Yes, Cadria is a small country, but she's proud and it's *our* duty to protect her. Keep her safe. So, yes. I understand your self-imposed duties, but it doesn't mean I like them any more than I like the golden chains linking me to my own set of duties."

He studied her for a long minute before speaking. When he did, he said only, "Quite a rant."

She huffed out a short laugh. "Apparently, I have what you Americans refer to as 'issues.'"

"I never use that word," he assured her, and reached out for her again.

Smiling, she let herself be held. Probably another monumental mistake, but she needed the comfort of his arms. The strength of him, wrapped around her. If she had one more thing to regret in the morning, then so be it.

"Why'd your father have to be a *king?*"

She laughed a little and linked her arms at the small of his back. "Your father was a King, too."

He gave her a squeeze. "Funny."

Tipping her head back, she looked up at him and whispered, "You may be willing to pretend that everything that happened tonight was a mistake, but I for one, enjoyed myself immensely."

"So did I, Alex. That's the problem."

"Doesn't have to be."

He shook his head. "I'm here to do a job and that doesn't include bedding *you*."

That barb hit home with a staggering force she didn't even want to admit to herself. So much for tender makeup scenes in the moonlight. "Yes," she said softly. "I wonder if you'll get a raise in pay for this? Maybe if I tell my father how very good you were?"

"Cut it out, Alex."

She felt like a fool. She'd spilled her heart out to him, laid it at his feet and he chose that moment to remind her that he was being paid by her father. How could she possibly *love* a man who only saw her as a job? How could she have forgotten, even for a minute, that he had lied to her from their first day together? That her father was paying him to watch over her?

Well, fine. If he wanted to turn his back on what they had together, then she wouldn't stop him. She might be fool enough to love him, but she wasn't so big a fool that she didn't know when to pull back from the edge of a very steep cliff. Releasing him, she steeled herself for the soul-deep cold that slipped inside her the instant she left the circle of his arms.

"You're the one who brought this up again," she reminded him.

"I just want you to understand is all. I didn't want to say yes to your dad, but he's a hard man to refuse."

"That much I know from personal experience."

He took a breath. "When I realized who you were, I was worried. I called your father and told him I was uncomfortable with you out on your own with no protection. And so was he. I talked to your mother, too."

She closed her eyes briefly and he felt the tension in her body tighten. "So they double-teamed you."

"Yeah," he said with a sharp nod. "Guess you could say that."

"They're very good at it," she mused, a half smile blooming and disappearing from her mouth in a fraction of a second. "It's how they deal with my brothers and me, as well."

"Then you can see why—"

"I can see why you said yes to my father," she cut him off neatly and speared him with a glance that had gone icy. "What I don't see is why you *lied* to me."

"I lied because I had to. Your father told me you're adept at escaping your guards."

"And because you lied, I never even tried to escape you," she whispered.

"I couldn't risk you escaping me, Alex. I had to keep you safe. As for fighting what was happening between us..." He paused and shook his head again as if he couldn't believe they were in this situation. "In my job, when I get distracted, people tend to *die*. I won't let that happen to you, Alex."

"Garrett, if you don't *live,* you might as well be dead already. Don't you see that?"

"What I see is that I let you get to me," he said, gaze moving over her face. "Didn't mean to. Didn't want you to. But you did anyway."

A part of her thrilled to hear it. But the more rational voice in her mind warned against it. The look in his eyes was far from warm and fuzzy. The set of his jaw and the tension in every line of his body screamed that he was a man who'd made his decision. Alex had come in second to his sense of honor. What he said next only defined it.

"As much as I want you, I can't let this happen again, Alex. Not while I'm responsible for your safety."

There it was. Duty first. She should respect that sentiment, seeing as she had been raised to believe the same. But somehow, that didn't make her feel any better.

A chill swept over her that had nothing at all to do with the cold wind still flying toward them. Garrett couldn't have made himself clearer.

"No worries, Garrett," she told him, keeping her voice light in spite of the knot of pain clogging her throat. "You're absolutely safe from me now as I'm just not interested anymore."

"Liar."

She laughed shortly. "Amazing that you even feel comfortable using that word against someone else."

"Amazing that you can be so pissed at me for doing something you're pretty good at yourself."

She ignored that and turned for the bedroom, suddenly more than ready for this conversation to be over. "Before you go, want to check the bathroom for hidden assassins?"

"Funny."

Stepping into the bedroom, she walked to the dressing table, picked up her hairbrush and started drawing the bristles through her tangled hair. Staring into the mirror, she caught his reflected gaze. "You're making far too much of this situation. You're assuming I want this 'relationship' to continue. But I don't."

"Lying again."

She tossed the brush down. "Stop telling me when I'm lying. It's rude."

"Then stop lying."

"Same to you."

"I'm not lying now," he said. "I still want you."

"Me, too."

"Damn it, Alex."

"Shut up and kiss me, Garrett."

He did and Alex's brain went on hiatus again. Soon,

she would be able to sit back and regret this at her leisure. But at the moment, all she could think was how right it felt. How good it was to be in his arms again. To have his mouth fused to hers.

He lifted her and carried her to the bed and when he set her down onto the mattress, she looked up into icy-blue eyes that sparked and shone with the kind of need that shook her to the bone.

For now, that was enough.

Three days later, Garrett was on the edge with no way out.

Now that she knew who he was, Alex seemed to delight in making him nuts. She insisted on walking down crowded sidewalks, going shopping through packed malls and even driving to San Diego to visit SeaWorld. It was as if she had determined to make him earn every dime of his paycheck from her father.

It was a security expert's nightmare.

Garrett knew damn well it was only a matter of time before her identity was revealed. Someone, somewhere, was going to recognize her and then he'd be hip-deep in paparazzi, reporters and general nutcases, all trying to get close to the visiting princess.

But short of locking her into her penthouse, he didn't have a clue how to keep her from being noticed. A woman like Alex got people's attention. She was tall, gorgeous and had a perpetual smile on her face that seemed to welcome conversations with strangers. He hovered as closely as he could and still it wasn't enough.

His mind filled with ugly possibilities. He'd seen enough damage done over the years to be prepared for the absolute worst—his brain dredging up any number of horrific scenarios. And it killed him to think of anything happening to Alex.

Which was only natural, he assured himself. After all, she was in his care. Of course he'd be worried about her—that was his *job*. And that was all it was.

Garrett's trained gaze swept the room as he deliberately tried to become invisible, as any good bodyguard would. But, being the only man in a homeless shelter that catered to women and kids made Garrett's job harder. He stood out like Death at the Party. He caught the glances tossed his way and was sorry to know he was making some of the women here really uncomfortable. But damned if he was going to let Alex out of his sight.

The woman continued to press her luck and push him closer and closer to the ragged edge of control. Today, she had insisted on visiting a women's shelter to compare their setup with the program she knew at home.

Jane, the woman in charge, hadn't had a problem with his presence—but she had asked him to stay out of the way and that he was willing to do. Better all the way around for a protection detail to blend into the background as much as possible. It gave him eyes and ears to the place without attracting attention himself.

Watching Alex move around the room with the director, Garrett felt his admiration for her grow. She wasn't here as a princess. She had introduced herself as a fellow volunteer, visiting from Europe. And in a few short minutes, she and Jane had been chatting like old friends.

While Alex looked at the facility and met a few of the residents, Garrett watched *her*. She fit in any damn where, he thought and wondered at how easily Alex dismissed *what* she was in favor of *who* she was. She was so much more than some dilettante royal. She was eager and involved and she *cared* for people and what she might do to help. It had nothing to do with her crown. This was her soul he was watching, and damned if he could look away.

"You a cop?"

Garrett jolted out of his daydreams, gave himself a mental kick for being caught unaware and then looked down at the little boy staring up at him with wide brown eyes. "No, I'm not a cop."

"Look like one," the boy said, giving Garrett a gap-toothed smile. "You're all straight and stiff like one."

Great. He was doing such a good job being invisible that a five-year-old had made him. Alex really was throwing him off his game.

One corner of his mouth lifted in a smile. "You stand up straight, you get taller."

Those brown eyes went as big as saucers. "Tall as you?"

"Taller," Garrett assured him and instantly, the kid squared his shoulders, straightened his spine and lifted his chin. All forty pounds of him.

"Is she your girlfriend?"

That question came unexpectedly, though why it had, he didn't know. He'd spent enough time around his cousin's kids to know that they said pretty much whatever popped into their heads. "No," he said, shifting his gaze back to Alex. "She's a friend."

"She's nice," the boy said. "Pretty, too, and she smells good."

"Yeah," Garrett said, still watching Alex. "You're right."

"You should make her your girlfriend."

Intrigued, he shot the kid a look and asked, "Yeah? Why's that?"

"Because she smiles when she looks at you and that's nice. Besides, she's *pretty*."

"Timmy!" A woman shouted from across the room and the little boy trotted off, leaving Garrett staring after him.

Out of the mouths of babes, he mused. He looked up, caught Alex's eye and she flashed him one of those smiles that seemed designed to knock him off balance. In a flash, he remembered her under him, over him. The feel of her skin, the taste of her mouth, the scent of her, surrounding him.

As if she knew exactly what he was thinking, her smile slipped into something more private. More…intimate. And Garrett was once again hit with the knowledge that he'd fallen into a hole that just kept getting deeper.

Alex very much enjoyed watching Garrett go quietly insane at the beach. It was a lovely day to sit on the sand and enjoy the last of summer. There were only a handful of people there, including a few children busily building sand walls in an attempt to hold back the inexorable rush of the tide. Sandpipers and seagulls strutted along the shoreline and surfers sat atop their boards waiting for the perfect ride.

Everyone was having a good time, she thought. Everyone, that is, but Garrett King.

Honestly, it was simply too easy to push the man's buttons. And Alex had discovered just how much fun it could be. The man was determined to keep her at a distance. He hadn't touched her since that one night they'd spent together. Her heart hurt and her body ached for his and so, she had decided to make him as uncomfortable as possible with his decision to leave her alone.

If she was going to be miserable, then she would do everything she could to make sure he was, too. She challenged him, worried him and in general made his time with her as difficult as possible. She flirted with him outrageously and watched him fight his own desires to keep his professionalism at the fore.

With his serious "bodyguard" expression, he kept most people at bay. But those who weren't the least bit intimidated slipped past him, much to Alex's delight. Because then she flirted with other men, just to watch Garrett's instant, infuriated response.

Take for example the surfer who was right now giving her a wink and a smile before heading for the water. If she weren't in love with a perfectly infuriating man, she would very well be tempted to take the other man up on his not-so-subtle offer.

"He's short," Garrett muttered from behind her.

She smiled to herself, nodded at the surfer and said, "He's at least six feet tall."

"Shorter than me, then," Garrett said tightly.

"Most people are," she returned. "Hardly a crime."

"He's at least thirty and he's at the beach in the middle of the week."

"So are you," she pointed out, glancing over her shoulder at the man in black who was glowering at the rest of humanity. Honestly, he looked like the Grim Reaper. No wonder most people tended to give her a wide berth.

"Yes, but I'm *working,*" he told her.

"And you never let me forget that, do you?" Alex gritted her teeth and turned her head back to watch the handsome surfer carry his board out to the water. His black wet suit clung to a fairly amazing body and his long, light brown hair was sun-streaked, telling her he spent most of his days in the sun. Perhaps Garrett was right and he was a layabout. She frowned at the thought.

"Alex, don't start that again."

"I didn't start it, Garrett," she told him, now ignoring the surfer to concentrate on the conversation she was having with the man who refused to get close to her. "I never do. You're the one who consistently reminds me that I'm your *responsibility*. And I simply can't tell you how flattering that is."

He sighed. She heard it even from three feet away.

"But, even though it's your *job* to watch over me," she added, not for the first time, "it doesn't give you the right to chase away any man who dares to look at me."

"It is if I think they're dangerous."

She laughed outright at that comment and turned to stare at him. "Like the college student yesterday at the art gallery? That sweet young man who was so nervous he dropped his bottle of water?"

Garrett frowned. "He kept touching you."

"It was *crowded* in that shop."

"That's what he wanted you to think. He wasn't nervous, Alex. He was on the prowl. He kept bumping into you. *Touching* you." Scowling, he picked up a handful of sand and let it drift through his fingers. "It wasn't that crowded."

"Well, certainly not after you threw the poor soul up against a wall and frisked him!"

He smiled at the memory. "Did discourage him quick enough, didn't it?"

"And half the gallery," she pointed out. "People scattered, thinking you were a crazy person."

"Yeah..." He was still smiling.

"You're impossible. You know that, don't you?"

"If I hadn't known it before I met you, I do now. You tell me often enough."

"And yet you don't listen." Pushing up from the sand, Alex dusted off the seat of her white shorts and snatched up the sandals she had kicked off when they first arrived. Walking to him, she looked down into Garrett's eyes and said, "You might want to ask yourself why you take it so personally when another man looks at me. Or talks to me."

"You know why," he muttered, keeping his gaze fixed on hers.

"Yes, the job." She went down to one knee in front of him. "But I think it's more than that, Garrett. I think it's much more, but you're too much of a coward to admit it."

His features went like granite, and Alex knew she'd struck a nerve. Well, good. Happy to know it.

So quickly she hardly saw him move, he reached out, grabbed her and pulled her close. Then he gave her a brief, hard kiss before letting her go again. Shaking his head, he stood up, then took her hand and drew her to her feet as well.

"You keep pushing me, Alex, and you never know what might happen."

"And that, Garrett," she said, licking her lips and giving him a small victory smile, "is the fun part."

Eleven

"I quit."

"I beg your pardon?"

Garrett winced at the snooty tone the King of Cadria could produce. He had known going in that this phone call wouldn't go well, but there was nothing to be done about it. Garrett was through working for the king, and Alex's father was just going to have to deal with it.

"You heard me correctly, your majesty," he said, leaning back in his desk chair. The study in his home was dark, filled with shadows in every corner. A single lamp on his desk wasn't enough to chase them away—seemed like a pretty good metaphor for his life at the moment, he thought, surprised at the poetic train his mind was taking. But there were shadows in Garrett's past, too. Always there. Always ready to pounce. And the light that was Alex—though damn brighter than anything he'd ever known—still couldn't get rid of all those dark places.

So there was really only one thing to do. "I quit as your daughter's bodyguard."

The king blustered and shouted and Garrett let him go. He figured he owed it to the man to let him get it all out of his system. And while a royal father thousands of miles away ranted and raged, Garrett's mind turned to that afternoon on the beach. The look in Alex's eyes. The taste of her.

These past few days had been torturous. He couldn't be with her without wanting her and he couldn't have her as long as he was responsible for her safety. But the whole truth was, he couldn't have her, *period.*

Even if he gave in to what he wanted, what would it gain either of them? Soon she'd be going home to a damn palace. He would be here, in California running his business. He wasn't looking to be in love or to be married. But even if he were, she was a princess and there was just no way Garrett could compete with that. Oh, he was rich enough to give her the kind of house and servants she was used to. But he didn't have the pedigree her family would expect of a man wanting to be with Alex.

He was a King, and he was damn proud of it. The problem was, she was the daughter of a *king*.

No. There was nothing ahead for them but more misery and, thanks very much, but he'd rather skip that part of the festivities.

Sitting forward, he braced his elbow on the desktop and only half listened to the king on the other end of the line. Whatever the man said wouldn't change Garrett's mind. He already knew he was doing the only thing possible. For both of them.

"Mr. King," Alex's father was sputtering, "you cannot simply walk away from my daughter's safety without so much as a warning. I will need time to—"

Enough was enough.

"Sir, I won't take money from you to watch over Alex," Garrett finally interrupted the king and the other man's abrupt silence told him the king wasn't used to that kind of treatment. Just one more nugget of proof that Garrett King and royalty were never going to be a good mix. "But, that said," he continued into the quiet, "I won't leave her out there alone, either. On my own, I'll watch out for her until she's on a plane headed home."

"May I ask *why* you've decided to leave my employ?"

Touchy question, Garrett told himself. He could hardly confess to the king that he didn't want to be taking money from the father of the woman he wanted in his bed. That might be enough for a beheading in Cadria, for all Garrett knew.

"Let's just say, Alex and I have become friends. And I feel badly taking money from her father."

There was a long silence, and then the king gave a tired sigh. Garrett sympathized. Couldn't be easy being thousands of miles away from someone you worried about. "Fine then. I appreciate your help in this, Mr. King, and it won't be forgotten."

Long after the king hung up, Garrett sat in his darkened study and stared at nothing. No, he thought. None of this would be forgotten.

Ever.

The late-night knock on Alex's door startled her.

She tossed the book she had been reading to the sofa cushion beside her. Jumping up from the couch, she tugged at the belt of her blue silk robe and crossed the room with hesitant steps. She wasn't expecting anyone and the desk always called before they disturbed her. And just who would have been able to get onto the penthouse elevator besides… She looked through the peephole and saw Garrett staring back at her.

Her heart did a slow roll in her chest as her nerves drained away and an entirely different emotion charged to the surface. She leaned her forehead on the cool, painted surface of the door and took a breath. Would the man always have this effect on her? Would one look at him always be enough to turn her knees to water?

Shaking her head, she steadied herself, then fumbled with the locks and opened the door to him. "Garrett. I didn't expect to see you until tomorrow."

"Yeah," he muttered, stepping past her to enter the suite. "Something's come up."

She frowned as he walked into the room, careful not to get close enough to brush against her. Alex noticed that his features were grim, his cheeks shadowed by beard stubble and his hair looked as if he'd been running his fingers through it for hours.

"Garrett? Is something wrong?"

He laughed shortly and turned to look at her. His eyes were dark and filled with charged emotions too deep to name. Shoving his hands into the back pockets of his worn jeans, he just looked at her for a long minute before saying, "Just came to tell you something. You win."

"What?"

Shaking his head, he blew out a breath and said, "I talked to your father a while ago. Told him I quit."

"You did?" All right, she should be pleased, and yet, the look on his face told her that more was coming and that she wasn't going to like it.

"Told him I couldn't take money from him for keeping you safe."

She took a single step toward him. "Why, Garrett? Why would you do that?"

"You know why." His gaze swept her up and down before settling on her eyes again. "But that doesn't mean I'm backing off, Alex. I'm still going to be there. Every day. Making sure nothing happens to you."

"Garrett." She reached up and cupped his cheek in her palm. "Nothing's going to happen to me."

He caught her hand in his and held on. His shadow-filled eyes locked with hers and flashed with steely determination. "Damn straight, it's not."

Her hand trapped in his tight grip, she could only stare up at him. "Garrett, you're even more crazed about protecting me than the palace guards. Why?"

"Because I won't fail again."

"Fail? Fail how?"

He released her, turned and walked to the couch and looked down at the book, spine up on the cushions. He snorted. "Romance novel?"

"There's nothing wrong with a happy ending," she said.

"Happy endings are fictional, Alex."

"They don't have to be."

He turned back to face her. "You don't get it." A choked off laugh shot from his throat. "No reason why you should."

Alex was standing not two feet from him and yet she felt distance stretching out between them. The pale light of her reading lamp was a golden circle in the darkness, reaching for Garrett and not quite making it. Absently she noted the soft roar of the ocean, like an extra heartbeat in the room.

"Then explain it to me, Garrett. Tell me what's driving you."

He reached up, scraped both palms across his face and then shoved them through his hair. When he'd finished, he looked at her and his eyes were bleak, sending a thread of worry sliding through Alex's body.

When he spoke, his voice was rough and low, as if he regretted saying the words even before they were out of his mouth. "About ten years ago, I was hired to be a bodyguard for the daughter of a very wealthy man."

Alex held her breath and stayed perfectly still. Finally, she was going to get to the heart of the problem and she didn't want to risk interrupting him. Yet at the same time, she couldn't fight the notion that once he said what he had to, nothing would be the same. For either of them.

"Her name was Kara." A smile briefly twisted his mouth and was gone again in a blink. "She was beautiful and stubborn and smart. A lot like you, really."

A trickle of cold began to snake down her spine and still, she remained quiet.

"I got…distracted," he said and once again shoved a hand through his hair as if somehow he could wipe away the memories swarming in his mind. "I fell in love with her—"

Pain was swift and sharp. Jealousy dug its talons into her heart and twisted. And just as quickly, it all faded away. He had loved, but it was ten years ago and obviously it hadn't ended well. She forced herself to ask, "What happened?"

"I quit my job," he said, and swept the room with his troubled gaze before looking back at her. "Knew I couldn't protect Kara with my focus splintered. Told her father I wouldn't be responsible for her life anymore and I left. Two days later, Kara ditched her new guard and ran away. The letter she left behind said she was running to me. She never got there. She was kidnapped and killed."

"God, Garrett…"

"I won't let that happen to you."

Sympathy briefly warred with frustration inside her. Frustration won. "What makes you think it would? One tragedy doesn't always signal another."

"I know. But even getting past that, it's not just Kara. It's you and me. We're too different, Alex. Our worlds are light years apart." He shook his head and she felt the finality of that one single action. His features were tight, implacable. His voice a promise as he added, "I'm not looking to fall in love, Alex. What would be the point?"

Her heart gave a sudden lurch in her chest, and it felt as if a ball of lead had dropped into the pit of her stomach. He was walking away from her. Without even trying. Without a backward glance. Tears filled her eyes but she furiously blinked them back. She wasn't about to let him see her *cry*. What would be the point anyway?

Whatever she had convinced herself they shared, in reality, it was no more than a holiday fling. A summer romance doomed to die at the end of the season. She loved a man determined to not love her back, and there didn't seem to be a thing she could do to change it.

And would she if she could?

She had her pride after all. And that emotion was leading the charge when she snapped, "I never said anything about love, Garrett."

"Please." He gave her a patient, tired smile that made her want to kick something. "I can see it in your face, feel it in your touch. Alex, you're looking for something I can't give you."

She felt the sting of those words, and actually swayed in place when they hit her. But she kept her chin lifted and her eyes defiant as she corrected, "Not can't. *Won't*."

"Same thing," he said, folding his arms across his chest and glaring down at her.

"For a man who prides himself on seeing every possible angle of every possible situation, you're surprisingly blind."

"Is that right?"

"It is," she answered and took a step closer to him. Her gaze fixed with his. "This isn't even about *me*, Garrett. It's about you and how you look at your life. I'm sorry about Kara. But that wasn't your fault. Bad things happen. You can't stop them. You can only live your life in spite of them."

"She left her guards because of me," he told her flatly. "If I hadn't gotten involved with her, she'd be alive today."

"You don't know that," she told him and saw denial in his eyes. "You're not God, Garrett. You don't have the power of life and death, and you can't personally protect everyone you care about."

"But I can limit those I care about," he said softly.

"So rather than love and risk the pain of losing it, you would make your own world smaller so maybe danger won't notice you? Maybe your circle of loved ones will be tiny enough that nothing bad will touch you?"

He didn't say anything to that, but then, he didn't have to. Alex knew now for certain that what they had was over. He could stay and watch over her as he'd said he would, but there would be no more lovemaking. No more flirtatious fun. No more laughter. There would be only Garrett, in his role of knight errant ready to do battle in defense of his charge.

And that wasn't enough for Alex. Not nearly enough.

Sadly, she shook her head and said, "The difference between you and me is, I won't deny myself something wonderful for fear of losing it."

"That's because you've never lost."

"Wrong again," she said, a half smile curving her mouth. "I just did."

"Alex—"

"I think you should go," she said, though the words tore at her.

This was over. He couldn't have made himself plainer. He didn't want her—he saw her only as his responsibility—and she wanted the magic.

The gulf lying between them was wider than ever.

"Fine. I'll go. But I'll be back in the morning," he said. "Don't leave the hotel without me."

She didn't answer because an order didn't require one. She simply stood, alone in the dim light and listened to the door close behind him.

First thing in the morning, though, the plan changed.

Griffin needed some backup with a client and Garrett had already dumped so much of the company work on his twin lately, he couldn't turn him down. Besides, he figured it might do both he and Alex some good to have some space.

He'd been up half the night, reliving that scene in her penthouse suite. He could still feel the chill in the room when he told her he wouldn't love her. Could still see her eyes when she told him to leave. A low, deep ache settled in his chest, but Garrett accepted it as the price he had to pay for screwing this up so badly.

And he knew that the pain was going to be with him a long, damn time. He was halfway to San Diego when he thought it was late enough that he could call Alex without waking her up. Punching in the phone number, Garrett steered his car down the 405 freeway and waited for what seemed forever for Alex to answer the damn phone. The moment she did, the sound of her voice sent another ping of regret shooting through him.

Mentally, he explained it away. Of course he regretted

that she'd be leaving. Why the hell wouldn't he? He'd spent practically every day with her for more than a week. Why wouldn't he be accustomed to her smile, her laughter? It was only natural that he'd listen for the sound of her accent and get a buzz when he knew he was going to see her.

Didn't mean he cared. Didn't *mean* anything. When she was gone, things would settle down. Get back to normal, he assured himself. Which was all he wanted. The regular world that didn't include runaway princesses.

"Alex, it's me," he said shortly, changing lanes to pass an RV moving at a snail-like speed in the sun-washed morning.

"What is it, Garrett?"

Her voice was clipped now, as if anger was churning just below the surface. He hated to hear it, but it was probably best, he told himself. If she was mad, then she wasn't hurting. He'd never meant to hurt her, God knew. But it had happened anyway and now the best thing he could do was keep up the wall he'd erected between them the night before.

"I won't be able to come over this morning," he said tightly. "Griffin needs some help on a case, and I—"

"No need to explain. I'm sure you're very busy."

The words might be right, but her tone said differently. He scowled at the phone. "Yeah. Well, anyway. You won't be alone. I sent one of our best agents over there. Terri Cooper. She's in the lobby now, waiting for a call from you to the front desk. She's the best in the business, so I know she'll keep you safe."

"Garrett, I don't need a babysitter."

"She's a bodyguard, Alex, and until I get back, she's sticking to you like glue."

"And I've no say in it."

He frowned to himself and downshifted as the flow of

traffic picked up a bit. "If you don't want to see Terri, don't leave the hotel. I'd prefer that anyway. I should be able to be back before dinner."

"I see," she said, her accent a little sharper, "and I'm to await you at your convenience, is that it?"

He punched the accelerator and swung around another car, which had no business driving in the fast lane. "Alex, don't start with me. We've been over this. You know it's not safe."

"No, Garrett," she argued, "*you* know it's not safe. But I've a mind of my own and am in no way burdened with your overwhelmingly cautious nature."

"Damn it, Alex." He thought about hitting the first off-ramp and heading back. Then he realized his twin was in La Jolla waiting for him, and Garrett was stuck between the proverbial rock and a hard place.

And he did *not* have a cautious nature.

Made him sound like some old lady afraid to leave her house. Nothing could be further from the truth. He faced down danger every damn day of his life. It was *Alex* facing danger he couldn't bear the thought of.

"I'm in charge of your safety."

"No, you're not. You said yourself last night that you're no longer working for my father. That makes you nothing more than a bossy ex-bed partner. And I don't take orders from my exes."

"You're making me crazy, Alex. Terri will be with you if you leave the hotel."

Someone cut him off and Garrett honked at them. Didn't do any good, but made him feel a little better.

"I won't promise anything. And if that makes you crazy, then I'll admit to enjoying your misery as a side benefit."

She was enjoying it, too. He heard it in her voice. God knew what she would do today just to prove to him that she could take care of herself. He didn't even want to think about it.

The stream of traffic was slowing down. Brake lights flashed ahead and cars were stacked up behind him, too. Just another day on Southern California's freeways. Once he was stopped dead, he muttered, "I'll be back as soon as I can. Just—be careful, okay?"

There was a long pause and, for a moment, he half wondered if she'd hung up on him and he hadn't noticed. Then finally, she said only, "Goodbye, Garrett."

Car horns blared, the radio in the car beside him was set to a volume probably audible in space and the only sound Garrett really noticed was the hum of the dial tone, telling him she was gone.

"She's making me nuts."

"In her defense," Griffin said helpfully, "she didn't have far to go."

"Thanks for that." Garrett gave his twin a dark look. "You're supposed to be on my side, remember? Blood thicker than water and all that?"

"Yeah, we're family, blah, blah," Griffin said, kicking back in the leather booth seat and pausing long enough to take a long pull on his bottle of beer. "But if the princess is getting to you this badly, then I'm all for it."

Garrett stared down at his own beer and then lifted his gaze to look around the half-empty pub. It was supposed to look Irish, but Garrett had seen the real thing not long ago when he did a job for his cousin Jefferson. Still, it wasn't bad, just touristy. Lots of dark wood, flags of Ireland all over the place and even a bronze leprechaun crouched on the bar.

He and Griffin had finished with their client early and had stopped in here for some lunch before facing the long drive home again. He was still worried about Alex, but she'd been on her own for hours already, doing God knew what—because the damn woman wouldn't answer her damn phone. All Terri sent him was a brief text saying everything was fine. So him taking a half hour for lunch wasn't going to make that much difference at this point.

"And did I mention," Griffin said with a knowing leer, "you look like *hell?*"

He had known that talking to Griffin about all of this wouldn't get him any sympathy. And maybe he didn't need any. What he needed was somebody to talk to.

He should have picked someone smarter.

"Doesn't matter if she's 'getting' to me or not—which she isn't," he added, after a pause for a sip of beer. "The point is she's a princess, Griff. Would never work."

"Man, I really did get all the brains," Griffin mused with a slow shake of his head. "The way you talk about her, she seems damn near perfect. And you don't want her because she's a princess? What is that?"

"It's not a question of want."

"Then what is it?"

"Even if I did admit to wanting Alex, the fact that she's a princess pretty much cools that whole idea."

"Because…"

Irritated, Garrett glared at his twin. "You think her family would want her with a security expert?"

"Who better?"

"Nice try. But royals prefer royals, and everyone knows that. Her father's probably got her future husband all picked out for her." The thought of that made him want to break something.

"Uh-huh. And what else?" Griffin shook his head. "There's more here, Garrett."

"Kara." He'd loved once and lost her. He wasn't sure he was willing to go through that again.

"Here we go," Griffin muttered. "You know, I've been hearing that excuse for years, and I'm just not buying it anymore."

"What the hell's that mean?"

"It means, that you've been hiding behind Kara. Yeah, it was terrible what happened to her. But you know damn well it wasn't your fault."

Garrett shifted in his seat, took a swig of beer and set the bottle down again.

"You loved her, and she died."

"Thanks for the news flash. But I don't need you to tell me that. I lived it."

Griffin ignored him. Leaning on the tabletop, he said, "Somewhere along the way, though, you died, too. Or at least you stopped living, which amounts to the same thing."

Garrett glared at his twin again, but it didn't do any good. Nothing could shut Griffin up if he had something to say and clearly he did. Seemed he'd been building up to this little speech for years.

"Now along comes the princess, shakes you up, makes you notice, *hey, not a bad world out here,* and *boom.*" He clapped both hands together for emphasis. "You shut down. Start pulling Kara out of the past and using her as a shield or some damn thing. The problem isn't Kara, Garrett. Never was. The problem is *you.*"

The waitress arrived with their lunch and while Griffin flirted and got an extra order of fries for his trouble, Garrett did some fast thinking. His twin might actually have a point. He had been enjoying his time with Alex. Had been relaxing the guard around his heart and the minute she got close, he'd pulled back. So was he using Kara as a shield? If that was true, then Alex had been right the night before when she'd accused him of making sure his world was small enough that tragedy would have a harder time striking.

When it was just the two of them again, Griffin noted, "Hmm. Looks like a lightbulb might have gone off in your head."

"Maybe," Garrett admitted, then added, "but even if you're right—"

"Can't hear that often enough," Griffin said with a grin just before popping a French fry into his mouth.

"—it doesn't change the fact that Alex is a princess and lives in a palace for God's sake. I live in a condo at the beach—"

"No, you don't," Griffin interrupted.

"Excuse me?" Seriously, he knew where he *lived.*

Taking another pull of his beer, Griffin said, "You don't live there. You live out of suitcases. Hell, you spend more time on King Jets than you do in that condo."

"What's that supposed to mean?"

"Means you don't live anywhere, Garrett. So what's keeping you here?"

He just stared at his twin. Was he the only one who could see the problems in this? Alex was oblivious and now Griffin, too? "Our *business?*"

"More excuses." Griff waved one hand at his brother, effectively dismissing him, then picked up his burger and took a bite. After chewing, he said, "We can run our place from anywhere. If you wanted to, you could set up a European branch and you damn well know it."

His chest felt tight. The noise in the pub fell away. All he could hear was himself, telling Alex that he wouldn't love her. That he couldn't. The problem was, he *did* love her.

A hell of a thing for a man to just be figuring out. But

there it was. He'd had to quit working for her father because he couldn't take money for protecting the woman he loved. He had kept his distance from her because he couldn't sleep with her knowing that he'd have to let her go.

But did he have to?

What if he was wrong? What if there was a chance a commoner might have a shot with a princess? Was he really ready to let Alex go without even *trying* to make it work? His brain raced with possibilities. Maybe he had been short-sighted. Stupid. But he didn't have to stay that way.

His phone rang, and he glanced at the readout. Instantly, he answered it and fought the sudden hot ball of worry in his guts. "Terri? What is it?"

"Boss, I'm sorry, but you *did* tell me to stick to her and—"

"What happened?" In his mind, he was seeing car wrecks, holdups, assassins...

"She had me drive her to L.A. and—"

"Uh, Garrett..."

"Shut up," he muttered, then to Terri he said, "L.A.? Why L.A.?"

"Garrett!"

His gaze snapped to Griffin.

Pointing to the bar, his twin said, "You need to see this."

He turned to look. Terri was still talking in his ear, but he hardly heard her. There was a flat screen TV above the bar, the sound muted. But he didn't need the sound. What he saw opened a hole in his chest. He snapped the phone shut and stared.

Alex was on the TV. But an Alex he hardly knew. Her long, thick hair was twisted into a complicated knot at the top of her head. Diamonds winked at her ears and blazed at the base of her throat. She wore a pale green dress that was tailored to fit her beautifully and she looked as remote as a...well, a *princess*.

Garrett pushed out of his seat, crossed the room and ordered the bartender to, "Turn it up, will you?"

The man did and Garrett listened over the roaring in his own ears. Someone shoved a microphone at Alex and shouted, "Princess, how long have you been here and why the big secret?"

She smiled into the camera, and Garrett could have sworn she was looking directly at him. His hands curled around the edge of the polished wood bar and squeezed until he was half afraid he was going to snap the thick wood in two.

"I've been in America almost two weeks," she said, her voice low, moderate, regal. "As for the secrecy of my visit, I wanted the opportunity to see the *real* America. To meet people and get to know them without the barriers of my name and background getting in the way."

People in the bar were listening. Griffin had moved up alongside him, but Garrett hardly noticed. His gaze was fixed on Alex. She looked so different. And already so far away.

"Did it work?" someone else shouted.

"It did," she said, her gaze still steady on the camera, staring directly into Garrett's soul. "I've enjoyed myself immensely. This is a wonderful country, and I've been met with nothing but kindness and warmth."

"You're headed home now, Princess," a reporter called out. "What're you going to miss the most?"

There was a long, thoughtful pause before Alex smiled into the camera and said, "It's a difficult question. I loved Disneyland, of course. And the beach. But I think what

I loved most were the people I met. *They* are what I'll miss when I go home. *They* are what will stay with me. Always."

She was leaving.

And maybe, he told himself darkly, it was better this way. But even he didn't believe that.

The camera pulled away and an excited news anchor came on to say, "Princess Alexis of Cadria, speaking to you from the Cadrian Consulate in Los Angeles. I can tell you we were all surprised to get the notice of her brief press conference. Speculation will be rife now, as to just where the princess has been for the last week or more.

"But this afternoon, a private jet will be taking her back to her home country. A shame we didn't get to see more of the lovely Princess Alexis while she was here."

Garrett had already turned away when the woman shifted gears and launched into another story. Walking back to their booth, Garrett sat down, picked up his burger and methodically took a bite. There was no reason to hurry through lunch now.

"Garrett—"

He glared his twin into silence and concentrated on the burger that suddenly tasted like sawdust.

Twelve

Everything was just as she'd left it.

Why that should have surprised Alex, she couldn't have said. But it did. Somehow, she felt so…changed, that she had expected to find the palace different as well.

Standing on the stone terrace outside the morning room, she turned to look up at the pink stone walls of the palace she called home. The leaded glass windows winked in the early morning sunlight and the flag of Cadria, flying high atop the far turret, snapped in the breeze.

She was both comforted and irritated that life in Cadria had marched inexorably on while she had been gone. But then, her emotions were swinging so wildly lately, that didn't surprise her, either. Since coming home a week ago, she had slipped seamlessly back into the life she had so briefly left behind. She had already visited two schools and presided over the planting of new trees in the city's park.

The papers were still talking about her spontaneous visit to the U.S. and photographers still haunted her every step.

Now, when she wanted to go shopping, she couldn't just walk to the closest mall or wander down to the neighborhood shops. A shopping excursion became more of a battle strategy. There were guards, which she told herself, Garrett would thoroughly approve of, there were state cars and flags flying from the bumpers. There were stores closed to all other shoppers and bowing deference from shopkeepers.

God, how she missed being a nobody.

Of course, her family didn't see it that way. They were all delighted to have her back. Her oldest brother was about to become engaged, and the other two were doing what they did best. Immersing themselves in royal duties with the occasional break for polo or auto racing. Her parents were the same, though her father hadn't yet interrogated her about her holiday and Alex suspected she had her mother to thank for that.

And she appreciated the reprieve. She just wasn't ready to talk about Garrett yet. Not to anybody. She was still hoping to somehow wipe him out of her mind. What was the point in torturing herself forever over a man who saw her as nothing more than an anvil around his neck?

"Bloody idiot," she muttered and kicked the stone barrier hard enough to send a jolt of pain through her foot and up her leg. But at least it was *physical* pain, which was a lot easier to deal with.

"Well," a familiar voice said from behind her, "that's more like it."

Alex looked over her shoulder at her mother. Queen Teresa of Cadria was still beautiful. Tall and elegant, Alex's mother kept her graying blond hair in a short cut that swung along her jawline. She wore green slacks, a white silk blouse and taupe flats. Her only jewelry was her wedding ring. Her blue eyes were sharp and fixed on her daughter.

"Mom. I didn't know you were there."

"Clearly," Teresa said as she strolled casually across the terrace, "care to tell me who the 'bloody idiot' is? Or will you make me guess?"

The queen calmly hitched herself up to sit on the stone parapet and demurely crossed her feet at the ankles. Alex couldn't help but smile. In public, Teresa of Cadria was dignified, elegant and all things proper. But when the family was alone, she became simply Teresa Hawkins Wells. A California girl who had married a king.

She had bowed to some traditions and had livened up other staid areas of the palace with her more casual flair. For instance, when she became queen, Teresa had made it clear that the "old" way of raising royal children wouldn't be happening anymore. She had been a hands-on mother and had remained that way. Naturally, there had also been governesses and tutors, but Alex and her brothers had grown up knowing their parents' love—and there were many royals who couldn't claim that.

None of Teresa's children had ever been able to keep a secret from her for long. And not one of them had ever successfully lied to their mother. So Alex didn't even bother trying now.

"Garrett King," she said.

"As I suspected." Teresa smiled as encouragement.

Alex didn't need much. Strange, she hadn't thought she wanted to talk about him, yet now that the opportunity was here, she found the words couldn't come fast enough. "He's arrogant and pompous and bossy. Always ordering me about, as bad as Dad, really. But he made me laugh as often as he made me angry and—"

"You love him," her mother finished for her.

"Yes, but I'll get over it," Alex said with determination.

"Why would you want to?"

The first sting of tears hit her eyes and that only made Alex more furious. She swiped at them with impatient fingers and said, "Because he doesn't want me." She shook her head and looked away from her mom's sympathetic eyes to stare out over the palace's formal gardens.

She focused on the box hedge maze. The maze had been constructed more than three hundred years ago, and Alex smiled, remembering how she and her brothers used to run through its long, twisting patterns at night, trying to scare each other.

The maze was so famous it was one of the most popular parts of the castle tour that was offered every summer. But the most beautiful part of the garden was the roses. They were Alex's mother's pride and joy. Teresa had brought slips of California roses with her when she'd given up her life to be queen. And she still nurtured those plants herself, despite grumblings from the head gardener.

Their thick scent wafted to them now, and Alex took a deep breath, letting the familiar become a salve to her wounded pride.

"Alex," her mother said, reaching out to lay one hand on her daughter's arm, "of course he wants you. Why else would he refuse to take money for protecting you?"

"Stubbornness?" Alex asked, shifting her gaze to her mother.

Teresa smiled and shook her head. "Now who's being stubborn?"

"You don't understand, Mom." Alex turned her back on

the garden and pushed herself up to sit beside her mother. The damp cold from the stones leached into her black slacks and slid into her bones, but she hardly noticed. "It was different for you. You met Dad at Disneyland, and it was magic. He fell in love and swept you off your feet and—"

She stopped and stared when her mother's laughter rang out around her. "What's so funny?"

"Oh, sweetie," Teresa said as she caught her breath again. "I didn't mean to laugh, but…maybe your father was right. When you were a little girl, he used to tell me I was spinning too many romantic stories. Filling your head with impossible expectations."

Confused, Alex just looked at her mother. "But you did meet at Disneyland. And you fell in love and became a queen."

"All true," her mother said, "but, that's not *all* of the story."

Intrigued, Alex let her own troubles move to the background as she listened to her mother.

"I did meet Gregory at Disneyland," she said, a half smile on her face. "I was working at the Emporium and he came in and bought half the merchandise at my station just so he'd have an excuse to keep standing there talking to me."

Alex could enjoy the story even more now that she had been to the famous park and could imagine the scene more clearly.

"We spent a lot of time together in the two weeks he was in California and, long story short, we fell in love." She smiled again, then picked up Alex's hand and gave it a squeeze. "But it wasn't happily ever after right away, sweetie."

"What happened?"

"Your dad left. He came back here, to the palace." She swept her gaze up to take in the pink castle and its centuries of tradition. "He told me he was going to be a king and that he couldn't marry me. That we couldn't possibly be together. His parents wouldn't have allowed it, and his country wouldn't stand for it."

"What? That's ridiculous!" Alex immediately defended her. "Cadria *loves* you."

"Yes," her mother said with a laugh. "*Now.* Back then, though, it was a different story. I was heartbroken and furious that he would walk away from love so easily."

She and her mother had more in common than Alex knew, she thought glumly. But at least her mom had eventually gotten a happy ending. But how? "What happened?"

"Your father missed me," Teresa said with a grin. "He called, but I wouldn't speak to him. He sent me gifts that I returned. Letters that went back unopened." Nudging Alex's shoulder with her own, Teresa admitted, "I drove him crazy."

"Good for you. I can't believe Dad walked away from you!"

"Centuries of tradition are hard to fight," Teresa said. "And so was your grandfather who had no interest in a commoner daughter-in-law."

"But—"

"I know, sweetie. Your grandfather loved me. Once he met me, everything was fine." She sighed a little. "But, your dad actually had to threaten to abdicate before his father would listen to reason."

"Dad was willing to give up the throne for you?"

"He was," Teresa said with another sigh of satisfaction. "Thankfully, it didn't come to that, since he's a very good king. But once his father saw how serious Gregory was, he promised to make it work. He went to the Law Chambers himself to see that the country's charter was rewritten to allow for a commoner as queen."

"Wow." She didn't know what else to say. Alex had had no idea of the intrigue and passion and clashes that had been involved in her parents getting together.

"Yes, wow," Teresa said, laughing again. "When it was all settled, in a record amount of time, thanks to your father being an impatient soul, Gregory came back to California with his grandmother's ring in hand and the rest, as they say, is history."

Holding up her left hand as proof, Teresa wiggled her fingers, letting the ancient diamond wink and glitter in the sunlight.

"I had no idea."

"Of course you didn't, and I should have told you the whole truth sooner. But, Alex, I had a point in telling you this now," her mother said and reached out to give her a one-armed hug. "And that is, don't give up on your young man. Love is a powerful thing and, once felt, it's impossible to walk away from. If your Garrett is anything like my Gregory…" She smiled again. "There's always hope."

"Excuse me, your majesty."

Teresa looked to the open doorway into the morning room. A maid stood in the shadows. "Yes, Christa?"

"I've laid the tea out, ma'am, for you and her highness."

"Thank you, Christa," Teresa said, "we'll be right in."

A quick curtsy and the maid was gone again. A moment later, Teresa scooted off the parapet, dusted off the seat of her slacks and said, "I'll pour the tea. You come in when you're ready, okay?"

Nodding, Alex watched her mother go, as her mind

whirled with possibilities. Was her mom right? Was there hope? Yes, her parents' love story had turned out well in the end, but the King of Cadria had been in love.

Whereas Garrett King *refused* to be in love with her.

She turned her head to stare out over the gardens, to the ocean beyond and to the man on the other side of the world. Hope, she thought wistfully, could be a both a blessing and a curse.

"She sent it back."

"What?" Griffin looked up as Garrett stormed into his office.

Tossing a small package onto his brother's desk, Garrett complained, "The necklace I sent to Alex two days ago. She returned it!"

"And this is my problem because…"

"You're my brother, and it's your job to listen to me," Garrett told him as he stalked the perimeter of his brother's office.

"Actually, it's my job to look into the file we just got on our Georgia client and—"

"Why would she return it?" Garrett asked no one in particular, thinking of the platinum and onyx piece he'd had commissioned just for her. He hadn't asked himself why it was so important for him to give her a memento of their time together. It simply was. He couldn't have her, but damned if he could entirely let go, either.

These past two weeks without her had nearly killed him. Nothing felt right to him anymore. Without Alex in his life, everything else was just white noise. He kept as busy as possible and *still* her absence chewed at him, widening the black hole inside him every damn day.

His fingers closed around the box that had been returned to him just a few minutes ago. Shaking it for emphasis, he blurted, "It was a trinket. Sort of a souvenir. You know, help her remember her holiday."

Griffin gave up and sat back in his chair. "Maybe she doesn't *want* to remember."

Garrett stopped dead and glared at his twin. "Why the hell wouldn't she want to remember? She had a great time."

"Yeah, but it's over, and she's back home at the palace."

"So, close the door? That's it?" Could she really cut him out of her life, her memories, that easily?

"Aren't you the one who closed the door?" Griffin asked.

"Not the point." Hell, Garrett knew he wasn't making any sense. He didn't need his twin stating the obvious.

Two weeks without her. Didn't seem to matter that he knew he'd done the right thing. Didn't matter that he knew there was no way they could have worked out anything between them. He missed her like he would an arm. Or a leg.

She was as much a part of him as his damn heart and without her, it was like he didn't have one.

This had not been a part of the plan. He'd expected to miss her, sure. But he hadn't counted on not being able to sleep or keep his mind on his damn work. He hadn't counted on seeing her everywhere, hearing her voice, her laugh in his mind at odd moments during the day.

"You're just going to prowl around my office, is that it?" Griffin asked.

Garrett stopped and glared at him. "What the hell am I supposed to do?"

"You know what I think you should do. Question is, what are you *going* to do?"

"If I knew that," he muttered darkly, "I'd be doing it."

"Well then, maybe this will help you decide," Griffin said and pulled the morning paper out from under a stack of files. "Wasn't going to show you this—but maybe you should see it after all."

"What?" Garrett took the paper, glanced at the picture on the front page and felt his heart stop.

Front and center, there was a photo of Alex, dressed in a flowing gown and a crown, holding on to the arm of an impossibly handsome man in a tux, wearing a damn sash across his chest that was loaded down with medals. The tagline above the photo screamed, Royal Engagement In The Wind?

"Oh, *hell* no," Garrett muttered.

"Looks to me like you'd better go get your woman back before it's too late," Griffin said, clearly amused at Garrett's reaction.

Garrett's vision fogged at the edges until all he could see was Alex's face staring up at him from the paper. He was about to really lose her. Permanently. Unless he took a chance.

Clutching the newspaper tight in one fist, Garrett grabbed the returned package and said, "Call the airport for me. Have one of the King Jets fueled up and ready to go when I get there."

Griffin was laughing as he made the call, but Garrett was already gone.

"Where is he?" Garrett stormed past the footman at the door to the castle and stomped loudly across the marble flooring. His head turned as if on a swivel as he scanned every hallway for signs of the king.

"If you'll follow me," the butler said, "his majesty is in the library."

Garrett hadn't slept in nearly twenty-four hours. He felt ragged and pushed to the edge of his endurance, but damned if he was going to wait another minute to talk to Alex's father. He'd gotten past the palace guards on the strength of his having done work for the crown before. But getting an audience with the king this easily was a plus.

The air smelled of roses and beeswax, and Garrett took a deep breath to steady himself for the coming confrontation. The sound of his footsteps as he followed after his guide rang out hollowly in the air, thudding like a heartbeat. He had a plan, of course. Wasn't much of one, but he'd use whatever he could. Alex was here, somewhere, and no matter what happened between him and the king in the next few minutes, he wasn't leaving until he spoke to her.

He stepped into the library and the butler left him with the king. The room was imposing, as it was meant to be. Dark paneling, bloodred leather furniture and floor-to-ceiling windows with a view of the sea. The man standing before a crackling fire was just as imposing. King Gregory was tall, muscular and the gray in his hair only made him look more formidable.

"Garrett, this is a surprise."

About to be an even bigger one, he thought and cut right to the chase. "Your majesty, Alex can't marry Duke Henrik."

"Is that right?" One eyebrow lifted.

Hell, Garrett couldn't believe the man would allow Alex *near* the duke. A quick online search had been enough to show Garrett that the man was more known for his string of women than for any work done in the House of Lords.

Well, the king might be okay with that, but damned if Garrett would let Alex end up with someone who didn't deserve her.

"How is this any of your business, Garrett?"

"It's my business because there's a good chance Alex is pregnant with my child."

Risky move, he told himself, since there was no way Alex was pregnant. But it was the one sure way he knew to delay any kind of wedding but for the one Garrett now wanted more than anything.

The king's face went red. "You——"

"Pregnant?"

Garrett whirled around at the deep voice behind him and was just in time to watch Alex's older brother Prince Christopher's fist collide with his face. Pain exploded inside his head, but he ducked before the prince could land another one.

Then he threw a fast right himself and watched the prince stagger backward. The other man recovered quickly and came at Garrett again, still furious.

The king was shouting, "Pregnant? *Pregnant?*"

Two more men ran into the room. They took in the scene at a glance and immediately joined their older brother in the fray.

"Perfect," Garrett muttered, turning a slow circle so he could keep an eye on all three of them. Seemed he wasn't going to come out of this without a few bruises. But he'd give as good as he got, too.

He blocked another blow, threw a punch himself and smiled when the youngest of the princes was laid out flat on his back. The king pushed past one of his sons and threw a punch of his own that Garrett managed to avoid.

He wasn't about to hit a king, either, so he focused on protecting himself and doing a lot of dodging.

As Garrett avoided another blow, he yelled, "Just let me talk to Alex and we can straighten this out."

"You stay away from my sister." This from the prince pushing up from the floor.

"No one is talking to anyone until I have some answers," the king shouted again.

"Why is everyone yelling?" Alex called into the mix.

Garrett turned at the sound of her voice and Christopher landed another solid jab on his jaw. "Damn it!"

Hands clapped loudly, followed by a sharp, feminine command. "Stop this at once! Christopher, no more fighting. Help Henry off the floor, and Jonathon, get your father some water."

The king was sputtering in rage, but everyone else moved to follow the queen's orders. Everyone but Alex. She just stood there in the doorway, staring at him as if she'd never seen him before. Her hair was tidy, her elegant dress and tasteful jewelry made her seem unapproachable. But somewhere beneath that cool exterior was *his* Alex. And Garrett wasn't leaving until he'd had a chance to reach her.

The capper for Garrett, though, was seeing the damn duke standing right behind her. That settled everything. No way in hell was Garrett letting his woman go. And she *was* his. Had been from that first day at Disneyland.

"Who's pregnant?" Alex demanded.

"Apparently, *you* are," Christopher told her.

"I'm *what*?" She fired a furious look on Garrett and he just glared right back.

"I said you could be."

"Pregnant?" Henrik repeated from behind her. "You're *pregnant?* I'll be leaving."

"Henrik!" The king's shout went unanswered as the duke scuttled out the door to disappear. Probably forever.

"What is going on here? I could hear the shouts all the way to the garden." The queen looked from one face to the next, her silent, accusatory stare demanding answers.

"Garrett King claims Alexis is pregnant with his child," the king managed to say through gritted teeth.

"And I was just about to beat him to a pulp," Christopher said helpfully.

"In your dreams," Garrett muttered, never taking his eyes off Alex.

"Well, it's a lie," she snapped. "I'm not pregnant."

No one was listening. The princes were arguing among themselves, the queen and the king were locked into battle and Alex was looking at Garrett through furious eyes. When she turned to leave, he bolted across the room, grabbed her hand and tugged her into the hall, away from her arguing family.

"Don't," she said, pulling her hand free. Looking up at him, she said, "You don't belong here, Garrett. Go home."

"No."

"You had your choice, and you made it. Now it's time we both live with it."

He grabbed her again, holding on to her shoulders half worried that she'd run if he let her go. It could take him *weeks* to find her again in this place. "Why did you return the package I sent you?"

"Because what we had is over. Now please, just *go*."

"I'm not going anywhere," he murmured and pulled her in close. Wrapping his arms around her, to hold on tight when she started to squirm, Garrett kissed her. He poured everything he'd been feeling for the last two weeks into that kiss. The longing. The pain. The regret. The joy at being with her again. For the first time in too damn long, he felt whole. As if the puzzle pieces of his life had fallen into place.

Her tongue tangled with his, her breath slid into his lungs and her heartbeat clamored in time with his own. Everything was right. He just had to convince her that he was a changed man.

Finally, he broke the kiss, stared down into those amazing eyes of hers and said, "Alex, I don't give a damn about your crown. I don't care that you're a princess. Don't care that our worlds are so different. I'll convince your father to let us be together. We can make it work, Alex. We *will* make it work."

"Garrett…" She sighed, and said, "I want to believe you. But you made yourself perfectly clear before. You didn't want me in California. So why now? What's changed?"

"Me," he told her, lifting his hands to cup her face. His thumbs moved over her cheekbones and just the feel of her soft, smooth skin beneath his eased the pain that had been tearing at him for what seemed forever. "I've changed. And I did want you in California, Alex. I always wanted you. From the first time I saw you in Disneyland, I wanted you. I was just too busy looking for trouble to see what I'd already found."

She shook her head, and Garrett's heart stopped briefly. But a King never backed away from a challenge. Especially one that meant more to him than his life.

"Alex, I know now what's really important." God, he had to make her believe him. Those eyes of hers were so deep, so rich with emotion, with *love*. Seeing it gave him enough hope to continue. To tell her everything he wanted her to know.

And he still hadn't even said the most important thing. "I love you. I *love* you, Alex, Princess Alexis Morgan Wells. I really do."

Her breath caught and a single tear rolled from the corner of her eye. He caught it with his thumb as if it were precious. Sunlight speared in from an overhead window and lay on her beautiful hair, now tightly controlled in a twist on top of her head.

"I love your laugh." His gaze moved over her and then he reached up to tug a few pins loose, letting her hair fall down around her shoulders. "And I love your hair, all wild and tangled. I love the way you find something beautiful in everything. I love your clever brain and your smart-ass mouth. I love that you're willing to call me out when you think I'm being an idiot."

Her lips quirked.

"And I love that you want to help women in need and I'd like to be a part of that."

She took a sharp breath.

"I want to be with you, Alex. Always. I want to build a life with you. In California *and* Cadria."

"How—"

"I'm opening a branch of King Security right here in Cadria. We'll be the European division."

"Garrett—" She shook her head sadly. "You're not used to this kind of life. I'm followed by reporters and photographers. We wouldn't be able to just buy a house in town and move in. We would have to live here in a wing of the palace. You'd hate that, you know you would."

He laughed shortly. "First off, you forget. I'm one of the Kings of California. We've got paparazzi following us all the damn time looking for a story. I'm used to life in a fishbowl. It's not always pretty, but if you want to badly enough, you can carve out a private life."

"But—"

"And it doesn't matter where we live, Alex," he said, "as long as we're together." He gave a glance around the wide hallway, with its priceless art hanging on the walls and the gleam of marble shining up at them. "I could learn to love the palace."

She laughed, and God, it sounded like music to him.

"I'll miss good Thai food at one in the morning, but if the craving gets bad, I'll have Griffin send me some on a King Jet."

"Oh, Garrett," she said on a chuckle.

"It'll work, Princess," he said quickly, giving her a quick kiss as if to seal a promise. "We'll blend our lives and build one together that will suit both of us."

Alex's breath caught in her chest. Everything she had ever dreamed of was right here, in front of her. All she had to do was reach out and take it. Returning the package he had sent her hadn't been easy, but she'd hoped that he would come to her, repeating family history. Now, here he was and Alex was half afraid to believe in it.

"I love you, Alex," he said softly. "Marry me. Love me back."

She sighed and lifted both arms to wrap them around his neck. "I do love you, Garrett King."

"Thank God," he said on a laugh, dropping his forehead to hers. "When you returned the necklace…"

"It was a necklace?"

"I brought it with me." He dipped one hand into his pocket and pulled out a flat, dark green jeweler's box.

Alex took it, opened the lid and sighed with pleasure.

"It's a seagull," he told her unnecessarily. "I had it made to remind you of the ocean. Of all the time we spent at the beach."

Tears stung her eyes as she lifted the beautifully crafted piece free of the box. She turned and lifted her hair so that he could put it around her neck and when it was lying against the base of her throat, she touched it and whispered, "I love it, Garrett, though I don't need a reminder. I'll never forget a moment of my time with you."

She had everything she had ever dreamed of, right there in her arms. Garrett King was looking at her with more love than she could have imagined possible. She felt the truth of it in his touch. Saw it plainly in his beautiful eyes that were no longer shadowed with old pain. Her heart felt full and yet...

"I'm still a princess, Garrett," she warned. "That won't change, ever. There will still be the chance of danger surrounding me and my family. It will still drive you crazy."

"Yeah," he said solemnly. "I know. But I'll be here to make sure you're safe. All of you." A small smile crooked one corner of his mouth. "King Security can be the palace's personal protection detail.

"Marry me, Alex. Together, you and I can do anything."

"I know we can," she said and went up on her toes to kiss him. "So yes, Garrett, I'll marry you."

He grinned and blew out a relieved breath. "Took you long enough."

Shaking her head, she said, "I can't believe you told my father I was pregnant."

"It was the only thing I could come up with on short notice."

She smiled up at him. "You used to be a much better liar, Mr. King."

"It's all in the past, Princess. No more lies. Not between us."

"Agreed," she said, a grin she felt might never go away curving her mouth.

"So," he asked as he leaned in to kiss her, "how do you feel about Disneyland for a honeymoon?"

"I think that sounds perfect."

Then he kissed her, and the world righted itself again. Alex reveled in the sensation of everything being just as it should be. She gave herself up to the wonder and the joy and wasn't even aware when her brothers and father burst into the hall to see why things had gotten so suddenly quiet.

And she didn't see when her mother ushered her men back into the study to allow her daughter time to enjoy the magic of a lifetime.

* * * * *

A GROOM WORTH WAITING FOR

SOPHIE PEMBROKE

For Emma, Helen & Mary.

CHAPTER ONE

'WHAT DO YOU MEAN, he's coming here?' Thea Morrison clasped her arms around her body, as if the action could somehow hide the fact that she was wearing a ridiculously expensive, pearl-encrusted, embroidered ivory wedding dress, complete with six-foot train. 'He can't!'

Her sister rolled her big blue eyes. 'Oh, calm down. He just told me to tell you that you're late to meet with the wedding planner and if you aren't there in five minutes he'll come and get you,' Helena said.

'Well, stop him!'

No, that wouldn't work. Nothing stopped Flynn Ashton when he really wanted something. He was always polite, but utterly tenacious. That was why his father had appointed him his right-hand man at Morrison-Ashton media. And why she was marrying him in the first place.

'Get me out of this dress before he gets here!'

'I don't know why you care so much,' Helena said, fumbling with the zip at the back of the dress. 'It's not like this is a real wedding anyway.'

'In two days there'll be a priest, a cake, some flowers, and a legally binding pre-nup saying otherwise.' Thea wriggled to try and get the strapless dress down over her hips. 'And everyone knows it's bad luck for the groom to see the bride in the wedding dress before the big day.'

It was more than a superstition, it was a rule. Standard Operating Procedure for weddings. Flynn was not seeing this dress a single moment before she walked down the aisle of the tiny Tuscan church at the bottom of the hill from the villa. Not one second.

'Which is why he sent me instead.'

Thea froze, her blood suddenly solid in her veins. She knew that voice. It might have been eight years since she'd heard it, but she hadn't forgotten. Any of it.

The owner of that voice really shouldn't be seeing her in nothing but her wedding lingerie. Especially since she was marrying his brother in two days.

Yanking the dress back up over her ivory corset, Thea held it tight against her chest and stared at him. 'I thought you weren't coming.' But there he was. Large as life and twice as... Hell, she couldn't even lie in her brain and finish that with *ugly*. He looked...grown up. Not twenty-one and angry at everything any more. More relaxed, more in control.

And every inch as gorgeous as he'd always been. Curse him.

Helena laughed. 'Eight years and that's all you have to say to him?' Skipping across the room, blonde hair bouncing, she wrapped her arms around him and pressed a kiss against his cheek. 'It's good to see you, Zeke.'

'Little Helena, all grown up.' Zeke returned the hug, but his gaze never left Thea's. 'It's good to see you too. And rather more of your sister than I'd bargained on.'

There was a mocking edge in his voice. As if she'd planned for him to walk in on her in her underwear. He wasn't even supposed to be in the country! Flynn had told her he wouldn't come and she'd been flooded with relief—even if she could never explain why to her husband-to-be.

But now here Zeke was, staring at her, and Thea had never felt so exposed.

She clutched the dress tighter—a barrier between them. 'Well, I was expecting your brother.'

'Your fiancé,' Zeke said. 'Of course. Sorry. Seems he thought I should get started with my best man duties a few days early.'

Thea blinked. '*You're* Flynn's best man?'

'Who else would he choose?' He said it as if he hadn't been gone for eight years. As if he'd never taunted Flynn about not being a real Ashton, only an adopted one, a fall-back plan. As if he hadn't sworn that he was never coming back.

'Anyone in the world.' Quite literally. Flynn could have appointed the Russian Prime Minister as his best man and Thea would have been less surprised.

'He chose his brother,' Helena said, giving Thea her usual *are you crazy?* look. She'd perfected it at fifteen and had been employing it with alarming regularity ever since. 'What's so weird about that?'

Helena hadn't been there. She'd been—what? Sixteen? Too young or too self-absorbed to get involved in the situation, or to realise what was going on. Thea had wanted to keep it from her—from everybody—even then. Of course with hindsight even at sixteen Helena had probably had a better idea about men than Thea had at eighteen. Or now, at twenty-six. But Helena had been dealing with her own issues then.

'So, you're here for the wedding?' Thea said.

Zeke raised his eyebrows. 'What else could I possibly be here for?'

She knew what he wanted her to say, or at least to think. That he'd come back for her. To tell her she'd made the wrong decision eight years ago and she was making a worse one now. To stop her making the biggest mistake of her life.

Except Thea knew full well she'd already made that. And it had nothing to do with Zeke Ashton.

No, she had her suspicions about Zeke's return, but she didn't think he was there for her. If he'd come back to the family fold there had to be something much bigger at stake than a teenage rebellion of a relationship that had been dead for almost a decade.

'I need to get changed.'

Keeping the dress clasped tight to her body, Thea stepped off the platform and slipped behind the screen to change back into her sundress from earlier. She could hear Helena and Zeke chatting lightly outside, making out his amused tone more than the words he spoke. That was one thing that hadn't changed. The world was still a joke to him—her family most of all.

Hanging the beautiful wedding dress up carefully on its padded hanger, Thea stepped back and stared at it. Her fairytale dress, all sparkle and shine. The moment she put it on she became a different person. A wife, perhaps. That dress, whatever it had cost, was worth every penny if it made her into that person, made her *fit*.

This time, this dress, this wedding...it had to be the one that stuck. That bought her the place in the world she needed. Nothing else she'd tried had worked.

Shaking her head, Thea tugged the straps of her sundress up over her shoulders, thankful for a moment or two to regroup. To remind herself that this didn't change anything. So Zeke was there, lurking around their Tuscan villa. So what? He wasn't there for *her*. She was still marrying Flynn. She belonged with Flynn. She had the dress; she had the plan. She had Helena at her side to make sure she said, wore and did the right thing at the right time. This was it. This villa, this wedding. This was where she was supposed to be. Everything was in its right place—apart from Zeke Ashton.

Well, he could just stay out of her perfect picture, thank you very much. Besides, the villa was big enough she probably wouldn't even notice he was in residence most of the time. Not a problem.

Sandals on, Thea smoothed down her hair and stepped back out. 'Now, if you'll excuse me, I have a meeting with the wedding planner to attend.'

'Of course,' Zeke said, with that infuriating mocking smile still in place. 'We wouldn't dream of delaying the blushing bride.'

Thea nodded sharply. She was *not* blushing.

She'd made a promise to herself eight years ago. A decision. And part of that decision meant that Zeke Ashton would never be able to make her blush again.

That part of her life was dead and buried.

Just two days until the wedding. Two more days—that was all. Two days until Thea Morrison got her happily-ever-after.

'In fact,' Zeke said, 'why don't I walk you there? We can catch up.'

Thea's jaw clenched. 'That would be lovely,' she lied.

Two days and this miserable week would be over. Thea couldn't wait.

She barely looked like Thea. With her dark hair straightened and pinned back, her slender arms and legs bronzed to the perfect shade of tan…she looked like someone else. Zeke studied her as she walked ahead of him, long strides clearly designed to get her away from his company as soon as physically possible.

Did she even remember the time when that had been

the last thing she'd wanted? When she'd smile and perform her hostess duties at her father's dinner parties and company barbecues, then sneak off to hide out somewhere private, often dark and cosy, with him…? Whoever she'd pretended to be for their parents—the good girl, the dutiful daughter—when they were alone Zeke had seen the real Thea. Seen glimpses of the woman he'd always believed she'd become.

Zeke shook his head. Apparently he'd been wrong. Those times were gone. And as he watched Thea—all high-heeled sandals, sundress and God only knew what underneath, rather than jeans, sneakers and hot pink knickers—he knew the girl he'd loved was gone, too. The Thea he'd fallen in love with would never have agreed to marry his brother, whatever their respective fathers' arguments for why it was a good idea. She'd wanted love—true love. And for a few brief months he'd thought she'd found it.

He'd been wrong again, though.

Lengthening his own stride, he caught up to her easily. She might have long legs, but his were longer. 'So,' he asked casually, 'how many people are coming to this shindig, anyway?'

'Shindig?' Thea stopped walking. 'Did you just call my wedding a *shindig*?'

Zeke shrugged. Nice to know he could still get under her skin so easily. It might make the next couple of days a little more fun. Something had to. 'Sorry. I meant to say your fairytale-worthy perfect day, when thou shalt join your body in heavenly communion with the deepest love of your heart and soul. How many people are coming to *that*?'

Colour rose in her cheeks, filling him with a strange sense of satisfaction. It was childish, maybe. But he wasn't going to let her get away with pretending that this was a real, true love-match. It was business, just like everything else the Morrisons and the Ashtons held dear.

Including him, these days. Even if his business wasn't the family one any more.

'Two hundred and sixty-eight,' Thea said, her tone crisp. 'At the last count.'

'Small and intimate, then?' Zeke said. 'Just how my father likes things. Where are you putting them all up? I mean, I get that this place is enormous, but still…I can't imagine *your* guests doubling up on camp beds on the veranda.'

'We've booked out the hotel down the road. There'll be executive coaches and cabs running back and forth on the day.'

A small line had formed between her eyebrows, highlighting her irritation. That was new, too.

'Why do you care, anyway?'

'I'm the best man,' he reminded her. 'It's my job to know these things.'

That, apparently, was the line that did it. Spinning round to face him straight on, Thea planted her hands on her hips and scowled at him. 'Why are you here, Zeke? And don't give me some line about brotherly duties. I know full well what you think about Flynn.'

Did she? Maybe she could enlighten *him*, then. Zeke had long since given up trying to make sense of his relationship with his adopted brother. After he'd left home he'd spent months lying awake thinking about it. Wondering if he could have changed things if he'd realised sooner, before that last conversation with his father that had driven him away for good… But in the end the past was the past. He'd had to move on. Besides, this wasn't about him and Flynn. It was about Flynn and Thea.

'Well, if you're not going to buy brotherly affection,

I doubt you'll go for family loyalty either.' He shrugged. 'I'm far more interested in what our fathers said to get you to agree to marry the Great Pretender.'

'Don't call him that,' Thea snapped. 'It wasn't funny when we were kids, and it's not funny now. And is it so hard to believe that I might actually *want* to marry Flynn?'

'Yes,' Zeke said automatically. And not just because she wasn't marrying *him*, whatever his business partner, Deb, said.

'Well, I do.' Thea stared at him mulishly, as if she were barely resisting the urge to add, *So there!*

Zeke leant back against the sunny yellow stone of the hallway, staring down through the arches towards the terrace beyond and the green vines snaking up the trellis. Clearly they were no longer in a hurry to get to the meeting, which gave him a chance to find out what had been going on around here lately.

'Really?' he said, folding his arms across his chest. 'So you're saying that the fact that your marriage will merge both sides of the business for all time, and give your heirs total control, hasn't even crossed your mind?'

Thea pulled a face. 'Of course it has.'

'And if it hadn't I'm sure your father would have made it very clear.' Thomas Morrison was always very good about making his daughter understand the implications of her actions, as Zeke remembered it. Especially when they could benefit him—or threatened to inconvenience him.

'But that doesn't mean it wasn't my decision,' Thea said.

And suddenly all Zeke could think about was the last decision Thea had made, right before he'd skipped out on the family, the business and the rest of his life.

'Of course not,' he said, with a sharp, bitter taste in his mouth at the words. 'I know you like to weigh your decisions very carefully. Make sure you're choosing the most beneficial option.'

Thea's jaw dropped slightly. What? Had she expected him not to notice exactly how mercenary her behaviour was? Maybe eight years ago she might have fooled him, but he knew better now. He knew exactly what mattered to her—and it wasn't him.

'What, exactly, are you trying to say?' She bit the words out, as if she were barely holding back a tirade of insulted pride. 'And I'd think very carefully before answering.'

Zeke gave her his most blinding smile. 'Exactly what you think I'm trying to say. That suddenly it makes an awful lot of sense why you chose to stay here instead of coming away with me eight years ago. What was the point once you knew I wasn't the heir any more?' He shrugged, nonchalantly, knowing it would irritate her even more. 'Gotta say, though…I'm surprised it took you this long to bag Flynn.'

She was going to explode. Literally just pop with rage and frustration, spilling bitterness and anger all over the expensively rustic scrubbed walls of this beautiful villa.

Except that would probably make Zeke Ashton smirk even more. So, instead, Thea took a deep breath and prepared to lie.

'As hard as it may be for you to believe, I am in love with your brother.' Her voice came out calm and cool, and Thea felt a small bubble of pride swelling up amongst all the fury. There'd been a time when any words Zeke had spoken to her had provoked an extreme reaction. When they were kids it had usually been annoyance, or anger. Then, when they were teenagers, that annoyance had suddenly become attraction, and then anger, arousal… By the time he'd left… all sorts of other complicated reactions had come into play.

But not any more. Now she was an adult, in control of

her own life and making her own decisions. Zeke Ashton's barbs and comments had no power over her any longer. It felt incredibly freeing.

'Love?' Zeke raised an eyebrow. 'You know, I'm starting to think you've got your definition of that word wrong.'

'Trust me, I know *exactly* what it means.' Love meant the incredible pain of loss when it was gone. Or the uncertainty of never knowing if it was returned. It baffled Thea why so many people thought love was a good thing.

'Really? Well, I'm sure I'm just thrilled that you've finally found true love. Guess I was just a practice run.'

Thea's stomach rolled at the reminder. It wasn't that she'd thought he'd forgotten their teenage fling, or even forgiven her for the way it had ended—he'd made it very clear in the half-hour he'd been in the villa that neither had happened. But she hadn't expected him to want to actually *talk* about it. Weren't men supposed to be strong and silent on matters of the heart? Suffering in silence, and all that?

Except Zeke had always loved the sound of his own voice. Apparently that hadn't changed, even if nearly everything else had.

'That was a long time ago, Zeke. We were kids.' Too far in the past to bring up now, surely? Even for Zeke, with his ridiculous need to *talk* about everything. 'We've both moved on. We're different people now.'

'Want to throw in a few more clichés with that?' Zeke shook his head. 'Look, you can rewrite history any way you like. And, trust me, I'm not here to try and win you back—even to get one over on Flynn. But you're not going to convince me that this is anything but a business deal with rings.'

'You're wrong,' Thea lied. 'And you'll see that. But…'

'But?' Zeke asked, one eyebrow raised again in that mocking expression that drove her crazy. 'But what?'

'Even if it was a business deal…what would be wrong with that? As long as we both know what we're getting into…' She shrugged. 'There are worse reasons to get married.'

'Maybe.' Zeke gave her a slow smile—the one that used to make her insides melt. 'But there are so many better reasons, too.'

'Like love,' Thea said, apparently still determined to stick to her story.

Zeke didn't buy it, and knew he wouldn't, no matter how hard she tried to convince him. He knew what Thea in love looked like, and this wasn't it.

At least not his Thea. The old Thea. He shook his head. He couldn't let doubt in now. The only thing in his life that had never let him down was gut instinct. He had to trust himself, especially since he couldn't trust anyone else. Not even Thea.

'Love's the big one,' Zeke agreed. 'But it's not the only thing that counts. Trust. Respect. Common values—'

'We have those too,' Thea broke in.

'Sexual compatibility,' Zeke finished, smirking when her mouth snapped shut. 'That's always important for long-term happiness, I find.'

Her gaze hardened. 'Really? And how's that working out for you? I can't help but notice you've come to my wedding alone, after all.'

He had a comeback for that somewhere, he was sure. But since Flynn arrived at that moment—cool, collected, and always an inch and a half taller than Zeke—he didn't have to search for it.

'Zeke! You made it.' Flynn stepped up and held out a hand, but before Zeke could even take it Thea had latched on to her fiancé's other arm, smiling up at him in a sickeningly adoring manner.

Keeping the handshake as perfunctory as possible, Zeke moved out of their circle of love and into his own space of scepticism. 'How could I resist the opportunity to be the best man for once? Might be the only chance I get.'

Flynn's smile stiffened a little at that, but he soldiered on regardless. Always so keen to play up the family loyalty—to be a part of the family he'd never really thought he belonged in. Zeke would have thought that their father choosing Flynn over him would have gone a long way to convincing his brother that there was only one golden boy in the family, and that blood didn't matter at all.

'I wouldn't want anyone but my brother beside me on such an important day,' Flynn said.

He didn't even sound as if he was lying, which Zeke thought was quite an accomplishment.

'Really? Because I have to admit I was kind of surprised to be asked.' Zeke glanced at Thea, who gave him an *I knew it!* look. 'Not as surprised as Thea was to see me here, of course,' he added, just because he could. She glared at him, and snuggled closer against Flynn's arm. There was absolutely no chemistry between them at all. And not a chance in hell they'd ever slept together. What on earth was Thea doing with him?

'You said he wasn't coming,' Thea pointed out—rather accusingly, Zeke thought.

'I wasn't sure he would,' Flynn admitted, glancing down at Thea with an apologetic smile.

Zeke wasn't sure he liked the idea of them talking about him in his absence. What had she said? How much had she told him?

'But, Zeke, you were the one who left us, remember? Not the other way round. Of course I asked you. You're my brother.'

'And that's the only reason?' Zeke asked. An uncomfortable feeling wriggled in his chest at the reminder of his disappearance, but he pushed it aside. He hadn't had a choice. His father had made his position very clear, and that position had taken any other options Zeke might have had off the table. He'd only hung around long enough to waste his time talking to Thea that same night, then he'd been gone. And nobody looking at Zeke now, at how far he'd come and how much he'd achieved, could say that he'd made a mistake by leaving.

Flynn didn't answer his question. With a sigh, he said, 'Dad's got a dinner planned for tonight, by the way. To welcome you home.'

Zeke appreciated the warning too much to point out that a luxury Tuscan villa belonging to some client or another wasn't actually 'home', no matter how many swimming pools it had. 'A prodigal son type thing? Hope he's found a suitably fatted calf.'

'I'm sure there was some poor animal just *begging* to be sacrificed on your behalf,' Thea said. 'But before then don't we have a meeting with the wedding planner to get to, darling?'

The endearment sounded unnatural on her tongue, and Flynn actually looked uncomfortable as she said it. Nobody would ever believe these two actually loved each other or wanted to see each other naked. Watching them, Zeke couldn't even see that they'd ever met before, let alone been childhood friends. He could imagine them on their wedding night—all unnatural politeness and a wall of pillows down the middle of the bed. If it wasn't Thea doing the marrying, it would be hilarious.

'She had to leave,' Flynn said. 'But I think we sorted out all the last-minute details. I said you'd call her later if there was anything you were concerned about.'

'I'm sure it's all fine,' Thea said, smiling serenely.

Even that seemed false. Shouldn't a woman getting married in two days be a little bit more involved in the details?

A door opened somewhere, slamming shut again as Hurricane Helena came blowing through.

'Are you guys still here?' she asked, waves of blonde hair bobbing past her shoulders. 'Shouldn't you all be getting ready for dinner? Thea, I had the maid press your dress for tonight. It's hanging in your room. Can I borrow your bronze shoes, though?'

'Of course,' Thea said, just as she always had to Helena, ever since their mother had died.

Zeke wondered if she even realised she did it.

'Come on, I'll find them for you now.'

As the women made their way down the corridor Helena spun round, walking backwards for a moment. 'Hope you brought your dinner jacket, Zeke. Apparently this welcome home bash is a formal affair.'

So his father had been sure he'd come, even if no one else had. Why else would he have set up a formal dinner for his arrival?

Helena turned back, slipping a hand through her sister's arm and giggling. Thea, Zeke couldn't help but notice, didn't look back at all.

Beside him, Flynn gave him an awkward smile. He'd always hated having to wear a bow tie, Zeke remembered suddenly. At least someone else would be miserable that evening.

'I'll see you at dinner,' Flynn said, setting off down another corridor.

'Can't wait.' Zeke's words echoed in the empty hallway. 'Gonna be a blast.'

CHAPTER TWO

THEA SHOULD HAVE known this wasn't just about shoes.

'So...Zeke coming home. Bit of a shock, huh?' Helena said, lounging back on Thea's ridiculously oversized bed.

'Yep.' Thea stuck her head in the closet and tried to find her bronze heels. Had she even packed them?

'Even though old Ezekiel Senior has planned a welcome home dinner?'

'I told you—Flynn didn't think he'd come,' Thea explained. 'So neither did I.'

'So Flynn was just as shocked?' Helena asked, too innocently.

'Probably,' Thea said. 'He just hides it better.'

'He hides *everything* better,' Helena muttered. 'But, to be honest, he didn't seem all that surprised when I told him Zeke had arrived.'

Thea bashed her head on the wardrobe door. Rubbing her hand over the bump, she backed out into the room again. 'Then maybe he just had more faith that his brother would do the right thing than I did. I really don't think I brought those bronze shoes.'

'No? What a shame. I'll just have to wear my pewter ones.' Helena sat up, folding her legs under her. 'Why don't you trust Zeke? I thought you two were pretty close before he left.'

Thea stared at her sister. She'd known all along she didn't have the stupid shoes, hadn't she? She'd just wanted an excuse to quiz her about Zeke. Typical.

'We were friends,' she allowed. 'We all were. Hard not to be when they were over at our house all the time.'

'Or we were there,' Helena agreed. 'Especially after Mum…'

'Yeah.'

Isabella Ashton had quickly taken pity on the poor, motherless Morrison girls. She'd been more than happy to educate fourteen-year-old Thea in the correct way to run her father's household and play the perfect hostess. At least until Thea had proved she wasn't up to the task and Isabella had taken over all together. Thea would have been relived, if she hadn't had to bear the brunt of her father's disappointment ever since.

And been made to feel like an outsider in my own home.

Thea swallowed and batted the thought away. Helena probably didn't remember that part of it. As far as she was concerned Isabella had just made sure they were supplied with any motherly advice they needed. Whether they wanted it or not.

Thea moved over to the dressing table, looking for the necklace Isabella had given her for her eighteenth birthday. The night Zeke had left. She'd wear it tonight, along with her own mother's ring. Isabella always appreciated gestures like that.

'And you've really not spoken to Zeke at all since he left?' Helena asked.

Thea wondered how much her sister suspected about her relationship with Flynn's brother. Too much, it seemed.

'Not once,' she said firmly, picking up Isabella's necklace. 'Not once in eight years.'

'Strange.' Helena slipped off the bed and came up behind her, taking the ends of the chain from her to fasten it behind her neck. 'Do you think that's why he's come back now? Because you're getting married?'

'Well, he was invited, so I'm thinking that was probably the reason.'

'No,' Helena said, and something about her sister's quiet, firm voice made Thea look up and meet her eyes in the mirror. 'I meant because *you're* getting married.'

Thea swallowed. 'He didn't come and visit the last time I almost got married.'

'Or the time before that,' Helena said, cheerfully confirming her view of Thea as a serial fiancée. 'But then, those times you weren't marrying his brother.' The words *And you didn't go through with it...* went unsaid.

Thea dropped down onto the dressing table stool. Wouldn't that be just like Zeke—not to care that she might marry someone else as long as it wasn't a personal slight to him? But did he even know about the others? If he did, she predicted she'd be subjected to any number of comments and jibes on the subject. *Perfect.* Because she hadn't had enough of that at work, or from her friends, or even in the gossip pages.

Only Helena had never said anything about it. Her father had just torn up the pre-nups, asked his secretary to cancel the arrangements, and said, 'Next time, perhaps?' After the last one even Thea had had to admit to herself that she was better off sticking to business than romance.

It was just that each time she'd thought she'd found a place she could belong. Someone to belong to. Until it had turned out that she wasn't what they really wanted after all. She was never quite right—never quite good enough in the end.

Except for Flynn. Flynn knew exactly what he was getting, and why. He'd chosen it, debated it, drawn up a contract detailing exactly what the deal entailed. And that was exactly what Thea needed. No confused expectations, no unspoken agreements—this was love done business-style. It suited her perfectly.

Zeke would think it was ridiculous if he knew. But she was pretty sure that Zeke had a better reason for returning than just mocking her love life.

'That's not why he's back.'

'Are you sure?' Helena asked. 'Maybe this is just the first time he thought you might actually go through with it.'

'You make me sound like a complete flake.' Which was fair, probably. Except she'd always been so sure... until it had become clear that the men she was supposed to marry weren't.

Helena sighed and picked up a hairbrush from the dressing table, running it through her soft golden waves. Thea had given up wishing she had hair like that years ago. Boring brown worked fine for her.

'Not a flake,' Helena said, teasing out a slight tangle. 'Just...uncertain.'

'"Decisionally challenged", Dad says.'

Helena laughed. 'That's not true. You had a perfectly good reason not to marry those guys.'

'Because it turned out one was an idiot who wanted my money and the other was cheating on me?' And she hadn't seen it, either time, until it had been almost too late. Hadn't realised until it had been right in front of her that she couldn't be enough of a lover or a woman for one of them, or human enough to be worth more than hard cash to the other. Never valuable enough in her own right just to be loved.

'Because you didn't love them.' Helena put down the

brush. 'Which makes me wonder again why exactly you're marrying Flynn.'

Thea looked away from the mirror. 'We'll be good together. He's steady, sensible, gentle. He'll make a great husband and father. Our families will finally be one, just like everyone always wanted them to be. It's good for the business, good for our parents, and good for us. This time I know exactly what I'm signing up for. That's how I know that I've made the right decision.'

This time. This one time. After a lifetime of bad ones, Thea knew that this decision had to stick. This was the one that would give her a proper family again, and a place within it. Flynn needed her—needed the legitimacy she gave him. Thea was well aware of the irony: he needed her Morrison bloodline to cement his chances of inheriting the company, while she needed him, the adopted Ashton son, to earn back her place in her own family.

It was messed up, yes. But at least they'd get to be messed up together.

Helena didn't say anything for a long moment. Was she thinking about all the other times Thea had got it wrong? Not just with men, but with everything…with Helena. That one bad decision that Helena still had to live with the memory of every day?

But when she glanced back at her sister's reflection Helena gave her a bright smile and said, 'You'd better get downstairs for cocktails. And I'd better go and find my pewter shoes. I'll meet you down there, okay?'

Thea nodded, and Helena paused in the doorway.

'Thea? Maybe he just wanted to see you again. Get some closure—that sort of thing.'

As the door swung shut behind her sister Thea wished she was right. That Zeke was ready to move on, at last, from all the slights and the bitterness that had driven him away and kept him gone for so long. Maybe things would never be as they were when they were kids, but perhaps they could find a new family dynamic—one that suited them all.

And it all started with her wedding.

Taking a deep breath, Thea headed down to face her family, old and new, and welcome the prodigal son home again. Whether he liked it or not.

It was far too hot to be wearing a dinner jacket. Whose stupid idea was this, anyway? Oh, that was right. His father's.

Figured.

Zeke made his way down the stairs towards the front lounge and, hopefully, alcohol, torn between the impulse to rush and get it over with, or hold back and put it off for as long as possible. What exactly was his father hoping to prove by this dinner?

Zeke couldn't shake the feeling that Flynn's sudden burst of brotherly love might not be the only reason he'd been invited back to the fold for the occasion. Perhaps he'd better stick to just the one cocktail. If his father had an ulterior motive for wanting him there, Zeke needed to be sober when he found out what it was. Then he could merrily thwart whatever plan his dad had cooked up, stand up beside Flynn at this ridiculously fake wedding, and head off into the sunset again. Easy.

He hadn't rushed, but Zeke was still only the second person to make it to the cocktail cabinet. The first, perhaps unsurprisingly, was Thomas Morrison. The old man had always liked a martini before dinner, but as his gaze rose to study Zeke his mouth tightened and Zeke got the odd impression that Thea's dad had been waiting for him.

'Zeke.' Thomas held out a filled cocktail glass. 'So you made it, then.'

Wary, Zeke took the drink. 'You sound disappointed by that, sir.'

'I can't be the only person surprised to see you back.'

Zeke thought of Thea, standing in nothing but the underwear she'd bought for his brother, staring at him as if he'd returned from the dead. Was that really how she thought of him? In the back of his mind he supposed he'd always thought he *would* come back. When he was ready. When he'd proved himself. When he was *enough*. The wedding had just forced his hand a bit.

'I like to think I'm a pleasant surprise,' Zeke said.

Thomas sipped his martini and Zeke felt obliged to follow suit. He wished he hadn't; Thomas clearly liked his drinks a certain way—paint-stripper-strong. He put the glass down on the cocktail bar.

'Well, I think that depends,' Thomas said. 'On whether you plan to break your mother's heart again.'

Zeke blinked. 'She didn't seem that heartbroken to me.' In fact when she'd greeted him on his arrival she'd seemed positively unflustered. As if he was just one more guest she had to play the perfect hostess to.

'You never did know your mother.' Thomas shook his head.

'But *you* did.' It wasn't a new thought. The two families had always been a touch too close, lived a little too much in each other's pockets. And after his wife's death…well, it hadn't been just Thomas's daughters that Zeke's mother had seemed to want to look after.

'We're old friends, boy. Just like your father and I.'

Was that all? If it was a lie, it was one they'd all been telling themselves for so long now it almost seemed true.

'And I was there for both of them when you abandoned them. I don't think any of us want to go through that again.'

Maybe eight years had warped the old man's memory.

No way had his father been in the least bit bothered by his disappearing act—hell, it was probably what he'd wanted. Why else would he have picked Flynn over him to take on the role of his right-hand man at Morrison-Ashton? Except Zeke knew why—even if he didn't understand it. He had heard his father's twisted reasoning from the man's own lips. That was why he'd left.

But he couldn't help but wonder if Zeke leaving hadn't been Ezekiel Senior's plan all along. If he'd *wanted* him to go out in the world and make something of himself. If so, that was exactly what Zeke had done.

But not for his father. For himself.

'So, you think I should stick around this time?' Zeke asked, even though he had no intention of doing so. Once he knew what his father was up to he'd be gone again. Back to his own life and his own achievements. Once he'd proved his point.

'I think that if you plan to leave again you don't want to get too close while you're here.'

The old man's steely gaze locked on to Zeke's, and suddenly Zeke knew this wasn't about his father, or even his mother.

This was about Thea.

Right on cue they heard footsteps on the stairs, and Zeke turned to see Thea in the doorway, beautiful in a peacock-blue gown that left her shoulders bare, with her dark hair pinned back from her face and her bright eyes sharp.

Thomas clapped him on the shoulder and said, 'Welcome home, Zeke.' But the look he shot at Thea left Zeke in no doubt of the words he left unsaid. *Just don't stay too long.*

The air in the lounge felt too heavy, too tightly pressed around the stilted conversation between the three of

them—until Helena breezed in wearing the beautiful pewter shoes that had been a perfect match for her dress all
along. She fixed drinks, chatting and smiling all the way,
and as she pressed another martini into their father's hand
some of the tension seemed to drop and Thea found she
could breathe properly again.

At least until she let her eyes settle on Zeke. Maybe that
was the problem. If she could just keep her eyes closed
and not see the boy she remembered loving, or the man
he'd turned into, she'd be just fine. But the way he stood
there, utterly relaxed and unconcerned, his suit outlining
a body that had grown up along with the boy, she wanted
to know him. Wanted to explore the differences. To find
out exactly who he was now, just for this moment in time,
before he left again.

Stop it. Engaged to his brother, remember?

Flynn arrived moments later, his mother clutching his
arm, and suddenly things felt almost easy. Flynn and Helena both had that way about them; they could step into a
room and make it better. They knew how to settle people,
how to make them relax and smile even when there were
a million things to be fretting about.

Flynn had always been that way, Thea remembered.
Always the calm centre of the family, offset by Zeke's
spinning wild brilliance—and frustration. For Helena it
had come later.

Through their whole childhood Thea had been the responsible eldest child, the sensible one, at least when people were looking. And all the while Helena had thrown
tantrums and caused chaos. Until Thea had messed up
and resigned her role. Somehow Helena had seemed to
grow to fill it, even as Isabella had taken over the job of
mother, wife and hostess that Thea had been deemed unsuitable for. If it hadn't been for her role at the company,

Thea wondered sometimes if they'd have bothered keeping her around at all. They certainly hadn't seemed to need her. At least not until Flynn needed a bride with an appropriate bloodline.

'Are we ready to go through for dinner?' Isabella asked the room at large. 'My husband will be joining us shortly. He just has a little business to finish up.'

What business was more important than this? Hadn't Ezekiel insisted on this huge welcome home feast for his prodigal son? The least he could do was show up and be part of it. Thea wanted nothing more than for Zeke to disappear back to wherever he'd been for eight years, and *she* was still there.

Thea glanced up at Zeke and found him already watching her, eyebrows raised and expression amused. He slid in alongside her as they walked through to dinner.

'Offended on my behalf by my father's tardiness?' he asked. 'It's sweet, but quite unnecessary. The whole evening might be a lot more pleasant if he *doesn't* join us.'

'I wasn't…it just seemed a little rude, that's all.'

'Rude. Of course.'

He offered his arm for her to hold, but Thea ignored it. The last thing she needed was to actually touch Zeke in that suit.

'That's why your face was doing that righteously indignant thing.'

Thea stared at him. '"Righteously indignant thing"?'

'Yeah. Where you frown and your nose wrinkles up and your mouth goes all stern and disapproving.'

'I…I didn't know I did that.'

Zeke laughed, and up ahead Helena turned back to look at them. 'You've always done it,' he said. 'Usually when someone's being mean about me. Or Flynn, or Helena. It's cute. But like I said, in this case unnecessary.'

Thea scowled, then tried to make her face look as neutral as possible. Never mind her traitorous thoughts—apparently now she had to worry about unconscious overprotective facial expressions, too.

There were only six of them for dinner—seven if Ezekiel managed to join them—and they clustered around one end of the monstrously large dining table. Her father took the head, with Isabella at his side and Flynn next to her. Which left Thea sandwiched between Zeke and her father, with Helena on Zeke's other side, opposite Flynn. Thea couldn't help but think place cards might have been a good idea. Maybe she could have set hers in the kitchen, away from everybody…

They'd already made it through the starter before Ezekiel finally arrived. Thea bit her lip as he entered. Would he follow the unspoken boy-girl rule and sit next to Helena? But, no, he moved straight to Flynn's side and, with barely an acknowledgement of Zeke's presence in the room, started talking business with his eldest son.

Thea snuck a glance at Zeke, who continued to play with his soup as if he hadn't noticed his father's entrance.

'Did he already welcome you back?' Thea asked. But she knew Ezekiel Senior had been locked in his temporary office all day, so the chances were slim.

Zeke gave her a lopsided smile. 'You know my father. Work first.'

Why was she surprised? Ezekiel Ashton had always been the same.

'Well, if he's not going to ask you, I will.' Shifting in her seat to face him a little, Thea put on her best interested face. 'So, Zeke… What have you been up to the last eight years?'

'You don't know?' Zeke asked, eyebrows raised. 'Aren't you supposed to be in charge of PR and marketing for the company? I'd have thought it was your business to keep on top of what your competitors are up to.'

Too late Thea realised the trap she'd walked straight into. 'Oh, I know about your *business* life,' she said airily. 'Who doesn't? You set up a company purposely to rival the family business—presumably out of spite. It's the kind of thing the media loves to talk about. But, really, compared to Morrison-Ashton This Minute is hardly considered a serious competitor. More a tiny fish.'

'Beside your shark?' Zeke reached for his wine glass. 'I can see that. But This Minute wasn't ever intended to be a massive media conglomerate. Big companies can't move fast enough for me.'

That made sense. Zeke had never been one for sitting in meetings and waiting for approval on things he wanted to get done. But according to industry gossip even his instant response news website and app This Minute wasn't enough to hold his attention any more.

'I heard you were getting ready to sell.'

'Did you, now?' Zeke turned his attention across the table, to where his father and Flynn were still deep in conversation. 'That explains a lot.'

'Like?'

'Like why my father added his own personal request that I attend to my wedding invitation. He wants to talk about This Minute.'

So *that* was why he was back. Nothing to do with her, or Flynn, or the wedding. Not that she'd really thought it was, but still the knowledge sat heavily in her chest. 'You think he wants to buy it?'

'He's *your* CEO. What do you think?'

It would make sense, Thea had to admit. Their own twenty-four-hour news channels couldn't keep up with the fast response times of internet sites. Buying up This

Minute would be cheaper in the long run than developing their own version. And it would bring Zeke back into the family fold…

'Yes, I think he does.'

'Guess we'll find out,' Zeke said. 'If he ever deigns to speak to me.'

'What would you do?' Thea asked as the maid cleared their plates and topped up their wine glasses. 'Would you stay with This Minute?' It was hard to imagine Zeke coming back to work for Morrison-Ashton, even on his own terms. And if he did he'd be there, in her building, every day…

'No.' Zeke's response was firm. 'I'm ready to do something new.' He grinned. 'In fact, I want to do it all over again.'

'Start a new business? Why? Why not just enjoy your success for a while?'

'Like your father?' Zeke nodded at the head of the table, where Thomas was laughing at something Isabella had said.

Thea shook her head. 'My dad was never a businessman—you know that. He provided the money, sat on the board…'

'And left the actual work to my father.' He held up a hand before Thea could object. 'I know, I know. Neither one of them could have done it without the other. Hasn't that always been the legend? They each brought something vital to the table.'

'It worked,' Thea pointed out.

'And now you and Flynn are ready to take it into the next generation. Bring the families together. Spawn the one true heir.'

Thea looked away. 'You need to stop talking about my wedding like this.'

'Why? It's business, isn't it?'

'It's also my future. The rest of my life—and my children's.' That shut him up for a moment, unexpectedly. Thea took advantage of the brief silence to bring the conversation back round to the question he'd so neatly avoided. 'So, you didn't tell me. Why start up another new business?'

Zeke settled back in his chair, the thin stem of his wine glass resting between his fingers. 'I guess it's the challenge. The chance to take something that doesn't even exist yet, build it up and make it fantastic. Make it mine.'

It sounded exciting. Fresh and fun and everything else Zeke seemed to think it would be. But it also sounded to Thea as if Zeke was reaching for something more than just a successful business venture. Something he might never be able to touch, however hard he tried.

'You want to be a success,' she said slowly. 'But, Zeke, you've already succeeded. And you still want more. How will you know when you've done enough?'

Zeke turned to look at her, his dark eyes more serious than she'd ever seen them. 'I'll know it when I get there.'

But Thea was very afraid that he wouldn't.

CHAPTER THREE

So NOW HE KNEW. Had Thea told his dad about the rumours, Zeke wondered, or had the old goat had his own spies on the lookout? Either way, his presence in Italy that week suddenly made a lot more sense. Ezekiel Senior wanted This Minute.

And Zeke had absolutely no intention of giving it to him.

As the rest of the guests enjoyed their dessert Zeke left his spoon on the tablecloth and studied his father across the table. How would he couch it? Would he make it sound as if he was doing Zeke a favour? Or would he—heaven forbid—actually admit that Zeke had achieved something pretty great without the backing of Morrison-Ashton? He'd have to wait to find out.

After dinner, Zeke decided. That would be when his father would finally acknowledge the presence of his youngest son. Probably he'd be summoned to the study. But this time he'd get to go on his own terms. For once Ezekiel wanted something he, Zeke, possessed, rather than the other way round.

That, on its own, made it worth travelling to Flynn and Thea's wedding.

Zeke only realised he was smiling when Flynn suddenly looked up and caught his eye. Zeke widened his grin, raising an eyebrow at his brother. So, had dear old dad just broken the news to the golden boy? And did that mean Thea *hadn't* told her beloved about the rumours she'd heard?

Flynn glanced away again, and Zeke reached for his spoon. 'You didn't tell Flynn, then?'

Thea's dropped her spoon against the edge of her bowl with a clatter. 'Tell Flynn what?' she asked, eyes wide.

Interesting. 'Well, I meant about the This Minute sale,' he said. 'But now I'm wondering what else you've been keeping from your fiancé.'

Thea rolled her eyes, but it was too late. He'd already seen her instinctive reaction. She was keeping things from Flynn. Zeke had absolutely no doubt at all.

'I didn't tell Flynn about the sale because it doesn't directly affect him and it's still only a rumour. If your father decides to make a bid for the company I'm sure he'll fill Flynn in at the appropriate time.' Thea looked up at him through her lashes. 'Besides, we don't talk about you.'

'At all?' That hit him somewhere in the middle of his gut and hit hard. Not that he'd been imagining them sitting around the dining table reminiscing about the good old days when Zeke had been there, or anything. But still, despite his initial misgivings over them talking about him in his absence, he thought this might be worse. They didn't talk about him *at all*?

'Apart from Flynn telling me you weren't coming to the wedding? No.' Thea shrugged. 'What would we say? You left.'

And she'd forgotten all about him. Point made. With a sharp jab to the heart.

But of course if they didn't talk about him… 'So you never told Flynn about us, either?'

She didn't look up from her dessert as she answered. 'Why would I? The past is very firmly in the past. And I had no reason to think you would ever come back at all.'

'And now?'

Raising her head, she met his gaze head-on. 'And now there's simply nothing to say.'

'Zeke.'

The voice sounded a little creakier, but no less familiar. Tearing his gaze away from Thea's face, Zeke turned to see his father standing, waiting for him.

'I'd like a word with you in my office, if you would. After eight years…we have a lot to discuss.'

They had one thing to discuss, as far as Zeke was concerned. But he went anyway. How else would he have the pleasure of turning the old man down?

Ezekiel had chosen a large room at the front of the villa for his office—one Zeke imagined was more usually used for drinks and canapés than for business. The oversized desk in the centre had to have been brought in from elsewhere in the house, because it looked utterly out of place.

Zeke considered the obvious visitor's chair, placed across from it, and settled himself into a leather armchair by the empty fireplace instead. He wasn't a naughty child any more, and that meant he didn't have to stare at his father over a forbidding desk, waiting for judgement to be handed down, ever again.

'Sit,' Ezekiel said, long after Zeke had already done so. 'Whisky or brandy?'

'I'd rather get straight down to business,' Zeke said.

'As you wish.' Ezekiel moved towards the drinks cabinet and poured himself a whisky anyway. Zeke resisted the urge to grind his teeth.

Finally, his father came and settled himself into the armchair opposite, placing his glass on the table between them. 'So. You're selling your business.'

'So the rumour mill tells me,' Zeke replied, leaning back in his chair and resting his ankle on his opposite knee.

'I heard more than rumour,' Ezekiel said. 'I heard you were in negotiations with Glasshouse.'

Zeke's shoulders stiffened. Nobody knew that, except Deb and him at the office, the CEO at Glasshouse and his key team. Which meant one or other of them had a leak. Just what he *didn't* need.

'It's true, then.' Ezekiel shook his head. 'Our biggest competitors, Zeke. Why didn't you just come to me directly? Or is this just another way of trying to get my attention?'

Zeke will never stop trying to best his brother. The words, eight years old, still echoed through Zeke's head, however hard he tried to move past them. But he didn't have time for the memory now.

'I haven't needed your attention for the last eight years, Father. I don't need it now.'

'Really?' Ezekiel reached for his whisky glass. 'Are you sure? Because you could have gone anywhere, done anything. Yet you stayed in the country and set up a company that directly competed with the family business.'

'I stuck to what I knew,' Zeke countered. Because, okay, annoying his father might have been part of his motivation. But only part.

Ezekiel gave him a long, steady look, and when Zeke didn't flinch said, 'Hmm…'

Zeke waited. *Time to make the offer, old man.*

'I'm sure that you understand that to have my son working with Glasshouse is…unacceptable. But we can fix this. Come work with us. We'll pay whatever Glasshouse is paying and you can run your little company under the

Morrison-Ashton umbrella. In fact, you could lead our whole digital division.'

Somewhere in there, under the 'let me fix your mistakes' vibe, was an actual job offer. A good one. Head of Digital… There was a lot Zeke could do there to bring Morrison-Ashton into the twenty-first century. It would give him enough clout in the company in order not to feel as if Flynn was his boss. And he would be working with Thea every day…

'No, thanks.' Zeke stood up. He didn't need this any more. He'd grown up now. He didn't need his father's approval, or a place at the table, or even to be better than Flynn. He was his own man at last. 'I appreciate the offer, but I'm done with This Minute. Once I sell to Glasshouse I'm on to something new. Something exciting.'

Something completely unconnected to his family. Or Thea's.

'Really?'

Ezekiel looked up at him and Zeke recognised the disappointment in his eyes. It wasn't as if he hadn't seen that peculiar mix of being let down and proved right at the same time before.

'And if I appeal to your sense of family loyalty?'

Zeke barked a laugh. 'Why would you? You never showed *me* any. You gave Flynn all the chances, the job, the trust and the confidence. You wanted me to find my own road.' He crossed to the door, yanking it open. 'Well, Dad, I found it. And it doesn't lead to Morrison-Ashton.'

'Well,' Flynn said, dropping to sit beside her on the cushioned swing seat. 'That was a day.'

'Yes. Yes, it was.' Thea took the mug he offered her and breathed in the heavy smell of the coffee. 'Is this—?'

'Decaf,' Flynn assured her. 'You think I don't know what my wife-to-be likes?'

'Less "likes",' Thea said, taking a cautious sip. Everyone knew that on a normal day she'd be on her third double espresso well before lunch. 'More that I don't need anything else keeping me awake at night right now.'

'Hmm...' Flynn settled against the back of the seat and, careful of her coffee cup, wrapped an arm around Thea's shoulders, pulling her against him. 'Want to tell me what's keeping you awake?'

Thea tucked her legs up underneath her, letting Flynn rock the swing seat forward and back, the motion helping to relax the tension in her body.

They didn't share a room yet; it hadn't really seemed necessary, given the agreement between them. So he didn't have to know exactly how many hours she spent staring at the ceiling every night, just waiting for this wedding to be over, for the papers to be signed and for her future to be set and certain. But on the other hand she was marrying the man. He'd be her companion through life from here on in, and she wanted that companionship badly. Which meant telling him at least part of the truth.

'I guess I'm just nervous about the wedding,' she admitted.

'About marrying me?' Flynn asked. 'Or getting through the day itself?'

'Mostly the latter.' Thea rested her head against his comfortable shoulder and sighed. 'I just want it to be done. For everyone else to leave and for us to enjoy our honeymoon here in peace. You know?'

'I really, really do.'

Thea smiled at the heartfelt tone in his voice. This was why a marriage between them would work far better than any of the other relationships she'd fallen into, been passionate about, then had end horribly. They were a fit—a pair. If they actually loved each other it would be a classically perfect match.

But then, love—passion, emotion, pain—would be what drove them apart, too. No, far better this friendship and understanding. It made for a far more peaceful life.

Or it would. Once they got through the wedding.

'Feeling the strain, huh?' Thea patted Flynn's thigh sympathetically. 'Be grateful. At least my sister didn't walk in on you in your wedding lingerie this morning.'

'I don't have any wedding lingerie,' Flynn pointed out. 'I have the same boring black style I wear every day. Hang on. Did Zeke…?'

'Yep. He said you sent him to fetch me to meet with the wedding planner. So you wouldn't see me in my dress before the big day.'

'Sorry,' Flynn said, even though it obviously wasn't really his fault. 'I just know how important the traditions are to you. I didn't want to upset you.'

Thea waved a hand to brush away his apology, and Flynn reached over to take her empty coffee cup and place it safely on the table beside him. 'It's not your fault. Just something else to make this day difficult.'

'That does explain why he was in such an odd mood this afternoon, though,' Flynn mused. 'All those defensive jokes. He always did have a bit of a crush on you, I think. Even when we were kids.'

A bit of a crush. Thea ducked her head against Flynn's chest to hide her reaction. Had there ever been such an understatement? She'd assumed at first that Flynn had known something of her relationship with his brother—despite their attempts at secrecy it seemed that plenty of others had. But it had quickly become clear he'd no idea.

And they'd never talked about him, so she'd been perfectly happy to consign it to the realms of vague memory.

'I don't think that's why,' she said. 'I'm sure it's just being here, seeing everyone again after so long. It must be strange.'

'It was his choice.' Flynn's voice was firm, unforgiving. 'He could have come home at any time.'

'Perhaps.' What had *really* brought Zeke back now? *Was* it his father's summons? Not to satisfy the old man, of course, but to show him how much Zeke no longer needed him. To deny him whatever it was he wanted just out of spite?

The Zeke she'd seen today hadn't seemed spiteful, though. He was no longer the angry boy, lashing out, wanting revenge against his family, his life. Her. So why was he here?

Thea didn't let herself believe Helena's theory for a moment. If Zeke had really wanted to see her he'd had eight years. Even if he hadn't wanted to see his family again he could have found her—made contact somehow. But he hadn't. And by the time Thea had known where he was again any lingering regret or wish to see him had long faded. Or at least become too painful to consider. That wound was healed. No point pulling it open again.

Except now he was here, for her wedding, and she didn't have a choice.

Flynn shifted on the seat, switching legs to keep them swinging. 'Anyway... Talking about my prodigal brother isn't going to help you feel any more relaxed about the wedding. Let's talk about more pleasant things.'

'Like?'

'Our honeymoon,' Flynn said decisively, then faltered. The swing stopped moving and his shoulder grew tense under her cheek. 'I mean... I don't mean...'

Thea smiled against his shirt. He was so *proper*. 'I know what you mean.'

'I was thinking about the day trips we might take—that sort of thing,' Flynn explained unnecessarily. 'There are some very fine vineyards in the region, I believe. I don't want you to think that I'm expecting…well, *anything*. I know that wasn't our agreement.'

Thea pushed herself up to see his face. The agreement. It had been written, signed, notarised months ago—long before the wedding planning had even begun. They both knew what they wanted from this marriage—the business convenience, the companionship, fidelity. The document had addressed the possibility of heirs—and therefore sex—as something to be negotiated in three years' time. That had been Thea's decision. Marriage was one thing. Children were something else altogether. She needed to be sure of her role as a wife first.

But now she wondered if that had been a mistake.

'Maybe we should… I mean, we can talk again about the agreement, if you like?'

Flynn's body stilled further. Then he started the swing moving again, faster than before. 'You've changed your mind?'

'I just…I want our marriage to be solid. I want the companionship, and everything else we discussed, but more than anything I want us to be partners. I don't want doomed passion, or anger and jealousy. I want true friendship and respect, and I know you can give me that.'

'And children?' Flynn asked, and Thea remembered just how important that was to him. How much he needed a family of his own—she suspected not just to make sure there was a legitimate Morrison-Ashton heir for the business.

'In time,' she said, 'yes, I think so. But I'd still like a

little time for us to get to know each other better first. You know…as husband and wife.'

Was that enough? Would he get the hint?

'You want us to sleep together?' Flynn said. 'Sorry to be blunt, but I think it's important we both know what we're saying here.'

Another reason he'd make a good husband. Clarity. She'd never had that with Zeke. Not at all. 'You're right. And, yes, I do.'

'Okay.'

Not exactly the resounding endorsement she'd hoped for. 'Are you all right with that?'

Flynn flashed a smile at her. 'Thea, you're a very beautiful woman and I'm proud that you're going to be my wife. Of course I'm okay with that.'

'You weren't sounding particularly enthusiastic.'

'I am. Really.' He pulled her close again and kissed the top of her head. 'Who knows? Maybe we'll even grow to love each other as more than friends.'

'Perhaps we will,' Thea said. After all, how could she tell her husband-to-be that the last thing she wanted was for either of them to fall in love with each other. Sex, marriage, kids—that was fine. But not love.

Hadn't it been proved, too many times already, that her love wasn't worth enough?

The corridors of the villa were quieter now. Zeke presumed that everyone was lingering over after-dinner drinks in the front parlour or had gone to bed. Either way, he didn't particularly want to join in.

Instead, he made his way to the terrace doors. A little fresh air, a gulp of freedom away from the oppression of family expectation, might do him some good.

Except the terrace was already occupied.

He stood in the doorway for a long moment, watching the couple on the swing. Whatever he'd seen and thought earlier, here—now—they looked like a real couple. Flynn's arm wrapped around Thea's slender shoulders… the kiss he pressed against her head. She had her legs tucked up under her, the way she'd always sat as a teenager, back when they'd spent parties like this hiding out together. The memories were strong: Thea skipping out on her hostessing duties, sipping stolen champagne and talking about the world, confiding in him, telling him her hopes, plans, dreams.

It hurt more than he liked, seeing her share a moment like that with someone else. And for that someone else to be his brother…that burned.

It shouldn't, Zeke knew. He'd moved past the pain of her rejection years ago, and it wasn't as if he hadn't found plenty of solace in other arms. She'd made her choice eight years ago and he'd lived by it. He hadn't called, hadn't visited. Hadn't given her a chance to change her mind, because he didn't want her to.

She'd chosen their families and he'd chosen himself. Different sides. Love had flared into anger, rejection, even hate. But even hate faded over the years, didn't it? He didn't hate her now. He didn't know what he felt. Not love, for certain. Maybe…regret? A faint, lingering thought that things might have been different.

But they weren't, and Zeke wasn't one for living in the past. Especially not now, when he'd finally made the last cut between himself and his father. He'd turned down the one thing he'd have given anything for as a boy—his father's acceptance and approval. He knew now how little that was worth. He was free, at last.

Except for that small thin thread that kept him tied to the woman on the swing before him. And by the end of the week even that would be gone, when she'd tied herself to another.

His new life would start the moment he left this place. And suddenly he wanted to savour the last few moments of the old one.

Zeke stepped out onto the terrace, a small smile on his lips as his brother looked up and spotted him.

'Zeke,' Flynn said, eyes wary, and Thea's head jerked up from his shoulder.

'I wondered where you two had got to,' Zeke lied. He hadn't given it a moment's thought, because he hadn't imagined they could be like this. *Together.* 'Dinner over, then?'

Thea nodded, sitting up and shifting closer to Flynn to make room for Zeke to sit beside them. 'How did things go? With your father?'

'Pretty much as expected.' Zeke eyed the small space on the swing, then perched on the edge of the low table in front of them instead.

'Which was...?' Flynn sounded a little impatient. 'I don't even know what he wanted to talk to you about. Business, I assume?'

'You didn't tell him?' Zeke asked Thea, eyebrow raised.

'We were talking about more important things,' Thea said, which made Flynn smile softly and kiss her hair again.

Zeke's jaw tightened at the sight. He suspected he didn't want to know what those 'more important things' were. 'Your father wanted to try and buy my business,' he told Flynn.

'He's your father too,' Flynn pointed out.

Zeke laughed. 'Possibly not, after tonight.'

'You told him no, then?' Thea guessed. 'Why? To spite him? You've already admitted you want to sell.'

'He wanted me to come and work for Morrison-Ashton.'

'And that would be the worst thing *ever*, of course.' Sarcasm dripped from her voice. 'Are you really still so angry with him?'

Tilting his head back, Zeke stared up through the slats of the terrace roof at the stars twinkling through. 'No,' he answered honestly. 'This isn't… It's not like it was any more, Thea. I'm not trying to spite him, or hurt him, or pay him back for anything. I just want to move on. Sever all ties and start a whole new life. Maybe a new company, a new field. A new me.'

'So we won't be seeing you again after the wedding, then?' Flynn said, and Zeke realised he'd almost forgotten his brother was even there for a moment. He'd spoken to Thea the same way he'd always talked to Thea—with far more honesty than he'd give anyone else. A bad habit to fall back into.

'Maybe you two would be worth a visit,' he said, forcing a smile. 'After all, I'll need to come and be favourite Uncle Zeke to your kids, right?'

At his words Flynn's expression softened, and he gave his fiancée a meaningful look. Thea, for her part, glanced down at her hands, but Zeke thought he saw a matching shy smile on her face.

Realisation slammed into him, hitting him hard in the chest until he almost gasped for breath. *That* was what they'd been talking about—their 'more important things'. Children. He'd been so sure that this marriage was a sham, that there was nothing between them. But he hadn't imagined kids. Even when he'd made the comment he'd expected an evasion, a convenient practised answer. Another sign that this wasn't real.

Not *this*. Not the image in his head of Thea's belly swollen with his brother's child. Not the thought of how much better parents Flynn and Thea would be than his own father. Of a little girl with Thea's dark hair curling around a perfect face.

'Well, you know you'll always be welcome in our home,' Flynn said.

The words were too formal for brothers, too distant for anything he'd ever shared with Thea. And Zeke knew without a doubt that he'd never, ever be taking them up on the offer. Maybe he didn't love Thea any more, but that tightly stitched line of regret inside him still pulled when she tugged on the thread between them.

He couldn't give Thea what she wanted—never had been able to. She'd made that very clear. And in two days she'd be married, that thread would be cut, and he'd never see her again.

'I should get to bed,' Thea said, unfolding her legs from under her. 'Another long day tomorrow.'

Flynn smiled up at her as she stood. 'I'll see you in the morning?'

Thea nodded, then with a quick glance at Zeke bent and kissed Flynn on the lips. It looked soft, but sure, and Zeke got the message—*loud and clear, thanks*. She'd made her choice—again—and she was sticking with it.

Fine. It was her choice to make, after all. But Zeke knew that the scar of regret would never leave him if he wasn't sure she was happy with the choice she was making. If he wanted the freedom of that cut thread, he had to be able to leave her behind entirely. He had to be sure she knew what she was doing.

Zeke got to his feet. 'I'll walk you to your room.'

CHAPTER FOUR

THIS WAS EXACTLY what she didn't want. Which, in fairness, was probably why Zeke was doing it.

It had been too strange, sitting there with the two brothers, talking about her future as if Zeke might be part of it—in a role she'd simply never expected him to take. Hard enough to transition from fiancée to wife to mother with Flynn, without adding in her ex as her brother-in-law. It had all been so much easier when she'd imagined he was out of her life for good. That she'd never have to see him again. She'd got over the hurt of that loss years before.

The villa was in darkness, and their footsteps echoed off the tiled floors and painted stone walls. The place might be luxurious, but in the moonlight Thea couldn't help but find it creepy. From the hanging tapestries to the stone arches looming overhead, the shadows seemed oppressive. And it felt eerily empty; everyone else must have gone to bed hours before.

She'd expected Zeke to talk, to keep up the banter and the cutting comments and the jokes, but to her surprise they walked in a companionable silence. She could feel him beside her, the warmth of his presence a constant reminder of how close he was. If she stretched out a finger she could reach his hand.

But she wouldn't.

As they climbed the stairs, Zeke only ever one step behind her, his hand next to hers on the banister, she catalogued all the questions she wanted to ask.

Why are you back?

Why didn't you call?

Are you really going to stay?

What do you want from me now?

There had to be a rhyme and reason to it all somewhere, but Thea couldn't quite put her finger on it. Maybe he didn't know the answers, either. Maybe that was why he seemed always on the edge of asking a question he wasn't sure he wanted her to answer.

'I'm just down here,' she whispered as they reached the top of the stairs. 'You're over that way, right?'

Zeke nodded, but made no effort to head to his own room. After a moment Thea moved towards her door, very aware of him still behind her.

Hand on the door handle, she stopped again. 'What do you want, Zeke?' she asked, looking at the door in front of her.

She felt his sigh, a warm breath against her neck. 'I want to be sure.'

'Sure of what?'

'Sure that you're…happy. That this is really what you want. Before I leave.'

'You're not going to come and visit again, are you?' She'd known that even as he'd talked about being Uncle Zeke. She'd known the truth of it all along. She already knew the answers to all her questions in her heart.

Zeke was here to say goodbye.

'No.'

She turned at the word, and found herself trapped between Zeke's body and the door. He had one arm braced against the wood above her head, the other at his side, fist clenched.

'Why?' More of a breath than a question.

'I need…I need to move on. Away from my family, from yours. For good.'

'Eight years wasn't long enough for you to stop hating us, then?'

'I didn't—'

He stopped short of the lie, which Thea appreciated even as his meaning stabbed her heart. She'd known he hated her. She couldn't let herself be surprised by the confirmation.

'It's not about that any more,' Zeke said instead. He gave a low chuckle. 'I've spent so long caught up in it, in proving myself to my father even as I hated him. So long living my life because of my past, even if I didn't realise I was doing it. And it's time to stop now. Time to build a life for myself, I guess.'

Without us, Thea finished for him in her head.

'So what I need to know is—*are* you happy? Is this really what you want? Or is it just what you think you're supposed to do?'

Zeke's gaze caught hers as he asked his questions, and Thea knew she couldn't look away from those dark eyes even if she'd wanted to.

Was this what she wanted? She thought about Flynn. About how easy it was with him compared to in her previous disastrous attempts at relationships. About everything she could have with him. This wasn't just for their fathers, this time, or even for Helena. This was for her. To give her security, the safety of knowing her place in the world. Knowing where she belonged.

She blinked, and told Zeke, 'This is what I want.'

Time stretched out between them as he stared into her

eyes as if scanning for truths. Finally his eyelids fluttered down, and Thea snapped her gaze away.

'Okay…' Zeke spoke softly, and she was sure she heard relief in the word. 'Okay.'

When she looked back he lowered his lips and kissed her, soft and sweet, before stepping away.

'I hope to God you're not lying to me this time, Thea,' he said, and he turned and walked away to his room.

Thea stood and watched him go, the wood of the door at her back and her grip on the door handle the only things holding her up.

'So do I,' she whispered when his door had closed behind him.

Loosening his tie, Zeke threw himself onto the bed and pulled out his phone. He'd promised Deb an update when he arrived, but between Thea in her underwear and thwarting his father he hadn't had much of a chance.

He checked his watch; London was behind them anyway. She'd still be up.

'So?' Deb said when she answered. Her usual greetings and pleasantries were apparently not deemed necessary for him. 'How's it going?'

'My father wants to buy This Minute.'

'He heard we were selling to Glasshouse?' Deb asked, but there didn't seem to be much of a question in her words. More of a sense of inevitability.

Suspicion flared up. 'Yeah. Any idea how that might have happened?'

'Not a clue,' she replied easily. 'But it's kind of handy, don't you think?'

'No.' Had she leaked it? Why? He should be mad, he supposed, but he trusted Deb. She always had a perfectly logical reason for her actions, and he was kind of curious to find out what it was this time.

'I do,' she said. 'I mean, with two interested parties the price will go up, for starters. And, more than that, this gives you a chance to decide what you really want.'

'Other than to get out of here?'

'That's one option,' Deb said. 'The other is to return to the family fold.'

Zeke remembered the look on his father's face when he'd turned him down. That had felt good. 'I think I already burnt that bridge tonight.'

'That works too.' Deb sounded philosophical about the whole thing. 'At least it was your choice to make this time.'

Sometimes Zeke really regretted the occasional late-night drinking sessions with his business partner. His tongue got loose after alcohol, and she knew him far too well as a result.

'Anyway, it's done,' he said, steamrollering past any analysis of his relationship with his father that she had planned. 'Now I just need to get through the wedding and then I can get back to my real life again.'

'Ah, yes. "The Wedding".' Her tone made it very clear that it had capital letters.

'That is what I came here for.'

'And how was it? Seeing Thea again?'

A vision of her standing there, wedding dress around her waist, flooded his mind. But Deb really didn't need to know about that. 'Fine.'

'You think she really wants to marry your brother?'

'I do.' He was just unsure about her motives.

'Then do you really have to stay?'

'I'm the best man, Deb. Kinda necessary to the proceedings.'

'Zeke…' Her voice was serious now, and he knew it was time to stop joking.

'It's fine. It's just a couple of days and I can put it all behind me.'

'You don't have to put yourself through this, you know. If you're satisfied that she's not being coerced into this by your father—'

'Oh, I'm pretty sure she is.'

'But you said—'

'Which doesn't mean she doesn't want to go through with it.' He sighed. Explaining the peculiarities of the Morrison and Ashton families to outsiders was never easy. 'Look, I need to stay. I need to see this through. It's the only way I'm ever going to…I don't know.'

'Have closure?' Deb said, knowing his own thoughts better than himself as usual. That was always disturbing. 'Fine. But if you need me to manufacture a work emergency to get you out of there…'

'I know where you are. Thanks, Deb.'

'Any time.' She paused, and he got the impression she wasn't quite done with him yet. 'Just…don't stay just to punish yourself, okay?'

'Punish myself for what?'

'Leaving her in the first place.'

The phone went dead in his hand. Apparently goodbyes were no longer necessary, either. He tossed it onto the bedside table and flopped back onto the bed.

This time Deb didn't know what she was talking about. Zeke had absolutely nothing to feel sorry for.

He just hoped Thea knew that, too.

Thea didn't sleep.

She dotted concealer under her eyes the next morning, knowing that Helena would spot the dark shadows anyway.

She'd just have to tell her that it was pre-wedding nerves. Which would no doubt lead to another rousing rendition of the *'It's not too late to back out'* chorus. Still, that had to be better than telling her sister the truth.

The truth about the past, that was. Thea wasn't even sure if *she* understood the truth of her and Zeke in the present.

Helena had laid out her chosen outfit for Thea to wear the day before her wedding and Thea slipped into the pale linen dress without question. One of the advantages of having a younger sister with an eye for style, colour and fashion was never having to worry if she'd chosen the right outfit for an occasion. This week, more than ever, she needed the boost to her confidence of knowing she looked good.

She appreciated it even more when, as she reached the bottom of the stairs, she was accosted by Ezekiel Ashton, Senior.

'Thea! Excellent. I just need a little word with you, if you wouldn't mind.'

Whether she minded or not, Ezekiel ushered Thea into his temporary office—away from the tempting smells of hot coffee and pastries.

Ezekiel's desk was covered in papers and files, his laptop pushed away to the corner, precariously balanced on a stack of books. Thea cleared a ream of paper covered in numbers from the visitor's chair and sat down. His office at the company headquarters was usually neat to the point of anal. Had he been up all night working after his meeting with Zeke? Or was he just missing his terrifyingly efficient PA Dorothy? And, either way, what exactly did he think he needed Thea for?

What if this wasn't business? What if this was some sort of *'welcome to the family, don't hurt my son'* talk? And, if so, how could she be sure which son? Because he was a little late for one of them...

Laughter bubbled up in her chest and Thea swallowed it down as Ezekiel creakily lowered himself into his chair. This was Ezekiel Ashton. Of course it was going to be about business.

'Now, Thea. I appreciate that work might not be your highest priority today, given your imminent nuptials. But this wedding has given us a unique opportunity. One I need you to take full advantage of.'

He gave her a meaningful look across the desk, and Thea's heart sank. This was business, yes, but it was personal, too. This was about Zeke.

'What are you hoping I'll be able to do?' Thea crossed her legs and stared back at her father-in-law-to-be. She couldn't promise anything when it came to Zeke. She'd burnt that bridge long ago. But how to explain that to Ezekiel without telling the whole miserable story?

Ezekiel leant back in his chair, studying her. 'Zeke has always been...fond of you.'

He waited, as if for confirmation, and Thea forced a nod.

'We were friends. When we were younger.'

'I'm hoping you might be able to utilise that friendship.'

No sugarcoating it, then. Not that she'd really expected any such thing from Ezekiel.

'We haven't seen each other in eight years,' Thea pointed out. 'And we didn't...we weren't on the best of terms when he left.'

A slightly raised eyebrow was the only hint that this came as a surprise to Zeke's father. 'Still. After all this time I'm sure you can both forgive and forget.'

Forgive? Thea thought she'd managed that years ago, until Zeke had shown up and reminded her of all the reasons she had to be angry with him. Almost as many as he had to be angry with her.

Forget? Never.

Thea took a breath. Time to refocus the conversation. 'This is about This Minute, right?'

Ezekiel gave a sharp nod. 'I'm sure you can understand the value to Morrison-Ashton of bringing Zeke's little business under the company umbrella.'

'I'd hardly call it a "little business",' Thea said. Its turnover figures for last year had been astronomical. Far higher than their own digital news arm. 'And I think the detrimental effect of *not* buying This Minute is of far higher importance to you.'

'True.'

His gaze held a hint of grudging appreciation. *Good.* In her five years working her way up to running the PR department of Morrison-Ashton Ezekiel had never given her a single sign that he appreciated the work she did, or believed it really added value to the company. It was about time he realised she brought more than a name and some money to the table. She wasn't her father, after all.

'Which is why I need you to persuade him to sell This Minute to us,' Ezekiel finished.

Any satisfaction Thea had felt flew away. *Why did he have to choose this day to suddenly have faith in my abilities?*

'I was under the impression that Zeke had already declined your offer.' And he would continue to do so. She might not have seen him in eight years, but she knew Zeke. He'd never give his father what he wanted without a fight.

'Of course he has,' Ezekiel said, impatiently. 'Otherwise why would I need you? Zeke's letting his pride get in the way, as usual. He knows that the best thing for him and This Minute is to become part of Morrison-Ashton, and for him to take up his rightful role here.'

The role you refused to give him eight years ago. 'He seems very set on moving on to something new.'

'And selling This Minute to Glasshouse.'

'Glasshouse?'

That would be a disaster. For Morrison-Ashton, at least. This Minute would give their main competitor a huge advantage in the digital arena, and the PR fallout from Zeke Ashton defecting to Glasshouse would run and run. It would certainly eclipse any positive coverage her wedding to Flynn was likely to garner.

'Precisely,' Ezekiel said, as if he'd heard every one of her thoughts. 'We need Zeke to sell to Morrison-Ashton. For the family as much as the business. So, you'll do it?'

Could she? Would Zeke listen to her? Would he care? Or would he go out of his way to do the opposite of anything she asked, just as he did with his father? If she could make him see reason...if she could win this for them... This wouldn't just be a business victory. This would assure her place in the Ashton family more than marrying Flynn could achieve.

But even if he did listen...could she ask this of him? Could she choose the business and the family over Zeke all over again, knowing it would hurt him?

Only one way to find out.

'I'll do it.'

Zeke had never given very much thought to weddings beyond showing up in an appropriate suit and whether or not there'd be a free bar. But sitting at a small wrought-iron table at the edge of the villa's huge entrance hall, taking his time over coffee, he had to conclude that, really, weddings were a whole lot of palaver.

The villa had been humming with activity since dawn, as far as he could tell. Before he'd even made it downstairs garlands of flowers and vines had been twisted round the banisters of the staircase, the floors had been polished, and potted trees with ribbons tied around their trunks had been placed at the base of each arch that spanned the hall.

He had no doubt that every other room in the villa would be receiving similar treatment over the next twenty-four hours, but they'd started with the area most likely to be seen by the greatest number of people that day.

And, boy, were there a lot of people. Guests had started arriving very early that morning, flying in from all over the world. From his chosen seat he had a great view of the front door, through a large arch that opened onto the hall-way. Clearly not everyone was staying at the hotel down the road, as several couples and families with suitcases had pitched up already and been shown to their rooms. Family, Zeke supposed. He recognised some and recognised the looks he received even better. First the double-take, checking that it really was him. Then the raised eyebrows. Then a whisper to a companion and the whole thing started over again.

Zeke had seriously considered, more than once, taking a pen to the linen napkin he'd been given and fashioning some sort of sign.

Yes, it would say, *it really is me. Zeke Ashton Junior, black sheep, passed-over heir, broke his mother's heart and had the cheek to come back for his brother's wed-ding. And, no, I'm not selling my father my company, ei-ther. Shocking, isn't it?*

The only thing that stopped him was that, even if he managed to fit all that on a napkin, no one would be able to read it from the sort of distance they were keeping. So instead he smiled politely, raised his coffee cup, and refused point-blank to leave his table. People wanted to stare? Let them.

As the hour became more reasonable other people started to stop by, ostensibly to drop off presents but probably to gawp at the villa and try and catch a glimpse of the bride. Zeke wished them luck; he hadn't seen hide nor hair of her since he'd said goodnight the evening before.

That, Zeke thought ruefully, had been a mistake. Swilling the dregs of his coffee around at the bottom of his cup, he tried not to remember the way Thea had smelled, so close in the darkness, and failed. Just as he'd failed to forget every moment of that last night he'd spent with her before he left.

The way she'd smiled at him before the party. The way she'd kissed him and sworn that it didn't matter when he told her about Flynn taking his job. The way she'd supported him when he'd decided to go and face his father, tell him what he really thought of him.

How his rage had bubbled to the surface as he'd approached his father's office. How unprepared he'd been for what he'd heard there.

Mostly he remembered the moment he'd known he had to leave. Right then—that night. He remembered climbing up to Thea's window to ask her to come with him, and her tears as she told him she couldn't. Wouldn't. The way his heart had stung as he'd realised she really meant it.

Eight years and he couldn't shake that memory.

Couldn't shake the hurt, either.

Catching the eye of the maid, Zeke gave her his most charming smile. She frowned, but headed off to fetch the coffee carafe anyway. Zeke supposed she had other things she was supposed to be doing today, and he was stopping her. But no one had told *him* what to do. He might be the best man, but it seemed the title was wholly ceremonial.

Flynn had disappeared out earlier with one of their cousins, apparently not even spotting Zeke at his table. Whatever tasks there were to be performed today, Flynn seemed to have plenty of help.

Which left him here, drinking too much coffee, and overthinking things. Not ideal.

Across the wide hallway he heard heels clicking on stone and looked up, already knowing somehow who it was.

Thea looked tired, Zeke thought. Was that his fault? Had she been kept awake thinking about exactly where everything had gone wrong between them as he had? He motioned to the maid for a second coffee cup and waited for Thea to cross the hall and sit down at his table. Even if she wanted to avoid him he knew the lure of coffee would be too strong for her.

It took her a while, because another crowd of people had arrived with gifts wrapped in silver paper and too much ribbon and she'd got caught up playing hostess. Zeke watched her smiling and welcoming and thanking and thought she looked even less like the girl he remembered than she had in her wedding dress. The Thea he'd known had hated this—all the fake smiles and pretending to be delighted by the third set of champagne flutes to arrive in the last half-hour. She'd played the part well enough after her mother died, at her father's insistence, the same way she'd acted as a mother to Helena and run the Morrison household for the three of them. But she'd always escaped away upstairs at Morrison-Ashton company parties, as soon as it was at all polite. These days it seemed she relished playing the part.

Eventually Isabella arrived, her smiles and gestures even bigger than Thea's. As his mother took over the meet-and-greet, Thea stepped back from her guests, a slightly disappointed frown settling onto her forehead, looking suddenly out of place. After a moment she moved across the hallway towards him. And the coffee. Zeke had no doubt that the caffeine was more appealing to her than his presence.

'Good morning, Zeke.' Thea swept her skirt under her as she sat, and smiled her thanks at the maid as she poured the coffee. 'Did you sleep well?'

'Like a baby,' Zeke lied. 'And yourself?'

'Fine, thank you.'

'Up early on wedding business?' he asked, waving his coffee cup in the direction of the new arrivals.

'Actually, I was just catching up on a few work things before tomorrow.' Thea picked up her cup and blew across the surface. 'I'll be off for almost a month for the honeymoon, so I'm trying to make sure everything is properly handed over.'

'I'd have thought you'd have more important things to do today than work. Wedding things,' he added when she looked confused.

Thea glanced down at her coffee cup again. 'To be honest, I've been able to leave most of that to the wedding planner. And Helena and Flynn.'

'Most brides *want* to be involved in their wedding plans, you know.' At least, the ones who wanted to get married. Who were marrying a man they loved. And Zeke was beginning to think that Thea didn't fall into *either* of those categories, whatever she said.

'I didn't say I haven't been involved,' Thea said, her voice sharp. 'But at this point it's all the last-minute details and fiddly bits, and Helena is much better at making things look good than I am.'

'So, what *are* you doing today, then?' Zeke asked.

'Actually, I do have one very important wedding-related task to do,' Thea said. 'And I could really use your help.'

Zeke raised his eyebrows. 'Oh?'

Thea nodded. 'I need to buy Flynn a groom's gift. I thought you might be able to help me find something he'd like.'

He hadn't seen his brother in eight years, and he'd had precious little clue what the man liked before then. But if this was the excuse Thea needed to talk to him about whatever was really on her mind, he'd play along. It might even be fun.

'Okay,' he said, draining his coffee. 'I'll bring my car round while you get ready to go.'

But Thea shook her head. 'Oh, no. *I'm* driving.'

CHAPTER FIVE

THE MORE SHE thought about it, the more Thea was convinced that this was a brilliant idea. She could use the shopping trip to sound Zeke out on his plans for This Minute before she approached the more difficult task of convincing him to sell it to Morrison-Ashton. And at the same time she could prove exactly how happy she was to be marrying Flynn by choosing her husband-to-be the perfect wedding gift.

Plus, it got her out of the villa—*and* she got to drive. That was almost enough to assuage the twinges of guilt that still plagued her about her mission that morning.

'Why am I not surprised?' Zeke asked as she pulled up outside the front door in her little red convertible.

'I like to drive.' Thea shrugged, her hands never leaving the wheel as Zeke opened the passenger door and lowered himself into the seat. 'It was an engagement present from Flynn.'

Well, he'd given it to her anyway. She rather suspected that Helena had helped him choose it. Flynn's idea of appropriate gifts tended to be more along the line of whatever the jeweller recommended.

'Of course it was.' Zeke buckled up his seat belt and rested his arm along the side of the door.

He looked casual enough, but Thea knew he was gripping the seat with his other hand. He'd complained regularly about her driving in the eleven months between her passing her test and him leaving.

'So, where are we going?'

'There's a small town just twenty minutes' drive or so away.' Smoothly, Thea pulled away from the villa and headed down the driveway, picking up speed as they passed another load of guests coming up. She'd just have to pretend she hadn't seen them later. 'It has some nice little shops, and there's a wonderful trattoria where we can stop for lunch.'

'Sounds nice. And I'm honoured that you're choosing to spend your last day of single life with me. Really.'

Thea rolled her eyes and ignored him. There was plenty of time to deal with Zeke and his terrible sense of what counted as funny once they reached the town. For now, she just wanted to enjoy the drive.

Zeke fiddled with the car stereo as Thea turned off onto the main road, and soon they were flying through the gentle hills and green and yellow fields of the Tuscan countryside to the sound of the classic rock music he'd always insisted on.

'I *know* I don't own this CD,' Thea said—not that she cared. Somehow it sounded right. As if they'd fallen back in time to the day she'd passed her driving test, just a few weeks after her seventeenth birthday, and Zeke had let her drive his car for the first time.

Zeke held up his phone, connected to the stereo by a lead she hadn't known existed. 'You know me. I never travel without a proper soundtrack.'

The summer sun beamed down on them as they drove along the winding road, past farms and other villas and the occasional vineyard. She'd have two weeks to explore this land with Flynn, Thea thought. Two whole weeks to get used to the idea of being his wife, to get to know him as her husband, before they headed back to London to set up their new home together. It would be perfect.

The heat on her shoulders relaxed her muscles and she realised that Zeke was blissfully silent beside her, not even commenting on her speed, as any other passenger might have done. Maybe he was remembering that first trip out, too. Maybe he was remembering what had happened afterwards, when they'd found a ruined barn on the edge of a nearby farm and he'd spread his jacket out over the hay as he laid her down and kissed her...

Thea glanced at the speedometer and relaxed her foot off the accelerator just a touch.

Time to think of calmer things. Like Flynn, and their honeymoon.

Eventually she slowed down to something approaching the speed limit as they passed rows of stone houses on the outskirts and joined the other traffic heading over the bridge into the town. Thea pulled into the same parking space she'd used the last time she'd visited, just outside the main *piazza*. She grabbed her handbag, waiting for Zeke to get out before she locked the car.

'So,' he asked, pushing his sunglasses up onto his head as he stepped into the shade of the nearest building, 'where first?'

Thea stared down the street, through its red stone arches and paving, and realised she hadn't a clue. What *did* you buy your future husband as a wedding gift, anyway? Especially one who, even after decades of friendship, you didn't actually know all that well?

Glinting glass caught her eye, and she remembered the jeweller's and watch shop she and Helena had found down a winding side street off the *piazza*. Surely there'd be something there?

'This way,' she said, striding in what she hoped was the right direction through the crowds gathered to watch a street entertainer in the *piazza*.

'Where you lead...' Zeke said easily, letting her pass before falling into step with her.

Thea's stride faltered just for a moment. He didn't mean anything by it, she was sure—probably didn't even remember the song. But at his words a half-forgotten melody lodged in her head, playing over and over. A promise to always follow, no matter what.

Her mum had sung it often, before she died. And Thea remembered singing along. The tune was as much a part of her childhood as bickering with Helena over hairbands and party shoes. But more than that she remembered singing it to Zeke, late at night, after half a bottle of champagne smuggled upstairs from the party below. Remembered believing, for a time, that it was true. That she'd follow him anywhere.

Until he'd actually asked her to leave with him.

Shaking her head to try and dislodge the memory, she realised they were there and pushed open the shop door. There was no time for dwelling on ancient history now. She was getting married tomorrow.

And she still needed to find her groom the perfect gift.

'Right,' she said. 'Let's see what this place has that screams *Flynn*.'

The answer, Zeke decided pretty quickly, was not much.

While Thea examined racks of expensive watches and too flashy cufflinks he trailed his fingers over the glass cases and looked around at the other stuff. Flynn wasn't a flashy cufflinks kind of guy, as far as he remembered. But maybe Thea knew better these days.

He glanced over and she held up a gold watch, its oversized face flashing in the bright overhead lights. 'What about this?'

'Flynn has a watch,' Zeke pointed out.

'Yeah, but maybe he'd like a new one. From his wife.'

'Wife-to-be. And I doubt it. The one he wears was Grandad's.' He'd spotted it on his brother's wrist the night before, at dinner, and stamped down on the memory of the day their father had given it to him.

'Oh.' Thea handed the watch back to the assistant. 'Maybe we'll look at the cufflinks instead, then.'

With a sigh, Zeke turned back to the other cases, filled with precious gems and metals. Maybe he should get something for his mother. Something sparkly would probably be enough to make up for any of the apparent pain Thomas had said she'd felt at his departure. Not that Zeke had seen any actual evidence of that pain.

Maybe she was just too caught up in the wedding festivities to remember that she'd missed him. It wouldn't be the first time that other people, other events, had taken precedence over her own sons.

A necklace caught Zeke's eye: pale gold with a bright blue sapphire at the centre. The same colour as Thea's dress the night before. He could almost imagine himself fastening it around her neck as they stood outside her room—a sign that he still...what? Cared? Remembered what they'd had? Regretted how things had ended? Wanted her to be happy? Knew that even though they'd both moved on they'd always be part of each other's past?

That was the hardest thing, he decided. Not even knowing what he wanted to tell Thea, what he needed her to understand. It wasn't as simple as hating her—it never could be, with Thea. But it wasn't as if he'd shown up here this weekend to tell her not to marry Flynn, to run away with him at last instead. As they should have done eight years ago.

No, what he felt for Thea was infinitely more complicated. And if there was a single piece of jewellery that could convey it to her, without him having to find the words, he'd buy it for her in a heartbeat—no matter the cost. But there wasn't.

With a sigh, Zeke dragged his gaze to the next case, only to find tray after tray of sparkling diamond solitaires glinting up at him.

Engagement rings. *Not helpful, universe. And why choose now to get a sense of humour, huh?*

Besides, she already had one of those. He'd glimpsed it flashing in the candlelight at dinner, recognising it as his grandmother's, and had barely even managed to muster any surprise about it. What else would the favoured Ashton heir give to his fiancé-cum-business partner? They were building an empire together, based on their joint family history.

A history Zeke had all but been written out of eight years ago.

'I'm going to have to think about it,' Thea told the shop assistant apologetically, and Zeke, realising he was still staring at the engagement rings, spun round to face her.

'We're leaving?'

'For now,' Thea said.

Zeke followed her out of the shop, letting the door swing shut behind him. 'Nothing that screamed *Flynn*, huh?'

'Not really. He's not really a flashy cufflinks kind of guy, is he?'

Something tightened in Zeke's chest, hearing her echo his thoughts, but he couldn't say if it was because she knew Flynn better than he'd thought or because her thought processes still so closely resembled his.

'So, where next?' he asked, trying to ignore the feeling.

'Um, there's a leather shop down here somewhere.' She waved her hand into an arcade of small, dark but probably insanely expensive shops, hidden under the arched stone roof. She hadn't even let Helena explore them properly last time. 'Do you think Flynn needs a new briefcase?'

'I think Flynn will love whatever you buy him, because it's from you.'

Thea gave him a look. One that suggested she was trying to evaluate if he might have been taken over by aliens recently. 'Seriously?'

'Okay, I think he'll pretend to love it, whatever it is, because that's the appropriate thing to do.'

'And Flynn *does* like appropriate.' She sighed and headed towards the leather shop anyway. 'Do you remember the hideous tie you bought him that last summer?'

'He wore it for his first day at work,' Zeke said, relishing the thought all over again. It had been the most truly horrendous tie he'd been able to find anywhere. Expensive, of course, so that his mother couldn't object. But hugely inappropriate for the serious workplace with its neon tartan. The perfect graduation gift for the perfect brother. Zeke had known Flynn would wear it just so as not to offend him. And that Flynn would never realise it was a joke gift.

'He changed it on the train before going into the office,' Thea told him, thus ruining a perfect memory.

'Seriously? That's a shame. I did love thinking of him sitting in meetings with the board wearing that tie,' Zeke said wistfully.

'He's probably still got it somewhere,' Thea said. 'He might not be stupid enough to wear it for work, but he's definitely sentimental enough that he won't have thrown it away. After all, it was the last thing you gave him before...'

'Before I left,' Zeke finished for her. 'Yeah, I don't think he was as bothered by that as you think.' Seemed like no-body had been.

She gave him a small sad smile. 'Then maybe I do know your brother better than you, after all.'

Did she? She should—she was marrying the guy. But the very fact she'd admitted she wasn't sure that she did… The contradictions buzzed around Zeke's brain, and at the heart of them was the disturbing thought that maybe Flynn *had* cared after all.

And another question. Had Thea?

The problem, Thea decided, wasn't that she didn't *know* what sort of things Flynn liked. It was just that he knew them better and had, in pretty much every case, provided them for himself. He already had the perfect briefcase, his grandfather's watch and a reliable pair of cufflinks. Whatever the item, he'd have researched it, chosen the best-quality one he required, and been satisfied with his purchase. Whatever she bought would be used a few times, to show his appreciation, then shoved to the back of a cupboard like that hideous neon tartan joke tie.

This whole trip had been a mistake. She'd wanted to show Zeke that she knew her fiancé, that they were in tune as a couple. Instead all she seemed to be proving was that whatever she brought to the marriage wasn't really required.

No. This wasn't about briefcases and watches. She brought a lot more to the table than material goods. She wasn't her father, just providing the money and then sitting back to watch the tide of success come rolling in. She was part of the company, part of Flynn's life, and part of their future together.

Which was great as a pep talk, but rubbish at helping her find a wedding present for her husband-to-be.

'What about this one?' Zeke held up a tan leather handbag. 'It's a man bag!'

'I'm pretty sure it's not,' Thea said. 'It has flowers decorating the strap.'

'Flynn's secure enough in his masculinity to carry it off,' Zeke argued, slinging the bag over his shoulder and pouting like a male model.

'I am *not* buying him the wedding present equivalent of a neon tartan tie, Zeke.' Thea turned back to the briefcases and heard him sigh behind her.

'Then what *are* you going to buy him?' Zeke picked up a black briefcase and flipped the latch open. 'Hasn't he already got one of these?'

'Yes.'

'So does he need a new one?'

'No.'

'Then can we go for lunch?'

Thea sighed. He did have a point, and she *was* hungry. She'd missed breakfast, thanks to Ezekiel Senior and his request.

She tensed at the memory. Never mind the perfect wedding gift, she had another job to do today. And lunch would be the perfect time to broach the subject. Preferably after Zeke had enjoyed a glass or two of wine. Or three. Three might be the magic number.

'Come on, then,' she said, opening the door and preparing to leave the cool shadows of the shopping arcade behind and step back out into the piazza. She waved a hand in the direction of a familiar-looking dark alleyway. 'The little trattoria I was talking about is down here somewhere.'

It wasn't fancy, but Zeke had never been one for the expensive restaurants and big-name places. He'd used to prefer hidden gems and secret spots that were just their own. She was always surprised, even after so long, when she caught a magazine photo of him at some celebrity chef's opening night at a new restaurant, or on the red carpet with some actress or another. That wasn't the Zeke she remembered. And now, spending time with him again, she wondered if it was even the Zeke he'd become. Was it just that being seen was the only way he had to let his father know that he was a success now, in his own right?

Maybe she'd ask him. After the wedding. And after she'd persuaded him to sell This Minute to his father.

So probably never, then.

Thea pushed open the heavy painted wood door under a sign that just read 'Trattoria' and let Zeke in first. He smiled at the nearest waitress and she found them a table next to the window without hesitation; only a few other tables were occupied. Thea couldn't help but think this was probably a good thing. If Zeke threw pasta all over her when she tried to talk to him about his father at least there wouldn't be too many witnesses. Helena would be cross about the dress, though...

'Can I get you some drinks?' the waitress asked, her English clearly far better than Thea's Italian had ever been. She let Zeke order a local beer before she asked for a soft drink. Alcohol really wasn't going to help the conversation they needed to have.

'So, you've been here before?' Zeke asked, looking around him at the faded pictures on the stone walls and the bare wooden tables.

The small windows had all been thrown open to let in air, but the heat of the day and the lack of breeze meant that not much coolness was moving around, save from the lazy spin of the lone ceiling fan. Thea's dress had started to stick to her back already, and she longed for that soft drink.

'I came here with Helena last week,' she said. 'Just

after we arrived. I can recommend the *pappardelle* with wild boar sauce.'

'With Helena? Not Flynn?' Zeke pressed.

Thea wondered why he cared anyway. He'd left, and had every intention of leaving again, without even the faint hope that he might return this time. What did he care if she married Flynn or not? Besides not letting his brother win, of course.

Maybe that was what this came down to. All Zeke wanted was to prove a point and then he'd move on. In which case she had pretty much no chance of talking him into selling them This Minute.

But she still had to try.

'No, not with Flynn. He didn't fly in until a couple of days ago. They needed him in the office.'

'But they didn't need you?'

Dammit. Why did Zeke always know exactly what niggled at her? And why did he always have to push at that point?

'My planning for the wedding kind of *is* part of my job at the moment.' Thea toyed with the menu in her hand so she didn't have to see his reaction to that.

'Of course,' Zeke said. 'The final union of the two biggest families in media. It's quite the PR stunt.'

'It's also my life,' Thea snapped back.

'Yeah, but after the last twenty-four hours I still can't tell which of those is more important to you.'

Thea looked up, searching for a response to that one, and gave an inward sigh of relief when she saw the waitress coming over with their drinks.

'Are you ready to order?' she asked, placing the glasses on the table.

Zeke smiled at her—that charming, happy-go-lucky

smile he never gave Thea any more. 'I'll have the wild boar *pappardelle*, please. I hear it's excellent.'

'The same, please,' Thea said. But she wasn't thinking about food. She was thinking about how she'd let her work become her life, and let her life drift away entirely.

Zeke sipped his beer and watched Thea, lost in thought across the table. He'd thought it would be fun, needling her about how her wedding was actually work. He'd had a run of honeymoon jokes lined up in his head—ones he knew she'd hate. But now…well, the humour had gone.

'I'm sorry,' he said, even though he wasn't sure he was, really. He'd only told the truth, after all. Something that happened far too little in their families.

'You're *sorry*?' Thea asked disbelievingly.

Zeke shrugged. 'Not really the done thing, is it? Upsetting the bride the day before her wedding.'

'I'm not upset.'

'Are you sure? Because you look a little…blotchy.' The way she always had moments before she started crying.

But Thea shook her head, reaching for her glass with a steady hand. 'I'm fine. Like you say, you've been back less than twenty-four hours. I don't expect you to understand the relationship and the agreement that Flynn and I have developed and nurtured over the past two years.'

'Two years? You've been with him that long?'

'Yes. You don't think marriage is something I'd rush into, do you?'

Actually, he'd assumed that the idea had come up in a board meeting, that their respective fathers had put forward a proposal document to each of them and they'd weighed up the pros and cons before booking the church. But Zeke didn't think she'd appreciate *that* analysis.

'You did last time,' he said instead. 'With What's-his-name.'

'Cameron,' she supplied. 'And how did you know about him?'

'I wasn't thinking about him.' How many guys *had* she almost married since he'd left? 'I meant the Canadian.'

'Scott.'

'Yeah. I read about him on our Canadian news site. Hockey player, right?'

'Right.'

'Whirlwind engagement, I heard.'

'And he was equally quick with the cheating, as it turned out.'

'Ah.' He hadn't known that. All that had been reported was that the wedding had been called off with hours to spare. So like Thea to protect the guy's reputation even as he was hurting her. 'So who was this Cameron guy, then?'

'A business associate. Turned out he loved my business, and my money, a lot more than he loved me.'

'Never mix business with pleasure, huh?' Zeke said, before remembering that that was exactly what she was doing with Flynn. 'I mean…'

Thea sighed. 'Don't worry. I am well aware of the disastrous reputation of my love-life. You can't say anything I haven't heard before.'

He hated seeing her like this. So certain she would make a mistake. Was that why she was marrying Flynn? The safest bet in a world full of potential mistakes?

Sometimes a woman has to choose the safest road, Zeke. We can't all afford to hike the harder trails if we want to arrive safely.' The words were his mother's, eight years old now, but he could see their truth in Thea's face. For the first time he wondered who Thea would have become if her own mother had lived. Or if Thomas Morrison had never met Ezekiel Ashton. Would she be happier? Probably, he decided.

'You weren't always rubbish at love,' Zeke said, the words coming out soft and low.

Her gaze flashed up to meet him, as if she was looking for a hidden jibe or more mockery. He tried to keep his expression clear, to show her that all he meant was the words he'd said.

Clearly he failed. 'Yeah, right. Funny man. Of course you know *exactly* how early my failure at love started.'

'I didn't mean—' he started, but she cut him off.

'My first love—you—climbed out of a window to escape from me on my eighteenth birthday, Zeke. I think we can all see where the pattern started.' Bitterness oozed out of her voice, but all Zeke could hear was her saying, *'No, Zeke. I can't.'* Eight years and the sound had never left him.

Hang on. 'Wait. Are you blaming *me* for your unlucky love-life?' Because as far as he was concerned he was the one who should be assigning blame here.

'No. Yes. Maybe.' She twisted her napkin in her hands, wrapping it round her fingers then letting it go again.

'I feel much better for that clarification.'

'I don't want to talk about this any more.'

She might not, but after eight years Zeke had some things he wanted to say. And she was bloody well going to listen. 'And, in the name of accuracy, I wasn't trying to escape you. In fact you might recall me begging you to come with me.' Standing on that stupid wobbly trellis, wrecking whatever that purple flower had been, clinging onto the windowsill. She'd looked out at him, all dark hair and big eyes, and broken his heart.

'I wouldn't call it begging,' Thea said, but even she didn't sound convinced.

'You said no. You chose to stay. You can't blame me for

that.' That moment—that one moment—had changed his entire life. Made him the person he was today. She could at least *try* to remember it right.

'You chose to leave me. So why can't I blame you? You're still blaming me. Isn't that why you're here? To make my life miserable because I made the right decision eight years ago and you hate that I was right for once?'

No. That wasn't it. That wasn't what he was doing. He was here to draw a line under everything there had ever been between them, under his bitter resentment of his family that had ruled his life for too long. Zeke was moving on.

But sometimes moving on required looking backwards. Closure—that was what this was.

'The right decision,' she'd said. 'You never once imagined what life might have been like if you' d left with me that night?' Because he had driven himself crazy with it even when he'd known it was pointless. Self-destructive, even. Had she been spared that?

Apparently not. 'Of course I did, Zeke! Endlessly, and a thousand different ways. But it doesn't change the fact that I was needed at home. That I was right to stay.'

And suddenly Zeke knew what it was he needed to move on. What it would take to get the closure he craved.

So he looked up at her and asked the question.

'Why?'

CHAPTER SIX

WHY?

As if that wasn't a question she'd asked herself a million times over the past eight years.

She knew the answer, of course. Helena. She'd needed a big sister right then, more than ever. Thea couldn't have left her, and she didn't regret staying for her for one moment.

But if she was honest that wasn't the only answer. And it wasn't the one she wanted to give Zeke. It wasn't her secret to tell, apart from anything else.

'Because we were too young. Too stupid. Zeke, I was barely eighteen, and you were asking me to leave my whole life behind. My family, my future, my plans and dreams. My place in the world. Everything.'

'I'd have been your family. Your place. Your future.'

Zeke stared at her, his face open and honest. For the first time since he'd come back Thea thought she might be seeing the boy she'd known behind the man he'd become.

'You know I'd have moved mountains to give you anything you wanted. To make every dream you had come true.'

The worst part was she did know that. Had known it even then. But she hadn't been able to take the risk.

'Perhaps. But, successful as you are now, I bet it wasn't like that to start with. You'd have had to struggle, work every hour there was, take risks with your money, your reputation.' She could see from his face it was true. 'And what did you think I'd be doing while you were doing that? I wanted to go to university, Zeke. I had my place—all ready and waiting. I didn't want to give that up to keep house for you while you chased your dream.'

'I wouldn't... It wouldn't have been like that.'

'Wouldn't it?'

'No.' He sounded firmer this time. 'Look, I can't change the past, and I can't say what would have happened. But, Thea, you know me. *Knew* me, at least. And you have to know I would never have asked you to give up your dreams for mine.'

'Sorry...' the waitress said, lowering their plates to the table. 'I didn't mean to... Enjoy!'

She scampered off towards the kitchen and Thea wondered how much she'd heard. How much she was now re-telling to the restaurant staff.

Zeke hadn't even looked at his lunch. 'Tell me you know that, Thea. I wouldn't have done that.'

Thea loaded pasta onto her fork. 'Maybe you wouldn't. Not intentionally. But it happens.' She'd seen it happen to too many friends, after they got married or when they started a family. At eighteen, she didn't think she'd have had the self-awareness to fight it.

'What about now, then?' Zeke asked, still looking a little shaken. 'Do you really think it will be different with Flynn?'

'Yes,' Thea said, without hesitation. She knew about business—knew what she needed to do there. Her marriage with Flynn would only enhance that. She wouldn't give it up just to be someone's wife. 'We've talked about it. About our future. We both know what we're getting into.'

Had it all written down in legalese, ready to be signed along with the marriage register.

Their conversation on the terrace the night before came back to her and she felt a jangle of nerves and excitement when she thought about what she'd agreed to now. Maybe that—a family—would be what she needed to make the whole thing feel real. She knew it was what Flynn wanted, after all. She frowned. But they hadn't spoken yet about what would happen then. Would he expect her to stay at home and look after the kids? If so, they had a problem.

Mentally, she added the topic to the list of honeymoon discussions to have. They had time. They hadn't even had sex yet, for heaven's sake.

The thought was almost amusing—especially sitting here with her fiancé's brother, a guy she had actually slept with. Lost her virginity to, in fact. *Along with my heart.*

Was that why none of the others had stuck? She had wondered sometimes, usually late at night, if Zeke had broken something inside her. If, when he'd left, he'd taken something with him she could never get back. But now he was here and she'd decided she was better off without whatever it was he'd taken. Better off choosing a sensible, planned sort of relationship. Maybe it didn't burn with the same intensity, but she stood a better chance of making it out without injury.

She might not have been able to fulfil the role her father had hoped she would, after her mother's death. Maybe she hadn't been a great hostess or housekeeper, or able to help Helena in the way a mother would have. But those were never supposed to be her roles, anyway. Not in her father's household. This time she'd found her own role. Her own place in her own new family. And she wasn't giving that up.

She couldn't. Not when she risked returning to that

empty, yawning loneliness that had followed Zeke's departure. With Zeke gone, Helena sent away for months, her father locked in his study and Isabella taking over everything Thea had thought was her responsibility...the isolation had been unbearable. As if the world had shifted in the wake of that horrible night and when it had settled there'd been no room for Thea any more. Nowhere she felt comfortable, at home.

And she'd been looking for it ever since. University hadn't provided it, and the holidays at home, with Helena floating around the huge house like a ghost, certainly hadn't. Working her way up at Morrison-Ashton, proving she wasn't just there because of her father, that had helped. But a corner office wasn't a home, however hard she worked.

Flynn...their marriage, their family...he could be. And Thea couldn't let Zeke, or anyone, make her question that.

She watched Zeke, digging into his *pappardelle* and wondered why it was he'd really come back. Not for her—he'd made that much clear. So what was he trying to achieve?

'Zeke?'

He looked up from his bowl, eyes still unhappy. 'Yeah?'

'Why did you come back? Really? I mean, I know it wasn't just for my wedding. So why now?'

With a sigh, Zeke dropped his fork into his bowl and sat back. 'Because...because it was time. Because I'm done trying to win against my father. I'm done caring what he thinks or expects or wants. I'm ready to move on from everything that happened eight years ago.'

'Including me?'

'Including you.'

Thea took a breath, held it, and let it out. After this week they'd be done with each other for good. She'd be married, and the past wouldn't matter any more. It felt…strange. Like an ache in a phantom limb. But she felt lighter, too, at the idea that everything could be put behind them at last.

Except, of course, she had one more thing to do before she could let him go.

Her gaze dropped down to her bowl as guilt pinged in her middle. This might be the one thing she could do to make sure Zeke never came back. But it was also one more step towards earning her place as an Ashton. And that meant it was worth it.

The way Thea's body relaxed visibly at his words left Zeke tenser than ever. Was she that relieved to be finally rid of even the memory of him? Or, like him, was she just so tired of lugging it all around every day? Was she happy to have the path clear for her happy-ever-after with Flynn? Or just settling for the safety of a sensible business marriage?

He'd ask…except those kind of questions—and caring about the answers—didn't exactly sound like leaving her behind.

One more day. He'd make sure she got down the aisle, said 'I do', and rode off into the sunset. Then his new life, whatever it turned out to be, could begin.

'Before you leave us all behind completely, though…' Thea said.

Zeke's jaw clenched. There was always one more thing with Thea.

'I need to talk to you about something.'

A hollow opened up inside him. This was it. Whatever reason Thea had for dragging him out to buy a stupid gift for his brother, he was about to find it out. And suddenly he didn't want to know. If he had to leave her behind for ever he wanted to have this last day. Wanted to leave believing that she'd honestly wanted to spend time with him before he went. For the sake of everything they'd had once and knew they could never have again. Was that so much to ask?

Apparently so.

'I spoke to your father this morning,' Thea said, and Zeke's happy bubble of obliviousness popped.

'Did you, now?' He should have known that. Should have guessed, at least. He'd let himself get side-tracked by the experience of being with Thea again, and now he was about to get blindsided. Another reason why being around Thea Morrison was bad for his wellbeing.

'He wanted me to talk to you about—'

'About me selling This Minute to Morrison-Ashton,' Zeke finished for her. It wasn't as if his father had any other thoughts in relation to him.

'Yes.'

One simple word and the hollow inside him collapsed in on itself, like a punch to the gut folding him over.

'No,' he said, and let the anger start to fill him out again.

How could she ask? After everything they'd been to each other, everything they'd once had…how did she even dare?

His skin felt too hot and his head pounded with the betrayal. He knew exactly why she was doing it. To make sure he left. To make sure her perfect world went back to the way she thought it should be. To buy her place in his family, at his brother's side.

Because Morrison-Ashton and their families had always mattered more to her than he had. And he should have remembered that.

Thea pulled the face she'd always used to pull when he'd been annoying her by being deliberately difficult. He'd missed that face until now. Now it just reminded him how little his feelings mattered to her.

'Zeke—'

'I'm not selling you my company, Thea.' He bit the words out, holding in the ones he really wanted to say. He wasn't that boy any more—the one who lost control from just being near her. This was business, not love. Not any more.

'Your father is willing to match whatever Glasshouse are offering…'

'I don't care.' *Just business*, he reminded himself.

'And even if you don't want to take up a position within Morrison-Ashton we could still look at share options.'

'I said no.' The rage built again, and he flexed his hand against his thigh to keep it from shaking.

'Our digital media team are putting together a—'

'Dammit, Thea!' Plates rattled as Zeke slammed his fist down on the table and the restaurant fell silent. 'Will you just listen to me for once?'

'Don't shout, Zeke,' Thea said, suddenly pale. 'People are looking.'

'Let them look.' He didn't care. Why should he? He'd be out of here tomorrow. 'Because I'm going to shout until you start listening to me.'

Thea's face turned stony. Dropping her fork into her bowl, she pulled out her purse and left several notes on the table. Then she stood, picked up her bag, and walked out of the restaurant.

The rage faded the moment she was out of his sight and he was Zeke Ashton the adult again. The man he'd worked so hard to become, only to lose him the moment she prodded at a sore spot.

Picking up his bottle of beer, Zeke considered his options. Then he drained the beer, dropped another couple of notes onto the stack and followed her, as he'd always known he would.

So had she known, it seemed, which irritated him more than it should have. Thea stood leaning against the wall of the restaurant, waiting for him.

'I left a very decent tip,' he said, watching her, waiting to see which way she'd jump. 'It seemed only fair since we walked out without finishing our meals.'

'Yelling suppresses the appetite.' Thea pushed away from the wall.

'It seemed the only way to get you to listen to me.'

Turning to face him, she smiled with obviously feigned interest. 'I'm listening.'

Suddenly his words felt petty, unnecessary. But he said them anyway. 'I will not sell This Minute to Morrison-Ashton.'

She gave a sharp nod. 'So you've mentioned. Now, if that's all, I want to go back to the villa.'

'What about Flynn's present?' Zeke asked, matching her stride as she headed for the car at speed.

'It can wait.'

'The wedding's tomorrow. I think you're pretty much out of time on this one.'

Thea opened the car door and slid into her seat. 'So I'll give him a spectacular honeymoon present instead.'

Zeke didn't want to think about what she might come up with for that. Except he already had a pretty good idea.

'Like the present you gave me for my twenty-first?' he asked, and watched Thea flush the same bright red as her car as she started the engine.

'You have to stop that,' she said, pulling away from the kerb.

'Stop what?' he asked, just to make her say it.

She glared at him. 'Look. I'm getting married tomorrow. So all this reminiscing about the good old days is getting kind of inappropriate, don't you think?'

'Oh, I don't know.' Zeke watched her as she drove, hands firm on the wheel, shoulders far more tense than they had been on the drive in. He was getting to her. And for some reason he really didn't want to stop. 'I think the question is whether Flynn thinks it's inappropriate.'

'Flynn doesn't know.'

'You mean you're not going to tell him about our shopping trip?'

'I mean he doesn't know about us at all. That we were ever…anything to each other.'

Thea took the last turning out of the town and suddenly their speed rocketed. Plastered back against his seat, Zeke tried to process the new reality she'd just confronted him with. She'd said they didn't talk about him, but he hadn't realised it extended this far. She'd written him out of their history completely, and the pain of that cut through his simmering anger for a moment.

'But…how?' How could anyone who knew them, who had seen them together back then, not known what they were to each other? They had been seventeen and twenty-one. *Subtle* hadn't really been in their vocabulary, despite Thea's requests to keep things secret. He hadn't cared who knew. Certainly their parents had known. How could Flynn have missed it?

'He was away at university, remember?' Thea said. 'And not just round the corner, like you. He was all the way up in Scotland. I guess he just…he was living his own life. I didn't realise at first, when we…started this. But it became clear pretty quickly. He just…didn't know.'

'And you didn't think it was important enough to tell him about?' Didn't think *he* was important enough. Suddenly Zeke wanted nothing more than to remind her just how important he'd been to her once.

'Why would I? You were gone. You were never com-

ing back as far as I was concerned. And even if you did…
even now you have…'

'Even now I have, what?'

'It doesn't change anything. You and I are ancient history, remember? What difference does it make now what
we might have had eight years ago?'

But it did make a difference. Zeke couldn't say how, but
it did. And suddenly he wanted her to admit that.

Thea tried to focus on the road, but her gaze kept slipping to the side, watching Zeke's reactions. It wasn't a
test, wasn't as if she'd said anything untrue, but he wasn't
reacting quite the way she'd expected.

She knew Zeke—had always known Zeke, it seemed.
She knew that for him to come back now, into this situation…whatever his reasons…he wouldn't pass up the opportunity to drag up the past. He'd want his brother to feel
uncomfortable, to know that he'd had her first. Punishment, she supposed. Partly for her, for not leaving with
him, for breaking their deal. And partly for Flynn, for taking everything Zeke had always assumed was his.

Not telling Flynn… It had seemed like the best idea at
the time. And when Zeke had returned she'd been so relieved that she hadn't. One less thing to drive her crazy
this week. Her relationship with Flynn might not be the
most conventional, but their marriage agreement did have
a fidelity clause, and she really didn't want to have an ex-
cruciatingly awkward conversation with her fiancé and
probably their lawyers, maybe even their fathers, about
whether Zeke's return would have any effect on that.

Of course it didn't. They'd both moved on. But Flynn
liked to be thorough about these things.

'It makes a difference,' Zeke said suddenly, and Thea

tried to tune herself back into the conversation, 'because you're lying to your fiancé. My brother.'

Thea gave a harsh laugh. 'Seriously? You're going to try and play the loving brother card? Now? It's a little late, Zeke.'

'I'm the best man at your wedding, Thea. Someone tomorrow is going to ask me if I know of any reason why you shouldn't get married.'

'You don't! Me sleeping with you eight years ago is not a reason for me not to get married tomorrow.'

Zeke raised an eyebrow. 'No? Then how about you lying to your fiancé? Or the fact you left your last two fiancés practically at the altar?'

'Why were you reading up on my love-life anyway?' She hadn't thought to ask when he mentioned Scott before. She'd been more concerned with getting the conversation away from her past romantic disasters. 'I don't believe for a second you just happened to stumble across that information on your site.'

'Did you think I hadn't kept up with you? Kept track of what was going on in your life?'

'Yes,' Thea said. 'That's exactly what I thought. I thought you left and forgot all about the people you left behind.'

'I didn't leave you behind.'

The countryside sped past faster than ever, but Thea couldn't bring herself to slow down. 'Zeke, you left and you didn't look back.'

'I asked you to come with me.' His mulish expression told her that even eight years couldn't change the fact that she'd said no. Too late now, anyway.

'And I told you I couldn't.'

Zeke shook his head. 'Not couldn't. Wouldn't.'

'It was eight years ago, Zeke! Does it really matter which now?'

'Yes!'

'For the love of God, why?'

'Because I've spent eight years obsessing about it and I need closure now, dammit! Preferably before you marry my brother and send me away again.'

Thea's head buzzed with the enormity of the idea. Eight years of obsession, and now he wanted closure. Fine. She'd give him his closure.

Slamming on the brakes, Thea pulled over to the side of the road, half into a field of sunflowers, and stopped the engine. Opening the door, she stepped out onto the dusty verge at the edge of the road, waiting for Zeke to follow. He did, after a moment, walking slowly around to where she leant against the car. She waited until he stopped, his body next to hers against the warm metal.

'You want closure?' she said.

'Yes.'

He wasn't looking at her—was choosing to stare out at the bright flowers swaying in the breeze instead. Somehow that made it all a little easier.

'Fine. What do you need to know to move on?'

Now he turned, his smile too knowing. 'I need to know that *you've* moved on. That you're not still making the same bad choices you made then for the same bad reasons.'

'I made the right choice,' Thea said, quietly. 'I chose to stay for a reason.'

'For Helena. For your father.'

'Yes.'

'You were living your life for other people to avoid upsetting your family, just like you are now.'

'No. I'm living my life for me.' And making the right

decisions for the future she wanted. She had to hang on to that.

'Really? Whose idea was it for you to marry Flynn?'

'What difference does it make? I'm the one who chose to do it.'

'It makes a difference,' Zeke pressed.

Did the man not know how to just let go of something? Just once in his intense life? Was it too much to ask?

'Fine. It was your father's idea,' Thea said, bracing herself for the inevitable smugness. Lord, Zeke did love being right.

'Of course it was.' But he didn't sound smug. Didn't sound vindicated. If anything, he sounded a little sad.

Thea turned to look at him. 'Why did you ask if you already knew?'

'Because I need you to see it. I need you to see what you're doing.'

His words were intense, but his eyes were worse. They pressed her, demanded that she look the truth in the face, that she open herself up to every single possibility and weigh them all.

Thea looked away, letting her hair fall in front of her face. 'I know what I'm doing.'

Zeke shook his head. 'No, Thea. I don't think you do. So, tell me. Why did you stay when I left?'

'Why do you think? We were too young, Zeke. And besides, my family needed me. Helena needed me.' More than ever right then.

'Why?'

'Oh, I don't know, Zeke. Why do you think? Why would a motherless teenage girl *possibly* need her big sister around to look out for her?' That wasn't the whole reason, of course, but the rest of it was Helena's secret to tell.

'She had your father. And my mother.'

A bitter laugh bubbled up in her throat. 'As much as she might pretend otherwise, your mother is not actually *our* mother.'

'Just as well, really,' Zeke said, his voice low, and she knew without asking that he wasn't thinking about her marrying Flynn. He was thinking about all the things they'd done in dark corners at parties, about his twenty-first birthday, about every single time his skin had been pressed against hers.

And, curse him, so was she.

'I had to stay, Zeke,' she said.

'Give me one true reason.'

Thea clenched her hand against her thigh. Did the man simply not listen? Or just not hear anything he didn't like? 'I've given you plenty.'

'Those weren't reasons—they were excuses.'

'Excuses? My family, my future—they're excuses?' Thea glared at him. 'Nice to know you hold my existence in such high esteem.'

'That's not what this is about.'

'Then what *is* it about, Zeke?' Thea asked, exasperated. 'If you don't believe me—fine. Tell me why *you* think I stayed.'

'Because you were scared,' he said, without missing a beat.

'Ha!'

'You stayed because other people told you it was the right thing to do. Because you knew it was what your father would want and you've always, *always* done what he wanted. Because you've never been able to say no to Helena ever since your mother died.' He took a breath. 'But mostly you stayed because you were too scared to trust your own desires. To trust what was between us. To trust *me*.'

The air whooshed out of Thea's lungs. 'That's what you believe?'

'That's what I know.'

When had he got so close? The warm metal of the car at her back had nothing on the heat of his body beside her.

'You're wrong,' she said, shifting slightly away from him.

He raised an eyebrow. 'Am I?' Angling his body towards her, Zeke placed one hand on her hip, bringing him closer than they'd been in eight long years. 'Prove it.'

'How?' Thea asked, mentally chastising her body for reacting to him. This was over!

'Tell me you don't still think about us. Miss us being together. Tell me you don't still want this.'

Thea started to shake her head, to try and deny it, but Zeke lowered his mouth to hers and suddenly all she could feel was the tide of relief swelling inside her. His kiss, still so familiar after so long, consumed her, and she wondered how she'd even pretended she didn't remember how it felt to be the centre of Zeke Ashton's world.

Except she wasn't any more. This wasn't about her— not really. This was Zeke proving a point, showing himself *and* her that he could still have her if he wanted. And he'd made it very clear that he didn't—not for anything more than showing his father and his brother who had the power here. She was just another way for him to get one over on the family business.

And she had a little bit more self-respect than that, thank you.

'Thea,' Zeke murmured between kisses, his arm slipping further around her waist to haul her closer.

'No.' The word came out muffled against his mouth, so she put her hands against his chest and pushed. Hard.

Zeke stumbled back against the car, his hands abandoning her body to stop himself falling. 'What—?' He stopped, gave her one of those ironic, mocking looks she hated.

'I said no.' Thea sucked in a breath and lied. 'I *don't* still think about us. I *don't* miss what we had. It was a childish relationship that ran its course. I was ready for my own life, not just to hang on to the edges of yours. That's why I didn't come with you.' She swallowed. 'And I certainly don't want *that*. Especially not when I'm marrying your brother tomorrow.'

For once in his life Zeke was blessedly silent. Thea took advantage of the miracle by turning and getting back into the car. She focussed on her breathing…in and out, even and slow. Strapped herself in, started the engine. Familiar, easy, well-known actions.

And then she said, 'Goodbye, Zeke,' and gave him three seconds to clear the car before she screeched off back to the villa.

CHAPTER SEVEN

ZEKE STARED AFTER the cherry-red sports car kicking up dust as it sped away from him. Thea's dark hair blew behind her in the breeze, and he could still smell her shampoo, still feel her body in his arms.

He was an idiot. An idiot who was now stranded in the middle of nowhere.

Pushing his fingers through his hair, Zeke started the long trudge up the path towards the villa. At least Thea had driven him most of the way home before kicking him out.

Not that he could really blame her. He knew better than to ambush her like that. He'd just been so desperate to hear her admit it, to hear her say that she'd made a mistake not going with him that night.

That she still thought about him sometimes.

But clearly she didn't. She stood by her decision. And he had to live with that. At least for the next couple of days. Then he'd be gone, ready to start his own life for once, without the memories and the baggage of trying to prove his family wrong.

He'd told Thea he wanted closure, and she'd given it to him. In spades.

It was a long, hot, depressing walk back to the villa. By the time he got there, dusty and sweaty, the only thing he wanted in the world was a shower. It was nice, in a way, to have his desires pared down to the basics. Simpler, anyway.

Of course just because he only wanted one thing, it didn't mean he was going to get it. Really, he should have known that by now.

'Zeke!' Helena jumped up from her seat in the entrance hall, blonde waves bouncing. 'You're back! Great. I wanted to— What happened to you?'

'Your sister,' Zeke said, not slowing his stride as he headed straight for the stairs. 'She's trying to destroy my life, I think.'

'Oh,' Helena said, closer than he'd thought. Was she going to follow him all the way to his room?

'Don't worry,' Zeke told her. 'I know how to thwart her.' All he had to do was not sell his company to Morrison-Ashton—which he had no intention of doing regardless—and let her marry Flynn—which he appeared to have no choice in anyway.

Even if both things still made him want to punch some poor defenceless wall.

'Right...'

Helena sounded confused, but she was still following him. Clearly he needed to address whatever her problem was if he were to have any hope of getting his shower before the rehearsal dinner.

Sighing, Zeke stopped at the top of the stairs and leant against the cool, stone wall for a moment. 'You wanted to...?'

Helena blinked. 'Sorry?'

'You said you wanted to...'

'Talk to you!' Helena flashed him a smile. 'Yes. I did. I mean, I do.'

'Can it wait until after I've had a shower?'

She glanced down at the elegant gold watch on her slender wrist. 'Um...no. Not really.'

'Then I hope you can talk louder than the water pressure in this place.' Zeke pushed off the wall and continued towards his room. 'So, what's up, kid?'

'I'm hardly a kid any more, Zeke,' Helena said.

'I suppose not.' She had been when he'd left. Barely sixteen, and all big blue eyes and blonde curls. Actually, she was still the last two, but there was something in those big eyes. Little Helena had grown up, and he wondered how much he'd missed while he'd been gone. What had growing up in this family, this business, done to her? Because he already knew what it had done to Thea, and he wouldn't wish that on anyone.

'In fact I'm the maid of honour tomorrow. And you're the best man.'

Zeke froze outside his bedroom door. What on earth was she suggesting?

Helena's tinkling laugh echoed off the painted stone of the hallway. 'Zeke, you should see your face! Don't worry—I'm not propositioning you or anything.'

Letting his breath out slowly, so she wouldn't suspect he'd been holding it, Zeke turned the door handle. 'Never thought you were.'

'Yes, you did,' Helena said, brimming with confidence. It was nice to see, in a way. At least that hadn't been drummed out of her, the way it had Thea.

'So, what are you saying?' Zeke kicked his shoes to the corner of the room, where they landed in a puff of road dust.

'We have responsibilities. We should co-ordinate them.' Letting the door swing shut behind her, Helena dropped down to sit on the edge of his bed, folding her legs up under her.

'As far as I can tell, other than an amusing yet inoffensive speech, I'm mostly superfluous to the proceedings.' Not that he cared. He knew his role here—show up and prove a point on behalf of the family that he was still a part of Morrison-Ashton. And he'd give them that for Flynn and Thea's wedding day. Not least because he knew it would be the last thing he ever had to give them. After tomorrow he'd be free.

'You're the best man, Zeke. It takes a little more than that.'

'Like dancing with you at the reception?' Stripping off his socks, Zeke padded barefoot into the bathroom to set the shower running. It took time to warm up, and maybe Helena would take the hint by the time it was at the right temperature.

'Like making sure the groom shows up.'

Zeke stopped. 'Why wouldn't he?' Did Helena know something he didn't? That *Thea* didn't?

'Because… Well…' Helena gave a dramatic sigh and fell back to lean against the headboard. 'Oh, I don't know. Because this isn't exactly a normal wedding, is it?'

That's what he'd been saying. Not that anyone—or at least not Thea—was listening. 'I'm given to understand that this is something they both want,' he said, as neutrally as he could.

Helena gave him a lopsided smile. 'She's been giving you the same line, huh? I thought maybe she'd admit the truth to *you*, at least.'

'The truth?' Zeke asked, when really what he wanted to say was, *Why me, 'at least'?*

'I know she thinks this is what she should do,' Helena said slowly. 'That it's the right thing for the company and our families. She wouldn't want to let anyone down—least of all Isabella or Dad.'

'But…?'

Tipping her head back against the headboard, Helena was silent for a long moment. Then she said, 'But…I think she's hoping this wedding will give her something it can't. And I don't think it's the right thing for her, even if she won't admit it.'

A warm burst of vindication bloomed in Zeke's chest. It wasn't just him. Her own sister, the one she'd stayed for eight years ago, could see the mistake Thea was making. But his triumph was short-lived. There was still nothing he could do to change her decision.

Zeke sank down onto the edge of the bed. 'If you want to ask me to talk to her about it…you're about two hours too late. And, as you can see, it didn't go particularly well.' He waved a hand up and down to indicate the state of him after his long, hot, cross walk home.

Helena winced. 'What did she do? Leave you on the side of the road somewhere?'

'Pretty much.'

'Dammit. I really thought…'

'What?' Suddenly, and maybe for the first time ever, he really wanted to know what Helena thought. Just in case there was a sliver of a chance of it making a difference to how tomorrow went.

Helena gave a little one-shouldered shrug. 'I don't know. I guess I thought that maybe she'd talk to you. Open up. There was always something between you two, wasn't there? I mean, she never talked about it, but it was kind of obvious. So I thought…well, I hoped… But she's so scared of giving Dad and Isabella something else to use against her, to push her out…'

'That's what I told her,' Zeke said, but then something in Helena's words registered. 'What do you mean, push her out? And what was the first thing they used against her?'

She stared at him as if it wasn't possible he didn't already know. But then she blinked. 'Of course,' she murmured. 'It was the night you left. I told her... I told her right before her eighteenth birthday party—talk about insensitive. But I guess she never told you...'

Zeke was losing patience now. He felt as if there was a bell clanging in his head, telling him to pay attention, that this was important, but Helena kept prattling on and he *needed to know.*

'What, Helena? What did you tell her?' And, for the love of God, could this finally be the explanation he'd waited eight years for, only to have Thea deny him?

Helena gave him a long look. 'I'll tell you,' she said, her tongue darting out to moisten her lips. 'But it's kind of a long story. A long, painful story. So you go and have that shower, and I'll go and fetch some wine to make it slightly more bearable. I'll meet you back here in a little bit, yeah?'

Zeke wanted to argue—wanted to demand that she just *tell* him, already—but Helena had already slipped off the bed towards the door, and it looked as if once again he wasn't being given an option by a Morrison woman.

'Fine,' he said with a sigh, and headed for the shower.

At least he wouldn't stink of sweat and sun and roads when he finally got his closure.

She had her wedding rehearsal dinner in two hours. She should be soaking in the bath with a glass of something bubbly, mentally preparing herself for the next thirty-six hours or so. She needed to touch up a chip in her manicure, straighten her hair, check that her dress for the evening had been pressed. There were wedding presents to open, lists of thank-you notes to make, a fiancé to check in with, since she hadn't seen him all day... And at some point she should probably check with Housekeeping that

Zeke had made it home alive—if only so she could slap him again later, or something.

But Thea wasn't doing any of those things. Instead she sat in Ezekiel Ashton's office, waiting for him to get off the phone with London. Just as she had been for the last forty minutes.

'Well, that's one way of looking at it, I suppose,' Ezekiel said into the receiver, and Thea barely contained her frustrated sigh.

Dragging a folder out of her bag she flipped through the contents, wishing she could pretend even to herself that they were in any way urgent or important. At least then she wouldn't feel as if she was wasting her time so utterly.

'The thing is, Quentin…'

Thea closed the folder. He could have asked her to come back later. He could have cut short his call. He could have looked in some way apologetic. But all Ezekiel had done was wave her into the visitor's chair and cover the receiver long enough to tell her he'd be with her shortly. Which had been a blatant lie.

She'd leave, just to prove a point, except he was almost her father-in-law and he already wasn't going to like the news she was bringing.

She sighed again, not bothering to hide it this time, and realised she was tapping her pen against the side of the folder. Glancing up at the desk, she saw Ezekiel raising his eyebrows at her.

Oops. Busted.

'I think I'm going to have to get back to you on that, Quentin,' he said, in his usual calm, smooth voice. The one that let everyone else know that as far as he was concerned he was the only person in the room that mattered. Zeke had always called it his father's 'Zeus the All-Powerful' voice. 'It seems that something urgent has come up at this end.'

Like the existence of his PR Director and soon-to-be daughter-in-law. Or perhaps the possibility of buying This Minute. Thea didn't kid herself about which of those was more important to the man across the desk.

'So, Thea.' Ezekiel hung up the phone. It was a proper old-fashioned one, with a handset attached by a cord and everything. 'Dare I hope that you're here with good news about my youngest son?'

Thea winced. 'Not…exactly.'

'Ah.' Leaning back in his seat, the old man steepled his fingers over his chest. 'So Zeke is still refusing to consider selling This Minute to Morrison Ashton?'

'I'm afraid so,' Thea said. 'He…he seems quite set on his decision, I'm afraid. And he says he's ready to move on from This Minute, so even offering him positions within the company didn't seem to help. He's looking for a new challenge.'

Ezekiel shook his head. 'That boy is always looking for an impossible challenge.'

He was wrong, Thea thought. Apart from anything else, Zeke was certainly no longer a boy. He'd grown up, and even if he'd always be twenty-one and reckless in the eyes of his family, *she* could see it. Had felt it in the way he'd kissed her, held her. Had known it when he'd told her the real reasons she hadn't left with him. He saw the truth even if she didn't want to face it. She *had* been scared. Even if in the end the choice had been taken away from her, and she'd had to stay for Helena, she knew deep down she'd never really thought she'd go. Hadn't been able to imagine a future in which she climbed out of that window and followed him.

Which was strange, because it was growing easier by the hour for her to imagine running out on this wedding and chasing after him. Not that she would, of course.

And not that he'd asked.

He'd wanted her to admit her mistake, had wanted to prove a point. But, kiss aside, there'd been no real thought or mention of wanting *her*.

Maybe Ezekiel was right. Maybe she was just his latest impossible challenge.

'Well, I can't say I'm not disappointed,' Ezekiel said, straightening in his chair. 'Still, I'm glad that you tried to convince him. That tells me a lot.'

Thea blinked at him. 'Tells you what, exactly?'

'It speaks to your commitment to the company—and to Flynn, of course. And it tells me that both you and Zeke have moved past your…youthful indiscretion.'

Heat flared in Thea's cheeks at his words. *Youthful indiscretion.* As if her history with Zeke was something to be swept under the carpet and forgotten about.

But wasn't that what she was doing by not telling Flynn about it?

Thea shook her head. 'I don't think that the childhood friendship Zeke and I shared would influence either of us in the matter of a business decision,' she said, as calmly and flatly as she could manage.

'Thea,' Ezekiel said, his tone mildly chastising. 'My son was in love with you once. He would have done anything for you. That he's said no to you on this matter tells me that he has moved on, that he no longer feels that way about you. And the fact that you asked him in the first place, knowing his…*feelings* for the family business—well, as I say, it's good to know where your loyalties lie.'

Nausea crept up Thea's throat as she listened to the old man talk. She knew he was right. She chosen work and business over a man she'd once thought hung the moon. Over someone who, whatever she might say to his face, still *mattered* to her. All because the old man across the desk had asked her to.

Worst of all was the sudden and certain knowledge that he'd known exactly what he was doing. This was the only reason Ezekiel had asked her to talk to Zeke about This Minute in the first place. It had been a test. Just like suggesting that she marry Flynn. Just like Zeke asking her for one true reason why she'd stayed. Just like her father, eight years ago, when she'd broken the news to him about Helena. Just like her first two engagements.

It was all a test—a way to find out if she was worthy of being a Morrison or an Ashton. Pushing her and prodding her to see how she'd react, how she'd cope, what decision she'd make, how she'd mess up this time. Her whole life was nothing more than a series of tests.

And the worst thing was she knew she was only ever one wrong answer away from failing. Just as she'd failed Helena.

Slowly, her head still spinning with angry thoughts, Thea got to her feet. 'I'm glad that you're satisfied, sir,' she said. 'Now, if you'll excuse me, I need to go and prepare for the rehearsal dinner.'

'Of course…of course.' Ezekiel waved a hand towards the door. 'After all, your most important role in this company is still to come tomorrow, isn't it?'

Thea barely managed a stiff nod before walking too fast out of the office, racing up the stairs, and throwing up in her bathroom.

When Zeke stepped out of the bathroom, a towel tightly tied around his waist, Helena was already sitting on his bed, halfway through a large glass of wine.

'Hang on.' Grabbing his suit hanger from the front of the wardrobe, he stepped back into the steam-filled bathroom and dressed quickly. At least he'd be ready for the rehearsal dinner early, and he'd feel better having whatever conversation this was fully dressed.

Helena handed him a glass of wine and he sat on the desk chair across the room, watching her, waiting for her to start.

She bit her lip, took another sip of wine, then said, 'Okay, so this isn't a story many people know.'

'Okay...'

'But I think it's important that you know it. It... Well, it might explain a bit about how Thea became...Thea.'

Anything that did that—that could explain how the free and loving girl he'd known had become the woman who'd left him at the side of the road today—had to be some story. 'So tell it.'

Helena's whole upper body rose and fell as she sucked in a breath. 'Right. So, it was a month or so before Thea's birthday. Before you left. I was sixteen. And stupid. That part's quite important.' She dipped her head, gazing down at her hands. 'Thea was babysitting for me one night. Dad was off at some business dinner, I guess. And even though I'd told him a million times that sixteen-year-olds don't need babysitters he was very clear. Thea was in charge. What she said went, and she was responsible for anything that happened while he was out.'

'Sounds like your dad,' Zeke murmured, wondering where this was going. 'I guess something happened that night?'

'I...I wanted to go out. I asked Thea, and she said no, so I nagged and whined until she gave in. I had a date with this guy a couple of years ahead of me in school. I knew Thea didn't like him, so I kinda left that part out when I told her I was going.'

Zeke had a very bad feeling about this story all of a sudden. 'What happened?' he asked, the words coming out raw and hoarse.

'He took me to his friend's house. There was beer, and

some other stuff. And the next thing I knew...' Helena
scrubbed a hand across her eyes. 'Anyway... They told me
it was my own fault—that I'd said yes and I just couldn't
remember. I was so ashamed that I didn't tell anyone. Not
even Thea. Not until six weeks later.'

'The night of her party?' Zeke guessed. She'd been crying, he remembered, when he'd climbed in her window to
tell her he was going and ask if she'd decided to come or
not. He'd thought it had been because she'd decided to stay.

'Yeah. I wouldn't have, but...I was pregnant.'

The air rushed out of Zeke's lungs. 'Oh, Helena...'

'I know. So I told Thea, and she told Dad for me, and then
I got sent away for the summer until the baby was born.'

Helena's voice broke at last. Zeke thought most people
would have given in to tears long before. Happy-go-lucky
Helena hid a core of steel.

'She was adopted, and I never saw her again.'

Zeke crossed the room in a second, wrapping an arm
around her as she cried. 'I should have been here.' Helena
had been a little sister to him in a way Thea never had
been. They'd been more. But Helena... Helena had been
important to him too, and he hadn't even said goodbye.
Hadn't dreamt of what she might be going through.

Helena gave a watery chuckle. 'What could you have
done? Besides, I had Thea.'

This was what she'd meant. Why she'd had to stay.
He'd always thought—believed deep down—that her
words about Helena and her family were excuses. But they
weren't. Helena really *had* needed her. Of course she'd
stayed. But why hadn't she told him?

'But there's a reason I've told you this,' Helena said,
snapping him back to the present. 'You have to understand, Zeke. Things changed after that night, and you
weren't there to see it. You remember how it was—how

Dad pushed her into taking over Mum's role after she died? He expected her to be able to do everything. School, the house, playing hostess for his clients, looking after me…'

'I remember,' Zeke said, bitterness leaking into his voice. She'd hated it so much. 'It was wrong. Hell, she was—what? Fourteen? Nobody should have that kind of responsibility at that age.'

'Well, she thought it *was* her responsibility. And so did he. So when all this happened…' Helena swallowed so hard Zeke could see it. 'He blamed her. Said that if she'd paid more attention it never would have happened. He took it all away from her. And that was when Isabella stepped in.'

'My mum?'

Helena nodded. 'She took over. She ran our house as well as yours. She became part of the family more than ever. She looked after me, played hostess for Dad…'

'She pushed Thea out,' Zeke finished for her. How had he not noticed that? Not noticed how little a place Thea seemed to have, even in her own wedding.

'Yeah. I wasn't here to start with, so I don't really know the whole of it. But ever since it's been like Thea's been trying to find her way back in. Find a place where she belongs.'

'And you think that's why she's marrying Flynn?'

Helena tilted her head to the side. 'I don't know. That's what I… I worry, that's all.'

And she was right to. Of *course* that was what Thea was doing. She'd practically admitted as much to him, even if he hadn't understood her reasoning.

'And the thing is, Zeke,' Helena went on, 'despite everything Thea blames herself for what happened to me and what happened next. She always has. Even though it isn't her fault—of course it isn't. But she was responsible for me that night. That's what Dad told her. And she thinks that if she hadn't let me go out that night everything would have been different.'

'*Her* fault?' Zeke echoed, baffled. 'How can she possibly…?'

'She calls it the biggest mistake she ever made.'

Suddenly Zeke was glad that Helena didn't know what Thea had given up to stay with her. He couldn't blame either of them any more. But could he make Thea see that one mistake didn't mean she had to keep making the same safe decisions her whole life?

'Thank you for telling me this, Helena.'

Helena gave a little shrug. 'Did it help?'

'Yeah. I think so.'

Pulling away, Helena watched his face as she asked, 'So, do you think you can talk Thea out of this wedding?'

'I thought I was supposed to be making sure the groom showed up on time?'

'If she decides to go through with it, yeah. But I want to be very sure that she's doing this for the right reasons. Not just because she's scared of being pushed out again for not doing what the family wants.'

Zeke grinned. 'Looks like we're on the same side, then.'

'Good.' Standing up, Helena smoothed down her dress and wiped her eyes. 'About time I had some help around here. Now, come on, best man. We've got a rehearsal dinner to get to.'

'And a wedding to get called off,' Zeke agreed, following her to the door.

He had his closure now, but he had far more, too. He had the truth. The whole story. And that was what would make all the difference when he confronted Thea this time.

CHAPTER EIGHT

THEA SCANNED THE dining room through the crack of the door, then glanced down at her deep red sheath dress, wondering why she felt as if she was walking into a business dinner. Of all the people she'd recognised in the room, waiting for them to walk in, only three had been family. Everyone else was someone she'd met across a conference table. This time tomorrow she'd be married, and her whole new life would start. But she was very afraid, all of a sudden, that her new life might be a little too much like her old one.

'Ready?' Flynn asked, offering her his arm.

He looked handsome in his suit, Thea thought. All clean-shaven and broad shoulders. Safe. Reliable. Predictable. Exactly what she'd decided she wanted in life.

'Or do you want to sneak into Dad's study for a shot of the good brandy before we face the gathered hordes?'

Thea smiled. 'Tempting, but probably not advisable. Besides, your Dad's almost certainly still working in there.'

'There is that.' Flynn sighed. 'I had hoped he'd see this as more of a family celebration than a networking opportunity.'

Nice to know she wasn't the only one who had noticed that. 'I guess he doesn't see any reason why it can't be both. I mean, he knows our reasons for getting married. He helped put together the contract, for heaven's sake.'

'Yeah, I know,' Flynn said, sounding wistful. 'It's business. I just… It would be nice if we could pretend, just for a couple of days, that there's something that matters more to us.'

Thea stared at him. She was going to marry this man tomorrow, and she'd never once heard him speak so honestly about their life or their relationship.

'Flynn? Are you…?' *Are you what? Getting cold feet? Unhappy with me? Not the time for that conversation, Thea.* 'Did you want to wait? To get married, I mean? To someone you're actually in love with?'

Because it was one thing to marry a man you didn't love because that was the deal. Another to do it when he was secretly holding out for more. She thought back to their conversation on the porch, about kids and the future. How happy he'd been at the idea of a family.

But Flynn shook his head, giving her a self-deprecating smile. 'Don't listen to me,' he said. 'We're doing the right thing here. For us and for the business. And, yeah, the fairytale would be nice, I guess. But it's not all there is. And who knows? Maybe you and I will fall in love one day.'

But they wouldn't, Thea knew, with the kind of sudden, shocking certainty that couldn't be shifted. As much as she liked, respected and was fond of Flynn, and as much as she enjoyed his company, she wasn't ever going to be in love with him. She knew how that felt, and it wasn't anything like this.

Thea tried to smile back, but it felt forced. 'Are you ready to go in?' she asked, wishing she'd just said yes when he'd asked her the same question. The knowledge she'd gained in the last two minutes seemed too much for her body—as if she could barely keep it inside on top of every other thought she'd had and fact she'd learned since Zeke came home.

'As I'll ever be,' Flynn said, flashing her a smile. 'Let's go.'

He pushed the door open and the volume level of conversation in the room dipped, then dropped, then stalled. Everyone stood, beaming at them, waiting for them to walk in and take their seats as if they were some kind of royalty. And all Thea could see was Zeke and Helena, standing together near the head of the huge table, leaning into each other. Helena murmured something Thea couldn't hear, and Zeke's lips quirked up in a mocking grin. Talking about her? Thea didn't care. All she knew was that she wanted to be over there, chatting with them, and not welcoming the fifty-odd other people who had somehow got themselves invited to her rehearsal dinner.

She let Flynn take the lead. His easy way with people meant that all she had to do was smile and nod, shake the occasional hand. She let him lead her to their seats, smiled sweetly at everyone around them as she sat down.

Her father nodded to Flynn, and Isabella said, 'Oh, Thea, you look so beautiful tonight. And those pearls are a perfect match! I'm so glad.'

Thea's hand unconsciously went to the necklace Isabella had given her. The perfectly round pearls were hard and cold under her fingers. You were supposed to wear pearls often, weren't you? To keep them warm and stop them cracking or drying, perhaps?

'Aren't pearls supposed to be bad luck?' Helena asked, topping up her glass of wine from the bottle on the table.

'Oh, I don't think so,' Isabella said, laughing lightly. 'And, besides, who believes those old superstitions, anyway?'

'"Pearls mean tears",' Helena quoted, her voice firm and certain. 'And you're the one who insisted on Thea having all the old, new, borrowed and blue stuff.'

'I like pearls,' Thea said, glancing in surprise at her sister. It wasn't like Helena to antagonise Isabella. For a moment it was almost as if the old teenage Helena was sitting beside her. 'I don't think they mean anything.'

There was silence for a moment, before the doors opened and a fleet of waiters entered, ready to serve the starters. They waited until every bowl was ready and in position, then lowered them all to the table at the same time, before disappearing again as silently as they'd come.

'Saved by the soup,' Zeke murmured from two seats down as he reached for the butter.

Thea studied him as he buttered his roll, and kept watching as Helena topped up his wine, too. He must have walked home, she supposed. His forehead was ever so slightly pink from the sun. But he didn't seem angry, or tense as he had earlier. He seemed calm, relaxed. Even happy.

Maybe he'd got the closure he needed. Maybe he was thinking ahead to leaving the day after tomorrow. To selling This Minute to Glasshouse and moving on to his new life. Thea could see how that might be appealing. Not that she had that option. She didn't want out of this family—she wanted in.

Besides, Zeke had been gone eight years already and still not really moved on. What reason was there to believe he'd be able to put it all behind him for real this time?

Isabella and Flynn kept up the small talk across the table through all three courses. Thea drank her wine too quickly and tried to pretend her head wasn't spinning. And then, as the waiters came round to pour the coffee, her father stood up and clinked his fork against his glass.

'Oh, no,' Thea whispered. 'What's he doing?'

Flynn patted her hand reassuringly, somehow managing to make her even more nervous.

'I know tonight isn't the night for big speeches,' Thomas

Morrison said. 'And, trust me, I'll have the traditional light, adoring and entertaining father of the bride speech for you all tomorrow. But I wanted to say a few words to-night for those of you who've been so close to our family all these years. Who've seen us through our dark times as well as our triumphs.'

'Which explains why almost everyone here is a business associate,' Helena muttered, leaning across towards Thea. 'We've barely seen any family since Mum died.'

'Shh...' Isabella said, without moving her lips or letting her attentive smile slip.

'You all know that getting here, to this happy event, hasn't always been a smooth path. And let me say candidly that I am both delighted and relieved that Thea has finally made a decision in her personal life that's as good as the ones she makes at work!'

The laughter that followed buzzed in Thea's ears, but she barely heard it. Her body felt frozen, stiff and cold and brittle. And she knew, suddenly, that even marrying Flynn wouldn't be enough. To her father she'd still always be a liability. A mistake just waiting to happen.

'And I want to say thank you to the person who has made all this possible,' Thomas went on, waving his arm expansively to include the food, the villa, and presumably, the wedding itself.

Thea held her breath, bracing herself for the blow she instinctively knew was coming next.

'My dear, dear friend, Isabella Ashton.'

More applause—the reverent sort this time. People were nodding their heads along with her father's words, and Isabella was blushing prettily, her smile polite but pleased.

Thea thought she might actually be sick.

'So, let us all raise our glasses to the mother of the

groom and the woman who has been as a mother to the bride for the last twelve years.'

Chairs were scraped back as people stood, and the sound grated in her ears. Wasn't it enough that she'd given them all what they wanted? She was marrying the families together, securing their future, their lineage, and the future of their business. And even today, the night before her wedding, she wasn't worthy of her father's approval, or love.

Thea staggered to her feet, clutching the edge of the table, as the guests lifted their glasses and chanted, 'Isabella!' Even Flynn, next to her, had his wine in the air and was smiling at his mother, utterly unaware of how his fiancée's heart had just been slashed with glass.

It was almost as if she wasn't there at all.

Zeke watched Thea's face grow paler as Thomas wound up his ridiculous speech. Who said something like that about his own daughter the day before her wedding? Especially when that daughter was Thea. He *had* to know how sensitive she was about her perceived mistakes, surely? And then to toast Isabella instead... That had been just cruel and callous.

Maybe he truly didn't care. Not if he could get in a good joke, amuse his business associates... Zeke ground his teeth as he waited for his coffee to cool. He'd never been Thomas Morrison's biggest fan, but right then he loathed the man more than he'd ever thought possible.

Thomas sat down to a round of applause and more laughter, and Zeke saw Thea visibly flinch. Flynn, however, was shaking his father-in-law-to-be's hand and smiling as if nothing had happened. As if he couldn't see how miserable Thea was. He was going to marry her tomorrow and he couldn't even see when her heart was breaking.

Zeke gulped down his rage at his brother along with

his coffee. All that mattered was getting Thea the hell out of there.

Helena appeared over his left shoulder suddenly, pushing something cold and bottle-shaped into his hand. 'Go on,' she said, nodding towards Thea. 'I'll cover for you both here.'

'Thanks,' Zeke murmured, keeping the bottle of champagne below table level as he stood. Catching Thea's eye, he raised his eyebrows and headed for the door, not waiting to see if she followed. Helena would make sure that she did.

Outside on the terrace the air held just a little bite— a contrast to the blazing sun he'd walked back in earlier. Dropping onto the swing seat, Zeke held up the bottle and read the label. The good stuff, of course. Old Thomas wouldn't serve anything less while he was insulting his daughter in front of everyone she'd ever met. Shame Helena hadn't thought to provide glasses... Although, actually, swigging expensive champagne from the bottle with Thea brought back its own collection of memories.

The door to the hallway opened and Thea appeared, her face too pale against her dark hair and blood-red dress. Her skin seemed almost translucent in the moonlight, and suddenly Zeke wanted to touch it so badly he ached.

'Have a seat,' he said, waving the bottle over the empty cushion beside him. 'I think your sister thought you might need this.'

'She was right.' Thea dropped onto the seat next to him, sending the whole frame swinging back and forth. 'Although why she decided I also needed you is beyond me.'

'Ouch.' Unwrapping the wire holding it in place, Zeke eased the cork out of the neck of the bottle. He didn't want the pop, the fizz, the explosion. Just the quiet opening and sharing of champagne with Thea. To show her that *he* knew tonight was about her, even if no one else seemed to.

'Oh, you know what I mean,' Thea said, reaching over to take the bottle from him. 'We're not having the best day, apart from anything else.'

'I don't know what you're complaining about,' Zeke said. 'You weren't the one left in the middle of nowhere in the blazing heat.'

Thea winced, and handed him the bottle back. 'Sorry about that.'

'No, you're not.' Zeke lifted the bottle to his mouth and took a long, sweet drink. The bubbles popped against his throat and he started to relax for the first time that day.

'Well, maybe just a little bit. You deserved it, though.'

'For telling the truth?'

'For kissing me.'

'Ah. That.'

'Yeah, *that*.'

Zeke passed the bottle back and they sat in silence for a long moment, the only sound the occasional wave of laughter from inside or the squeaking of the hinges on the swing.

'I'm not actually all that sorry about that, either,' Zeke said finally.

Thea sighed. 'Yeah. Me neither. Maybe we needed it. You know—for closure, or whatever you were going on about.'

'Actually, your sister helped me with that more than you did.'

Thea swung round to stare at him, eyes wide. 'Tell me you have *not* been kissing my sister this afternoon.'

'Or what?'

'Or I'll drink the rest of this champagne myself.' She took a long swig to prove her point.

Zeke laughed. 'Okay, fine. I have not been kissing Helena. This afternoon or any other.'

'Good.'

'Not that it would be any of your business if I had.'

'She's my sister,' Thea said, handing back the champagne at last. 'She'll always be my business.'

'But not your responsibility,' Zeke said. 'She's an adult now, Thea. She can take care of herself.'

'Perhaps.' Thea studied him carefully. 'When you said that Helena had helped you find closure…what did you mean?'

Zeke tipped his head back against the swing cushion. 'She told me some of what happened. Things I didn't know. About what really happened the night of your eighteenth birthday. Why you didn't come with me. And about what happened next.'

He heard the breath leave Thea's lungs in a rush. 'She told you? About the…?'

'About what happened to her. And about the baby.' He rolled his head to the left to watch her as he added, 'And how it really wasn't your fault.'

Thea looked away. 'That's up for debate.'

'No. It isn't.' No response. 'Thea. Look at me.'

She didn't. 'Why?'

'Because I'm about to say something that matters and I want to be sure that you're listening to me.'

Slowly she lifted her head and her gaze met his. Zeke felt it like a jolt to the heart—the connection he'd thought they'd lost was suddenly *right there*. Part of him again after all these years.

'Whatever mistakes you think you've made in your life, Thea, that wasn't one of them. You cannot make yourself responsible for what those boys did to her.'

'My father did,' Thea whispered. 'I was in charge. I was responsible. And I let her go out.'

'No.' He had to make her understand. Wrapping his arm around her shoulder, he pulled her closer, still keeping them face to face, until she was pressed up against his chest. 'Listen to me, Thea. It wasn't your fault. And you can't live your whole life as if it was.'

Thea stared up into his eyes for a long moment. They were filled with such sincerity, such certainty. Why could she never feel that way about her life? That unshakeable conviction that whatever choice she made was the right one. That fearlessness in the face of mistakes.

Of course in Zeke it also led to occasional unbearable smugness, so maybe she was better off without.

Swallowing, Thea pulled away, and Zeke let her go. 'Is that what you think I'm doing?'

'I know it,' Zeke said, unbearable smugness firmly in place.

'You're wrong, you know,' she said conversationally, looking down at her hands.

Part of her still couldn't believe that Helena had really told him everything. She'd barely discussed it with Thea ever since it happened. As far as she knew Helena had never willingly told anyone else about it—something their father and Isabella had been in full support of. After all, why make a scandal when you can hide one? And coming so soon after Zeke running away... Well, no one wanted to make headlines again. Thea assumed that Ezekiel Senior knew, but maybe not. Isabella had taken care of everything. Maybe she'd never seen the need to brief him on the shocking events.

'Am I? As far as I can see you stayed eight years ago for Helena, and because you were scared. And now—'

'I made the right decision eight years ago,' Thea interrupted. Because if he had to know everything at least he could admit that much. 'And I don't regret it for a moment.'

'Fair enough,' Zeke said, more amicably than she'd expected. 'And we'll never know how things might have worked out if Helena hadn't gone out that night, or if she'd waited one more day to tell you about it. But the point is Helena's all grown up now. She doesn't need you to protect her any more. And yet you're still staying.'

She shook her head. 'My whole life is here. My place is here.'

'Is it?' He gripped her arm, tightly enough that she had to pay attention. 'They pushed you out, Thea.'

The coldness that settled over her was familiar. The same chill she'd felt that whole summer after Zeke had left. 'You don't...you don't know what it was like.'

'Helena told me. She told me everything.'

But that wasn't enough. A description, a few words—it couldn't explain how it felt to have your whole existence peeled away from you. She wasn't sure if even she could explain it to him. But she knew she had to try...had to make him understand somehow.

'It was as if I'd stopped even existing,' she whispered in the end. 'I couldn't be what Dad needed, so there was no place for me any more. I wasn't good enough for him.'

Zeke's grip loosened, but just enough to pull her against his body. She could feel his heart, thumping away in his chest, and the memory of how his arms had always felt like home cut deeper now.

'Then why are you trying so hard to get back in? Surely you can see you're better off without him. Without all of them.'

'You think I should run away, like you?' She pulled back enough to give him a half-smile. 'This is my place. Besides, where else would I go, Zeke?'

'Anywhere! Anywhere you can be yourself. Live your own life. Not make decisions about your personal happiness based on what is best for the family business, or what

our fathers want you to do. Anywhere in the world, Thea.'
He paused, just for a moment, then added, 'You could even
come with me, if you wanted.'

Thea's heart stopped dead in her chest. She couldn't
breathe. She couldn't think. Couldn't process what he was
saying…

'I'm marrying Flynn tomorrow.' The words came out
without her permission, and she watched Zeke's eyes turn
hard as she spoke.

'Why?' he asked. 'Seriously, Thea. Tell me why. I don't
understand.'

'I love him.'

'No, you don't.'

'I might!'

Zeke laughed, but there was no humour in the sound.
'Thea, I'm sure you do love him—in a way. But don't try
and tell me you're in love with him, or vice versa. He didn't
even notice how distressed you were tonight.'

'*You* did.' She could hear the anger in his voice as he
talked about Flynn. Was that for her?

He gave a slight nod. 'Me and Helena. We're your team.'

'And you're leaving me tomorrow.' How could he offer
her a place in the world when he didn't even know where
he'd be tomorrow? Didn't he understand? She needed more
than that. Somewhere she could never be pushed out or
left behind. Somewhere she was enough.

'Yeah.'

'Great teamwork, there.'

Thea stared out into the darkness of the Tuscan hills
beyond. She hadn't answered Zeke's question—something
she knew he was bound to call her on before too long. But
what could she say? Whatever it was, he wouldn't agree or
approve. Should that matter? She didn't want Zeke to leave
hating her. But why not? She would never see him again

once she was married. He'd made that perfectly clear. If all she was protecting was the memory of something already eight years dead, what was the point?

'So?' Zeke asked eventually. 'The truth this time. Why are you so set on marrying Flynn tomorrow?'

'Maybe I think it'll make me happy,' Thea said.

Zeke shifted, turning his body in towards hers, one knee bent to let his leg rest on the seat. 'Do you? Think you'll be happy?'

She considered lying, but there didn't seem much point. Zeke never believed her anyway. 'I think I'll be safe. Secure. I'll have someone to help me make the right decisions. I think I'll have the agreement of all my friends and family that I'm not making a mistake.'

'Not all of them,' Zeke muttered.

'I think I'll have a place here again. A place I've earned…a place I belong. One that's mine by blood and marriage and can never be taken away from me. I'll be content,' Thea finished, ignoring him.

'Content? And is that enough for you?'

Thea shrugged. 'What else is there?' she asked, even though she knew the answer.

'Love. Passion. Happiness. Pleasure.'

'Yeah, you see, that's where I start to make mistakes. I know business. I know sensible, well thought out business plans. I know agreements, contracts, promised deliverables. Pleasure is an unknown quantity.'

Zeke shifted again and he was closer now, his breath warm against her cheek. Thea's skin tingled at the contact.

'You used to know about pleasure,' he said, his voice low.

'That was a long time ago,' Thea replied, the words coming out huskily.

'I remember, though. You used to crave pleasure. And

the freedom to seek it. To do what felt right and good, not what someone said you were supposed to do.'

His words were hypnotising. Thea could feel her body swaying into his as he spoke, but she couldn't do anything to stop the motion. The swing beneath them rocked forwards and back, and with every movement she seemed to fall closer and closer into Zeke. As if gravity was drawing her in. As if nothing she could say or do or think could stop it.

'Don't you miss it?' he whispered, his mouth so close to hers she could feel the words on her own lips.

'Yes,' she murmured, and he kissed her.

CHAPTER NINE

SHE TASTED JUST as Zeke remembered—as if it had been mere moments since his mouth had last touched hers. This wasn't the angry kiss of earlier that day, a kiss that had been more punishment than pleasure. This…this was something more.

Pleasure and pain mingled together. The years fell away and he was twenty-one again, kissing her goodbye even as he hoped against hope that she might leave with him.

Maybe this time it would end differently. Maybe this time he could persuade her. After all, he'd learnt a lot in eight years.

Slipping a hand around her back, he held her close, revelling in the feel of her body against his, back where she belonged. How had he let himself believe, even for a moment, that he could watch her marry someone else and then walk away?

Flynn… The thought of his brother stalled him for a moment, until he remembered him shaking Thomas's hand after that godforsaken speech. He didn't know Thea—didn't know what she needed, let alone what she wanted. He didn't love her any more than Thea loved him. Zeke knew that for sure.

Maybe he'd even understand. And even if he didn't… Zeke was close to the edge of not caring. Flynn didn't deserve her—he'd proved that tonight. And Zeke needed this. Needed her more than ever before.

Zeke ran his palms up Thea's back, deepening the kiss, and felt his heartbeat quicken at the little noises she made. Half moans, half squeaks, they let him know exactly how much more she wanted. And how much he planned to give her...

'Zeke,' Thea murmured, pulling back just a little. 'What about—?'

'Shh...' Zeke trailed his fingers over her neck, feeling her shiver against him. 'Just pleasure, remember?'

Thea gave a little nod, as if she couldn't help but agree, and Zeke took that as permission to kiss her again. First her lips, deep and wanting. Then her jaw, her neck, her collarbone, down into the deep V of her dress and the lacy bra beyond.

'Oh, Zeke.' Thea shuddered again as his hand crept up her thigh, under her skirt, and he smiled against her skin. He remembered this, too. Remembered how natural it felt to have her in his arms, how she responded to his every touch, every kiss. How she arched up against him, her body begging for more. How could she pretend that she wanted anything other than this, than *him*, when her whole body told him otherwise?

He wanted to get her upstairs. Wanted her in his bed, her naked skin against his. But he knew that he had only this moment to convince her, to change her mind, and he couldn't risk the pause being enough to break her out of pleasure's spell. No, he knew Thea. With cold air between them, and a whole staircase to climb to find a bed, she'd start doubting herself. He didn't have time for her to have second thoughts. She was supposed to get married tomorrow, and he couldn't let that happen.

So it would have to be here. He'd seduce her right here

on the terrace. Then she'd see she couldn't marry Flynn. And Flynn would understand that. Wouldn't he?

Tightening his hold on her, Zeke pulled Thea up from the swing across onto his lap, so her knees fell neatly either side of his thighs, all without breaking their kiss. Her body seemed to know exactly what he had planned, moving with his without hesitation. As if it had done it before... Which, of course, it had. Zeke smiled at the memory.

'This remind you of anything?' he murmured, kissing his way back up her throat.

Thea murmured in agreement. 'Your twenty-first birthday party.'

'Out on the balcony...'

'With the party going on right underneath us.'

'That was all *you*, you know.'

Thea pressed against him and he couldn't help but gasp.

'I seem to remember you being there, too.'

'Yeah, but you're the one who dragged me up there.' He could see it now, in his memories. The bright blue dress she'd worn, the naughty look in her eye, the way she'd bitten her lip as she raised her eyebrows and waited for him to follow her into the house...

'I didn't hear you complaining,' Thea said, her hands pushing his shirt up to get to his skin.

Zeke sucked in a breath at the feel of her fingers on his chest. 'I really wasn't.'

She stilled for a moment, and Zeke's hands tightened instinctively on her thighs, keeping her close. 'What is it?' he asked.

'I just... I've never felt that again. What I felt that night, with you...'

The words were a whisper, an ashamed admission, but Zeke's eyelids fluttered closed in relief at the sound of them. 'Me neither. It's never been like it was with you. Not with anyone.' Never felt so much like coming home.

She kissed him then, her hands on his face, deep and loving, and he knew for the first time in eight years that things were going to be okay again.

'Make love to me, Zeke,' Thea whispered, and Zeke looked up into her eyes and smiled.

'Always.'

Thea blinked in the darkness and wondered how it was possible that she'd forgotten this feeling. The sense that her whole body had relaxed into the place where it belonged. That moment of sheer bliss and an empty mind.

Maybe she hadn't forgotten. Maybe, as great as her memories were, it had never been like this for them before. Because, seriously, surely she'd remember something that good.

She breathed in one last breath of satisfaction…pleasure and *home*.

Then she sat up and faced the real world again.

Her senses and thoughts crashed in immediately—a whole parade of them, ranging from her complete idiocy to her goosebumps. It was cold on the terrace…colder than Thea had thought Tuscany could be in the summer. Of course it would probably be warmer if she was still wearing her dress… Beside her Zeke lay on the swing seat, his shirt unbuttoned to reveal a broad expanse of tanned chest.

Somehow this seemed far more dignified for men.

Reaching for her dress and slipping it over her shoulders, Thea tried to stop her mind spinning with the idea of what she'd just done. She'd cheated on her fiancé. She'd become *that* woman—the one who made a stupid mistake that might cost her everything. The night before her own wedding. At her rehearsal dinner! All because Zeke had started talking about pleasure and making her remember how good things had used to be... And hadn't she just finished telling him that wasn't what she wanted any more?

But she couldn't blame Zeke, however manipulated she felt. She'd wanted it. Asked for it, even. All he'd done was give her what she'd craved. What she'd spent eight years trying to forget.

Thea sighed and Zeke stirred at the sound, snaking an arm around her waist to pull her closer. She sank into him as if, having given in once, all her will power had gone.

This was the hardest part. If it was just great sex with Zeke she was giving up it would be easy. Well, maybe not easy, but certainly doable. But that wasn't all it was.

'You're thinking too loudly,' Zeke murmured against her ear, and she sighed again.

It wasn't the sex. It was the way her body felt in tune with his...the way he could anticipate what she needed before she knew she needed it. The way she felt right in his arms. The way she fitted—*they* fitted together. Not just physically, either.

It just felt so natural with Zeke, in a way she knew it never would with Flynn.

But was that enough?

Zeke might know what she needed, but there was no guarantee that he'd give it to her. As much as she'd loved him when they were younger, she knew him, too. Knew what mattered most to him. And while he might have proclaimed from the rafters that the only thing that mattered to him was her, in the end he'd still left her behind when she wouldn't fit in with his plans. Hadn't even listened when she'd tried to explain why she couldn't go.

Sometimes she wondered if it really had been love. It had felt like it, then. But they'd been kids. What had they known?

And even now Zeke didn't understand about doing the careful thing, the *right* thing. About not taking the risk of making things worse. For him, the risk was half the fun—always had been. He'd liked the thought of getting caught at his twenty-first birthday party. And she knew, from watching This Minute grow and develop through the business pages, that half the fun for Zeke was knowing that he was only ever one step, one chance, one risk away from it all coming down. He'd been lucky—brilliant too, of course—but it could have gone either way.

And Thea didn't have room for any more mistakes in her life. Couldn't risk being left with nothing, no place, again.

'Seriously,' Zeke said, shifting to sit up properly, his shirt flapping closed over his chest.

That might make it easier for her to think clearly, at least.

'What's going on in that head of yours?'

Thea sat up. 'I have to go. I need to… My guests are inside.'

Zeke's expression hardened. Reaching over, he picked up her bra and held it out to her, dangling from his fingers. 'You might need this.'

Thea snatched it from him. 'What did you think I was going to do next, Zeke? I'm supposed to be getting married tomorrow, and I'm out here with the best man! That's never a good decision.'

He shook his head ruefully. 'I should have known. You think I'm a mistake.'

'I didn't say that, Zeke.' She never would, knowing how much of his childhood he'd spent thinking that. That his parents would have been happier with just Flynn, their planned and chosen child, rather than the biological one who had come along at exactly the wrong moment. 'I just…

I need to tell Flynn.' That much was a given, surely? 'I need to sort all this out.'

Zeke blew out a breath and settled back against the swing. 'Yeah, okay. I guess disappearing in the middle of the night at some party never was your style, was it?'

'No, that was all you.' Thea gave him a sad smile, remembering that night eight years ago and knowing with absolute certainty, for the first time, that she could never have gone with him even if Helena hadn't needed her. She wasn't built for Zeke's kind of life.

She just hoped he realised that, too.

Zeke watched Thea walk back inside, her hair no longer so groomed and her make-up long gone. Would she go and fix herself up first? What was the point, if she was just going to tell Flynn that she couldn't marry him? Sure, Flynn would know exactly what they'd been doing, but was that such a bad thing? It gave a point-of-no-return sort of feel to things.

Settling back against the swing seat, Zeke pushed aside the guilt that flooded him at the thought of his brother. It wasn't a love match; he knew that. And this wasn't like when they were kids. He wasn't taking Thea just so that Flynn couldn't have her. She belonged with him—always had. Surely Flynn would understand that?

He hoped so. With conscious effort Zeke relaxed his muscles, feeling the happy thrumming that buzzed through his blood, the reminder of everything the evening had brought him. Who would have thought, when she'd dumped him on the roadside that afternoon, that the day would end here?

He should have known that appealing to her reasonable side wouldn't work. Thea wasn't like other people.

She needed to see the truth, *feel* it, not just be told it. Why hadn't he remembered that?

It didn't matter now. He'd shown her they belonged together. Even her most conservative, analytical, risk-averse side couldn't deny that now. She wanted a place to belong? He could give her that. He could give her everything she needed if she let him. Finally they'd get the life they'd been denied eight years ago, and he was going to make it so good for her. Make her loosen up a bit, reveal the Thea he knew was hiding in there somewhere.

Once the sale of This Minute went through to Glasshouse they could go anywhere, do anything. Maybe they'd just travel for a bit, see the world, get to know one another again as adults. He'd have to take things slowly, so as not to scare her. He knew Thea: even after the jump forward their relationship had taken this evening she was bound to scuttle a few paces back. But Zeke didn't care how slowly it went, how much he had to gentle her along. He'd have Thea in his arms every night, just as he'd always wanted. This time *he* was her choice. Not Flynn, not Helena, not the business, not her father or his. *Him.* Zeke. And he could live with everything in their past as long as he was her last choice.

Zeke smiled to himself as he listened to the sounds of the dinner finishing up and people starting to leave inside. He'd go back in soon, find Thea when she was ready for him.

Sure, there was a lot to figure out first—starting with calling off the wedding tomorrow. But once that was done there was a whole new future out there for them.

He was sure of it.

The sounds of the rehearsal dinner were fading. How many people must have left already without even seeing her? She should have been there, playing hostess, saying goodbye to people, looking excited about tomorrow. If Isabella would let her, of course. She had to start reclaiming that role if she was going to be Flynn's wife. People needed to see that she belonged there, at the head of table, running things.

Image was everything; she was the PR face of Morrison-Ashton and, however much this should have been a private event, it wasn't. These were clients, associates, investors, and she should have been there, working the room. Putting on a show.

And instead she'd been outside on the terrace, sleeping with the best man in the open air.

A shudder ran through her. What had she been thinking? Anyone could have walked out and seen them, and then everything would have been destroyed.

Of course, she reminded herself, it might still be once she told Flynn.

'Thea?' Helena clattered into the hall on her high heels. 'Are you okay? I kept everyone else off the terrace and they're all starting to leave now. Do you want to say goodbye? If not I can cover for you if you want to just go to bed?'

Thea gave her sister a half-smile. 'You take such good care of me.'

Helena shook her head and stepped forward to wrap her arms around Thea's waist. 'Not nearly as good as you take of me.'

Was that true? Thea wasn't sure. She'd stayed, yes, when Helena had needed her, and she'd done the best she could to help her. But she'd never pressed her sister to talk about what had happened, never pushed her to get counselling or other help. Whereas ever since she'd come back, thinner and paler, with her stomach still slightly rounded and hidden under baggy jumpers, Helena had made looking out for Thea a priority. She'd been there when her engagements had gone bad, she'd helped Isabella look after the house and Dad while Thea got on with climbing the corporate ladder, she'd smoothed out every difficult conversation, every awkward dinner party between the Morrisons and the Ashtons.

And tonight she'd protected Thea's privacy while she made another huge mistake.

'I need to talk to Flynn.'

Helena pulled back, frowning. 'Are you sure? Now?'

'Yes. Before I lose my nerve.'

'What are you going to tell him?' Helena asked.

Thea wondered how much her sister knew about her and Zeke. What Zeke had told her. What she imagined had happened out on the terrace.

Thea took a breath. 'Everything.'

Helena studied her for a long moment, then nodded. 'Okay, then. I'll fetch him. You go and wait in the library, yeah?'

'Okay.'

The library was shaded and dark, the tiny haloes of light around the table lamps barely enough to illuminate the chairs beside them, let alone the bookcases. Thea trailed her fingers across the shelves, waiting for Flynn, trying not to listen to the sounds of the guests leaving.

Helena's tinkling laugh caught her attention, though. 'She's been up since dawn! She's so excited about tomorrow. I think she's just crashed! I sent her to bed when she couldn't stop yawning. Can't have the bride looking anything but well rested on her wedding day, can we?'

Murmurs of amused agreement from the departing guests made Thea wince. How many lies had Helena told for her tonight?

The library door cracked open, and Thea spun away from the bookshelf.

'Thea?' Flynn asked, his voice as calm and even as it always was. 'Are you in here?'

Stepping into the light, Thea tried to smile. 'I'm here.'

Flynn closed the door carefully behind him with a click, then turned to her. 'Are you okay? Helena said you wanted to talk to me. I'd have come sooner, but our guests...'

Thea winced again. 'Yeah, sorry. I should have been there to talk with them. To say goodbye, at least.'

'Where were you?' Flynn asked. 'Helena's telling everyone you went to bed, but to be honest you don't look that tired. You look... I don't know...'

But Thea did. Her jaw tightened as she imagined what she must look like. Her hair would be rumpled, her dress creased, her make-up faded. She wished the library had a mirror for her to assess the damage. And maybe, a small part of her insisted, to see if she had that same glow, same radiance, that truly great sex with Zeke had always given her.

She kind of hoped not. She couldn't imagine that was something any man would want to see on his fiancée's face if he hadn't put it there. Even someone as affable and not in love with her as Flynn.

'I was on the terrace,' Thea said. 'With Zeke.'

'But Helena said...' Flynn's face hardened. 'Helena lied. What's going on, Thea?'

'I...I need to tell you some things.' Pacing over to the reading area, Thea placed her hands on the back of one leather wingback chair, her fingernails pressing into the leather. 'Perhaps you should sit.'

'You too, then,' Flynn said, motioning at her chair. When she hesitated, he added, 'Come on, Thea, you look like you're about to fall over.'

Thea slipped around and sat down, instantly regretting it as the stupid table lamp that gave only a glow to the rest of the room illuminated her completely. She could feel the light on her face and see the lamp opposite doing the same to Flynn's as he took his seat. It felt as if she was sitting in an interrogation room, which really didn't give her a good feeling about how the rest of this conversation was going to go.

'So...' Flynn said. 'Talk.'

She should have asked for a drink. Should have stolen the rest of the champagne she'd left outside with Zeke. Should have stayed at her rehearsal dinner if she was going to rewrite the evening.

Instead she took a breath and searched her mind for where to begin.

'Eight years ago,' she said—because wasn't that when everything had started?—'when Zeke left...he asked me to go with him.'

'Why?'

'Because we were in love.' Facts, even painful ones, were the only way to do this. The only way to make Flynn understand what had happened tonight.

Flynn shifted in his chair. 'I should have brought whisky.'

'Yeah. Sorry.'

'So. You didn't go with him. Why?'

'Because...' Could she tell him? It was Helena's secret. She'd told Zeke, but that had been her choice. Flynn deserved the truth... In the end she plumped for the simplified version. 'Helena needed me. She was sixteen, and she had a lot of stuff going on in her life. Our mother had died...she needed me. I couldn't leave her.'

'But if it hadn't been for Helena?'

The million-dollar question. 'I don't know.' Except she

did—in her heart. 'Zeke and I...we're very different people. Especially these days.'

'Okay. So what does this all have to do with tonight?'

Heat flooded Thea's cheeks as the shame of her actions hit home. 'I slept with Zeke tonight.'

'On the terrace? Where anyone could see?' Flynn's eyebrows shot up. 'That...doesn't sound very like you.'

Thea blinked at him. '*That's* your concern?'

Flynn sighed. 'Thea, I'm not an idiot. I knew the moment Zeke came back that there was unfinished business between you. I guess I was away at university when he left, so maybe I didn't know the ins and outs of it then. But seeing the two of you together this week, seeing how you act around me when he's there...neither of you are exactly subtle, Thea.'

'Oh. Okay.' Thea swallowed around the lump that had formed in her throat. 'Do you...do you hate me?'

Flynn's smile was gentle, far gentler than she deserved, and tears stung at Thea's eyes. 'Of course I don't hate you, Thea...' He sighed. 'Look. We know this isn't a love match. We're not married yet, so the fidelity clause isn't in effect.'

She'd forgotten all about that clause. One moment of Zeke's hands on her skin and she'd lost all reason.

'Quite honestly, if you have doubts like this and things you need to resolve, I'd far rather them happen now than in a year's time.'

'So...what happens now?'

'Well, that's up to you.' Flynn sat back in his chair and studied her. 'You need to decide what you want, Thea. If you think you could be truly happy with Zeke, that he can give you everything you need, then we'll go and talk to our parents and call the wedding off right now. But if you want the life we have planned—the business, the family support, kids, everything—if you still want that, then you need to forget about Zeke and marry me tomorrow.'

Thea stared at him, waiting for something more—something to make the choice for her, to make sure she made the right one. To tell her the right answer to this test.

But Flynn didn't offer advice. Didn't counsel…didn't help her reason it out. He just sat there and watched her. How could he be so impassive? But then, she'd wanted businesslike, detached, practical. She hadn't wanted Flynn to love her. He was giving her exactly what she'd always said she needed. And, against all the odds, she was still enough for him. She could still give him what he wanted, too, even knowing how much she'd messed up.

'It has to be your choice, Thea,' he said.

And, worst of all, she knew he was right.

CHAPTER TEN

'ARE YOU OKAY out here?'

Zeke turned at the sound of Helena's voice and saw the concerned crumple of her forehead as she stood in the door, watching him.

'I'm fine.' He patted the swing seat beside him. 'Wanna sit? Your sister has left us a little of the champagne.' He thought it wise not to mention exactly how Thea had been distracted from the champagne, right there on that very swing.

But Helena didn't sit anyway. Instead she leant against the railing opposite and reached out a hand for the bottle. Her high heels had been discarded, Zeke realised, and she seemed far smaller than the loss of a few inches should achieve.

'Everything okay in there?' he asked as Helena lifted the bottle to her lips. Of course what he really wanted to ask was, *Where's Thea? How did Flynn take it? When is she coming back?*

'Fine,' Helena said, passing the bottle back. 'The guests have all gone, or retired to their rooms. Thea and Flynn are in the library, talking. Your dad's in the study, and Isabella and Dad are sipping brandy in the back parlour, I think.'

That strange split again, Zeke thought. Everyone with the wrong person. Mum with Thomas, Thea with Flynn, and him out here with Helena.

'Do you know what they're talking about?' he asked.

Helena raised her eyebrows. 'Dad and Isabella? I dread to think.'

'I meant Thea and Flynn.' Zeke paused. 'And why dread to think?'

'Who knows what those two find to talk about?' Helena shrugged, but the look in her eyes told him there was more to it than a weird choice of phrase.

'Helena. What am I missing here?'

She tilted her head to look at him. '*Are* you missing it, though? Or just pretending you don't see it, like Thea?'

'I've been gone for eight years, Helena. I might have missed some stuff.' But he suspected. Always had. And the horrible certainty was already rising up in his gut.

'I knew when I was fourteen,' she replied.

How much more of life had Helena seen before she was an adult? What else had she been doing while Flynn had been at university and he and Thea had been sneaking around thinking that they were being so clever that no one knew about them?

'Knew what?' Zeke asked, even though he was sure he didn't want to know the answer.

'That my father and your mother were having an affair.'

Zeke grabbed the champagne bottle and drank deeply. 'Knew or suspected?' he asked, after wiping his mouth. Because *he'd* suspected, even when he hadn't wanted to. And he'd been very careful not to look any closer just in case he was proved right.

'Knew.'

Helena looked him straight in the eye, as if she wanted to prove the truth of her words.

'I saw them once. And once I'd seen…it was so obvious. I saw the proof of it in every single thing they did. It was a relief, in a way. At least I understood at last why Isabella was so determined to try and be my mother.'

'Yeah.' It explained a lot, even while Zeke wished that it didn't. What a mess. Tipping his head back against the wall behind the swing, he let his mind rerun the memories of twenty-one years of watching them but not seeing. Helena was right. Once you knew it was impossible not to see.

Was that how people had been with him and Thea?

The thought made him sit bolt-upright. 'Why are you telling me this now? I mean, there's no chance that I'm...' He couldn't even finish the sentence.

Helena's eyes widened. 'Our half-brother? God, no! That's...' She shuddered. 'No. Mum was still alive then, and I'm pretty sure it didn't start until after her death. Besides, Zeke, you look exactly like Ezekiel Senior. I don't think there's ever been any doubt about who your father is.'

'True.' Zeke's muscles relaxed just a little. 'Funny. For years I hated how much of him I saw when I looked in the mirror. Now...I'm profoundly grateful.'

'Hell, yes.'

'So why tell me now?'

Helena paused, her lower lip caught between her teeth. Suddenly she looked like the naughty schoolgirl he remembered, not the poised, sophisticated woman he'd found when he returned. Where had she gone, that Helena? Had all her rough edges and inappropriate comments been smoothed out by the things that had happened to her? By all the secrets she'd had to keep buried? He'd seen a glimpse of her at dinner, though, winding his mother up about the pearls. Maybe she wasn't gone for ever. He hoped not.

'Did you ever wonder why Isabella stayed with your dad?'

Zeke blinked. He hadn't, he realised. But he should have. 'I guess the money. The family. The business.'

'But if she'd left him for *my* dad...'

'They'd have had all of that, to some degree.' And Zeke would have grown up with Thomas Morrison as his step-father. He really couldn't be sure if that would have been an improvement, or not.

'Yeah.'

'So why?'

Helena shrugged. 'I don't know. I never asked. But maybe somebody should.'

'Why?' What did it matter now, anyway? He'd be gone tomorrow—leaving all this behind for his future with Thea.

'Because...' Helena took a deep breath. 'Because I think Thea is about to make the same mistake.'

Zeke's world froze. 'No. She's not. She's in there right now, telling Flynn she can't marry him.'

Helena's gaze was sad and sympathetic. 'Are you sure?'

'Yes,' Zeke lied. 'I'm absolutely sure.'

Isabella was waiting for her outside the library when Thea finally left Flynn alone with the books and headed for bed. It wouldn't do for the bride to look tired and distraught on her wedding day, after all. Just as Helena had said.

'Oh, my dear,' Isabella said, clasping her hands together at the sight of her. 'Come on. We'll go and have some tea.'

'Really, Isabella, I'm fine.' The last thing she wanted after the surrealism of her evening so far was to sit and sip tea with her future mother-in-law. 'I just need to get some sleep. It's been a long day.'

But Isabella wasn't taking no for an answer. 'You'll never sleep like this. Come on. Tea.'

Dutifully Thea trailed behind her, wondering how much longer this day could feasibly get. It had to be past mid-night already. Even if the wedding wasn't until tomorrow afternoon she couldn't imagine she'd actually get a lie-in, whatever happened. Apart from anything else she still had to talk to Zeke. Flynn had insisted she did, before making any final decisions.

The kitchens were in darkness, the last of the staff having gone home at last. The dishwashers were still running, though, so Thea suspected it had been a late night for all concerned. Isabella found the light switch without difficulty and flicked it on, before heading unerringly for a cupboard which, when opened, revealed a stock of different varieties of tea.

'Camomile?' she asked, glancing back at Thea. Then she frowned. 'Or maybe peppermint. Good for soothing the stomach.'

'My stomach is fine,' Thea replied. It was just her mind that was spinning and her heart that was breaking.

'As you say.' Isabella selected a tin then, opening another cupboard, pulled out a small silver teapot and two fragile-looking cups and saucers. 'I always make it my first priority to locate the teapot, wherever I'm staying. I just can't sleep without a soothing cup of something before bed.'

'I didn't know that.' Thea watched Isabella as she pottered over to the sink to fill the kettle then, while it was boiling, selected a couple of teaspoons and a tea strainer and stand from another drawer.

'Now, Thea...' Isabella placed the tea tray, complete with lace cloth, onto the kitchen table and took a chair opposite her. 'I want to talk to you about Zeke.'

'About Zeke?' Thea's fingers slipped on the handle of the teapot and she pulled back. She should let Isabella pour, anyway.

'Yes. I know you've always been...close to my son.'

'Your husband already asked me to talk to him about

This Minute,' Thea interjected, wishing she didn't sound as if she was babbling so much. 'And I tried—I did—but no dice. I think tomorrow he plans to leave and sell to Glasshouse, regardless of what we offer.'

'That's interesting,' Isabella said. 'But not what I wanted to talk about.'

'Then…what? Did you want to know where he's been? Because I have a pretty good idea, I think. Or what his plans are now? Because you'd really have to ask him, except…'

Except he was probably still waiting for her on the terrace. Did he know what she'd planned to tell Flynn? Or did he hope…? No. She couldn't think about it.

'I wanted to talk about your relationship with him. And my relationship with your father.'

Thea blinked. 'I don't understand.'

'Then you haven't been paying very close attention.' Isabella reached for the teapot and, placing the strainer over Thea's cup, started to pour. 'This should be brewed by now.'

'What exactly *is* your relationship with my father?' Thea asked, even though she suspected she already knew the answer. Should have known it for years.

'What exactly is *your* relationship with my youngest son?' Isabella didn't even look up from pouring the tea into her own cup as she turned the question round on Thea.

'I haven't seen him in eight years,' Thea said. 'I think that any relationship we did have will have been legally declared dead by now.'

'Except he was the one who came after you when you were upset tonight. And I suspect he's the one who's left you looking like your whole world is upside down.'

'Tell me about you and Dad.'

Placing the pot back on the tray, Isabella picked up her

teacup and saucer and sat back, surveying Thea over the rim of her steaming cup. 'I think, in some ways, our situation is very similar, you know.'

'I *don't* know,' Thea said. 'I don't know what you're talking about.'

'After your mother died your father was a wreck. I tried to help out where I could. And then, after that nastiness with Helena...'

'You saw your chance and pushed me out,' Thea said, her hackles rising. But Isabella merely raised her eyebrows a few millimetres as she sipped her tea.

'I did what was needed to keep things...settled.'

Sending Helena away and taking over Thea's home. Smoothing over the rough edges of the actual truth and providing a glossy finish. Thea shook her head. 'I don't see how this applies to me and Zeke.'

'Wait,' Isabella said. 'Drink your tea and listen. Over time, your father and I grew close. We talked a lot. We listened a lot. That was something we both needed. You might not have noticed, but my husband is not one of the world's great listeners and his only subject of conversation is the company. It was...different with Thomas.'

Thea's hands tightened around the warmth of her teacup. 'You fell in love.'

'We did. Very deeply.'

No wonder her father had chosen Isabella over her. For the first time Thea saw her past through new eyes. No, she hadn't been up to the job her father had thrown her into. But maybe that had been because it was a role that was never meant to be hers. Maybe he'd wanted Isabella there at his side all along.

Except he'd never got all of her, had he?

'You never left Ezekiel.'

'I never even considered it,' Isabella said without pause. 'And your father never asked me to.'

'Why?'

Isabella sighed. 'Because I was old enough and wise enough, by the time I fell in love for real, to know that love isn't everything. Thea, we all need different things in this life. Yes, we need someone to listen to us, to laugh with, to love. But we need other things, too.'

'Like money,' Thea guessed, not hiding the bitterness in her voice. How different might her life have been with Isabella as a real stepmother rather than someone who had to help out because Thea couldn't manage things on her own? 'Dad could have given you that, too, you know.'

'Not just money. Yes, Thomas could have given me that—and stability, and lots of other things. But what about the business? What about our social standing? My place in the world? What about Ezekiel and the vows I made?'

'You mean, what about the scandal?' Thea shook her head. 'Is that what it's always about with you? Was this just Helena all over again?'

'All I am saying is there are many aspects of a woman's life for which she has needs. You need to look at your requirements over the course of a lifetime when you're making a decision about whom to marry.'

'And Ezekiel gave you what you needed over the course of your lifetime? Because, if so, why did you feel the need to have an affair with my father?'

Isabella sipped at her tea delicately before responding. 'That's what I'm saying. Did it ever occur to you that perhaps it is unreasonable to expect one person to fulfil your every need?'

'No.' The response was instinctive, automatic. Even if she were willing to contemplate such a thing, neither Zeke nor Flynn was the sort of man who liked to share.

Isabella gave her a sad smile. 'You're young. You're still holding out for the dream. So, which of my sons do you think can give you that?'

Thea had no answer to that at all.

'If that's the way you feel you have only two options,' Isabella said. 'One: you marry Flynn as planned. Everyone is happy and no one needs to be any the wiser about your...indiscretion. You go about your life and probably never see Zeke again.'

'What's option two?' Thea asked, her mouth dry.

'You call off the wedding and leave with Zeke. You leave behind your career, your family and reputation, your chance at a stable and loving future, for a man who has already left you behind once. In an effort to put a good face on the company my husband will probably marry Flynn off to someone else pretty quickly. Helena, I imagine, would be the best candidate.'

'No.' The very idea chilled Thea's core. 'She wouldn't.'

'She would,' Isabella replied, with certainty in her voice. 'She couldn't bear to let everyone down *again*. Besides, surely you've noticed the way she looks at him.'

'No.'

Was Isabella just saying that to convince her to marry Flynn? Didn't she know that if she'd thought Helena wanted him she'd step aside in an instant? Probably not. Isabella had spent so many years watching Ezekiel drive a wedge between her sons she probably believed everyone wanted what their sibling had.

'I'd look closer, then.'

Thea shook her head. 'You're imagining things, Isabella. And it doesn't matter anyway.'

'Oh? Have you found a magical third path, then? Other than my original suggestion?'

'No.' Thea stared down into her teacup. If she was hon-

est, she'd known all along what she really had to do. For
her future and for her family. 'I'll marry Flynn, just as
we've always planned.'

Isabella watched her for a long moment, then nodded.
'Good. Now, more tea?'

'No. Thank you.' Thea pushed her chair away from the
table and stood. 'I need to go to bed. Lots to do tomorrow.'

Starting with explaining her decision to the one person
in the world who would never, ever understand it.

Zeke woke early the next morning. He'd waited up for
Thea on the terrace until he'd realised all the lights inside
had been turned off. Helena had kept vigil with him for
a while, before patting him on the shoulder and bidding
him goodnight. When he'd finally given up and gone to
bed he'd lingered outside Thea's door for long moments,
contemplating knocking and going in. But Thea had to
make this decision for herself—even he knew that much.

In the end he'd headed to bed alone, for a night of restless dreams and uncertainty. And now it was the morning of Thea and Flynn's wedding, and he still didn't know
her decision.

From the moment he woke he felt panic surge through
him at the realisation that he was alone again. Why hadn't
she come? He'd been so sure... Flynn must have said something. Threatened her, perhaps... Except that wasn't his
style. No, he'd have baffled her with logic. Probably had a
spreadsheet of reasons they should get married as planned.

Just what Thea didn't need.

Sitting up in bed, Zeke stamped down on the fear creep-
ing across his brain and contemplated his next move. He
could still fix this, still win, if he played the right hand.
Did he wait for Thea to come to him, or did he seek her
out? There was always the chance that she might not come

at all. If she'd made her decision—the wrong decision—what would be the point? But Zeke knew he couldn't live with the not knowing.

So what other choice did he have? He could just cut his losses now. He could go and say goodbye to Thea, give her one last chance to go with him, then leave if she said no.

In the end the choice wasn't his or Thea's. As he exited his bedroom, freshly showered and casually dressed—no way was he getting stuck in a tux this early in the day, even if the wedding went ahead and he actually attended—he saw Flynn, marching towards him.

'You and I need to talk,' his adopted brother said, face solemn. 'And then you need to talk to Thea.'

'Okay.' Zeke fell into step with Flynn, his heart rising slightly in his chest. Maybe he wouldn't need to convince Thea again after all. If Flynn wanted him to talk to her surely that meant he didn't approve of her decision. Well, he was damned if he thought Zeke would try to persuade her otherwise. 'What exactly do we need to talk about?'

Flynn gave him an exasperated look. 'Thea, of course.'

'Right.'

Zeke waited until Flynn had yanked open the door to the library and impatiently motioned him in before asking any more questions. Settling down into a wingback chair, he suddenly remembered Helena's words from the night before. This was where Flynn and Thea had talked after the interlude on the terrace. How he wished he could have heard what they'd said...

Maybe Flynn would tell him. If he asked right.

'So,' Zeke said, folding one leg up to rest his ankle on the opposite knee. 'What's up? Last-minute nerves?'

Flynn glared at him. 'In precisely six hours I'm supposed to marry Thea. If you have any interest at all in that event, however twisted, you need to stop playing *now*. I need you to be my brother, for once, and I need you to be honest with me.'

Zeke flinched under his brother's gaze. How had he become the kid brother again, the screw-up, the one who couldn't be serious about anything that mattered? Especially when he'd worked so hard to get away from that. Away from the bitter rivalry for something that had turned out not to matter at all—their father's approval.

'Fine. Then talk.'

'Thea told me that she slept with you last night.'

'She said she was going to.' Zeke looked Flynn right in the eye as he talked. He wasn't ashamed, even if he should be. Thea belonged with *him*, not in some soulless, loveless marriage of convenience. Getting her out of that was not a sin. Trapping her was.

'I still plan to marry her.'

'For the love of God, *why*?' Zeke grabbed the arms of the chair and sat forward. What else did he have to *do*? 'You don't love her—I know you don't. You couldn't be this calm right now if you did. And she doesn't love you!'

'Do you think she's still in love with you?'

'I know she is. And I know she deserves a lot better than what you have to offer.'

'And what, exactly, are *you* offering?' Flynn asked, staring at Zeke. 'The chance to say *screw you* to our father?'

'That's not...' Zeke sank back down into his chair. 'That's not why.'

'Are you sure?' Flynn tilted his head as he considered his brother. 'It's been eight years, Zeke. Why come back now, if not to prove a point?'

'Oh, I don't know—maybe to stop Thea making a huge mistake.'

'And you think you're the best judge of Thea's mistakes?'

'Better than her, at least,' Zeke said, thinking about Helena and all the guilt Thea carried on her behalf.

Flynn shook his head. 'You're wrong. But I told Thea last night she had to decide for herself what to do. I told her to think about it overnight, then talk to us both this morning. She'll be here any minute.'

And just like that the decision about how to approach Thea was taken away from him.

'Good,' Zeke said, hoping his surprise didn't show on his face.

He didn't want to have this conversation in front of his brother. Flynn made him a different person even now, after all these years. He needed it to be just him and Thea, so they could just be themselves, the people he remembered so well. But apparently his love life was now in the public domain. And before he could even object the library door opened and Thea was standing there, looking pale and lovely— and determined.

Zeke stood up. Time to win this.

CHAPTER ELEVEN

THEA SUCKED IN a breath as she opened the library door and saw Zeke and Flynn waiting for her. This was it. The moment that decided the rest of her life. Whatever she'd told Isabella, whatever she'd told herself in the dark of the night, her decision couldn't be final until she'd told the two men in this room. This might be the biggest choice and possibly the biggest mistake she'd ever made as an adult. So of course it involved Zeke Ashton.

'Thea, you're here. Good.'

Flynn gave her a gentle smile that made Thea's insides tie up in knots. She didn't want to be there *so much*.

But she was, and she was out of other options, so she moved to the centre of the room and took the chair Flynn indicated. This was his condition: he'd marry her today if she talked things through with both of them and still decided it was the best option. Since she'd slept with someone else the night before their wedding, Thea had to admit that this was more than fair. That was the thing about Flynn. He was always scrupulously fair. Even when she wanted him to just yell, or walk out, or make a decision for her.

'Okay, so here's what I'm thinking.' Flynn settled into his own chair, looking for all the world as if this was an everyday meeting or discussion. As if they weren't debating whether or not to get *married* that afternoon. 'We all know the situation. And we all agree that Thea has to be the one to make a decision about what happens next—correct?'

He glanced between them, focussing first on Zeke, who eventually nodded in a way that made it very clear he was doing so under duress, and then at Thea, who whispered, 'Yes,' even though she didn't want to.

'So… I think the best way to proceed is—'

'Oh, for God's sake!' Zeke interrupted. 'This isn't a board meeting, Flynn.'

'No,' Flynn replied, his voice calm and even. 'It's a meeting about my future. And since you're the one who's put that into the realm of uncertainty, I think you should just let me deal with it my own way, don't you?'

Zeke settled back into his chair at that, and Thea risked a glance over at him. His eyes were dark and angry, and she could see the tension in his hands, in the way they gripped the arms of the chair, even if his posture was relaxed. How he must hate this—must hate waiting to see if Flynn was going to beat him again. Because of course that was how Zeke would see it, even if it wasn't true. This wasn't about either of them, really, even if only Flynn seemed to realise that.

It was about Thea. About her making the right decision for once. Whatever that might be.

'So, here's what I propose,' Flynn said, and Thea tried to concentrate on listening to him instead of watching the way Zeke's jaw tightened with every word. 'Zeke and I will both lay out our arguments for why we feel you should choose our proposed course of action. You can listen, ask questions, and then we'll leave you alone to make your decision. The only thing I ask is that you decide quickly; once guests start arriving it will be a lot harder to cancel this thing, if you choose to.'

Thea nodded, and stopped looking at Zeke altogether.

'Okay. Shall I go first?' Flynn asked, and when no one answered he continued, 'Right. Thea, obviously I want to marry you today. I understand what happened last night, and I think, after talking with you yesterday, I can see why. But I don't believe that one impulsive action has to change the course of your whole life. We agreed to a contract—a marriage between us based on very sound reasoning and mutual desires. Everything we discussed and decided still stands. I can give you the security, the business, the future that you want. And marriage is only a small part of our lives; we have to consider the other people we love— what *they* want. I think we both know that everyone in this villa except Zeke wants a future with us as a couple in it. We can do so much together, Thea. And, quite honestly, I'd worry about your future if you left with Zeke today.'

He got up from the chair and came to stand by her side, gently taking her hand in his.

'Because, Thea, I care about you. Maybe we don't have that grand passion. But we have more. Mutual respect, caring, common interests and values. They matter too. And I suggest to you, right here, that they matter more for what we want to achieve in life.'

He wasn't just thinking about the business, Thea realised. He was talking about kids. Flynn would be a great father—calm and fair. And she was pretty sure he wouldn't ever sleep with his best friend's wife. Unlike her own father. Unlike Zeke, she thought, stealing a glance at him. Hell, he'd slept with her the night before her wedding. Morality had never been a strong motivation for him.

Or for her this week, it seemed.

Flynn seemed to be waiting for an answer, so Thea nodded and said, 'That all makes a lot of sense,' even though her poor muddled brain could barely remember what he'd said.

Maybe it didn't matter, she realised. Maybe, whatever they each had to say, it all meant nothing in the end. She couldn't weigh up the pros and cons of two people, could she?

Except she had to. And not just of the two men in front of her but of the whole lives they represented. She could see two futures for herself, branching off from this moment, and she simply didn't know which one was more terrifying.

But she still had to decide.

Flynn gave a sharp nod, then moved away to his own chair, yielding the floor to his brother. 'Zeke. Your turn.'

Zeke looked up slowly, his dark gaze finally meeting hers. 'I don't know what you want me to say.'

'Neither do I,' Thea admitted. Did she want him to talk her out of marrying Flynn—really? Or did she want him to say something so awful that she stopped feeling guilty about marrying Zeke's brother in the first place? She wasn't sure.

He blew out a long breath. 'Okay. I don't want you to marry Flynn. I think it's a mistake.'

Thea flinched at the word, even though she tried not to. 'It's mine to make, though.'

'It is,' Zeke conceded. 'I just... I really don't want to do this with him in the room.'

'He's your brother. And he's right—he does have kind of a big stake in this conversation.'

'I know.' Zeke took another breath. 'Okay, fine. I know you think you're doing this for the family, to prove yourself to them somehow. And I know you believe that everyone will be happy if you just go along with their plans. But you're wrong.'

'And our happiness is suddenly of such importance to you? Zeke, you haven't cared about us for the last eight years. I find it hard to believe that we suddenly matter that much to you.'

'Of course I've cared!' Zeke yelled, and Flynn's gaze shot to the door, as if he was worrying about who might be listening. It was a fear that seemed all the more reasonable when Zeke's words were followed by a knock on the library door a moment later.

'Ah, here you all are,' Isabella said, giving them all her best hostess smile. 'Thea, darling, there's a small question about the table settings that we could use your input on, if you have a moment.'

Isabella's eyes were knowing, but Thea refused to meet them.

'I'll deal with it,' Flynn said, getting to his feet. 'Thea and Zeke are just reminiscing about old times, Mother. Something they won't have much of a chance to do once we're married.'

She had to know it was a lie, but Isabella let it go nonetheless. 'Come on, then. And once this is sorted, perhaps you can help me with the question of the gift table.'

Flynn shut the door firmly behind them, and Thea felt as if he'd taken all the air in the room with him. Now it was just her and Zeke and every moment of their history, weighing down on them like the books on the shelves.

'That's better,' Zeke said. 'Now we can do this properly.'

How could she look so poised and calm, when he felt as if his insides were about to combust? For Thea this might as well be just another business meeting. Maybe she was a perfect match for Flynn after all.

No. If this was his last chance to try and uncover the Thea he'd known and loved, the one he'd glimpsed again as he'd made love to her on the terrace last night, then he was grasping it with both hands. He had to make her see sense.

'Maybe we should wait until Flynn gets back,' Thea said, as if she truly believed that any part of this discussion really did involve his brother.

'This isn't about Flynn,' Zeke said. 'He could be anyone. Any poor bloke you'd roped in to try and make your life safe and predictable. Just like the last two. No, this is about you and me, and it always has been.'

Thea's gaze shot up to meet his, dark and heated. 'You mean it's all about *you*. You proving a point to your father. Just like it always is.'

'Last night wasn't just about me,' Zeke replied, enjoying the flush of red that ran up her neck to her cheeks. 'In fact I distinctly remember it being all about you more than once.'

'This isn't about sex, Zeke,' Thea snapped. 'This is my future you're playing with.'

'Who said I'm playing?' Because he wasn't—not one bit. He knew exactly how important this moment was. But with Thea sometimes you had to get her mad to see the truth. To let her true self break out from all the rules and restrictions she'd tucked herself in with like a safety blanket.

Thea gave a bitter laugh. 'It's always been a game to you—all of it. You've always cared more about beating your father and Flynn than anything else. If you'd paid any attention at all you'd know that Flynn isn't even competing. He's just getting on with his life, like an ordinary, good man.'

'And that's what you want, is it? Ordinary?' If she thought it was, she was wrong. Thea deserved much, much more than ordinary.

'I want to not be a trophy! I want to not be one more

thing you can use against your family for some misguided slight almost a decade ago!'

The words hit him hard in the chest. 'That's not what I'm doing.'

'Isn't it? Are you sure? Because it seems to me that coming back here—right when you're about to sell your company to our competitor, just when I'm about to get on and make a success of my life—is far more about you and your need to win than anything else.'

'You're wrong.'

'Prove it.'

'How?'

'I don't know, Zeke! But if you really want me to throw over all my plans for the future, to upset both our families, probably damage the company's reputation…you need to offer me a little more than a cheap victory over your father and one night on a terrace.'

One night. Was that what it was to her? Was that all he'd ever been? A bit of fun, but never the one you chose for the long haul. No wonder she'd stayed eight years ago.

'Helena must have been a real handy excuse that night,' he said, letting the bitterness creep into his voice.

Thea blinked. 'What?'

'Tell me honestly. If it hadn't been for Helena would you have come with me when I asked, that night of your birthday party?'

The colour faded from Thea's cheeks and he knew the answer before she even spoke the word.

'No.'

Zeke tightened his muscles against the pain, stiffening into strength and resolve. With a sharp nod, he said, 'That's what I thought.'

'I just… I wanted…'

'You don't need to justify yourself to me.' A strange

calm had settled over him now. At last he knew, and to his surprise the truth made all the difference. 'I understand.'

'No! You don't,' Thea said, but Zeke just shook his head.

'Sure I do. You want a safe and predictable life, even if it makes you miserable.' How had he thought for so many years that Thea was different from the rest of them? He should have known that they were all the same at heart. More concerned with the appearance of the thing than the substance. Better that he realised that now, however belatedly, than go on believing she was something more than she was.

'That's not… It's not just that,' Thea said unconvincingly.

'Yeah, Thea, it is. Deny it all you want, but I know what's going on here. You're doing exactly what Daddy wants, as usual. You're going to marry Flynn to buy yourself the place you think you deserve.'

She looked away, but Zeke wasn't looking for shame in her expression. It was too late for that now, anyway. She'd made her choice and he knew his future now. But that didn't mean he couldn't open her eyes to a few home truths before he left.

'You realise you could be pregnant with my child already?' They hadn't used protection last night. Had been too caught up in the moment even to think of it.

'I know.'

'Does Flynn?'

'Yes.' A whisper…barely even a word.

'And he's happy to marry you anyway?' Of course he was. In fact he probably hoped that she was. 'Because that would give him the one thing he's never had, wouldn't it? Legitimacy. Raising a true Ashton blood heir with the Morrison heiress. Perfect.'

Thea sprang to her feet to defend her fiancé. 'You don't

have a clue what you're talking about! And anyway Flynn *is* the Ashton heir, remember? You gave it all up to run away and seek revenge.'

'Because my father chose him over me!' Zeke couldn't keep the anger from his voice this time. However far he moved past the pain, the sting of unfairness still caught him unawares sometimes.

'Your father made a business choice, not a personal one.'

Zeke flinched at her words. 'You're wrong there,' he said.

'Am I?'

He knew she was, but couldn't bring himself to explain, to argue. To revisit in glorious Technicolor the night he'd left. The things he'd heard his father say. What had really driven him away. Why he'd had to go even when Thea wouldn't leave with him. Why her rejection had been just one more slam to the heart.

What was wrong with him? He'd moved past this years ago. Wasn't that one of the reasons he'd come back in the first place? To prove that he'd moved on, that he had his own life now, that he didn't need his family or the business? So why was he letting her arguments get to him?

Was it the idea of a possible baby? The thought that *his child* might be brought up in the Morrison-Ashton clan, living its whole life waiting to see if it would be deemed *worthy enough* to inherit everything that Zeke had walked away from...? It made him sick to his stomach. No child— no person—deserved to go through that. But what were the honest chances that Thea was pregnant? Slim, he'd imagine. And she'd tell him, he knew. Thea might not be everything he'd thought she was, but she was honest. She'd told Flynn about sleeping with him, hadn't she? She'd tell Zeke if he were a father.

And then he'd be tied into this accursed family for ever. Perfect.

What had he been thinking, sleeping with her last night? Zeke wanted to beat himself up for it, except he knew exactly what he'd been thinking—that he might be able to save Thea from herself this time.

But Thea didn't want to be saved. She'd rejected him again, and this time it cut even deeper. She'd chosen Flynn. She wanted Flynn.

Fine. She could have him. But Zeke was making sure she knew exactly what she was letting herself in for first.

CHAPTER TWELVE

THEA THOUGHT SHE could bear anything except sitting one moment longer under Zeke's too knowing gaze. Who was he to judge her, to condemn her? To think he knew her better than she knew herself?

Except he just might.

No. She couldn't let herself believe that. After a sleepless night, spent with Flynn and Isabella's words resounding in her brain while her memories ran one long, sensual video of her evening with Zeke, she knew only one thing for certain: she was done with doing what other people said she should. Everyone in the whole villa thought they knew what was best for her, and Zeke was just the latest in a long line.

Well, she was done with it.

'You realise that you're choosing what other people expect of you over what you really want, right?' Zeke said, and she glared at him.

'How would you know what I want? And if you make one single innuendo or reference to last night after that comment I'm walking out right now.'

The smirk on his face told her that was exactly what Zeke had been about to do, but instead he said, 'Because I've seen you do it before, far too many times. You admitted you wouldn't have come with me even if Helena hadn't needed you. But why? I can tell you, even if you don't know yourself.'

Thea rolled her eyes. 'Enlighten me, oh, wise one,' she said, as sarcastically as she could manage.

'Because you're scared. Because you've spent your whole life doing what other people think is best for you and you don't even know how to stop. You can't make peace with your own desires because you think they might upset someone.'

'They upset *me*!' Thea yelled. 'Zeke! Do you think I want to be this person? The sort of woman who sleeps with the best man the night before her wedding? I hate myself right now! The best thing I can do is try and get back to my regularly scheduled life, without the chaos you bring into it. Is that so bad?'

'Not if the regularly scheduled life is what you really want.'

Zeke moved closer, and Thea's body started to hum at his nearness.

'But I don't think it is. I think that you want more. You want a life that makes your heart sing. You want it all.'

He swayed closer again, and before she knew it his hand was at her waist, pulling her towards him, and his lips were dipping towards hers...

She wanted this so badly. Wanted his mouth on hers, his body against her. But she couldn't have it. Not if she wanted all the other things she'd promised herself—her family, security, her work. This was her last chance to get things right—and she had to take it. However tempted she was to give in to desire over sense.

'No, Zeke.' She pushed him away, not letting her palms linger on his chest for a moment longer than necessary. 'I'm marrying Flynn.'

'Then you're a fool.'

Zeke stepped away, turning his back on her, but not before she saw the flash in his eyes of—what? Anger? Frustration? She couldn't be sure.

'I'm making the sensible decision,' Thea said, even though it felt as if her heart might force its way out of her sensible ribcage at any moment to fight its own case.

'You're making a mistake.'

'Am I?' Thea shook her head. This was going to hurt. And this was going to make him angry. But she needed to say it. Hell, she'd been waiting eight years to tell him this. It was past due. 'What about you? You say I'm relying on other people to tell me how to live, but how are you any better?'

'I live my life exactly the way I want.' Zeke ran his hand through his messy hair as he turned back towards her. 'By my own judgement. No archaic family loyalty rules or duty to manipulative men.'

'Really? Seems to me that everything you've done since you left—hell, even leaving in the first place—has all been more about your father than you.'

Zeke shook his head. 'You don't know what you're talking about.'

'I do,' Thea said firmly. 'Because I know you, Zeke. You said you wanted to leave Morrison-Ashton and everything it represented behind when you left. But what did you do? You went and worked for another media conglomerate and then set up your own rival company, for heaven's sake!'

'Stick with what you know, and all that,' Zeke said with a shrug, but Thea wasn't listening.

'And now you're here, still trying to prove to everyone that you don't need them. You're still so bitter about your father giving Flynn the job you wanted—'

'It's not just that!'

'You're so bitter,' Thea carried on, 'that you can't move

on. I bet even when you were away you were still checking up on your family. People keep saying that you walked out and left us, but you didn't. You've carried us with you every step of the way and, Zeke, that chip on your shoulder is only getting bigger and heavier. And until you let it go you're never going to be happy. Not even if I left with you right now.'

'You're wrong,' Zeke said, but even as he spoke he could feel the truth of her words resonating through his body. 'I'm done with the lot of you for good this time.'

Her smile was sad, but it enraged him. Who was she to tell him the mistakes he was making in his life? Thea Morrison—the queen of bad decisions. And, even if she didn't know it yet, this was the worst one. Well, she'd have a long, miserable marriage during which to regret it.

Zeke might have been willing to take a lot from Thea Morrison, but this was the last. The last rejection he'd ever face from anyone with the surname Morrison or Ashton.

He was done.

His chest ached as he realised this might be the last time he ever saw her. That he was walking away again and she wouldn't be coming with him this time, either. He choked back a laugh as he realised the awful truth. She'd been right all along. She'd been right not to leave with him eight years ago. They *had* been kids. And he knew now that he hadn't even understood what love was then.

He couldn't have loved Thea at eighteen—not really. He hadn't known her the way he did now, for a start. But mostly he knew it had to be true because, however much he'd thought it had hurt to leave her last time, it didn't come close to the pain searing through his body at the thought of leaving her now..

He loved Thea Morrison, the woman she'd grown up

to be, more than he'd ever believed possible. And it didn't make a bit of difference.

None of it mattered now. Not their past, not this horrific week in Tuscany, and certainly not their impossible future. When he left this time he wouldn't be coming back. And he knew just how to make sure that every atom of his relationship with these people was left behind too.

'Maybe you don't know it yet,' he said, keeping his voice calm and even, 'but you're going to make yourself, my brother, and everyone else around you desperately unhappy if you go through with this wedding. I love you. And I would have done anything to make you happy. Anything except stay here and live this safe life you think you want. But it will end up driving you mad. One day you're going to wake up and realise all that, and know what a mistake you've made. But, like you say, it's your mistake to make.'

He didn't look back as he walked to the door. He didn't want to see her standing there, beautiful, sad and resolved. She loved him—he knew it. But she wasn't going to let herself have the one thing that could make her happy.

Fine. It was her mistake, as she'd said.

But she couldn't make him watch.

'Goodbye, Thea,' he said as he walked out through the door.

The door shut behind him with a click, although it felt like an earth-shattering slam to Thea. She'd done it. She'd really done it. She'd sent him away, made the right decision for once. Avoided the oh, so tempting mistake she'd made so many times before. She'd won.

So why did she feel so broken?

Sinking into the chair, Thea sat very still and waited for whatever would happen next. The stylist would be here soon, she vaguely remembered, to do her hair and makeup. Helena would come and find her when it was time, wouldn't she? And in the meantime…she'd just wait for someone to tell her what she was supposed to do.

The irony of her thoughts surprised a laugh from her, and she buried her face in her hands before her laughter turned to tears. The decision was made and Zeke would leave now. She could get back to that regularly scheduled life she'd been hankering after for the past three days.

It was over at last.

Hearing a click, she looked up again in time to see the door open. For one fleeting moment her heart jumped at the thought that it might be Zeke, coming back to try and win her one last time. But, really, what else was there to say? They'd both said everything they needed to, everything they'd been holding in for the last eight years. That moment had passed. *Their* moment.

Flynn stuck his head around the door and, seeing she was alone, came in, shutting it behind him.

'Everything okay?' he asked, hovering nervously at a distance.

Poor Flynn. The things she'd put him through this week… He was such a good man. He didn't deserve it.

So she tried very hard to smile as she looked up at him, to make him feel wanted and loved. To feel like the winner he'd turned out to be. Her man, her choice, her future. Now and always.

'Fine,' she said, her cheeks aching. 'But I'm afraid you're going to need a new best man.'

The look of relief on his face was almost reward enough. 'I think I can arrange that.'

He moved towards her, settling on the arm of her chair, one hand at her shoulder in a comforting fatherly gesture. He'd be a brilliant dad, Thea thought again. It was important to focus on all the excellent reasons she had for marrying him, rather than the one uncertain and confusing reason not to.

'Are you okay?' Flynn asked, and Thea nodded.

'I'm fine. It was...a little difficult, that's all.'

'And you're sure you want to go through with this today? I mean, I appreciate you choosing me, Thea, I really do. And I think it's the right decision. We're going to have a great future together, I know. But it doesn't have to start today—not if you don't want. We could postpone—'

'No,' Thea interrupted. 'I've made my choice. I want to do this.'

Before she changed her mind.

Zeke didn't knock on his father's office door. He didn't need permission or approval from his father for what was going to happen next. In fact he didn't need anything from him. That was sort of the point.

Ezekiel Ashton looked up as Zeke walked in, and his eyebrows rose in amused interest. 'Zeke. Shouldn't you be off practising your best man's speech somewhere?'

'I believe that by now Flynn will have chosen a better man.' Zeke dropped into the visitor's chair, slouching casually. 'I'll be leaving as soon as I'm packed.'

Guests would start arriving soon, he was sure, for the pre-wedding drinks reception that Isabella had insisted on when she'd discovered that Thea planned a late afternoon wedding. He could probably grab one of the taxis bringing people up from the hotel to get him to the airport. He'd call his assistant while he packed and get her to book a flight.

This time tomorrow he'd be in another country. Another life.

'You're not staying, then.' Ezekiel shook his head sadly and turned his attention back to his paperwork. 'I don't know why I'm surprised.'

He doesn't matter. Nothing he thinks or does matters to me any more.

'I have one piece of business to conclude with you before I go,' Zeke said, watching in amusement as he became of interest to his father again.

'Oh, yes? I was under the impression that the very idea of doing business with your own father was distasteful to you.'

'It is,' Zeke said bluntly. 'But it has come to my attention that it may be the only way to sever my ties with you for good.'

'You make it sound so violent,' Ezekiel said. 'When really all you're doing is running away from your responsibilities. And, Zeke, we all know that you'll come back again eventually. We're family. That's what you do for family.'

Zeke shook his head. 'Not this one. Do you know why I left eight years ago?'

'Because you felt slighted that I'd given a position you considered rightfully yours to your brother.'

'No.' Zeke thought back to that horrible day and for the first time felt a strange detachment from the events. 'Because I finally understood why you'd done it. I heard you that day, talking to Thomas about us. I'd come to talk to you about you giving Flynn my job—the one I'd always been promised. I had all these arguments ready...' He shook his head at the memory of his righteous younger self. 'I heard you laugh and say that you realised now that perhaps it wasn't such a misfortune that Mum had fallen pregnant twenty-one years ago, just as Flynn's adoption was confirmed. That while you hadn't planned for two children perhaps it had all been for the best after all.'

He'd stood frozen outside his father's office door, Zeke remembered, his hand half raised to knock. And he'd lis-

tened as his father had ruined his relationship with his
brother for good.

'This way,' Ezekiel had said, 'they have built-in competition. In some ways it's better, having two sons. Flynn has
always felt he has to earn his place, so he fights for it—he
fights to belong every day. And as long as I let Zeke feel
that he's the disappointment, the second son, he'll keep
fighting to best his brother. It's a perfect set-up.'

'"I've told Zeke I've given Flynn the position as my
right-hand man,"' you said.' Zeke watched the memory
dawning in his father's eyes. '"Of course Zeke will get
the company one day. But I want him to fight his brother
for it, first."'

The words still echoed in Zeke's skull—the moment
his whole life had made horrifying, unbelievable sense,
and everything he'd ever thought he wanted had ceased to
matter. He'd had to leave—had to get away. And so he'd
run straight to Thea and asked her to go with him, only to
have his world, his expectations, damned again. That one
night had changed his whole life.

'Do you remember saying that, *Dad*?'

Ezekiel nodded. 'Of course I do. And what of it? Healthy
competition is good for the soul.'

'That wasn't healthy. Nothing you did to us was *healthy*.'

Zeke leant forward in his chair, gripping the armrests
tightly to stop himself standing and pacing. He wanted to
look his father in the eye as he told him this.

'What you did to us was unfair at best, cruel at worst.
You pitted two people who should have been friends, brothers, against each other. You drove a wedge between us
from the moment we were born. You made me feel rejected, inadequate. And you made Flynn believe that he
had to fight for every scrap from the table. You drove
your wife into the arms of your best friend, you drove me

to the other end of the country, and you drove Flynn and Thea to believe that marrying each other is the only way to serve the family business, to earn their place in the family. You are a manipulative, cold, uncaring man and *I am done with you.*'

Ezekiel was silent at his words, but Zeke didn't bother looking for remorse in his expression. He wouldn't find it, and even if by some miracle he did it didn't matter now.

'I am here today to undertake my final act of business with you, old man,' Zeke said, relaxing back in the chair. 'I am going to sell you This Minute, for twice what Glasshouse were offering.' He scribbled down the figure and pushed the scrap of paper across the table.

Ezekiel read it and nodded. 'I knew you'd see sense about this in the end.'

'I'm not done,' Zeke said. 'That's just the financial cost. I want something more.'

'A position at the company?' Ezekiel guessed. 'Would Director of Digital Media suffice for now?'

'I don't want a job. I never wanted to work for you in the first place. I want you to give Thea that role. I want you to make sure she has the freedom to run it her way, and to make her own mistakes. You cannot interfere one iota.'

Ezekiel gave a slow nod. 'That should be possible. As her father always says, her business decisions are far more credible than her personal ones. And she's due a promotion once the wedding is over.'

Zeke knew this game. By the time he left Ezekiel would have convinced himself that Thea's new job had been all his idea in the first place.

He'd have a harder time doing that with his second demand, Zeke wagered.

'One more thing,' Zeke said, and waited until he had his father's full attention before he continued. 'I want you to step down and appoint Flynn as the CEO of Morrison-Ashton. You can take a year for the handover,' he said, talking over his father's objections. 'But no more. By his first wedding anniversary Flynn will be in charge.'

'The company is supposed to come to you,' Ezekiel said.

Zeke shook his head. 'I don't want it. Flynn does. He's your son, as much as I am, and he's earned it a lot more than I have. It's his.'

Ezekiel watched him for a long moment, obviously weighing up how much he wanted This Minute against how much he hated his son right then. Zeke waited. He knew that his father's pride wouldn't allow him to let This Minute go to his main rival. Plus he probably thought he'd be able to get out of stepping down somehow.

He wouldn't. Zeke's lawyers were very, very good at what they did, and they would make sure the contract was watertight. But he'd let the old man hope for now.

'Fine,' Ezekiel said eventually.

Zeke jumped to his feet. 'I'll have my team draw up the papers. They'll be with you by next week.'

'And what about you? What are you going to do?'

Zeke paused in the doorway and smiled at his father. 'I'm going to go and live my own life at last.'

CHAPTER THIRTEEN

ISABELLA WAS WAITING for her in the hallway with the stylist when Thea finally pulled herself together for long enough to make it out of the library. Flynn still hovered nervously at her shoulder, but she tried to give him reassuring smiles when she could, in the hope that he might leave her alone for a few minutes.

'Thea! We're running behind schedule already, you know. And you look dreadful!'

'Thanks,' Thea said, even though she knew her mother-in-law-to-be was probably completely correct.

'Sorry. But…well, you do. Now, come with me and Sheila, here, will get you sorted out. Flynn, I think your father is looking for you. I saw Zeke come out of his office a few moments ago, so God only knows what that is about. Why don't you go and find out?'

Was Isabella just trying to get rid of Flynn for a moment? Thea wondered. Or did Ezekiel really want him? And, if so, why? Had Zeke finally agreed to sell This Minute to them?

And why did she still care?

It was business, that was all, Thea told herself. It was all business from here on in.

'Will you be okay?' Flynn asked.

'Oh, Flynn, don't be ridiculous. Of course she will! It's her wedding day.'

But Flynn was still looking at Thea, and ignoring his mother, so she nodded. 'I'll be fine. Go.'

Flynn gave her an uncertain smile. 'Okay. I'll see you at the church.'

'At the church,' Thea agreed weakly.

Sheila had set up in Thea's bedroom, so she followed the stylist and Isabella up the stairs, trying to focus on what happened next. One foot in front of the other—that was the way. One small step at a time until she was married and safe. Easy.

'So, what are we doing with your hair, then?' Sheila asked. 'Did you decide? I think all the styles we tried looked good on you, so really it's up to you.'

Thea tried and failed to remember what any of the practice styles had looked like. It had been days ago, before Zeke arrived. And everything before then was rapidly fading into a blur.

'I liked the curls,' Isabella said. 'With the front pinned up and the veil over the ringlets. It looked so dramatic with your dark hair. Don't you think, Thea?'

'Uh, sure. Sounds good.'

'Great!' Sheila said brightly, obviously used to brides almost comatose on their wedding day. Did everyone feel like this? Shell-shocked? Even if they hadn't been through the sort of drama Thea had in the last few days, did every bride have this moment of disbelief? This suspended reality?

Maybe it was just her.

Sheila started fussing with her hair and Thea sat back and let it happen, focussing on the feel of the strands as they were pinned, the warmth of the straighteners as the stylist used them to form ringlets. There was a strange calm in the room as Isabella flicked through a magazine and Sheila got to work, but still Thea had the feeling that she was being watched by her jailer as she was restrained.

Crazy. She'd shake her head to dispel the notion, but Sheila might burn her with the straighteners.

'Thea!'

The door burst open at the same time as Helena's shout came, and Sheila wisely stepped back before Thea spun round.

'What's happened?' Thea asked. Even Isabella closed her magazine for the moment.

'Zeke's leaving!'

Oh. That. 'I know.'

'He's supposed to be the best man!'

'Daniel's going to stand in, I think.'

'Right.' Helena leant back against the door. 'And… you're okay with this?'

'Helena,' Isabella said, putting her magazine aside and getting to her feet. 'Why don't we let your sister finish getting ready? Go and check on the centrepieces and the bouquets. Then you can come and have your hair done next. Okay?'

'Right. Sure.' Helena's brow crinkled as she looked at Thea. 'Unless you need me for…anything?'

Thea gave her a faint smile. 'I'm fine,' she lied. 'You'll come and help me get into my dress later, though, yeah?'

'Of course,' Helena promised as Isabella ushered her out of the door— presumably in case her little sister gave her the chance to reconsider her decision to marry Flynn.

Thea settled back into her chair, feeling comfortably numb and barely noticing that Isabella had left with Helena. It was almost time, and Zeke was almost gone.

There was nothing to reconsider.

Zeke had almost expected the knock at his door. Placing a roughly folded shirt on top of the clothes already in his case, he turned and called, 'Come in.'

His mother looked older, somehow, than she had since his return. Maybe it was just that she'd let the perma-smile drop for a moment.

'You're leaving me again, then?'

'Not just you,' Zeke pointed out, turning back to his wardrobe to retrieve the last of his shirts.

'I don't imagine you were planning on saying goodbye this time, either.'

Isabella moved to sit on the bed, to one side of his suitcase. The one place in the room he couldn't hope to ignore her.

'I wasn't sure you'd miss me any more this time than last,' he said, dropping another shirt into the case. 'What with the wedding to focus on. And I'm sure you have plans for marrying Helena off to someone convenient next.'

Picking up the shirt, Isabella smoothed out the creases as she folded it perfectly. 'I suppose I should be grateful that you're not staying to ruin Thea's wedding.'

Zeke stopped, turned, and stared. 'Thea's wedding? Not Flynn's?' He shook his head. 'You know, for years I never understood why you cared so much more about someone else's children than your own. I guess I thought it must be because they were girls, or because you felt sorry for them after their mother died. I can't believe it took me until now to realise it was because you thought they should have been yours.'

'I don't know what you're talking about,' Isabelle said, her gaze firmly fixed on the shirt. 'I loved all four of you equally. Even Flynn.'

'Ha! *That*, right there, shows me what a lie that is.' Grabbing the shirt from her, he shoved it into the case, making her look up at him. 'Why didn't you just leave, Mum? And marry Thomas? It can't have been for our sakes. We'd have been downright grateful!'

'My place is at my husband's side.' She folded her hands in her lap and met his eyes at last. 'Whatever else, I am his wife first and foremost.'

Zeke stared at her in amazement. 'You're wrong. You're *yourself* first.'

She gave him a sad smile. 'No, Zeke. That's just you.'

Zeke grabbed his case, tugging the zip roughly round it. He'd probably forgotten something, but he could live without it. He had his passport and his wallet. Everything else was replaceable. *Except Thea.*

'Do you even know how you made us feel all those years?' He wasn't coming back again. He could afford to tell her the truth. 'You let our father pit us against each other like it was a sport, and you ran off to another man's family whenever we weren't enough for you. For years I felt like an unwanted accident, every bit as much as Flynn felt like the outsider.'

'That's not…that's not how it was.'

'It's how it felt,' Zeke told her, pressing the truth home. 'And when I left… Thomas says that you missed me. That I broke your heart. But, Mum, how would I even know?'

'Of course I missed you. You're my son.'

'But you never thought to contact me. I wasn't hiding, Mum. I was right there if you needed me.'

'You made your feelings about our family very clear when you left.'

She still sounded so stiff, so unyielding. Zeke shook his head. Maybe her pride would always be too much for her to get over. Maybe his had been too, until now. But he'd already cut all ties with his father—could he really afford to do the same with his mother?

'I'm going now, Mum. And to be honest I'm not going to be coming back in a hurry. Maybe not ever. But if you mean it—about missing me—call me some time.' He lifted his carry-on bag onto his shoulder. 'Goodbye, Mum.'

But she was already looking away.

Outside his room, the corridors were cool and empty. He supposed most people would be in their rooms, getting ready for the wedding. A few were probably already down at the church, making sure they got a good seat for the wedding of the year. If he was quick he could grab one of the taxis milling about and be on his way to the airport before anyone even said 'I do'.

'Dad says that you're leaving.'

Zeke stopped at the top of the stairs at the sound of his brother's voice ahead of him. So close. And now he'd have to deal with all three family members in the space of an hour. At least it was the last time.

'Well, yeah,' he said, turning slowly and leaning his case against the wall. 'Not a lot of reason to stay now.'

'Is that truly the only reason you came back? For Thea?' Flynn asked. 'To try and win her back, I mean.'

'No. I thought…' With a sigh, Zeke jogged down a few steps to meet his brother in the middle of the staircase. 'I thought I'd moved on. From her, from the family, from everything. I came back to prove that to myself, I guess.'

'Did it work?'

Zeke smiled ruefully. 'Not entirely as planned, no. Turns out I was a little more tied in to things here than I thought.'

'And now?'

'Now I'm done,' Zeke said firmly. 'Ask our father.'

'I did.' Hitching his trousers, Flynn sat on the step, right in the middle of the stairs.

After a moment Zeke followed suit. 'I feel about five, sitting on the stairs,' he said.

Flynn laughed. 'We used to—do you remember? When

Mum and Dad had parties, when we were really little, we'd sneak out of bed and sit on the stairs, watching and listening.'

'I remember,' Zeke said. He must have been no more than four or five then. Had he known, or sensed, even then that he and Flynn were different? Or rather that their father believed they were?

'Dad told me your terms for selling This Minute to Morrison-Ashton.'

Zeke glanced up at his brother. 'All of them?'

Flynn ticked them off on his fingers. 'No role for you, Director of Digital Media for Thea, and…' Flynn caught Zeke's gaze and held it. 'CEO for me.'

'That's right.' Zeke dipped his head to avoid his brother's eyes.

'It was yours, you know,' Flynn said. 'I always knew that in the end Dad would give it to you. You're Ashton blood, after all.'

'I don't want it,' Zeke said. 'And you deserve it.'

'I'll do a better job at it, too.'

Zeke laughed. 'You will. I want to build things, then move on. You want to make things run smoothly. You're the best choice for it.'

'Was that the only reason?'

Zeke stared out over the hallway of the villa, all decked out in greenery and white flowers, with satin ribbons tied in bows to everything that stayed still long enough for the wedding planner to attack. 'No. I wanted to show Dad that his plan hadn't worked.'

'His plan? You mean, the way he always pitted us against each other?'

'Yeah. I wanted him to know that despite everything, all his best efforts, you were still my brother. Blood or not.'

Flynn stretched his legs out down the stairs and leant

back on his elbows. 'You know, that would sound a whole lot more sincere and meaningful if you hadn't slept with my fiancée last night.'

Zeke winced. 'Yeah, I guess so. Look, I'm…' He trailed off. He wasn't sorry—not really. He hadn't done it to hurt his brother, but he couldn't regret having one more night with Thea. 'That wasn't about you. It was about Thea and I saying goodbye to each other.'

'That's not what you wanted it to be, though, is it?'

'Maybe not.' Zeke shrugged. 'But it's the way it is. She wants a different life to the one I'm offering. And I need to live my life away from the bitterness this family brings out in me.'

'She told you that, huh?'

'Yeah.'

'So I guess I have her to thank for my promotion, really?'

'Hey! I played my part, too.'

'Let's just agree to call it quits, then, yeah?'

'Sounds like a plan.' Although Zeke had to think that all Flynn had got out of that deal was a company. He'd got to sleep with Thea. Clearly he was winning.

Except after today Flynn would get to sleep with Thea whenever he wanted. And Zeke would be alone.

Maybe Flynn was winning after all, even if he *did* have to deal with their parents and Morrison-Ashton for the rest of time.

'But, Zeke, after today… She's off-limits, yeah?'

'I know.' Zeke grabbed hold of the banister and pulled himself up. 'It's not going to be a problem. As soon as I'm packed I'll grab a cab to the airport and leave you guys to get on with your happy-ever-after.'

'You're not coming back?' Flynn asked.

Zeke shook his head. 'Not for a good while, at least. I

need to…I need to find something else to make my life about, you know?'

'Not really,' Flynn said with a half-smile. 'I've spent my whole life trying to get in to this family, while you've spent it trying to get out.'

'I guess so.' Zeke wondered how it would feel to finally get the one thing you'd always wanted. Maybe he'd never know. 'Something you and Thea have in common.'

Flynn tilted his head as he stared up at him. 'You really love her, don't you?'

Zeke shrugged, and stepped past his brother to climb the stairs to retrieve his suitcase. 'Love doesn't matter now.'

CHAPTER FOURTEEN

'Wow,' HELENA SAID as Thea stepped out from behind the screen. 'Maybe you should just walk down the aisle like that. I'm sure Flynn wouldn't complain. Or any of the male guests.'

Thea pulled a face at her sister in the mirror. She wasn't even sure she looked like herself. From the ringlets and veil, to the excess layers of make-up Sheila had assured her were necessary to 'last through the day'—despite the fact the wedding was at four in the afternoon—she looked like someone else. A bride, she supposed.

She let her gaze drop lower in the mirror, just long enough to take in the white satin basque that pushed her breasts up into realms they'd never seen before and the sheer white stockings that clipped onto the suspenders dangling from the basque. She looked like a stripper bride. She hoped Flynn would appreciate it.

Zeke would have.

Not thinking about that.

'Help me into the dress?' Thea said, turning away from the mirror. 'We're late already, and I think the wedding planner is about to have a heart attack. She's been calling from the church every five minutes to check where we are.'

Helena reached up to take the heavy ivory silk concoction from its hanger, then paused, biting her lip as she looked back at Thea.

'Don't, Helena,' Thea said, forestalling whatever objection her sister was about to raise. 'Just pass me the dress, yeah?'

Helena unhooked the dress and held it up for Thea to step into. Then, as Thea wriggled it over her hips, pulling it up over the basque, Helena said, 'Are you sure about this? I mean, really, *really* sure?'

Thea sighed. 'Trust me, Helena. You are not the only person to ask me that today. But I've made my decision. I'm marrying Flynn.'

'I'm glad to hear it.'

Thea spun around at the words, to see Flynn leaning against the doorframe.

'What are you *doing here*?' The last couple of words came out as a shriek, but Thea didn't care.

'I need to tell you something,' Flynn said, perfectly reasonably. 'It's important.'

'Not *now*!'

'You look beautiful, by the way,' Flynn added, as if that meant anything. The groom wasn't allowed to see the bride in her wedding dress before the wedding! It was terrible, *terrible* luck!

'Flynn, why don't you tell her what you came to tell her so she can stop freaking out?' Helena suggested. 'Plus, you should be down at the church already.'

Flynn nodded his agreement. 'Zeke has agreed to sell This Minute to Morrison-Ashton.'

Thea stopped trying to cover up her dress with her arms and stared at him. 'Seriously? *Why*?'

'Probably because someone convinced him he had to leave everything here behind and find his own path in life.'

'Ah,' Helena said, eyes wide. 'Thea, what—?'

'It doesn't matter.' Thea cut her off. 'Does that mean he's not taking the director job?'

'No. He insisted that Dad give that to you.'

Thea started to shake. Just a tremor in her hands and arms to start with, but she could feel it spreading.

'And he's made Dad agree to step down within the next year and pass the company to me,' Flynn finished. Even he looked a little shell shocked at that bit.

Thea dropped into the nearest chair as the tremors hit her knees. 'Why? Why would he do that?'

But she already knew. He'd given in. He'd given his father exactly what he wanted so he could walk away clear and free. Just as she'd told him he'd never be able to do.

'I think he wanted to make things right,' Flynn said, and Thea felt the first tear hit her cheek.

Zeke was free of them all at last. Even her. And she was being left behind again, still trying to prove she was good enough to belong. After today she'd be tied in for ever, never able to walk away.

Was she *jealous*?

'Thea? Are you okay?' Helena asked.

'*No!*' Thea sobbed, the word a violent burst of sound. 'I'm a mess. I'm a mistake.'

'That's not true,' Helena said soothingly, and Thea could see her giving Flynn looks of wide-eyed concern. 'What would make you think that?'

Thea gave a watery chuckle. 'Oh, I don't know. Maybe sleeping with the best man the night before my wedding? Perhaps having to have an intervention with my almost-mother-in-law about how it was better to have an affair than marry an inappropriate guy?'

Flynn swore at that, Thea was pleased to note.

'Or maybe sending away the guy I love so I can marry the guy I'm supposed to? And now, on top of everything else, Flynn's seen me in my wedding dress. That's not just like pearls! Everyone knows that's *absolute* bad luck! It's against all the rules!'

With another glance back at Flynn—who, Thea was frustrated to note, was still standing perfectly calmly in the doorway, with just a slight look of discomfort on his face—Helena knelt down beside her.

'Thea. I don't think this is about rules any more.'

'No. It's about me messing up again. I was so close to being happy here! And now I'm making a mess of everything.'

Helena shook her head. 'No, you're not. And today's not about family, or business, or any of the other things you seem to think this wedding should be about.'

Thea looked up at her sister. 'Then what *is* it about?'

'It's about love,' Helena said. 'It's about trusting your heart to know the right thing to do. And, since you're sitting here sobbing in a designer wedding dress, I think your heart is trying to tell you something.'

It couldn't, Thea wanted to say, because it had stopped. Her heart had stopped still in her chest the moment Zeke had walked out of the library that morning, so it couldn't tell her anything.

But her head could. And it was screaming at her right now that she was an idiot. She'd spent so long trying to find her place in the world, trying to force her way into a role that had never been right for her, she'd ignored the one place she truly belonged all along.

She looked up at Flynn, still so calm and serene and perfect—but not perfect for her.

'Go,' he said, a faint smile playing on his lips. 'You might still catch him.'

'But…but what about the wedding? Everyone's here, and our parents are waiting, and—'

'We'll take care of it,' Helena promised, glancing over at Flynn.

Was there something in that look? Had Isabella been right? Thea couldn't be sure.

'Won't we?'

'We will,' Flynn agreed. 'All you have to do now is run.'

Somewhere in the villa a door slammed, and Thea knew it had to be Zeke, leaving her again. But this time she was going with him.

Shoving the heavy wedding dress back down over her hips, Thea stepped out of it and dashed for the door, pausing only for a second to kiss Flynn lightly on the cheek. 'Thanks,' she said.

And then she ran.

Zeke shut the front door to the villa behind him and walked out into the late-afternoon Tuscan sun. Everyone must have already headed down to the little chapel at the bottom of the hill, ready for the wedding. His talk with Flynn had delayed him, and now there were no taxis hanging around. He might be able to find one down at the church, but he didn't want to get that close to the main event. Not with Thea due to make her grand entrance any time now. The wedding planner's schedule had her down there already, he remembered, unless they were running late.

No, he'd call for a cab and sit out here in the sunshine while he waited. One last glimpse of his old life before he started his new one.

Phone call made, he settled onto the terrace, sitting on the edge of the warm stone steps rather than the swing seat round at the side. Too many memories. Besides, he wouldn't see the cab arrive.

He heard a car in the distance and stood, hefting his carry-on bag onto his shoulder and tugging up the pull-along handle of his case. No car appeared, though, and he started to think it must have been another guest heading for the chapel. But he made his way down the driveway anyway, just in case.

'Zeke!'

Behind him the door to the villa flew open, and by the time he could turn Thea was halfway down the stairs and racing down the drive towards him.

He blinked in disbelief as she got closer, sunlight glowing behind her, making the white of her outfit shine.

White. But not her wedding dress.

'Isn't this where I came in?' he asked, waving a hand towards her to indicate the rather skimpy lingerie that was doing wonderful things for her heaving cleavage as she tried to get her breath back.

'Don't,' she said, scowling.

'Don't what?' Zeke asked. 'You're the one chasing me in your underwear. Five more minutes and my cab would have been here and I'd have been out of your life, just as you wanted.'

'Don't joke. Don't mock. I need you to…' She took a deep breath. 'I need you to stop being…you know…*you* for a moment. Because I need to tell you something.'

'What?' Zeke dropped his bag to the ground again. Apparently this was going to take a while.

'I don't want you out of my life.'

Zeke's breath caught in his chest—until he realised what she was *actually* saying. 'Thea, I can't. I can't just stick around and be Uncle Zeke for Christmas and birthdays. You were right; I need a fresh start. A clean break. Besides…' *I can't watch you live happily ever after with my brother when I'm totally in love with you myself.*

But Thea was shaking her head. 'That's not what I mean.'

'Then *what*, Thea?' Zeke asked, exasperated. He'd so

nearly been done. So nearly broken free for good. And here he was, having this ridiculous conversation with Thea in her underwear, when she was supposed to be getting married *right now*.

Unless…

'I've spent all day listening to people tell me what I should do. What's best for me. Where my place is. And I'm done. You were right—but don't let it go to your head. I need to make my own decisions. So I'm making one right now. I'm choosing my home, my place in the world. And it's the only choice that's going to matter ever again.'

She stepped closer, and Zeke's hands itched to take hold of her, to pull her close. But this was her decision, and she had to make it all on her own. And he had to let her.

'I'm choosing you,' she whispered, so close that he could feel the words against his lips. 'For better or worse, for mistake or for happily-ever-after, for ever and ever.'

Zeke stared into her soft blue eyes and saw no doubt hiding there. No uncertainty, no fear. She meant this.

'You're sure,' he said, but it wasn't a question. He knew.

'I'm certain. I love you. More than anything.'

Thea's hands wrapped around him to run up his back, and the feel of her through his shirt made him warmer.

'I should have known it sooner. *You're* my place. *You're* where I belong.'

'I can't stay here, Thea,' he said. 'Maybe we can come back, but I need some time away. I'm done obsessing about the past. It's time to start my own life.'

'I know.' Thea smiled. 'I'm the one who told you that, remember?'

'I remember.' Unable to resist any longer, Zeke dipped his head and kissed her, long and sweet and perfect. 'I love you. I thought when I came back that I was looking for the girl I'd known—the one I loved as a boy. But I couldn't have imagined the woman you'd become, Thea. Or how much more I'd love you now.'

Thea buried her laugh in his chest. 'I'm the same. I thought it would kill me, saying goodbye to you last time. But the thought of living the rest of my life without you...' She shook her head and reached up to kiss him again.

'Unacceptable.' Zeke finished the thought for her. And then he asked the question that had echoed through his mind for eight long years, hoping he'd get a different answer this time. 'Will you come with me?'

Thea smiled up at him and said, 'Always.'

And Zeke knew, at last, that it didn't matter where they went, or who led and who followed. They'd always be together, and that was all he needed.

* * * * *

RAPUNZEL IN NEW YORK

NIKKI LOGAN

To Carol and Marlon: I hope my Viktoria is
the kind of woman you'd have wanted
yours to grow into

CHAPTER ONE

"YOU'D better get up here, Nathan. There's a woman about to jump from your building."

Two sentences.

That's all it took to tear Nathan Archer away from his Columbus Circle office and send him racing uptown. Ironic that the A-line was quicker than a cab or even his driver could get him up to Morningside, but the subway spilled him out just one block from the West 126th Street building he'd grown up in. Grown old in. Well before his time.

He pushed through the gathered throng, shaking his head at the impatient crowd. Was there a whole population of people who hovered in alleys and bars just waiting for some poor individual to be nudged too far in life? To climb out onto a bridge or a rooftop?

Or a ledge.

He followed their collective gaze upward. Sure enough, there she was. Not exactly preparing for a swan dive; more crouched than standing. She looked young, though it was hard to tell from this distance.

She was staring at the sky with an intensity strong enough to render her completely oblivious to the crowd gathering below. He lifted his eyes to the popcorn clouds. Was she praying? Or was she just in her own tormented world?

"The crisis team is mobilizing," a nearby cop said, turning back to stare uselessly up to the tenth floor. "ETA twenty minutes."

Twenty minutes? She'd already been out there at least the quarter hour it had taken him to get uptown. The chances of her lasting another twenty?

Not high.

He glanced around at the many spectators who were doing exactly nothing to rectify the situation and swallowed a groan. There was a reason he was more of a behind-the-scenes kind of guy. Behind the scenes had served him well his whole life. You got a lot done when you weren't wasting time as the center of attention. He paid people to do the limelight thing.

Unfortunately, none of them were here.

He was.

Nathan looked back up at the looming building and the woman perched precariously on it. Hadn't these old walls contained enough misery?

He muttered a curse and his legs started moving. Had nobody thought of doing this sooner? He pushed past a gaggle of onlookers and headed toward the building, counting windows as he went. It took him three minutes to get into his own building and up to the eighth floor, and he passed three residents on the stairs up to the tenth—they had no clue about the drama unfolding in their own building. If they saw it on the news tonight they'd be kicking themselves they missed it. Not that it was making the news tonight, or any night while he still breathed. His development didn't need the bad press. He hadn't worked on it all this time only to have it turned upside down by a woman with a blown psychiatric fuse.

Nate burst through the stairwell door and turned left, counting the windows he knew to be on the outside of the building. *Nine...ten...eleven...*On twelve, he paused for only a second before delivering a strategic kick right at the weak point in the door of apartment 10B. As fragile as the rest of the century old building, it exploded inwards in a shower of splinters.

Inside, the apartment was neat and carefully decorated but

small enough that he was able to check all the five rooms in less than thirty seconds, even with a limp from the jar that had just about snapped his ankle. Three rooms had outside windows that were sealed tight—safety measures. But, apparently back at the turn of the twentieth century some architect had considered that only grown men needed to be saved from themselves, because every apartment had one more window—small and awkwardly positioned above the toilet cistern, but just big enough for a slight woman to wiggle through. Or a young boy.

He knew that from experience.

This one stood wide open, its tasteful lemon curtains blowing gently in the breeze, providing access onto 10B's sheltered ledge.

Nathan's heart hammered from way more than the urgent sprint up two flights of stairs. He took a deep, tense breath, climbed onto the closed lid of the toilet and peered out the window, sickeningly prepared to find nothing but pigeon droppings and a swirl of air where a woman had just been.

But she was still out there, her back to him as she stretched out on the ledge on all fours, giving him a great view of her denim-clad behind…

…and the tangle of ropes and rigging that fixed her more than securely to the ledge.

Frustrated fury bubbled up deep inside. Of all the stupid-ass, time-wasting stunts… He boosted himself up and half through the window and barked to her butt, "Honey, you'd better be planning to jump, or I'm going to throw you off here myself."

Viktoria Morfitt spun so fast she nearly lost her careful balance on the ledge. Her reflexes were dulled through lack of use, but her muscle memory was still entirely intact, and it choreographed her muscles now to brace her more securely on the narrow stone shelf. Adrenaline pulsed through her bloodstream and her lungs sucked in an ache of cold air and then expelled it on a ripe curse as she spotted the man wedged in her bathroom window glaring at her like a maniac. His voice had drawn her attention, but his words whooshed away on the relentless New York sounds coming up from Morningside's streets.

What the—? She shuffled backward as far as the ledge allowed and knocked against the peregrine nest box she'd just been installing.

The stranger lurched farther forward, half hanging out the window, enormous hands stretched out toward her, and spoke more clearly. More slowly. "Easy, honey. Just a joke. How about you come back inside now?"

She wasn't fooled by those treacle tones for one moment. Or the intense eyes. Bad guys never turned up at your doorstep badly scarred, carrying violin cases and talking like Robert deNiro. They turned up like this: nice shirt, open collar, careless hair and designer stubble. Big, well-manicured hands. Good-looking. Exactly the sort of guy you'd think was okay to let inside your apartment.

Except that he'd already let himself in.

For one crazy second Tori considered leaping off the ledge. Her intruder could help himself to her stuff—whatever he wanted—and she could lower herself down to Barney's ledge. He'd be home for sure and his bathroom window was perpetually open so he could smoke out of it. Her hand slipped to the titanium fixings at her pelvis. Her rigging would hold. It always did.

A sharp pain gnawed deep and low. *Almost always.*

She raised her voice instead, hoping to alert a neighbour. "How about you get the heck out of my apartment!" Tension thumped out of her in waves that translated into quavers in her voice. Could he tell?

He reached forward again. "Look—"

Tori slid hard up against the corner of the building, clambering around the nest box. Dammit, any farther and she'd knock it off the ledge and have to start all over again. Well, that and possibly kill someone walking below...

She glanced easily over the ledge and met the intense stares of thirty or so passersby and a couple of NYPD officers. "Hey!"

she yelled down to the cops. "Get up here! There's a burglar in my apartment—10B!"

The stranger surged through the window and made a grab for her foot. She kicked it away, then stole a moment to glance back down. Two of the cops were running towards her building.

Heat poured off the contemptuous look he shot at her. "You know what? I have a meeting to get back to. So either go ahead and jump or get the hell back in here." With that, he disappeared back into her apartment.

Jump? She glanced back down at the crowd below, their expectant faces all peering up. *At her.*

Oh…no!

Heat surged up her throat. Someone must have called her in as a jumper when she was out on the ledge. *He* thought she was a jumper. But while most of them stood below waiting for the aerial show, only one had had the nerve to race up here and actually try to help her.

He deserved points for that.

"Wait!"

She scrabbled toward the now-vacant window and crouched to look inside. He was taller than he looked when he was squashed through her tiny window—broader, too—and he completely filled the doorway to her bathroom. Self-preservation made her pause. Him being good-looking didn't change the fact he was a stranger. And she wasn't much on strangers.

Tori peered in at him. "I'll come in when you're not there."

He rolled his eyes, then found hers again. "Fine. I'll be in the hall."

Then he was gone.

She swiveled on her bottom and slid her legs quickly through the tiny window, stretching down until her feet hit the toilet lid. Then she unclipped her brace-line with the ease of years of practice, clenched her abs, and brought her torso through in a twist that would have been right at home in Cirque du Soleil.

As good as his word, he'd moved out into the very public hallway. But between them lay a forest of timber shards.

"You kicked in my *door*?" She hit a pitch she usually heard only from the peregrine falcons that circled her building looking for somewhere to raise their chicks.

A frustrated breath shot from between his thin lips. "Apologies for assuming you were about to die."

He didn't look the slightest bit apologetic, but he did look stunningly well-dressed and gorgeous, despite the aloof arch of his eyebrows. Just then two uniformed officers exploded through the fire-escape doors and bolted toward them.

"He kicked in my door!" Tori repeated for their benefit.

Taller than either of the cops, he turned toward them easily, unconcerned. "Officers—"

They hit him like a subway car, slamming his considerable bulk up against the wall and forcing him into a frisk position. He winced at the discomfort and then squeezed his head sideways so that he could glare straight into her flared eyes.

Guilt gnawed wildly. He hadn't actually hurt her. Or even tried to.

He simmered while they roughly frisked him up and down, relieving him of his phone and wallet and tossing them roughly to the ground. He stared at her the whole time, as though this was her fault and not his. But that molten gaze was even more unsettling close up and so she bent to retrieve his property and busied herself dusting them carefully off while the police pressed his face to the wall.

"What are you doing here?" one asked.

"Same thing you are. Checking on a jumper."

"That's our job, sir," the second cop volunteered as he finished searching the stranger's pockets.

The man looked back over his shoulder at the first officer, his hands still carefully pressed out to both sides. "Didn't look like it was going to happen before nightfall."

"Protocols," the first cop muttered tightly, a flush rushing up his thick neck.

They shoved him back into the wall for good measure and Tori winced on his behalf. Okay, this had gone far enough.

"Are you responsible for this?" The taller cop spoke before she could, leaning around to have a good look at the gaping entrance to her apartment where the door hung from just one ancient, struggling hinge. "This is damage to private property."

"Actually I think you'll find it's my property," the man gritted out.

All three faces swiveled back to him. "Excuse me?" the taller cop asked.

The man slowly turned, his hands still in clear view. "My name is Nathan Archer. I own this building." He nodded at the wallet that Tori still held. "My identification's in there."

All sympathy for him vanished between breaths. *"You're* our landlord?" She held his property out numbly.

One of the officers pulled the man's driver's license from the wallet and confirmed his identification. "This confirms your name but not your ownership of this building."

He looked at Tori. "Who do you pay rent to?"

A money-hungry, capitalist corporate shark. Tori narrowed her eyes. "Sanmore Holdings."

The stranger looked back at the cop holding his wallet. "Back compartment."

The cop pulled out a crisp white business card. "Nathan Archer, Chief Executive, Sanmore Holdings."

The cops immediately eased their hold on him and he straightened.

Nathan Archer. The man responsible for the state of her building. Probably living below fifty-ninth himself, and way too busy and important to worry about elevators not working or torn carpet under their feet. She played the only card she had left and pleaded to the rapidly-losing-interest police.

"It's still my door. I must have rights?"

The second cop looked her over lazily while his partner answered for him. "I guess you could get him for trespass."

Archer immediately transferred the full force of his glare

onto the second officer. Insanely, Tori missed the searing ma-
levolence the moment it left her.

"Yes! Trespass. I didn't invite him in." She smiled trium-
phantly at her landlord for good measure.

That brought his eyes back to hers and her chest tightened
up fractionally.

"I was saving your life."

She shoved her hands on her hips and stood her ground. "My
life was just fine, thank you. I was fully rigged up."

"Not obvious from the street. Or from this side of the *locked*
door," he added pointedly, his blue, blue eyes simmering but no
longer furious. Not exactly. They flicked, lightning-fast, from
her head to her toes and back again, and the simmer morphed
into something a lot closer to interest—*sexual* interest. Breath
clogged her throat as he blazed his intensity in her direction,
every bit as naturally forceful as Niagara Falls.

In that moment the two cops ceased to exist.

It didn't help that a perky inner voice kept whispering over
her shoulder, seducing her with reason, weaving amongst the
subtle waves of his expensive scent and reminding her that he
had been trying to help. She didn't want to be seduced by any
part of this man. At all.

She wanted to be mad at him.

She straightened to her full height, shook off her conscience
and spoke slowly, in case one of those thumps his head had
taken at the hands of the local constabulary had dented his
greedy, corporate brain. "You broke my door!"

"I'll buy you a new door," he said, calm and completely
infuriating.

The police officers looked between them, bemused.

Tori glared up at him. "While you're buying stuff, how about
a new washer for the ancient laundry? Or a door buzzer that
works so we can quit calling messages up the stairwell."

The heat in his gaze swirled around her. He straightened and
narrowed his eyes. "Nothing in this building is below code."

"Nothing in this building is particularly above it, either.

You do just enough to make sure you meet the tenancy act. We have heat and water and electrics that aren't falling out of the ceiling, but that's about it. The elevator doesn't even go all the way to the top floor."

"It never has."

"So that's a good enough reason not to fix it now? The woman in 12C is eighty years old. She shouldn't be hiking it up four flights of stairs. And the fire code—"

His eyes glittered. "The fire code specifies that you use the stairs in an emergency. They work fine. I know because I just ran up them to save your life!"

She stepped closer, her chest heaving and dragged her eyes off his lips. This close she could practically feel the furnace of his anger. "Not if you're an octogenarian!"

"Then she should take an apartment on one of the lower floors."

Tall as he was, he had to lean down toward her to get in her face. It caused a riot in her pulse. She lifted her chin and leaned toward him. "Those apartments are full of *other* old people—"

The shorter cop growled behind them. "Would you two like some privacy? Or maybe a room?"

Tori snapped around to look at the cop and then back to the man in front of her. Sure enough, she was standing dangerously close to Nathan Archer and the hallway fairly sparkled with the live current swirling around the two of them.

"I have a room," she grumbled to the officer, though her eyes stayed on the tallest man in the hallway. "I just don't have a door."

Archer's deep voice rumbled through tight lips. A rich man's lips. Though she did wonder what they would look like if he smiled.

"I'll have that fixed by dinnertime."

Too bad if she wanted to take a nap or...relax...or something before then! "So you do have a maintenance team at your disposal. You wouldn't know it from the general condition of the building—"

"There you go," one officer cut in loudly. "Complete restitution. I think we're done here."

She spun back to him. "We're not done. What about the trespass?" The officer looked apologetically at Archer.

Oh, please... "Seriously? One waft of a fancy business card and now the rich guy is calling the shots?"

All three of them looked at her as if she was mad. Pretty much where she imagined they'd started an hour ago, back when she was up the ledge. "I want him charged with trespass. He entered my apartment without my permission."

Archer tried again. "Come on. I was trying to save your life."

She tossed her hair back. "Tell that to the judge."

"I guess I'll have to."

One officer reluctantly took her details while the other spoke quietly to Archer a few meters down the hall. He smiled while the cop shook his head and chuckled.

She wedged her hands to her hips again and spoke loudly. "When you're completely done with the testosterone bonding..."

Her cop took a deep breath and turned to the taller man. "You have the right to remain silent. Anything you say..."

As the Miranda unfolded, Tori handed Archer his cell phone and tried hard not to meet his eyes. She had a way of losing focus when she did that. But her fingers touched his as he wrapped them around his BlackBerry and she flinched away from the intimate brush of skin on skin.

Her pulse stumbled.

"...if you cannot afford an attorney..."

As if. He probably surrounded himself with attorneys. His fine white business shirt looked like it cost more than he spent on this building in a year.

The cops walked Archer back toward the stairs, finishing up their legal responsibilities. At some point someone decided handcuffs were overkill—*shame*—but Archer limped obediently between them anyway, speaking quietly into his phone and only half listening as his rights were fully enumerated.

As the cops sandwiched him through the door to the stairwell, he glanced back at her, a lock of dark hair falling across his forehead between those Hollywood eyes. He didn't look the slightest bit disturbed by the threat of legal action. For some reason, that only made her madder.

How often did this guy get arrested?

"Better save that single phone call they'll give you in lockup," she yelled down the hall to them. "You're going to need it to call someone about my door!"

CHAPTER TWO

"Your Honor—"

"Save it, Mr. Archer," the judge said, "I've made my ruling. I recognise that you meant well in going to the assistance of the plaintiff, however, the fact remains that you broke into her apartment and did material damage to her door and lock—"

"Which I fixed..."

The judge raised one hand and silenced him. "And that even though it was technically your own property, Ms Morfitt is afforded some protection under New York's Tenancy Protection Act, which makes her suit of trespass reasonable."

"If petty," Nate murmured. His attorney, business partner and best friend, Dean, counseled him to hold his tongue. Probably just as well or he'd end up behind bars for contempt. This whole thing was a ridiculous waste of his time—time that could have been better spent at his desk earning a bunch of zeroes for his company. All over a broken door that had been fixed the same day. If all his building's tenants were from the same planet as Viktoria Morfitt he'd be happy to see the back of them when he developed the site.

"I was trying to help her," he said flatly, for the hundredth time. No one but him seemed to care.

"Your file indicates that you specialize in Information Technology, is that correct?" the judge asked. She said that as though he was some kind of help-desk operator instead of the founder of one of the most successful young IT companies on the east coast.

Dean spoke just as Nate was about to educate her. "That is correct, Your Honor."

The judge didn't take her eyes off Nate's. Thinking. Plotting. "I'm going to commute your sentence, Mr. Archer, so that it doesn't haunt your record for the rest of your life. One hundred hours of community service to be undertaken within thirty days."

"Community service? Do you know what one hundred hours of my time *costs*?"

Dean swooped in to stop him saying more. "My client would be willing to pay financial compensation in lieu, Your Honor."

Willing was a stretch but he'd go with it.

The judge looked at Nate archly, and he stared solidly back at her. Then she dragged her eyes to his left. "No doubt, Counselor, but that's not on the table. The purpose of a service order is to give the defendant time to reflect. To learn. Not to make it all go away with the sweep of their assistant's pen." Nate could practically feel the order doubling in length. Or severity. She made some notes on the documentation in front of her, eyes narrowed. "Mr. Archer, I'm going to recommend you undertake your service on behalf of the plaintiff."

His stomach lurched. *Note to self: never upset a district judge.* "Are you serious?"

"Nate—" Dean just about choked in his haste to silence him, but then changed tack as the judge leaned as far forward as she could possibly go without tumbling from her lofty perch. "Thank you, Your Honor. We'll see that it happens."

But Nate spread his hands wide and tried one more time. "I was trying to help her, judge."

Dean's hand slid onto his forearm and gripped it hard. The judge's lips drew even tighter. "Which is why it's not a two-hundred-hour order, Mr. Archer. Counselor, please explain to your client that this is a judicial sentence, not a Wall Street negotiation."

Nate ignored that. "But what will I do for her?"

"Help her with her laundry? I really don't care. My order is set." She eyed the man by Nate's side. "Is that clear, Counselor?"

"It is, Your Honor, thank you." Dean whispered furiously in Nate's ear that a commuted service order was as good as invisible on his record.

"Easy for you to say," Nate growled. "That's not one hundred hours of *your* executive time." Spent in a building he preferred not to even think about.

The judge with super hearing lifted one arch brow. "I think you'll find that my time is just as valuable as yours, Mr. Archer, and you've taken up quite enough of it. Next!"

The gavel came down on any hope of someone seeing reason in all this lunacy.

Ten minutes later it was all over; Nate and Dean trod down the marble stairs of the justice building and shook hands. From an attorney's perspective it was a good outcome, but the idea of not only spending time in that building—with *her*...

Viktoria Morfitt's suit for trespass was ridiculous and everyone knew it. The cops. The judge. Even the woman herself, judging by the delicate little lines that had formed between her brows as the cops had escorted him from his own building.

But he'd spooked her out on the ledge and then made the tactical error of letting her know he was her landlord. If he'd kept his trap shut she probably would have let him off with the promise of restitution for the door. But no...He'd played the rare *do-you-know-who-I-am?* card, and she'd taken her first opportunity to let him know exactly what she thought about his building management.

Not very much.

And now he had a hundred hours of community service to think about how he might have done things differently.

"There's a morning we'll never get back," Dean grumbled

comfortably. "But don't worry about it, I'll get appeal paper-work straight off. Though you might have to do a few hours before that gets processed."

"When am I supposed to start this farce?"

"The judge's decree will be lodged after two-thirty today, but, reasonably, tomorrow will be fine. That'll give the public defender time to alert your jumper to the order."

"I'm sure she'll be thrilled."

"I'm sure she won't," his friend said, turning and trotting down the steps with a chuckle. "But the Archer charm hasn't failed you yet."

The fact that was true didn't really make things any better. One hundred hours with a human porcupine in a building he could barely stomach.

Great.

Tori filled her lungs behind her brand-new door and composed herself. The judge must have been having a badly hormonal day to task someone like Nathan Archer with community service. Either that or his smug confidence had got up Her Honor's nose as much as it had irritated *her* last week. Not hard to imagine.

Now or never... She pulled the door nice and wide and made a show of leaning on it. Showcasing it. "Mr. Archer."

The breath closest to her lips froze in its tracks at the sight of him filling her doorway and all her other breaths jammed up behind it in an oxygen pile-up.

Fortunately, he didn't notice as his blue eyes examined the door critically. "Could they have found anything less suitable?"

She looked at the modern, perfect door which was so out of place in a 1901 building. "I assumed you picked it specifically. But it locks, so I'm happy."

She'd forgotten how those eyes *really* felt when they rested on her. Like twin embers from a fire alighting on her skin.

Warm at first touch, but smoldering to an uncomfortable burn the longer they lingered.

"Well, one of us is, at least," he mumbled.

She couldn't stop the irritated sigh that escaped her. "I didn't ask for this community service, Mr. Archer. I'm no more thrilled than you are." The last thing she wanted was to be forced into the company of such a disagreeable stranger, with the uncomfortable responsibility of tasking him with chores.

Silence fell, and the only sound to interrupt it was 10A's television blaring out late afternoon *Sesame Street*.

He stared at her until finally saying, "May I come in?"

Heat broiled just below her collar. Leaving him standing in the hall... She stood back and let all six-foot-three of him into her home. "So how does this work?"

He shrugged those massive shoulders. "Search me, this is my first offence."

Tori winced, knowing that—truthfully—he'd done nothing more than try to help her. But one hundred hours was a small price to pay for how he'd neglected the building they both stood in. "Hey, service orders are the latest celebrity accessory. You can't buy that kind of street cred."

He turned and shot her a dark look from under perfectly manicured brows. Every glare he used was a glare wasted. She really didn't care whether or not he was happy. He was only her landlord.

She took his coat and turned to hang it on the back of her front door before remembering her new one didn't have a hook. She detoured via the sofa to drape it over the back. The contrast between the expensive fabric of his coat and the aged upholstery of her sofa couldn't have been more marked.

"Something's been bothering me," he said, turning those blue eyes on her. "About last week."

Only one thing? Quite a lot had been bothering her about it. Her reaction to his closeness not the least.

"What were you doing out on that ledge?" he continued.

"Not jumping."

"So I gathered."

She stared at him and then crossed to the large photo album on the coffee table. She spun it in his direction and flipped it open. "These are Wilma and Fred."

He leaned down to look at the range of photographs artfully displayed on the page. "Hawks?"

"Peregrine falcons. They live wild in this area."

Deep blue eyes lifted to hers. "And...?"

"And I was installing a nest box for them."

He blinked at her. "Out on the ledge?"

She clenched her teeth to avoid rolling her eyes. "I tried it in here, but it just didn't do as well." *Idiot.*

Archer grunted and Tori's arms stole round her midsection while he flicked through the various images in her album.

"These are good," he finally said. "Who took them?"

"I did."

His head came up. "Where from?"

She pulled back the breezy curtain from her living-room window to reveal spotless glass. "There's another window in the bedroom. Sometimes I use the roof. Mostly the ledge."

"So that wasn't your first dangerous foray out there?"

"It's not dangerous. I'm tethered at all times."

He lifted aristocratic eyebrows. "To a century-old building?"

A century-old building that's crumbling around you. He might as well have said it. It was perfectly evident to anyone who cared to look. The neglect wouldn't fly in Morningside proper, but being right on the border of West Harlem, he was getting away with it. Of course he was. Money talked around here.

"I pick the strongest point I can to fix to," she said.

He looked at the pictures again. "You must have some great equipment."

She shrugged. Let him believe that it was the camera that took the photo, not the person behind it. "I've always enjoyed wildlife photography." More than just enjoyed. She'd been on track to make a career out of it back when she'd graduated.

He reached the back pages of the album. "These ones weren't taken out your window." He flipped it her way and her heart gave a little lurch. An aerie with a stunning mountain vista stretching out in all directions behind it. An eagle in flight, its full wings spread three meters wide. Both taken from high points.

Really, *really* high points.

"I took those in the Appalachians and Cascades," she said, tightly, but then she forced the topic back to her city peregrines before he could ask any more questions. As far as she knew, this court order didn't come with the requirement for full disclosure about her past.

"Fred and Wilma turned up in our skies about three months ago, and then about four weeks ago they started visiting this building more and more. I made them a nest box for the coming breeding season so they don't have to perch precariously on a transformer or bridge or something."

So she could have a little bit of her old life here in her new one.

"Hawks…" He closed the album carefully and placed it gently back on the coffee table. Then he stood there not saying a word. Just thinking.

"So…" She cleared her throat. "Should we talk about how this is going to work? What you can do here for one hundred hours?"

His eyes bored into her and triggered a temperature spike. "I sense you've been giving it some thought?"

She crossed to the kitchen and took up the sheet of notepaper she'd prepared. "I made a list."

His lips twisted. "Really—of what?"

"Of all the things wrong with the building. Things that you can fix in one hundred hours."

The laundry. The elevator. The floors. The buzzer…

His eyebrows rose as he read down the page. "Long list."

"It's a bad building."

His long lashes practically obscured his eyes, they narrowed so far. "So why do you live here?"

Her stomach shriveled into a prune under his scrutiny. "Because I can afford it. Because it's close to the parks." Not that she'd visited those in a long time. But it was why she'd chosen this building originally.

He continued reading the list. "Just one problem."

"Why did I know there'd be a 'just'?"

He ignored her. "The judge's decree is firm on me not out-sourcing any of this service. It has to be by my own hand. Most of this list calls for tradesmen."

She stared at him. "It hadn't occurred to me that you'd actually follow the order. You struck me as a corner-cutter."

"Not at all."

She matched his glare. "The front-door buzzer's still faulty."

"That's not about cutting corners—*or costs*," he said just as she was about to accuse him of precisely that.

"What is it, then?"

He folded his arms across his chest, highlighting its vast breadth. "It's asset strategy."

Her snort was unladylike in the extreme. "Is your strategy to let the building and everyone in it crumble to dust? If so, then you're right on target."

Was that the tiniest hint of color at his collar? He laid the list down on the table. "I've accepted the terms of the order. I'll see it through. My way."

"So what can you do? What *do* you do?"

His grunt was immediate. "I do a lot of paperwork. I sign things. Spend money."

"Just not here."

He ignored that. "I'm in the information industry."

Tori threw her hands up. "Well, what's that going to be useful for?"

It took the flare of his pupils to remind her how offensive

he might find that. And then she wondered why she cared all about offending him. "I mean, here…in my apartment."

"Actually, I have an idea. It relates to your birds."

"The falcons?"

"Urban raptors are a big deal on Manhattan. There are a number of webcams set up across the city, beaming out live images to the rest of the world. Kind of a virtual ecotourism. For those who are interested."

The way he said it made it perfectly clear of how little interest they were to him.

"I guess. I was just doing it for me." And in some ways she'd enjoyed keeping the peregrine falcon pair a special thing. A private thing. Which was probably selfish. The whole world should be able to see the beauty of nature. Wasn't that what her photography was all about? "A webcam, you think?"

"And a website. One's pointless without the other."

Flutters fizzed up inside her like champagne and the strangeness of it only made her realize how long it had been since something had really excited her. A website full of her images, full of her beautiful birds. For everyone to see. She knew about the other falcon locations in New York but hadn't thought for a moment she might ever be able to do something similar in Morningside.

"You can design a website?"

His expression darkened. "Sanmore's mailboy can design a simple website. As can half the fifth graders on Manhattan. It's no big deal."

Not for him, maybe. She turned her mind to the ledge. "I guess it wouldn't be too hard to set a camera up on the ledge, focused on the nest box. If anything of interest happens, it'll probably happen there."

"How can you be sure they'll use the box?" he asked.

"I can't. But I'm encouraging them down every day. So I'm optimistic."

His eyes narrowed. "Encouraging?"

Might as well tell it as it was. "Luring. They're usually

pigeon eaters, but mice are easier to trap. This building has no shortage."

His lips thinned. "All buildings have vermin."

Her laugh was raw. "Not this many."

He stared at her, considering. "Excuse me a moment." Then he stepped into her small kitchen and spoke in quiet tones into the cell phone she'd held for him the week before. When he returned, his expression was impassive. "You may need to find a new source of bird bait."

She frowned. "What did you just do?"

"I took care of the vermin problem."

"With one phone call?"

"I have good staff."

One phone call. It could have been solved so long before this. "Good staff but not residential agents, I'd say. We've been reporting the mice for eighteen months."

He thought about that. "I trust our agent to take care of code issues."

"This is the same agent you trusted with my door selection?"

His eyes shifted back to the hideously inappropriate door and she felt a mini rush of satisfaction that she'd finally scored a point. But snarking at him wasn't going to be a fun way to spend the next hundred hours. And as much as she'd like to make him suffer just a little bit for the torn carpet and clunky pipes and glacially slow elevator, she had to endure it, too. And she had a feeling he would give as good as he got.

"Anyway," she said. "I'm sure raw meat will suffice in the unlikely event I run out of fresh food."

"Then what? They'll just…come?"

She slid her hands onto her hips. "Is this interest? Or are you just being polite?"

His left eye twitched slightly. "I have a court order that says I should be interested, Ms. Morfitt. No offense."

She arched a single eyebrow. People like him had no idea how offensive their very existence was to people like her. To every tenant who scraped together the rent to live in his shabby building. To the people who went without every day so he could have another sportscar in his parking space.

Her birds had no way of making him money; therefore, they didn't rate for Nathan Archer.

"None taken." She wouldn't give him the satisfaction. "I'm planning on moving the mice to the nest box tomorrow, to see how the falcons respond to it."

"Might as well get the camera set up and operating straight-away, then," he said.

"You're assuming I've agreed?"

"Haven't you? Your eyes twinkled like the Manhattan sky-line when I suggested it."

It burned her that he could read her so easily. And it bothered her that he was paying that much attention to what her eyes were doing. Bothered and…something else. Her chest pressed in tighter.

She shook the rogue thought loose. "Can we use something small and unobtrusive? I don't want to scare them away just as they're starting to come close. It took me weeks to get them accustomed to visiting the ledge, and any day now they'll need to start laying."

He moved to the window and looked out, examining the wall material. "I can probably core out one of the stone blocks in the basement and fit the camera into it. They'll barely know it's there."

She smiled. "There you go, then. You're not totally without practical skills."

He opened his mouth to argue, but then seemed to think better of it. "I'll need your bathroom."

She flinched. That seemed a stupidly unsettling and intimate request—not that the dictatorial words in any way resembled a request. The man was going to be here for one hundred hours—of course he was going to need the facilities at some point.

She stepped back from the doorway. "You know the way."

One brow twitched. "You're not coming?"

Both her own shot upward. "Uh...no, you'll have to manage by yourself." Who knew, maybe the man had assistants for that, too.

"You're going to play hardball on this court order, aren't you? Well, don't come crying to me if I pull out something I shouldn't."

What? Tori frowned after his retreating figure. Then, as she heard the exaggerated *ziiip,* her frown doubled and she muttered, "What, Mr. Corporate America isn't a door-closer?"

Seconds later she heard another metallic *ziiip* and she realized her mistake. Heat flared up her throat. The man wasn't peeing. He was measuring—with a steel tape measure. Probably the ledge window.

Of course he was.

And she'd just come across as the biggest moron ever to breathe. Things were off to a great start.

Just fabulous.

Nathan turned out of West 126th Street onto St. Nicholas Avenue and wove his way through the late-afternoon pedestrian traffic heading for the subway. It didn't matter that it was nearly evening—activity levels at nearby Columbia University didn't drop until much later, which meant the streets around it were perpetually busy during class hours. Even a few blocks away. He'd spent a lot of time out on these streets as a kid—more than most—so he knew every square inch.

Something about Tori Morfitt really got his people antennae twitching. What was a young, beautiful woman—a wildlife photographer—doing living alone in his shabby building, with no job or family that he could discern, spending her time hanging out with birds?

In a world where he tended to attract compliant yes-men—and *oh-yes* women—encountering someone so wholly unconcerned about appropriateness, someone who wore their heart so dangerously on their sleeve was a refreshing change. When she forgot to be angry with him she was quite easygoing: bright, sharp, compassionate. And the immediate blaze of her eyes as he'd suggested the webcam had reached out, snared him by the intestines and slowly reeled him in.

No doubt his interest would waver the moment he uncovered her mysteries, but for now... There were worse ways of spending time—and community service—than with a lithe, healthy young woman who liked to spar verbally.

He pulled out his phone as he walked.

"Dean," he said the moment his attorney answered his call.

"Hey, Nate."

"Forget the appeal, will you?"

"Are you serious?" He could almost hear the frown in his friend's voice—a full two-eyebrow job. What he was really asking was, *Are you insane*? "I can get you off."

"I'd rather see it out, Dean. It's a principle thing."

"You sure you can afford the moral high ground right now? We have a lot on."

His friend's gentle censure merged with the noise of the traffic. "I'll fit everything in. You know that. It's been a long time since I had anyone to get home to." He jogged between cars across the street and joined the salmon-spawn crush on the subway stairs. "Who's going to care if I pull some late ones at the office?"

"You're superhuman, Nate, not invincible."

"I don't want to lawyer my way out of this. Call it strategy—a good chance to get a handle on the lay of the land at Morningside, tenant-wise."

A good chance to get a handle on one particular tenant, at least.

Dean took his time answering. "Wow. She must be something."

Nate instantly started feeling tetchy. If he had to face an inquisition he might as well go back to Tori's. "Who?"

"Your jumper."

"She wasn't jumping."

"Don't change the subject. This is about her, isn't it?"

Nate surged forward as he saw the subway car preparing to move off. "This is about me remembering where I came from. How things were done before the money."

Dean sobered immediately. "The building's getting to you, huh?"

Nate shouldered his way between closing subway doors and leaned on the glass partition. "I just don't want to buy my way out of this."

"So you keep saying. But I'm not convinced. You worked hard all your life precisely so that you could have access to the freedom money buys."

"Yeah, but I'll do my hundred hours and then walk away knowing I did it the right way." Knowing that *she* knew it.

Dean thought about that. "Your call, buddy."

"Thank you. You can withdraw the appeal?"

"Consider it done."

Nate signed off and slid his phone back into his pocket.

One hundred hours with Tori Morfitt and he got to keep the moral high ground. A win-win. His favorite type of outcome.

He had some guilt about the effort they were about to go to in setting up the webcam but, at the end of the day, it was his effort to waste. He'd be doing most of the work. And it wouldn't be totally pointless. His plans to redevelop the building site wouldn't kick off for months so they'd get one good season out of the webcam, at least.

Of course, it meant spending more hours in the building where he was born than he particularly wanted to, but he'd control that. He'd managed the feelings his whole childhood, how hard could it be now? Memories started to morph from the gray haze he usually maintained into more concrete shapes and sounds.

He went for his phone again and dialed his office rather than let them take root in his consciousness.

"Karin, I'm heading back. What have I missed?"

As always, work did a sensational job of shoving the

memories to one side. It had served him well for fifteen years and it didn't fail him now as the subway rattled him back downtown to his own world.

CHAPTER THREE

"ARE you sure this is safe?"

Twenty-four hours later, Nathan was hanging out Tori's window again, watching her fit the stone block he'd brought with him into the corner of the ledge opposite the nest box. It was artfully hollowed out, and comfortably housed a small black camera, the lens poking discreetly out the front. The peregrines would notice nothing unusual when they returned after an evening's hunting and the camera would be protected from New York's wilder weather.

"It's safe. I've been much higher than this," Tori said through tight lips, not because she was frightened, but because she didn't like to talk about climbing. Sometimes she didn't even like to *think* about climbing. It made her feel things she was better off suppressing. She shifted her weight, wedged her scaling boot more firmly in the corner, and slid the block fully back into position.

"Better you than me," he murmured.

"Not good with heights?" she teased lightly.

"I love heights. My company's forty floors up. It's falling to my death I'm not so wild about."

Tori's body responded instantly to his words, locking up hard, squeezing her lungs so hard they couldn't inflate. It took all her concentration to will them open again so that air could rush in. She faked busy work with the camera to buy a couple of recovery seconds.

When she could speak again, she said, "You seemed ready enough to lurch out here last week."

"I thought you were in trouble. I wasn't really thinking about myself."

Sure. And hell had an ice-hockey team. Her money was on him thinking very much about the bad publicity that goes with a jumper. She turned and gathered up some of the scattered substrate from the nesting box and returned it to where it could do the birds more good.

"Won't it all just blow out again?" he asked, watching her clean-up effort. "It's gusty up here."

"It's heavier than it looks, so it doesn't blow. The peregrines toss it all out while investigating the box. They'll probably just do it again but at least it will have started fully set up for their needs. It's all I can do. They seem to like it this way."

He shrugged and mumbled, "The hawk wants what the hawk wants."

Curiosity drew her gaze back to him. So he did have a sense of humor, albeit a reluctant one. "Well, if they'd *want* a little more tidily that would be great for me." She sat back on her haunches and examined the now-tidy box, then looked at the hidden camera. A thrill of excitement raced up her spine. Nothing like the adrenaline dump of her climbing days, but it was something. "Okay. I think we're done."

She scooted backwards and twisted through the window, taking care not to snag the new cable that draped through it, connecting the camera to the small temporary monitor set up in her bathroom. Nathan stood back and let her back in.

"When I come next I'll hook it up to your TV so you can watch it with the flick of a switch," he said, shifting his focus politely from the midriff she exposed as her T-shirt snagged on the window latch.

"If I have a couple of nesting peregrines to watch, I'm not going to be switching anywhere," she said. Having the nest visible via closed circuit television would be a vast improvement on leaning out her window every day. Less likely to disturb the birds, too.

She lifted her gaze to him as she stepped down off the toilet seat and killed her height advantage. "That would be great, thank you."

Neither of them moved from the cramped bathroom, but Archer clearly had no more idea what to do with genuine gratitude from her than she did. A tiny crease marred the perfectly groomed place between his eyebrows. Her breathing picked up pace as she stared up at him, and her lips fell open slightly. His sharp eyes followed every move. Then his own parted and Tori's breath caught.

A rapid tattoo on the door snapped them both from the awkward place where silent seconds had just passed. A subtle rush of disappointment abseiled through her veins. Her face turned toward her new front door and then the rest of her followed, almost reluctantly. "That will be Mr. Broswolowski."

She squeezed past Nate's body carefully, failing at total clearance, and twisted slightly to avoid rudely shouldering him in the chest. That only served to brush her front against him as she moved through into the living room. If she'd been stacked instead of athletic it would have been totally gratuitous. As it was, his tight jaw barely shifted and his eyes only flicked briefly downwards.

While her breath tightened unaccountably.

She flung the front door wide as soon as she got to it.

"Aren't you the Queen of Sheba," the elderly man standing in the hall said as he admired her spotless new door. "Need to get yourself a peephole, though. This isn't the upper west side, you know."

Tori laughed as he entered. "I knew you by your knock, Mr. Broswolowski."

The man dumped a large hamper of clean laundry on her coffee table and commenced his standard grumble. "This basket doesn't get any lighter coming up two flights of stairs. What use is an elevator if it can't go to all floors?" He straightened uncomfortably.

"I keep telling you to bring them to me dirty. I can launder them for you before I iron them. Save your spine."

"I'm not so old that I'm prepared to have a pretty girl go through my dirty linens. The stairs are fine. But that washer isn't getting any more efficient."

Nathan chose that moment to fully emerge from the direction of the bathroom. Mr. Broswolowski looked up then turned in surprise to Tori.

"Mr. Broswolowski, this is—" for no good reason she hesitated to sic her acerbic downstairs neighbor on their landlord "—a friend of mine. He's helping me with the falcons."

"Is that so?"

Tori held her breath and waited for the awkward comment to come; some observation to the effect that her neighbor had never seen her with a man, let alone had one wander out of her bathroom as if he owned the place. Which, of course, he did. Not that she was going to share the fact. *Her* giving Nathan Archer grief was one thing, but exposing him to the collective grizzles of all her neighbors...

"Just the usual, Mr. B?"

The older man might struggle with his eyes and his arthritis, but his mind was in perfect working order. He let his curiosity dissipate, which was uncharacteristic; heavy hints usually only spurred him on. But he glanced more than once at Nathan's imposing figure and Tori realized this was the first time she'd seen Mr. B outgunned.

"Bless you, yes. There's a few more than usual," he said. "I'm spring-cleaning."

She nudged him toward the door. "Cranes or peacocks?"

He let himself be bundled out into the hall. "In a hurry, Tori?"

"Time is money, Mr. B."

"Like either of us needs to worry about time." He chuckled, before adding, "Peacocks."

Tori returned his smile. He was so predictable. "Done. I'll have them to you by tomorrow afternoon."

"Yes, yes. I wouldn't want to interrupt your date…"

She clicked the door shut behind them pointedly as she followed the older man into the hall, to lessen the chance of Nathan hearing. "It's not a date. It's business."

"*Some* kind of business, anyway," Mr. B mumbled, turning away happily.

"None of yours, that's for sure," she called after him. His laugh ricocheted back towards her down the dim hallway. She turned and pushed the door to go back in, but it didn't budge. Her lashes fell closed. That's right…new door.

New *self-locking* door.

She took a deep breath and knocked, steeling herself for the inevitable questions. If she got lucky, Nathan would have gone back to work on the camera and not heard a word Mr. B had said. If she got lucky he'd not be the slightest bit interested in what she and her neighbors got up to.

But it had been a long time since she considered herself lucky

An old sorrow sliced through her.

"Come in," Nathan said with a satisfied mouth-twist as he opened her door. His eyes travelled to the basket overflowing with linens still sitting on the coffee table. "You do his laundry?"

She shifted the clean linen over to the service cupboard that served as a closet and lifted her chin. "He has arthritis. Ironing hurts him."

The frown deepened. "What was with the peacock?"

Awkwardness leached through her. Speaking of *none of your business*… But his question seemed genuine enough. To an outsider it probably did seem crazy. "I like to make it special. Fun. I do a sort of hot-steam origami with his linen. He likes the peacock fan for his sheets."

"Doesn't that defeat the purpose of ironing?"

She smiled. "He doesn't seem to mind. I did it one Christmas as a surprise and it's kind of…stuck."

"*One* Christmas? How long have you been doing it?"

She frowned. Wow. Had it really been four years? "A while."

"Does he pay you?"

Heat surged. Was everything about money for him? "Worried I'm operating a home business without a license?"

"No," he said. "Just curious."

He shoved his hands into deep pockets, lifting the hem of his expensive coat and flashing the line of his dark leather belt where a crisp white shirt tucked neatly into a narrow waist. It had been a long time since she'd been this close to someone in formal business wear. And a long time since she'd seen someone whom business wear suited quite so much. She immediately thought of her brother dressed up to the nines on his first day at his first Portland job. He'd been so overly pressed and so excited.

Her chest tightened. A lifetime ago.

"We have a kind of barter system going. Mr. Broswolowski was a stage producer and he's still got connections."

"You're an actor?"

Her laugh then was immediate. The idea of her standing on stage in front of hundreds of strangers… Her stomach knotted just from the image. "No. But Angel on three is, and Mr. Broswolowski throws her opportunities every now and again in return for me doing his laundry."

"Wait… You do his laundry and someone else reaps the benefit?"

"I benefit. Angel babysits the deCosta boy half a day a week as a thank you for Mr. B's inside information, and in return Mrs. deCosta brings me fresh groceries every Monday when she does her own run."

If he frowned any more his forehead was going to split down the middle. "Just how many people are involved in this scheme?" he asked.

"Across the whole building? Pretty much everyone, one way or another."

He gaped. "Thirty-six households?"

"Thirty-five. 8B's been empty for years. But pretty much everyone else gets involved in one way or another. It suits our needs. And it's economical. Doing Mr. B's ironing keeps my refrigerator stocked."

"What happens when the deCosta boy gets too old for babysitting?"

Tori blinked. Straight to the weak link in the supply chain. No wonder he was a squillionaire. "Laundry's not my only trade. I have other assets."

His laugh was more of a grunt. "A regular domestic portfolio."

She fought the prickles that begged to rise. "Hey, I didn't start it. Some poor kid with an entrepreneurial spirit came up with it in the eighties as a way of making ends meet. But it works for me."

Inexplicably his whole face tightened. His voice grew tight. "You do know you can have groceries delivered to your door?"

Tori blinked at him. "Sure. But who would do Mr. B's ironing?"

The Captain of Industry seemed to have no good answer for that. He stared at her, long and hard. "I guess you have a point."

She fought down her instinctive defensiveness. The man was just trying to make conversation. "It's not like it's against the law, it's just neighbors getting together to help each other out."

He turned back on a judgmental eyebrow-lift. "You're exchanging services for gratuities."

Heat blazed. "I do someone's *ironing*. You make it sound like I'm selling sexual favours in the hallway. That hasn't happened in this building for a decade."

He spun toward the television, but not before she saw the

way his face rapidly dumped its color. All of it. Every part of her wanted to apologise, but…what for? *He'd* insulted *her.*

She sighed. "How about we just stick to what we're here for." She took a deep breath. "Tell me about this CCTV jig."

He took a moment before emerging from behind her modest television. "This doesn't have the inputs I need. I'll bring you a new one."

"A new what?"

"A new television."

"You will not!"

He blinked at her. "This one won't work with the CCTV gear."

"I'm not accepting a gift like that from you to get you out of community service."

His eyes narrowed. "Have I asked you to let me off the service order?"

"I'm sure you're working up to it." She lifted her chin and absorbed the tiny adrenaline rush that came with sparring with him.

"You really don't have a very high opinion of me, do you?"

Tori frowned. "I've been entrusted with…I feel like there's an obligation there."

"To do what?"

"To sign your attendance. Properly."

"Like some kind of classroom roll call?" The stare he gave her went on forever. "And you wouldn't consider just signing it off to be rid of me?"

Oh, how she'd love to be rid of him. Except someone had forgotten to tell her skin that. The way it tingled when she opened the door to him this afternoon… The way it prickled even now, under his glare.

She shrugged. "They're trusting me."

"You don't know them."

"It doesn't matter. *I* would know."

"Well if you want me to do this by the book you're going

to need to take the television, otherwise there can be no webcam."

"I can't accept a television."

"Ms Morfitt—"

"Oh, for crying out loud, will you call me Viktoria? Or Tori. You make me feel like an aging spinster." And that likelihood was something she tried very hard not to think about. Living it later was going to be hard enough…

She stood and moved toward the kitchen. Toward her ever-bubbling coffeepot.

"Viktoria…"

Nathan frowned, not liking the formal sound of it on his lips and tried again as she moved away from him. "Tori. I run an IT empire; we have monitors and televisions littering my office. Giving you one is about as meaningful to me as giving you corporate stationery."

Her nostrils flared and he felt like a schmuck. She'd done the very best she could with the bare bones of this apartment but there was no disguising the absence of money in her world. Not surprising if she was living on a barter system. And here he was throwing around televisions as if they were nothing. Which—brutal truth be told—they were, in his world. But waving his worth around wasn't usually his style. Money had come hard to him, but he wasn't so far gone he forgot what it felt like to live the other way.

One minute back in this building and it was all too fresh. Uncomfortably so.

"Look. You'll need it to monitor the web feed. I need it to get this community service order signed off." She looked entirely unmoved. He searched around for inspiration.

It wasn't hard for him to get into the trading spirit. That junior entrepreneur she spoke of living in the building twenty years ago had been *him*. He'd had a raft of creative schemes going to try and make something from the nothing of his youth. Not that he was going to tell her that. "I'll trade you if I have to."

Her gray eyes scanned his body critically and a tingle of honeyed warmth trailed everywhere she looked. He'd never been more grateful that he kept in good shape under the designer suits. Which was ludicrous—just because *she* was in perfect shape. The way she'd twisted in through that window—

His whole body twitched.

"You don't look like someone who needs their ironing done," she said, carefully. "What am I going to trade you for?"

The spark of defiance and pride in her expression touched him somewhere down deep. Enough to ask her seriously, "What can you offer me?"

She frowned. "Photography?"

As good as her images were, did she truly think she had nothing else to offer? He wanted to push her. To show her otherwise. A good brain ticked away beneath those tumbling auburn locks. Never mind the fact this was a great chance to learn a little more about her. "I don't need it. I have a whole marketing department for that stuff."

Her delicate brows dipped. "Well…if we're talking something you *need*…"

Crap. He should have taken the photography.

"…how about I show you around your building?" she continued. "Introduce you to people. Show you the human face of this towering *asset*."

Nate's heart doubled in size and pressed hard against his lungs. Despite what he'd told Dean, getting to know his tenants was the last thing he wanted. Not when he was about to rip the building out from under them. But it did mean Tori would take the new television and that meant he'd get his life back ninety-five hours from now. And as a side bonus, he could get to know her better.

"Not that I can see how that actually benefits me, but I accept." Whatever it took. He'd just stall her indefinitely on her part of the bargain.

"Of course it benefits you. I'm sure you know your tenants

are an asset too. Some of them have lived here all their lives. You don't get more loyal customers than that."

…all their lives.

That meant some of them might have lived here back when *he* lived here. And when *she* lived here. His mother. Nate's skin tingled. Meeting those tenants was definitely out of the question. And therefore getting chummy with the natives was categorically not on his radar.

Except maybe this one. Surly or not, Tori grabbed his attention in a way no other woman had. A two-handed grab.

"I'll have the television delivered tomorrow," he cut in, shaking the image free. "Will you be home?"

"Yep."

"I haven't given you a time yet."

She shrugged. "I'll be home. I have a date with a *Battlestar Galactica* marathon and Mr. B's ironing, remember?"

For some reason, the thought of the same hands that took such artistic wildlife photos sweltering behind a steam iron all day made him uncomfortable. But what Viktoria Morfitt chose to do with her spare time was entirely her own business.

And her business was none of his business.

"Tori Morfitt, door!"

A man in a hemp beanie flung the front door wide and let Nate into the ground floor of his own building the next day, then hollered Tori's name up the stairwell. Somewhere upstairs, someone else echoed the call. And then someone else as the message passed up the building frontier-style.

"Buzzer doesn't work," the man finally said by way of awkward conversation and then turned back to scanning his mail.

Nate's smile was tight. What could he say? That was *his* buzzer doing such a bad job of providing security for his tenants. Fortunately, the neighbors had it covered—this guy wasn't letting him go anywhere until Tori appeared and vouched for him.

Security by proxy.

"She's jogging so she shouldn't be long," the guy eventually said, taking an exaggerated amount of time sorting through his post. Nate turned and looked outside, confused. He hadn't passed her in the street... Then again, Morningside was a campus district, full of people at all hours, and she might prefer the ease of the public parks. He turned more fully to watch the path that led up from the sidewalk to the foyer door.

Anyone would think he was looking forward to it.

The stairwell door burst open behind him, snapping his head back around. Tori came through flushed, sweating and kitted out in tight running gear. Her eyes flared as they hit him and she stumbled to a halt. "You're early."

Her chest rose and fell heavily with each breath. He concentrated extra hard on keeping his focus high, but it wasn't easy, given her training top was more bandage than clothing and her skin glistened with sweat along her breast line. "I had a meeting in Jersey. I figured there was no point going back downtown for only half an hour."

He took in the way she ran her palms down her tight-fitting workout gear. She looked as though she wanted to be anywhere else than here—with him. "Sorry. Is it a problem?"

"No. I just..." She pushed her fingers through damp hair. "Come on up."

As they turned, she threw a smile at beanie guy. "Thanks, Danny."

Danny gave her a keen smile and Nate immediately stood straighter as a surge of territoriality hit him out of nowhere. *Ridiculous.* As if she'd go for the half-washed hippie type anyway.

As he headed for the elevator, he realized he had no idea what type of guy she did go for. Not his type, judging by how quickly she took offense at just about everything he did.

"You're taking the stairs?" he said as she let him enter the elevator alone.

"I'll meet you up there," she said. "I'm nearly done with

my workout. And you really don't want to be locked in a small space with me right now. The rate that elevator moves I might even get there before you."

She turned and disappeared back through the door, leaving Nate to enter the elevator alone. As it happened, he couldn't think of anything better than being closed in a small space with Tori Morfitt—sweat or no sweat. Something about standing so close to all that radiating heat while he was buttoned up in his best three-piece... His subconscious slapped him for the pleasurable twinge that flicked through him, low and sharp.

She hadn't meant to get caught out in Lycra, all hot and bothered.

He pulled out his phone the moment the old doors slid shut and—as he had every time he got into this elevator—he picked a spot of carpet to focus on and kept his eyes glued there rather than look at himself in the age-speckled mirrors lining the walls. This little box held all kinds of memories for him—none of them good.

"Karin?" he greeted his assistant when she picked up. "I want you to get onto Tony Ciaccetti and have him sort out the door security at Morningside."

It was crazy that the residents of his building had to pass messages up the stairwell like a warfront. It was secure enough, just not convenient. Which hadn't really troubled him before, but now that he saw it in action he realized how difficult it could make things, especially for older residents. Even for Tori.

Just because he'd dreaded the knell of the buzzer as child didn't mean every tenant in the place had to suffer the consequences.

He lurched to a halt on the eighth floor and optimistically pressed Tori's floor again. The doors opened then closed, and for one hopeful moment he thought the elevator was going to rise. But no, the doors reopened impotently, as silently judging as Tori was every time she'd mention some failing part of the building.

"I'll see you tomorrow, Karin."

He stepped out into the hallway and disconnected his call, then turned with determination to the stairwell before daring to lift his eyes again. Today he just didn't need the shadows of the apartment where he grew up. In the relative silence of the stairwell his ears tuned in to the steady thump of feet coming closer. He trod the two flights and held open the door with her floor number painted on it in flaking blue.

A moment later Tori appeared, sprinting heavily up the final flight. She jogged straight past him onto the tenth floor. She didn't smell nearly as bad as she probably feared. Actually she smelled pretty good. An image of rumpled sheets twisted his gut, rough and distracting, before he shut it down.

"I'm sure someone would have told me if we'd installed a gym in the building."

She slowed to a walk and let him catch up and spoke between heavy puffs of breath. "I run the stairs every day."

He looked at her, frowning. Significant heat stained her perfect skin, but it didn't detract from the fine lines of her bone-structure. "All twelve floors?"

"Three times each."

His feet ground to a halt. Well, that explained her legs. "Why not run the streets? The parks? You have enough of them nearby."

Her lashes dropped. "I don't like to run alone, even during the day." She pulled a key from a chain that hung disguised in cleavage he wouldn't have expected to be there and opened her front door.

Nate closed it behind them. "It's just dawned on me that you've been very relaxed about having me in your home. Given you don't know me from Adam. And given your...interest...in security."

If by *interest* one meant *fixation*...

"Relaxed? No." Her smile was tight. "But you own the building. I figure if you had anything nefarious in mind you could get a key to any of our doors without any difficulty." The smile mellowed into a sweet twist. "Or just kick it right in."

His gut twanged. Here was he imagining her naked and meanwhile she was finally softening to him.

Schmuck.

"I'm not sure, but that sounded almost like...trust?"

"Or resignation to my fate."

Her husky laughter heightened the streak of color still high in her cheeks. She stood straighter to pat a towel down the bare, glistening parts of her body. His own tightened. Just slightly. It had been a long time since any woman got anything other than designer-sweaty in front of him. Exertion just wasn't in with the women in his social circles. Except one kind of exertion and even that was often carefully orchestrated. Yet that wasn't what was holding his attention—at least not entirely.

It was the warmth in Tori's eyes. He hadn't realized before that anything had been missing from her steady gaze, but seeing it now full of light and laughter, he knew he'd miss it terribly if it vanished again.

"I'll take trust," he said.

They fell to silence, standing awkwardly in her neat living room, staring at each other.

"I should..." She waved her hands at her state of dress, then glanced around nervously.

She wanted to take a shower, but not while he was in her home. So trust was a measured thing, then. He crossed to the giant box dumped in the middle of her floor. If he couldn't get absent, he'd get busy. "I'll get your TV hooked up while you're gone."

"I hope that's all box," she said, eyeing the monolith. "I probably can't afford the electricity for anything bigger."

Again the vast gulf between them came crashing home to him. He hadn't even thought about running costs for a big-screen plasma. So maybe he wasn't still as attuned to his roots as he liked to believe. "It's mostly packing foam. Don't worry."

At least he really, really hoped so.

She shifted nervously, then seemed to make a decision, and disappeared into her bedroom. He heard the spray of water and then the very definite snick of a lock being turned. At least she hadn't consigned him to the hall as she had that first day.

He'd spent enough time in hallways for one lifetime.

He took the opportunity to look around. The floor plan was identical to the apartment he'd grown up in, two floors down, and beneath the layer of bright, contemporary paint he still recognized the essential design. Tori's careful application of color and light helped to make this stock-standard apartment into a cozy, feminine home. Much nicer than the one he grew up in.

On the mantel, she'd displayed a number of framed photographs: a blissfully happy-looking gray-haired couple in front of a large RV named *Freedom*; a stunning print of a bald eagle in flight silhouetted against a blazing sky and one of Tori herself, fully kitted up in climbing gear but relaxed and pouring two mugs of steaming coffee from a campfire pot and laughing up at the camera, her cheeks flushed with cold and vibrant life.

Her parents. Her mountains. And, presumably, her life. The look of total comfort and adoration on her face as she looked at whoever was taking the photo—whoever the second cup of coffee was for—squirreled down deep into his soul.

A lover?

Again the slither of jealousy coiled low in his belly. What kind of a man would Tori Morfitt choose? Not the beanie guy, surely. She'd appreciate someone outdoorsy, not too precious to pitch a tent out in the woods somewhere. Maybe an alpha type. A smart guy? A rich guy?

He looked around again, frowning. No other evidence that anyone else lived here with her or ever had. No photos of a man. More important…why was a creature as intrinsically *wild* as Tori Morfitt living in a cruddy building in upper Manhattan?

And…why did he care?

Behind him the shower shut off, so Nate got busy tearing into the shipping box his firm had delivered. He wrestled the

TV from its container, said a tiny whisper of thanks that it truly was moderate in size and busied himself disconnecting the old one.

By the time Tori emerged from her shower, clean and fresh and feeling infinitely more respectable in a T-shirt and jeans, Nathan was tuning the new television. It was spectacular. Not enormous, but flat-screen, which made it far less obtrusive in her small apartment than its clunky predecessor, which presently dominated the coffee table. That had been her parents' before they'd sold up everything and committed themselves to a life roaming around North America in their mobile home. She'd been happy to take it, though. She'd had to replace everything when she moved in here with only the bare essentials five years ago.

It had been years since she'd had anything shiny and new in her apartment. Just the smell of the packaging was exciting.

Pathetic, Morfitt.

Nathan spun around as she cleared her throat and spoke. "Wow. I may also have to introduce you to the tenants in the next building over for a truly fair trade."

Not that she knew anyone in the next building or could even visualize it anymore. She frowned.

He picked up the remote control and crossed to stand beside her. "Ready for a show?"

He thumbed the remote and the screen filled with the vision-feed from her ledge—just like the image in the bathroom monitor but vastly larger. Her ledge—complete with side-opening nest box, scattered substrate and scrubbed clean of pigeon poop—filled her living room in glorious high definition. On-screen, a curl of residual steam from her shower drifted out the open bathroom window.

"I should have done this years ago," Tori whispered as she sank into her sofa, misty-eyed. "It's awesome."

As they watched, a heavily feathered, brown-and-black hawk appeared on the edge of the screen. Nathan sucked in a breath.

Tori leaned sideways as though it might improve the framing, then she scooted to the front of her sofa.

"Wilma, I think."

He slid down next to her, just as captivated. "How can you tell?"

"Her coloring is different and she's smaller."

"That's small?"

Tori laughed. "She looks huge on screen, but peregrines are smaller than most of the other birds of prey. Fred's a good deal bigger than her. He needs to be to provide for his family."

Wilma's patterned head turned close to 360 degrees as she scanned her environment relentlessly, but her clawed feet took her closer to the box. Step by cautious step.

"She's here to check it out," Tori whispered.

They watched in silence—as though the slightest noise from inside the apartment would somehow disturb Wilma's investigations—and she patrolled the ledge, inching ever closer to the box. She plucked what little substrate was left out of the box and then stepped into it, exploring it thoroughly but keeping a hawk eye on possible predators.

Left of screen another dark blur touched down.

"Fred!" Tori leaned even farther forward and Nathan was right beside her. His thigh pressed hard against hers, drawing her glance down for a heartbeat. But she forced it up to watch the screen.

The larger bird had alighted on the ledge blurrily close to the camera. But they could still make him out as he crossed back and forth in front of the camera lens, studying this foreign arrival while Wilma continued to toss substrate out of the box in the background. The camera stayed focused on the nest box.

"Easy buddy..." Nathan whispered as Fred pecked at the lens with his savage hooked beak and gnawed on the rubber surround. But the bird's curiosity soon waned and he turned his attention to his mate. Wilma stood in the nest box apparently satisfied with what she had found.

Tori held her breath. In her peripheral vision she saw Nathan turn to watch her face. But she couldn't take her own eyes off the screen.

"Come on...come on..."

Then it happened. Casually as you like, Wilma picked up a random piece of tossed substrate from the ledge and carried it back to the box. She tossed it straight out again the moment she put it down, but then went and selected another more acceptable to her.

"What's she doing?" Nathan asked.

Tori's throat was too thick to speak. She swallowed hard and then tried again. "Starting a nest."

It was the most beautiful thing she'd seen. Up in the mountains she'd seen majestic aeries but they'd all been fully formed. Renovations of last year's eroded nests. This was the first time she'd seen a bird choose and build a nest from scratch.

And they'd chosen *her* ledge. If not for Nathan and his television she wouldn't have seen any of this.

She turned her face to him as Wilma continued searching for exactly the right piece of substrate. "This is so special. I'm so sorry I've been such a pain in the butt about all of this. Thank you, Nathan."

His blue eyes were steady, but somehow they made her critically aware of how naked she'd been just moments before as water sluiced down over her hot skin while he worked just beyond her bathroom wall. And how naked she would be now if not for the thin layers of cotton-blend fabric separating them. Yet his eyes never so much as left hers.

He smiled. "You know, I've been here three times and that's the first time you've said my name. I was beginning to wonder if you knew what it was."

Heat rushed up her newly showered neck. "Of course I knew it. It's on your business card...Nathan..." She stumbled to a halt, cursing that just using his name should feel so intimate. But it did. As though she'd whispered it. "I mean... Yes, I knew it. I'm sorry."

"I'm not after an apology. I just like the way you say it."

The pulse in her throat started to thump. In her periphery, the birds continued exploring the ledge. But a pterodactyl touching down to join them couldn't have torn Tori's gaze from his.

"How do other people say it?"

"Most people call me Nate. Or Mr. Archer."

This is where she should make a flippant comment about him being accustomed to being called *sir*. But flippancy was beyond her. She murmured instead, "What would you like me to call you?"

He stared at her for an eternity and her breath thinned out to almost nothing. He licked his dry lips and the tiny motion transfixed her. The last of her breath evaporated.

"Nathan is perfect," he finally said, husky and low. "Unique to you."

His phone trilled and the two falcons on-screen took urgent flight at the sudden sound through the bathroom window. She and Nathan snapped their focus to the empty screen and, when Tori's drifted carefully back, his had lost all hint of the warm depth she'd briefly glimpsed.

He silenced the trilling. "Archer."

His brows immediately dropped as he held the phone to his ear and then his lips tightened. He turned away from her but not before his eyes drifted shut with what looked like pain. Or exquisite relief.

"Thank you, Karin," he said quietly before hanging up. "I'll come right back. Yes, let him know I'll be right down."

"Bad news?" Tori said brightly, trying to drag things back on a professional footing. Trying to regulate her pounding heart.

"No. The opposite. A business deal I've been waiting on has finally come through."

"Oh. Well… Yay business!" She tightened her hands in her lap. Was she more annoyed that the phone call had interrupted the strange moment they'd almost shared or that he was so easily yanked away from it?

"Anyway," he said, sliding his phone back into his coat pocket and clearing his throat, "Nathan it is. It seems awkward if I'm calling you Tori and you're calling me Mr. Archer."

Tori's stomach dropped away. *Awkward.*

Huh.

Just like this moment.

What had just happened? What had just ended before it began? There was no hint now in Nathan's body language of the momentary connection she'd felt. Or had she imagined it? Could she be that sad?

"Will they be back?" He nodded his head at the television.

The birds. That's right…the whole point of them being here together.

"I'll liberate some straw from Marco deCosta's gerbil," she said, as eager to move on as Nathan suddenly seemed to be. Maybe his eyes had dropped closed with sheer relief that they'd been interrupted by the phone call? "Hopefully Wilma will like that more than the substrate."

He stood, almost stumbling in his haste. "I need to cut today's visit short, I'm sorry. I'll see you tomorrow."

Tori shook her head back to full sensibility, reluctantly stepping free of the fine threads of attraction that had unexpectedly tangled around her feet.

It took him about fifteen seconds to gather himself together and disappear out the door, and Tori got the feeling if there'd been a big red eject button in her apartment he seriously would have thought about pressing it to get out of here more quickly. She held the door open for him and he was through it and gone before she could do more than hastily say goodbye.

Wow. The last time she'd had that effect on a man, she was eighteen and Rick had warned off one of her friends so badly he'd practically paled when she next spoke to him. And given that her overprotective brother wasn't around to scare off any man who looked sideways at her, she could only assume she'd managed to put Nathan Archer off all by herself.

Which was fine, since she wasn't keen to indulge the schoolgirl flutters she got whenever he was around, but still…

That took a particular breed of talent.

* * *

His car pulled up in front of the building and Nate leaped in, hoping that Tori wasn't watching out her window. He really didn't need any more rich-guy black marks from her this week.

"Mr. Archer," his driver said.

"Hi Simon. Back to the office, please."

He felt an indescribable fraud turning up at his childhood building in the company limo. Like some guy who'd spent a month's wages hiring the car for the day to make a good impression. Except he had another one just like it in Sanmore's parking garage and no one to make a good impression on, particularly.

If anything, it would have made a bad impression on Tori had she seen it. He'd never thought he'd be more self-conscious of having money than he ever was of not having it. But then he'd never thought he'd be hanging out in his old building again, either.

The streets of Morningside and then the Upper West Side cruised by as the limo headed downtown. Nate pulled up the document Karin had emailed him and read it through twice. Confirmation that his demolition strategy had finally been approved by the city. A year's worth of negotiations and compliance hoop-jumping in order that he could redevelop his building in Morningside. The building he'd grown up in. The building Tori and all her batty neighbors now lived in.

But not for long.

He'd bought the building because he could. It had been a suitably poetic use for his first bunch of profit zeros. More than cars or women or planes—to buy out the building that they'd been so poor in and know that no-one could ever take it away from them. And becoming his mother's landlord...

Stupidly gratifying.

He'd never before—or again—felt so valued by Darlene Archer as he had the day she'd realized she could hit him up for free rental. It was as though he'd finally been some good to her. After she took her last selfish breath, he'd closed up her apartment and focused one hundred percent of his attention on to growing Sanmore Holdings. It wasn't until Dean had quizzed him about this sole piece of real estate in his portfolio three years ago that he'd started to wonder what else he could put on this site. Something shiny and modern. Something with a future…

…and no past.

The practical demolition application had been easy enough to get through City Hall but recent changes to the Tenancy Act meant he had to give the thirty-five households in his building more notice than he wanted to once the idea of development had taken root. And now that he held the actual permissions in his hands he wasn't prepared to wait at all.

He'd rehouse all thirty-five families in the Ritz if it meant getting this building emptied faster. They could live out the final months of their lease elsewhere courtesy of Sanmore Holdings and he could get on with upgrading the site. The bomb it would cost was more than worth it.

The fact his memories would finally be exorcised from his soul…pure bonus.

Simon pulled the limo up in front of Nate's Columbus Circle office tower to let him out before driving off to do the compli- cated four-block double-back to access the building's rear car park. With the downtown traffic and the monolithic Trump Towers next door, Nate would be at his desk before Simon even started heading back this way.

Karin met him at the elevator, her handbag on her shoulder and a guilty expression on her face.

"Nice to see you were sticking around in case I needed anything," Nate said dryly.

"It's Friday night, Nathan Archer. Just because you have no life doesn't mean all of us want to work late. I have babies to feed."

She rattled off a few of the afternoon's highlights and thrust a document into his hands. "How did it go?" Her kind eyes knew him so well. "Hostilities ceased?"

Viktoria Morfitt.

"We don't have to be best friends, Karin. I'll just do my time and we'll be back to our regular programming at Sanmore."

Karin lifted a single brow. "Uh-huh."

He'd worked with his assistant long enough to know most of her nuances. She saved her best Harlem gestures for when she had a real point to make. He leaned forward and pushed the down button on the elevator for her. "It's going to be fine."

"You don't have time for this, Nate. You have the merger and the StarOne software trials coming up this month."

"Don't frown at me Karin. I'm the Good Samaritan on this one." He jiggled the elevator button again.

"So fight it. You have right on your side."

He still could. Dean had the appeal paperwork sitting in a file just in case. But standing in Viktoria Morfitt's apartment this afternoon as his body answered the call of all her post-workout pheromones he knew he wouldn't be changing his mind.

There was just something about her. Something he needed some time to figure out.

But arguing with Karin in the hallway wasn't going to get him that. "Okay, I'll go talk to Dean."

"Thank you," Karin said with all the righteousness of a mother of four who was right very often. Except not this time. "Have a good night. Don't stay too late."

She said that every night. And every night he said, "I won't."

But the amount of work he left for her in the mornings probably told her a whole different story.

Nate saw her safely into the elevator and then turned down the hall away from his own office and poked his head around the door of his best friend's.

Dean looked up from whatever legal tome he was reading. "Hey. You're back early."

"Can you have your team get onto something for me?" The two of them had a lot of history together, but their friendship worked so well because they both knew how to maintain clean lines between work and personal.

Dean snapped straight into employee mode. "Name it."

Nate rattled off his plan for rehoming his Morningside tenants to expedite the demolition. Paying out their lease and finding alternative accommodations for every one of them.

"Expensive," Dean murmured. In the circles they both moved in vast dollars didn't scare them but they were still noted.

Nate countered. "Worth it, though."

He watched the lawyer in Dean war with the friend in him. They'd been through so much together. Everything.

"Yeah, it probably is," Dean said with a sigh. "I'll take care of it."

Nate's shoulders instantly lightened up. "Thanks, buddy. I'll give you more information as I can. Good night. Go home and start your weekend."

Back in his own office, Nate signed off on the few things Karin had left for him and returned one quick phone call to an overseas banker. Someone had said "The world never sleeps' and it was never truer. There were half a dozen ways the world could get hold of Sanmore's CEO, 24/7—office phone, home phone, cell phone, email, text, Twitter, couriers—and often at the same time. There hadn't been such a thing as *silence* on this planet since the internet was first wrestled from the hands of the military and went public.

But since he was as responsible for that as everyone else involved in the online boom he really couldn't complain.

He moved over to his floor-to-ceiling windows and stared out at Columbus Circle, but it didn't take long for his eyes to track right…uptown towards Morningside. Towards Tori.

She was someone who would appreciate silence.

Lots of silence.

He could imagine her scaling the face of some mountain with nothing but the sounds of her own exertion and the wind in her ears. No phones. No email. No relentless accessibility.

What would that be like?

He could have a taste of it if he turned off his phone when he was at her place. If he took the subway instead of the car so no one knew where he was. It would be as close to invisible as he got. As close to private. Although being *private* with Tori Morfitt was not necessarily a good idea.

As tempting as it was.

CHAPTER FOUR

"SETTLE, GRETEL."

The humongous dog returned to her mat in Tori's living room and curled back up in a neat, gigantic heap.

"Good girl."

Gretel's big brown Great Dane eyes watched every move Tori made and blinked happily from time to time before finally closing for yet another doggie nap. Life would be so much easier if humans could get away with napping as much as dogs did.

"It's a rough life, kid," Tori murmured, working at her computer on her latest falcon images.

Thirteen out of fourteen days Gretel's owners, the Radcliffes, managed to coordinate their respective work so one of them was home to feed, love and walk their small horse of a dog during the day. Every second Saturday that was Tori's job. Except for the walking part, but Gretel didn't seem to mind the absence of exercise just that once. She happily traded it for pats and snacks on Tori's mat. And Tori traded Gretel's nurse mother, Tracey, for medical assistance, as she needed it. So far, she hadn't really required more than checkups, flu advice and the occasional herbal for when her insomnia was particularly bad. And for anything bigger there were house-call medical services.

Thank God for New York. A supplier for everything, no need too obscure. On call 24/7. The relentless, too-close noise of the city was a small price to pay for that kind of service.

She fiddled with the saturation on a particularly pretty digital shot of Wilma landing on the ledge, some tufts of feather and twig in her hooked beak during her first, aborted, nest-building phase. Nathan wanted lots of images for the website, to make it really special. Fortunately, although she lacked the technical expertise to make this website a reality, gorgeous photos she could definitely provide. In abundance.

Gretel let out a corker of a snore over on her mat.

"Nice, Gretel," Tori twisted her lips but didn't take her attention off screen. "Your dad teach you those manners?"

By midafternoon, she filed away the last of the images she'd selected for the website and glanced at her watch. Her heart gave a little lurch. Nathan would be here soon and her tranquil afternoon would be shot. He'd swan in, dominate her apartment, her time and generally take up clean air. Then he'd find some unique way of making her feel inadequate and remind her of how busy and important he was, and his work would be done!

And all the while she'd be mooning about how good he smelled or looked in a suit.

Crazy.

Tori snapped her attention away from the blank wall and forced it back onto the computer. She had time, maybe she could do a bit of Mrs. Arnold's memories album. Yet another trade. This one for clothing alterations. Most of the catalogue clothes she ordered fitted just fine around her hips but were a bit loose around her waist. She still had a small, hard, climber's midriff courtesy of the ab cruncher hooked to the base of her bedroom door—fabulous for fashion but not if you wanted your pants to stay up. Mrs. Arnold was a deft touch with a sewing machine and—thanks to her desire to have her memories captured digitally, which she was *not* a deft hand with—kept all Tori's pants politely in position by way of thanks.

She glanced at her watch again. *Screw it.* This was her Saturday, too…she wasn't going to wait around for someone to call up the stairwell to tell her Nathan had arrived. He wasn't the only one whose time was worth something. She fired up her image software and the screen peppered with Mrs. Arnold's long lifetime of scanned memories. But then, down in the corner of the screen, another folder displayed by default—her personal one—and Tori fought hard to ignore it. But the more she ignored, the more it seemed to pulse and grow. Begging her attention. Without taking her eyes off Mrs. Arnold's black-and-white wedding photos, her hand slid the cursor over to her personal folder and readied to shush it back to where it came from.

But her fingers didn't make the minute depression needed to click the file shut. They hovered anxiously over it instead. She glanced around the room as though someone would catch her looking and then, with tight breath, slid her wrist slightly to the left and clicked. The whole time frowning, knowing this wasn't smart. Knowing it was going to hurt.

But unable not to.

Mrs. Arnold's folder minimized, and Tori's personal images unpacked like a picnic on her screen. Her life in rich, high-res pixels. Tori as a child, dirty and bloody and having a fabulous time down some hole or another. Her school friends, always trying to turn Tori into the girl she resisted being. Images of her gray-haired parents sent from all over America, each one crazier than the one before, most of them featuring some over-sized monument on some long, busy interstate. The adventure of their lifetime. Love saturating each one.

Then Rick's folder. The one she tried to avoid but knew she wouldn't.

One click spilled her brother's beautiful face across her screen. Rick smiling. Rick on horseback. Rick looking back down to her from halfway up a rock face, the wind in his brown, tossed hair, the world in his bright, living eyes. So much like her own. The ache in her chest swelled out to encircle her lungs, too, stealing her breath. She'd taken all of these pictures. They'd spent so much time together and she'd captured so much of it by habit she literally had hundreds of photographs of her twin stored in her computer. But none in her apartment.

Losing him all over again in the waking moments of every day was hard enough without stretching it out across twelve hours. She liked to keep the memories contained.

She looked at them now, her mouse-finger clicking through all the different versions of her brother. Happy Rick. Frustrated Rick. Crazy Rick. Triumphant Rick. Rick in crisis. Rick in love. She'd grown up in his pocket and then shared a house with him until they were twenty-one—there wasn't an expression he had that she hadn't memorized.

Including the one in the split second when he'd realized he was going to die.

Behind her, something screeched and she jumped almost as high as Gretel who issued an urgent bark before galloping to the door. Heart thumping, she spun around and stared at her kitchen counter. Specifically at the great pile of cookbooks that were stacked there against the wall, against the—

The books buzzed again.

Tori quickly shifted the books and a vase of Mr. Chen's fresh-cut flowers away from the defunct intercom and stared at it as though it were alien technology. In so many ways it was. It had never worked in for five years here. Now it was making noise all of a sudden.

"Hello?" She pressed the blue button and shouted overly loud into the speaker. Alexander Bell couldn't have done better.

"Tori? It's Nate. Can you buzz me in?"

She blinked at the unit and muttered to herself. "I have no idea." She poked the blue button again and spoke loudly into the box. "Why is this working?"

His pause reeked with frustration. "I had it fixed." She heard him rattle the front door. "Try again."

She depressed the button marked with a bell and heard a clicking sound. He didn't call her back so she assumed he was in the building.

Her eyes went to the door where Gretel stood like a sentinel, eyeballs fixed on the shiny timber. It took her a few seconds to realise she was staring with the same vigilance, her heart pattering away in anticipation of Nate's brisk, confident knock.

"Do you have no pride?" she said to a tail wagging Gretel, but really it was for herself. She forced her attention back to her kitchen counter, now in disarray. Now that it was fully exposed, the intercom was really quite dusty so Tori quickly wiped it down and then set about making alternative space for her cookbook collection. She moved the flowers down to the coffee table.

First CCTV and now a working intercom. Way too much technological excitement for one week.

Gretel issued one of her booming barks and Tori snapped her head around to her apartment entrance as her heart burst into a furious thumping. She shoved her hip between the excited dog and the door and used her weight to force Gretel out of the way so she could open the door inwards, muttering to her, "It's not your parents, dopey. Too early."

Gretel's booming bark must have prewarned him, but still Nathan's eyebrows almost disappeared into the hair flopping over his forehead when he stepped into her apartment and saw the size of her other guest. He warily eyed the grinning, drooling monster that followed him in.

"I hope you get something amazing in return for that," he said, and then looked up at her. "What?"

Tori stared. He had exchanged his dark, tailored corporate clothes for a faded New York casual—well-loved jeans bunched around beaten boots, an earthy green hooded sweat, and a short suede jacket that matched the boots. His hair was finger-combed and loose, and free of whatever fifty-dollar-a-tube product usually kept it architecturally perfect. No doubt a lot of money went into making him look as though he'd just been throwing a ball for kids in the park. But it sure was well-spent.

For the first time, the gulf between them seemed to shrink. Monday-to-Friday Nathan screamed *hands off* in a way that made sidelining her hormones possible. But Saturday Nathan…

Her eyes tracked him into her tiny apartment. Breathless awareness surfed down her arteries, spreading a chaos of confusion to every cell in her body. She straightened self-consciously, just shy of giving Gretel a run for her money in the drool stakes.

…*this* Nathan was positively edible.

He courteously offered the dog the back of his hand, and Gretel swung around to give it an investigatory sniff, her muscled tail waving frantically. Tori snapped clear of her hormonal haze and dived for the coffee table just as the Dane's tail whipped the footing out from under the flowers she'd just moved there. In spite of her keen reflexes, the vase and its contents went flying. Water surged over the edge of the table and trickled onto the floor, but before she could do more than shout Gretel's name in exasperation, Nate tossed his jacket aside, hauled his sweater off and pressed it straight down into the spreading puddle, stemming the flow onto her carpet.

By the time Tori had wrestled an excited Gretel back to her mat and got her to drop and stay, Nate had the spill well and truly under control and three of the loose cut flowers in his hand. She joined him and picked up a few more from the floor. His sweatshirt was a ruined, soggy mess on the table, leaving him in just his T-shirt. Tori struggled not to appreciate the way the cotton fitted to his well-shaped torso and concentrated on plucking errant flower stalks from her sofa.

She'd hung out with climbers; buff torsos weren't anything new to her. Maybe it had just been a long time since she'd seen one. That's why her pulse was falling over itself suddenly.

That and the fact that he smelled different today. Killer cologne. She filled her lungs with his scent. Something…woodsy. She stared at him curiously. *Woodsy?* Why the change from his slick Fifth Avenue original?

"A dog like that should be out in the suburbs," Nathan said, breaking the silence she only just realized had stretched out.

"It was my fault. I shouldn't have put the flowers so low."

He straightened and stared at her. "Wow. I broke your door and you took me to court. Godzilla over there destroys your furniture and you give it full amnesty."

Heat threatened to peek over her collar. "*Gretel* didn't mean to do it."

"Excitement of the moment?"

Tori frowned, knowing exactly the same could be said for the day he broke her door down. "Okay, look. I'm sorry about everything that happened. You came lurching at me when I was out on the ledge. It freaked me out and I…" *I really don't like surprises.* "I may have overreacted a bit."

"Just a bit?"

"You have no idea how smug you were standing in that hallway with two cops eating out of your hand."

He glanced up at her. "Smug? Not something I was aware was in my professional repertoire."

"Seriously? No one's told you that before? You have this whole…lip-twist thing going on. It's extremely irritating."

Just like the tiny smile he gave her now. The way he saw right through her. His eyes sparkled. "Getting under your skin, Tori?"

Yes.

The toss of her head said the idea was laughable. "No. But you seem to be very accustomed to getting your own way. I don't like that in a person." God, she'd so nearly said *man*. Was his lumberjack cologne messing with her mind now, as well?

He studied her hard and finally spoke. "If I've railroaded you with anything, I apologize. Occupational hazard."

Should she tell him about that other annoying look he had—the whole innocent and earnest thing? Trouble was *that* look actually worked on her. Like right now. She thrust out her hand. "Give me your sweater, I'll wring it out."

"I'm here for a few hours. Hopefully it will dry out in that time."

In her north-facing windows? Not a chance. She wrung the

worst of the water out in her kitchen sink. "I'll take it up on to the roof—it'll get more sun there. Gretel needs a toilet stop anyway."

"You toilet the dog on the roof?" His cautious glance spoke volumes. "Is that hygienic?"

She had to laugh. "It's fine, Nathan. Wait and see."

It *was* fine. The roof was a mini haven for the residents of their building. One of the first things Tori had done when she moved in was install a big patch of turf alongside Mr. Chen's rooftop vegetable garden. Just turf—but a lush, large, elevated square. Mr. Chen let her piggyback off his reticulation and the Davidson kids' two pet rabbits kept the patch mowed with their daily visits and fertilized with their castings, so, while Gretel's fortnightly visits weren't great for it, it had plenty of recovery time in between.

"This is amazing," Nate said, looking around the crowded roof space. Tori's turf, Mr. Chen's veggies, a couple of deck-chairs, a small outdoor table, an empty wading pool, a washing line, and a rickety old telescope. It was a hive of activity—when it wasn't just the two of them.

Gretel crossed immediately to the grass, sniffed around briefly and did what she'd come for. While Nathan looked around, Tori carefully pegged his sweater on the sunny side of the washing-line to swing in the breeze.

"It wasn't like this when I liv—" He frowned darkly and flicked his eyes back to her. "When I bought the building."

Tori kicked off her shoes. "I wanted something to tend. I'd helped Mr. Chen build his vegetable garden so he helped me make this." She stepped onto the grass across from where Gretel had peed and sunk her bare toes into the thick green blades. Amazingly healthy given its containment. Although not given the massive amount of spoiling it got from Tori. It had to be the most expensive patch of lawn on Manhattan, inch-for-inch.

"I guess Gretel benefits," he smiled. "Of course, you know there's a park right at the end of the street?"

Her belly balled up tight and she frowned. "Right. But

Gretel's not mine and we weigh almost the same, I'd hate to lose her out in the street if something happened."

Nate's gaze narrowed but he accepted her word. "She seemed easy enough to handle on the stairs."

"That's because she was coming up. You wait till we have to take her back down."

Nate followed Tori's gaze to the dog and then upward to the telescope. He crossed to it and swung it around to look back toward lower Manhattan. "I'd forgotten what the view was like up here," he murmured.

"Not a patch on your office's outlook, I'm guessing."

He lifted his eyes and rested them on her. "Depends on what you value looking at."

For the life of her she couldn't tear her own eyes away. The air suddenly thinned like that on the highest mountain peaks and screws she barely knew she had began to tighten deep and low inside her. But then Gretel trotted over and saved the day, nudging Tori for a pat, providing the perfect, polite excuse to break the traction of Nathan's gaze.

"I prefer the rivers and parks," she said, slightly breathless. The upstate wilderness she hadn't visited since she'd lost Rick.

He swung the telescope around toward Riverside and picked out a few highlights to study. The rising arc of the telescope told her he'd spotted a hawk just before he asked "Why didn't you build your nest box up here?"

A tiny part of her mourned the return to the subject of the falcons. It only reminded her of the real reason he was standing with her on this roof. Duress. Couldn't they go on pretending they were just…friends…a little bit longer?

"Too exposed. They like cover on a couple of sides if they can. Also too much traffic up here."

He straightened. "Well, let's ease the congestion, shall we? Your website isn't going to design itself."

Tori sighed and followed him to the stairwell door, whistling for Gretel to follow. It took both of them to manhandle the dog back inside once she realized her rooftop visit was being cut unnaturally short, but she finally acquiesced.

On the tenth floor, Tori tossed her key to Nate.

"It's about time for me to drop her home," she said, her hand on the dogs smooth, warm head. "Let yourself in, I'll be right back."

Nate watched as she wrestled the small pony down the next flight of stairs. She hadn't been kidding when she'd spoken of the difficulty she'd have out in public if Gretel took it into her head to bolt. It was possible the dog actually *did* weigh more than its lithe human companion. She might have the taut array of climber's muscles, but Tori Morfitt was still half air.

And she blew as hot and cold as the most changeable winds. Today—lukewarm; he felt vaguely welcome. Maybe she mellowed on weekends? Maybe the presence of the dog chilled her out a bit? Whatever, standing on the roof with her was the first time he'd felt any kind of mutual respect between them. A reciprocal connection. Not the connection he kept stumbling over—the one he had no business feeling—but an intellectual one. Today he felt truly relaxed in her company.

He frowned and stumbled to a halt. *In this building.*

The residents had done something special up on that rooftop. Not complicated, not high-tech, but special. And clearly most of his tenants loved to spend some time up there. Just one more thing that would press on his conscience the day the demolition crew moved in.

Still, they were all on leases. Every single one of them knew nothing was forever.

Tori's door swung noiselessly inwards and Nate propped it open with a footstool, then poured himself a coffee from the simmering pot in the kitchen and made himself comfortable at Tori's computer ready for a long haul of web design. He was sure she had assumed he'd build the website in the comfort of his own home, on his own laptop, and then just upload it, finished, to her PC. That had been his plan, too, right up until the moment he found himself giving the doorman of his building a farewell salute this afternoon and turning left for the subway uptown. To Morningside. But, no. He was going to build the whole thing on her computer, downloading what he needed online, coding from scratch. The website he wanted to give Tori was old-school. Classic. Like her.

The long-forgotten rush of staring at a blank page of code hit him again now. Man, how long had he been out of his zone? Another thing he'd exchanged for success. He used to live on air and the thrill of programming back when he was starting out.

Nate wiggled the mouse to bring Tori's hibernating screen back to life and then sucked in a breath as he slowly sank back in his seat. Dozens of photos of the same man splayed out on the screen like a pack of cards. As if she'd just been poring over them in privacy. A good-looking, athletic man. A really happy man. A man literally on top of the world in some of the photographs.

A climber.

He flicked through them. Insanely, it had never seriously occurred to him that Tori might have a boyfriend. The absence of pictures in the apartment—of a man in the apartment—had given him a false sense of security. *Here* were the photos most girlfriends splashed all over their living rooms. Their phones. Their social networking accounts. The way the women he risked relationships with liked to carry him around like a social handbag.

A boyfriend. He'd been stupid to assume—

"What are you doing?

Her quiet, pained words brought him round sharply, as guilty as if he'd been caught digging through her underwear drawer. Heart thumping from way more than just the surprise of being caught.

Tori had a boyfriend.

"Sorry, were you working on something?"

The darkness of her gaze lifted slightly as she cleared her throat. "No. I was just…" She stepped forward and pressed slightly against him as she leaned in to close the file. The hairs right along that side of his body gravitated towards her. Her trembling hand missed the first attempt. But then the images sucked back into the file and disappeared into darkness. Which is exactly where she'd be hoping the subject could stay. He saw it in the way her eyes rested everywhere but on his.

He spun in the chair as she hurried into the kitchen to wash her hands. "Who was that, Tori?"

Her body stiffened and stumbled, but she forced her hands to reach for the simmering coffeepot.

He tried again. "Someone special?"

It had to be, the way she was going all out to pretend the images were of no consequence. She finished pouring her coffee and wiped down the spotless kitchen counter, then the coffeepot. Then a nonexistent mark on her refrigerator door. He watched her rinse the cloth thoroughly and lay it carefully over the edge of the sink to dry. He'd seen this kind of delay tactic in the boardroom; the corporate equivalent anyway. Silence was his best friend right now, he knew if he waited long enough she'd spill.

Eventually.

She turned to him, seemingly desperate for a task, and opened her mouth to ask him something, but her gaze fell on his still-steaming cup of coffee and the words dried up. But she was looking at him with speech trembling on her lips and he was steadily watching her. Waiting. She had to say something if she couldn't offer him a coffee.

She turned, reached into her tiny pastry, retrieved a packet of shortbread biscuits and placed a couple on a plate. Then, on still-bare feet, she brought him the offering and placed it silently next to him on her desk.

Still he waited.

The computer whirred, oblivious, in the awkward silence.

"My brother, Rick," she finally said.

Relief pumped through him in a steady, controlled feed. His eyes fell briefly shut. Not a boyfriend. Not a lover.

A brother.

Maybe all sisters kept hundreds of photos of their brothers. He wouldn't know, happy families were so far outside his field of experience.

He scrabbled around for something normal to fill the next silence. "Good-looking guy."

Pain flashed across her face in a hundred tiny muscle shifts and he knew, somehow, he'd said the wrong thing. Again.

"Yes."

"Good genes in your family."

The lameness of his words was only amplified by the silence with which they were met. *Christ, Archer, why don't you just ask her how she likes her eggs in the morning and be done with it...* He really was out of practice. How hard could it be to get someone to start talking about something more personal than the neighbors?

Attempt number two. "Where does he live?"

Tori stared at him, carefully neutral, then at the now-blank computer screen. Then she straightened and offered him a watered-down facsimile of a smile that barely twitched a cheek before speaking softly. "In my heart."

Nate's stomach sank. That explained the photos. "He's dead?"

She nodded.

When? How? And most importantly...*Are you okay?* But he only risked, "I'm sorry."

She lifted her coffee to her lips and her still-trembling fingers sloshed it in its cup. "Me, too."

"Were you close?"

She nodded again. Barely.

Okay, he was prepared to do this twenty-question fashion if he had to. The chance to peek inside Tori Morfitt's heart was too golden an opportunity to politely step back from. He scrabbled around for something lateral to ask.

"Did he teach you to climb?" Those photos that looked out over massive expanses of American landscape...

Tori's nostrils flared and she seemed to collapse in on herself like a tumbling building, walls of defense blocking him out. *Clang, clang, clang*...like the best system firewall, as the opportunities for him to advance slammed shut one by one. But he knew the best way through a crashing system was forward. Steady and unpanicked. Fewer mistakes that way.

"I taught him," she croaked.

Steady and unpanicked... "Did you both live in New York?"

"No. We're from Oregon." She was like a rusted piece of machinery oiled for the first time in thirty years. Slowly, painfully, her speech was coming more freely.

"Not from Manhattan?" he asked. Though he already knew the answer.

Her lips twisted and he almost heard the protesting squeak. "Most of Manhattan's not from Manhattan."

"I am." The words were out before he even knew they were forming.

Her almond eyes elongated and creased slightly at the corners. "I know. Your accent's a dead giveaway. Where did you grow up?"

His senses went on full alert. *Uh-uh. This is my inquisition, not yours.* "Not far from here. What part of Oregon?"

She leaned down over him and opened another photo album on the desktop. A heap of rugged wilderness shots scattered across the screen. Oregon, presumably.

"Medford, originally. Though Rick and I shared my grandmother's place on the edge of Portland when we moved out of home." Her conversation unwound along with some of the visible tension in her body.

"Good climbing district." He had no idea if that were true but she accepted it easily enough. "What brought you to New York?"

She stared long and hard. No longer tense but a million miles from relaxed. It only tweaked his instincts further. He wanted to tease the pain he could see right out of her, carefully and controlled. He wanted to see what she looked like without the perpetual shadow in her gaze.

"It wasn't Oregon."

He kept his smile light. "Florida would have been further."

"Geographically maybe."

Interesting. So what was she after by coming here? "Fresh start?"

"Something like that."

"Do you miss the wilderness?"

A sharp kind of pain flashed across her eyes, and then it was gone. "Every day."

"Why not go back?"

"There's nothing there for me now. After Rick... When he was gone, my parents sold up and hit the road. They're official Gray Nomads now."

"Was that their way of coping?"

A frown formed on her smooth brow. "It's their way of honoring Rick. By living their lives to the fullest."

"What's your way?"

The shutters dropped again. This time instant and entire. He'd pushed too far. But short of quizzing her on the finer details of how a healthy young man dies so young, he was going to have to ease back on trying to twist his way into her inner psyche. She'd tell him when she was ready.

Or not... Which would be quite telling in itself.

"They visited once but didn't like bringing the RV into Manhattan. We talk by phone all the time."

A spectacularly obvious change of subject but he let it go. "It's nice that you're close to your parents."

"Where's your family?"

Unprepared for the question, it took his defenses by surprise. A tiny thread of old pain took its chance and weaseled out between the cracks from the place he kept it carefully contained, tightening his whole body. "I'm all that's left."

Surprise lightened Tori's features, followed almost immediately by compassion. It was such a welcome change from the shadows he'd caused her he forgot to be defensive about her pity. "Really? I had imagined you as one in a big family of successful Manhattan achievers."

His snort rivaled that of the half-dog-half-horse that had just left. "No. I was born in the city but my mother wasn't. She moved here back in the eighties to pursue…"

Wow. How was he going to put this…?

"Her dreams?" Tori stepped in.

He couldn't credit the woman he remembered with possibly having aspirations and dreams. Certainly she'd never encouraged him to have any. "Her *job*. She never spoke of her family. Or where she'd come from." Or where he had. Though he had a pretty good idea about that.

"They're *your* family, too. You never asked about them?"

"All the time at the beginning. But my mother wasn't a woman who believed in looking backwards." Plus she had no idea at all which of dozens of men had actually fathered her child.

Tori stared. "Huh. Not what I imagined at all," she said.

Uncomfortable, suddenly, with the false image she must have had of his halcyon childhood in an up-market neighborhood surrounded by opportunity and wealth and love, he shifted decisively in the chair. He flicked casually through more of her on-screen photographs, scrabbling for a subject change.

"Is that Potsdam?" he asked, enlarging one of her images on-screen. It was a wilderness shot with a river twisting through the background and a pretty village on its banks taken from high up in a mountain range. "I went to school there. Clarkson. Upstate, at the base of the Adirondack Mountains. That's definitely New York State."

She leaned in over him slightly to look at the image, and her heat radiated deliciously. And her scent—lightly floral, intensely seductive.

"That's where I took it. I climbed the Adirondacks with—" She stumbled. "It looks like a beautiful place to go to school."

Six hundred acres on the banks of the Raquette River. "It was."

"Far from home." Her gray eyes slid sideways to search his. "Almost across the Canadian border."

"Almost across the universe. That's what I loved about it."

"You really weren't happy here. Why Clarkson?"

"Because they took me. I was early admission and on scholarship." *Hardship* scholarship seemed too pathetic to add.

"Early admission...? You must have been a bright kid."

"I studied and read relentlessly." And half the high-school faculty wanted him the heck out of his mother's orbit and, collectively, pulled every string they could to find him an opportunity.

"Then what happened?"

"I discovered the opposite sex." Those years at Clarkson were the first good years he'd ever had.

"And that was the end of the reading and the studying, I'm sure."

"Not at all. Every girl on campus wanted to take the young kid under their wing. They all thought I needed some kind of bridging tutoring. It was a great way to meet girls." A lot of girls. And volume meant he could keep them all at a nice, safe distance. Where they all belonged.

Tori laughed. "How early was your admission?"

"Only a year. But a year means a lot when you're seventeen. And I was happy not to let on that I was already aceing my classes."

Tori smiled. "My landlord, the player."

"Landlord?" He winced. "You make it sound like I have a paunch and a cardigan." It was more than just vanity that made him want that image of him stripped from her mind, permanently. He took a lot of pride in being a leader in the world's fastest-growing industry.

She backpedalled immediately. "Not at all. You're in great shape—"

The blush that stole up her neck only endeared her to him

more. Nate's lips twisted in exactly the way she hated. "Coming from a rock-climber that's quite a compliment."

"Ex rock-climber."

"You wouldn't know it. There's not an inch of fat on you."

Her eyes flew to his and flared as he watched. Okay, not his most subtle moment but totally worth it to see the dawning of awareness in her gray depths. Time slowed to molasses as he brushed his glance over every part of her face. The doe lashes. The smooth bridge of her nose with its peppering of freckles. The perfect shape of her mouth. Made for kissing...

As his focus lingered there, she sucked a corner of her bottom lip between pearly teeth, and tiny creases roosted in the corners of her eyes. Tiny, *anxious* creases.

He pushed away from the computer slightly, giving them both some much-needed oxygen. "How about you show me what you've pulled together for the website graphics and we'll start planning what kind of feel you want it to have? How we can bring the world into Morningside."

She regarded him thoughtfully, but then she crossed to the tiny dining alcove and selected one of two barely used chairs and brought it over to sit next to him. Close enough that her clothed arm pressed against his bare one, and her warmth radiated out and gently heated that part of him that was cold and empty from everything he'd not revealed.

A place where warmth seldom reached. Seldom survived.

He let the welcome glow soak in and did nothing to shift politely away. As she opened the computer file with her astounding falcon imagery he tried not to indulge the satisfaction of knowing that she hadn't moved away either.

She didn't like him smug.

CHAPTER FIVE

IN late afternoon, the stairwell spat Nate out on the eighth floor and, as he always did, he kept his eyes low and headed directly for the elevator, intentionally avoiding the far end of the hall. But as he drew close to the silver antique he slowed... wavered.

He should check. What if the place had been vandalized? What if a water pipe had burst? What if someone had been secretly living here the entire time it had been boarded up? Going back into his mother's apartment was not high on his list of favorite things to do, but it was probably necessary. Besides, how long could he hang out in this building and pretend apartment 8B didn't exist?

He wiped his damp palms on his jeans as he walked down the hall, fished the cluster of keys out of his pocket and then slid the tarnished bronze one carefully into the lock.

And then he stopped.

Hand poised. Lungs aching. Just staring at the tarnished letter B that hung crookedly on the outside of the door.

Every miserable memory of the woman—the men, the drinking, the wailing and moaning, the *other* moaning, the fighting—it all came back to him in a blinding, sickly rush. He recalled every reason he'd ever sealed up this door and not looked back.

He braced his hands on the door frame and let his head sag forward. If the pipes were damaged or the place was full of

vermin or squatters then that was going to have to be someone else's job to discover. He'd taken many risks in his life,
overcome many hurdles; he didn't consider himself lacking in
strength or courage, but nothing short of a force of nature was
getting him through that door.

He pulled his phone out to get Karin to arrange an
inspection.

"I think she's out," a quiet voice said behind him.

He turned to see a small, folded-over woman in a neat, faded
dress.

A violent rattle started up deep inside. "I'm just…uh…"

"She's probably gone for cigarettes. Smokes like a chimney,
that one." The old woman had a pruned smile, and bright,
vacant eyes. Kind and deep but…vacant. And disturbingly familiar. Nate's stomach coiled tighter.

"Nancy! There you are." Tori's head popped out of the stairwell and huffed with relief. "I just got a call to say you were
out. We've been looking for you all over the building."

The woman turned slowly. "I'm helping this delivery man.
He needs someone to sign for the parcel for 8B."

Tori looked at Nate curiously, then glanced around for a
delivery. There was no point denying it—that wouldn't help
the older woman's confusion. Nancy's ancient gaze drifted to
the phone he still held clutched in his hand. Clearly, she wasn't
moving until he had a signature.

"I'll take care of that," Tori said, putting her hand out for
the phone. She took it from him and pretended to sign it. The
old woman smiled again and stepped closer. Nate froze as the
complicated mix of smells reached out to him. Talcum powder.
Citrus. And old lady.

"Would you like to come on up with me?" she said to
him.

His chest clenched. Immediately. Painfully.

Conclusively.

"We'd love to, Nancy, thank you," Tori soothed. "It's a long
climb. Will you be okay?"

"The elevator's broken," she said, curling her arm for Tori to take.

His gut squeezed again. Something clearly was not right here.

"I know," Tori said. "But we'll help you. Wait a moment, Nancy, while I get the door." She moved down the hall. Nate took the older woman's arm.

"Miss Smith?" He hadn't meant to say it out loud and he barely did. The ancient ears certainly didn't hear him and neither did Tori. She was too busy propping the stairwell door open twenty feet away.

Would you like to come up?

It had become a regular offer when she'd step out of the lift on the eighth floor to swap to the stairwell and find Nate there, curled against the wall after school while his mother... worked. Nancy, according to Tori, but he'd only ever known her as Miss Smith. He spent the better part of most afternoons hanging out at her place—doing his homework, watching TV, watching her cook a meal. Occasionally he'd slept on her sofa when his mother went out all night and forgot to leave the key for him. Although he'd never eat with her no matter how hungry he was or how amazingly good her food smelled. Accepting sanctuary was one thing; accepting charity...

God, he hadn't thought about her in years. He hadn't let himself.

They were one long, exhausting flight up before she lifted her thin silver curls to look at Nate. "I should sign for that parcel."

"Perhaps when we get to your door," he said, lending her as much of his strength as he could and glancing over her head at Tori, who smiled tightly at him.

It took close to ten minutes to shuffle her up to the twelfth floor. Nate had long since realized that this was the eighty-something-year-old woman Tori had referred to on the first day they'd met. She was right. This climb would kill Miss Smith one day.

He held her arm tighter.

"Here we are," Tori smiled as they emerged on to the top floor of the twelve-story building. Nate's chest cramped up hard. God knows how the old lady's must be feeling. But his chest-squeeze was uncomfortable for way more than just his exertion, as twenty years in full tackle gear rushed headlong at him.

"You left your door open," Tori gently admonished as they stepped Nancy across the hall to 12C's entry.

He looked around. Nothing about this place had changed one bit. The furniture was even still where it had been two decades before. Like a museum display built to haunt him. But Miss Smith was changed. Had she always been this tiny? She made Tori seem positively robust. Or had he just grown so much?

In a building where everything felt as recent as last week, seeing Miss Smith so aged was a shock. A reminder that time actually had passed since that day when he was seventeen and he'd walked out of this building without a backward glance. He'd never even said goodbye to Miss Smith.

"Lemonade, dear?"

His head came up fast enough to give him whiplash, but she wasn't speaking to him. She was smiling at Tori, who closed the door carefully, properly, behind them.

That was straight out of his childhood, too. Miss Smith's lemonade. A sweet, tangy port in the relentless storm of his miserable childhood.

"I'd love some, Miss—" The words *Miss Smith* so nearly spilled from his lips until he remembered that he only knew her first name as far as Tori was concerned. "Nancy. Thank you."

Tori caught his eye apologetically as the older woman wandered into her kitchen. He split his frozen lips into something he hoped resembled a smile. But Tori's frown suggested maybe he hadn't quite pulled it off.

She dropped her voice. "I'm sorry Nathan. I hope this won't take long."

"She's got Alzheimer's?"

She glanced toward the kitchen. "Dementia. Mild enough she can still live on her own, but severe enough she might wander out of the building and forget where she lives. She's been stable for a few years, but it's been worse this past year. Inside her apartment she's generally okay. Or in the building. Everyone here looks out for her." Her eyes narrowed slightly. "You're extremely special. She would normally never invite a stranger up. Ever."

Nathan averted his eyes immediately and, grief welling, watched the tiny, blue-rinsed woman pottering in her kitchen. Miss Smith had given him shelter when he'd needed it—never a question asked—and he'd barely thought of her these past two decades. He remembered her as old twenty years ago, but logically she could only have been in her mid-sixties back then. Somewhere deep in his subconscious he'd convinced himself she'd have died by now. So to find her still living, but in such poor health... And all alone...

"Here you are, dear. No sugar." She reappeared and passed one of two tall glasses of home-squeezed lemonade to Tori, and then turned to him. "And extra for you."

Nate reeled as the soft, wrinkled hands extended a pebbled glass straight from his past. Extra sugar. Just how he'd always taken it. He glanced up between chest thumps but her pale eyes showed no recognition whatsoever. Whatever functioning part of her clouded brain remembered how he took his lemonade, it wasn't communicating with the part that would remember a face. Or a name. Or, God forbid, his circumstances.

She remembered him, but apparently she didn't.

His hand shook as he took the glass, and his eyes flicked to Tori.

She glanced openly and quizzically between him and Miss Smith. He didn't dare hold the older woman's gaze in case the spark of recognition should suddenly form. In case she'd re-member and blurt out what she knew. Instead, he took his lemonade and wandered over to the window to look out, keeping his back firmly to her.

The view didn't do much of a job of taking his mind off the imminent exposure that he risked by staying, but storming out now would only make it all more dramatic and obvious. The last thing he wanted or needed was for Tori to start asking questions about his childhood. He was as changed from the boy he'd been as Miss Smith was from the woman he remembered, but even through the haze of dementia she had recognized him on some unconscious level.

Tori sipped her lemonade and made quiet conversation with his old friend. Her tranquil goodness radiated outward and made him feel positively grimy for the kind of life he'd led here, for the decisions he'd made since leaving.

There was a reason he didn't like to go back into those feelings. They weren't productive.

The ice in his glass rattled and he realized how brutally he was holding his lemonade. He took a long, careful swig and half drained the contents, wincing. Memories flowed into him with the bittersweet liquid. The taste of citrus on his tongue as a boy, had become a balm against what he knew was going on downstairs, a psychological bridge to safety that he could cross as the drink crossed his lips, to enter Miss Smith's pillowed world. Somewhere normal. A thousand miles from the apartment four floors down where his mother sold her body to strangers three times a day.

Mission accomplished. These days he had money bursting out of metaphorical suitcases. More than any of them ever could have imagined. The life he lived now couldn't have been more different to the first two decades of his existence.

"Are you finished?" Tori's soft voice brought him around. She took his half-empty glass from his cold fingers. The warmth he'd admired earlier had completely vanished and a flat caution filled her expression instead. Understandable, given he'd been treating her to his back for the past ten minutes.

He nodded. "Let's get out of here." It was straight from his aching heart. From the part of him that still carried shame. But it visibly pierced her skin.

Her brows dropped and her eyes darkened. "I'm sorry to have kept you. But thank you for helping me get her back upstairs."

Disapproval leached through the tightness of her expression. She couldn't understand his haste, of course. She had no idea how many agonies it was for him, standing here, smelling these smells, reliving the memories. So unprepared.

In front of *her*.

"I'll start on the website tomorrow afternoon," he murmured. There was no way he could stay today.

"It's Sunday."

"Doesn't matter. The faster I get this done..." *The faster I get the hell out of this building.*

A dark shaft flashed across her face. "Right. Of course. Time is money."

He nodded his farewell, glanced at Miss Smith and hurried out into the relative silence of the hallway where his memories didn't shriek at him.

As he pushed open the stairwell door, he imagined Miss Smith's frail wrists trying to do it. Remembered how they'd had to proceeded slowly as a funeral cortège up the four flights from the eighth floor where she'd found him. He kept his eyes down as he switched from the stairs to the elevator, but then made himself raise them as he stepped in. He couldn't go on studying the carpet forever.

He glanced around at the aged inner furnishings and let himself go back where he seldom did. His sixteenth birthday. The cheaply dressed woman turning to him with a smile as fake as the nails that stalled the elevator in middescent. How he'd pressed his clenched fists to the polished glass throughout the whole encounter—wanting it and hating it at the same time— and stared into the reflection of his own anguished, fevered eyes until it was over.

But he never forgot it, nor forgave the woman who'd caused

it—not the stranger who'd popped the gum back into her mouth and tottered on high heels out of the elevator ahead of him, but her…his mother…the woman who'd gifted fifteen minutes of a fellow hooker's time to Nate for his sixteenth birthday. One of the rare times she'd given him anything.

And it had broken the final surviving fragment of his embittered young heart.

The next time he saw Darlene Archer was at her funeral. Dean's parents had offered him a no-questions-asked spare bed until his college scholarship kicked in. For months he'd been a model houseguest for them, so much so that Dean's mother had had to beg Nate not to do so much around the house. But he'd ignored her pleas; he was so desperate to stay. So damned desperate not to go back.

The lurch of the elevator snapped his thoughts back to the present. He shouldered his way through the aging doors and into the foyer before they were fully open, longing for fresh air all of a sudden. This was exactly why he'd locked those memories deep inside. It was bad enough growing up with the crippling lack of affection and interest from his mother. He didn't want to drag the anchors with him into his adult years.

And he hadn't. He'd stayed focused and on track right through college and into his career. That focus had brought him everything he wanted.

His mind threw up an image of the judgment leaching from perceptive gray eyes in Nancy Smith's apartment.

He pulled out his phone and dialed his office with unsteady fingers. "Karin," he said, and then cleared his voice so she could hear him more clearly. "Get someone to repair the elevator at Morningside, will you?"

Karin chose her words carefully. "That's not going to be cheap, Nathan. And you've just pressed the green light on demolition. Are you sure?"

It was unlike her to second-guess him, but then again, it was unlike him not to sound certain, to be reacting on emotion and not sound business sense. But his interest in making

Nancy Smith's day that little bit easier belonged one hundred percent in the past. His conscience and his judgment warred in a funnel of turbulent emotion deep inside. This was exactly why he never let emotion interfere with business.

He swore. "Get me three quotes, then. I'll see whether it's worth it." Then, because his assistant had been with him through thick and thin and because none of this was her fault, he softened his voice. "Thanks, Karin."

But somewhere deep inside he knew he'd do it. Or something better than fixing the elevator. He could make a difference for the woman who'd made such a difference to him, albeit years too late. He'd make sure she was re-housed somewhere better than his crappy old building—so she could be comfortable for the last years of her life.

It wasn't much of a thank-you, but it was something he could do.

CHAPTER SIX

"TORI, I'm sorry. Look at the time. I had no idea."

Tori straightened in her seat the following night and dropped her eyes to the computer's clock. How had four hours passed? One minute they were settling down to choose images and the next it was dark and Nathan's stomach had started vocalizing.

"Oh, wow. Me, neither. I got totally lost in the site."

She had. He'd used her images to start building a website that was elegant and clean, making stars of Fred and Wilma and building a simple text story around the two birds and the webcam. He did it in such a way that, later, when the birds bred, she'd be able to add their offspring easily. Tell a new generation of stories.

Though she had to admit he got visibly tense about the whole "future" part. Inexplicably.

But the moment passed and then so did the hours after it and now here they were, well after nine o'clock.

"Did you have plans?" she asked, mortified that some woman somewhere was tapping glossy acrylic nails on a counter top waiting for Nathan to appear.

"Nope." He finished a line of coding and turned to her, smiling with satisfaction. "You were my plans this evening."

That awkward pronouncement snapped her jaw shut audibly. She stared at him, speechless, a thick pleasure burbling upward.

I was?

"My goal was to finish this sucker tonight. A first draft, at least. No matter how long it took."

The broiling awareness thickened instantly to a hard, uncomfortable mass in her chest. He was going to stay up until all hours to get this project over with in the minimum amount of time. Her lips tightened. Of course he was. He had such a gift for making a girl feel *un*wanted.

"What if I'd had plans?" she asked, purely to be churlish.

His head came up. "Do you?"

No, but... "I might have."

He frowned at her prickly response. "Would you like me to go now? It's no problem."

Tori forced away the unexpected surge of defensiveness. She knew why he was here—the court order. Neither of them had pretended otherwise. Why the hell was she getting so offended by his haste? "No. Unless you want to? I'd understand."

It was ridiculous. Both of them stepping so carefully around the other's feelings.

Nathan chuckled first. "Let's start again." He sat up straighter. "Tori, it's late. Do you want to get some dinner?"

His smile melted her tension away to nothing. "Yes. Eating would be good."

"What do you like?"

"Anything but Portuguese chicken."

"What do you have against the Portuguese?"

"Nothing." She laughed. "Piri-Piri and I don't get along."

"I find it hard to imagine anyone or anything not getting along with you. You're very easy to be around."

More awkward silence. It was his color that rose this time, just slightly, in pinpricks high along his jaw. Tori scrabbled around for a distraction from just staring at him longer. "You wouldn't say that if you were with me right after I ingested Piri-Piri."

Oh, lord... The sort of thing you said around a campfire

after a long day climbing with your buddies, not around a hot man you couldn't stop staring at.

But Mr. Smooth took it in his stride. "Well, I've got a hankering for some Mexican. How about we clear our heads, take a walk and see if we can find somewhere with an outdoor table?"

Everything in her tightened up. She waved a carefully casual hand. "Why walk when we can dial? Eat in."

"Are you serious? We've been fixed in one position for four hours. We should probably be doing some yoga to unkink."

Immediately Tori thought of more collaborative ways of working the knots out of their muscles. A part of her longed to suggest it.

"Plus it's a beautiful night," he went on. "Come on, Tori, I'll take you to dinner. Somewhere with a view."

Again with the clenching muscles deep inside. What was going on with her? Was she really so out of touch with how this was done in normal circles? Not that anything was being done here tonight. This was just a practical necessity. They both had to eat.

"We've got one of the best views around right here," she said. "Why don't I set up the table on the roof while you pick up the takeout?"

The lines between his brows doubled. He shrugged. "Sure. Okay. Got any recommendations?"

Tori crossed to her fridge, relieved to be away from Nathan's scrutiny, and rifled through an enormous bundle of restaurant fliers pinned to its front.

"I should rephrase that," he said, deceptively light. "Any recommendations you *don't* have?"

She looked at the ridiculous wad in her hand and fought the bristle of discomfort at his gentle teasing. "I enjoy eating in."

"But not eating out?"

Her mouth dried up. She blinked at him urgently then stammered to speech. "W-wait till you've sat up there. You'll understand."

His eyes held hers while his brain ticked over. They nearly broiled with the intensity of his gaze. "You'd better make it special, then. Worth it."

And just like that it was a date.

What should have been a casual, convenient take-out meal had suddenly become a *special* tryst for two on the top of a New York building. He'd already seen the rooftop so she'd have to do more than just throw out a clean table cloth. And there was no electric light up there so they'd have to have candles.

Ugh…!

Not that a long-suppressed, girlie part of her wasn't thrilling at the idea of being on a date. After…how long? Even if it wasn't really a *date*-date. She hadn't sat across a dinner table from a man in five years. She wasn't even sure she remembered what people did on a date. Talked. Ate. Shared.

Kissed.

Her stomach flip-flopped. It was very telling that the idea of *sharing* with Nathan Archer was infinitely scarier than the idea of kissing him. Not that she'd given much thought to what it would be like to kiss him. Not truly. Okay, a few times…just casually wondering… Nothing serious.

Although now that the fantasy was in her head she had trouble shaking it.

"Yes." She thrust him the advertisement of the best TexMex in the area, just a few blocks over. "It'll be worth it."

Tori didn't take the word *special* any more lightly than the challenge she'd seen in Nathan's eyes as he headed out to buy the food. Whatever she did, she knew it had to be inspired.

Seven years ago she'd been hiking the Canadian Rockies and she'd had the best Mexican food she'd ever tasted in an Irish pub, of all places. They'd served sizzling meals on scorching hot tiles straight out of the fire, and margaritas in moonshine jars. Tonight she was desperate enough to recreate every part of that experience.

She'd loved it then, maybe Nathan would love it now.

She finished pouring margarita mix over a pitcher of hastily crushed ice, loaded up a couple of clean preserve jars and a crazy cowboy-hat candle her parents had sent her from Texas, and raced up the stairs. Then she came back down for the pizza stones she'd baked to blazing in her oven. She stacked them on top of each other and used the lifters to carry them carefully up the two flights of stairs. By the time she emerged, even her climbing arms were trembling from the strain.

She placed them carefully onto tiny terracotta blocks to protect the table. Then stood back to admire her handiwork.

Special. No denying it.

"Food's up," a deep voice said, behind her. She spun, still breathless from dashing around and kicking herself she hadn't dashed faster so she could have dedicated just sixty seconds to freshening up. So that, just once, he could see her at her best rather than her worst.

But then she remembered this wasn't a date-date. This was just dinner. "How did you get back in?"

"One of the perks of owning the building. I finally signed myself over a key."

Tori's heart fluttered. Just the idea that he could let himself in whenever he wanted… Was that uncertainty or excitement curling her stomach. Or was it just hunger?

She distracted herself with pouring slushy-ice margarita into the large empty jars while Nathan unloaded six containers of Mexico's finest. Then they both sat and got busy serving up rice, burritos, chili, tamales, stuffed peppers and skillet-fried fish onto their piping-hot stone tablets. The mouth-watering odors wafted around them. They loaded up their forks and sampled.

Nathan took a long, appreciative swallow from his moon-shine jar to wash down the first mouthful of food and looked around before letting his contented eyes rest back on hers through the flicker of candlelight. "Okay, you win. This is without question the best way to eat Mexican *ever*."

Tori waved a hand. "I do it like this all the time."

"You do not," he laughed. Though he looked as if he'd have believed her if she said she really did. "When you didn't want to come with me I wondered if I'd done something to…" He frowned. "But this is great. I appreciate the effort you've gone to."

She knew she'd offended him by not going with him to dinner. Not that she could explain why when she didn't even know herself. She'd just been listening to her body. And her body said stay. "You're welcome. It is nice, huh?"

To illustrate the point she took a big swig from her moonshine jar. Then she bit into a piping-hot tamale. "Okay, wow. That's better than…"

"Than?"

The spicy heaven filled her mouth with excited juices. She rolled her eyes with pleasure. "Everything."

He lifted one sexy eyebrow. "Not everything, surely?"

She sat back in her seat and chewed a tamale appreciatively. "I'm struggling to think of something better."

Nathan selected one from the tray, trying for himself. "It is good," he nodded slowly then his mouth split into a heart-stopping grin. "But not that good."

Tori smiled to cover the sudden pounding of her heart. What she wouldn't give just to lean forward and wipe the tamale grease right off his lips…with her own. Slowly and thoroughly. Lingering on the bottom one. Her tongue slipped out onto her own lips in sympathy. "Well, you'd know, I guess!"

"Meaning?"

She stiffened her back. "Meaning I imagine you've had a lot of…everything…to compare to."

He smiled. "You're talking about sex."

Thump, thump… "No, *you* were talking about sex. I was talking about everything else."

His narrowed gaze saw too much. "But not sex?"

It had to come up sooner or later. "If these tamales are like sex then I can understand what all the fuss is about."

Nathan stared at her and she took another healthy swig of margarita then finally met his eyes silently.

His blazed back at her. "You've never had sex?"

"Try and contain your disbelief. It's insulting." Her words would have been, too, if she hadn't punctuated them by casually popping another tamale between her tingling lips and smiling. Way more casually than she felt.

He seemed to shake himself free of his stupor. "I'm sorry. I'm having a hard time believing it."

"Why?"

The blue in his gaze boiled as furiously as a hot spring. "Have you seen yourself, Tori?"

She shrugged. "Maybe my body is my temple?"

He put down his fork and leaned forward. "Come on. Seriously?"

"Why do people who've had sex always find it inconceivable that someone else hasn't?" And on what planet did she sit across the table from a relative stranger talking about her nonexistent sex life?

Planet Nathan, apparently.

He considered that in silence. "You're right. I just..." He shook his head. "How old are you?"

That question had only just occurred to him? She'd looked him up on the internet him almost immediately after she'd met him to find out the essentials. Which had seemed stupid at the time. "I'm twenty-six."

"Huh." He shook his head.

"You're really struggling with this." Amazing. And insanely flattering. Her whole body tightened in response. "I was one of the boys at prep school, then I spent most of my teen years in sports clubs." And why the heck was she defending herself so vigorously? "Then on the peaks I was just one of the boys again. Maybe I missed my window of opportunity."

"Uh, no, Tori, that window is still *wide* open for you."

She stared at him as his lashes blinked, apparently at half speed. Or was everything around her just happening sluggishly?

Certainly the blood in her veins and what air was in her lungs were thickening up dangerously.

"All those climbers, Tori. All that testosterone…"

The glow dissipated just a bit. "The last person in the world you want to climb with is someone you're emotionally involved with." She topped up her rice and got stuck into it, hoping to change the subject.

"Why?"

Hoping in vain. "It's like brain surgery. You should never do it on someone you love. Makes it hard to stay objective."

"You climbed with your brother."

The food in her mouth congealed into a tasteless paste. She chewed it carefully then took care swallowing so that it stayed down. "We had rules. To keep things separate."

Mostly.

"What kind of rules?"

"We'd climb in groups and always partner someone else. If we were climbing together we'd only do novice peaks." That was the rule. But the moment they set it, they'd started breaking it. Incrementally. Which could only lead to one thing…

"Defeats the purpose, I would have thought," Nathan said.

"Not many people get that." She looked at him differently in that moment, but then she remembered in his own industry he was the risk-taker. The first one to the highest peaks. "So we'd try for groups whenever we could so we could really climb."

"And no-one wanted to…get closer?"

Some of the taste in her food returned and she smiled gently. "With them, Rick was like a rottweiler on patrol. I think he'd heard too many of their stories."

"Ah. Big brothers."

"Physically, definitely. He out-muscled all of them. But I was older than him by fifteen minutes."

That stilled the fork halfway to his mouth. "You and Rick were twins?"

Her chest ached. Five years meant nothing to the ball of pain still resident in her chest. "We were the full cliché. Finishing each other's sentences, being sensitive to each other, sharing a house..." She felt the darkness hovering and took a deep breath to stave it off. "I even wore his clothes until puberty hit and he shot up four sizes. It drove him nuts."

"He was lucky to have you." Blue eyes held hers as he got used to that idea. A chili-like warmth spread through her body and added to the sluggish mix. "So that explains how you stayed under the radar until you were twenty-one. You haven't met anyone since you came to Manhattan?"

Tori's muscles coordinated to squeeze the last bit of oxygen from her lungs. Okay, when the conversation started working its way around to him it was definitely time to stop talking about sex. She forced a chuckle. "Mr. B's not really my type and Marco deCosta isn't old enough yet."

He laughed. "You think you're joking. The day will come when that kid's not going to be able to look at you without a cushion in his lap."

Tori spluttered, surprised by the unfamiliar sound of her own full belly laugh, and intrigued by the sudden forked frown lines that appeared between Nathan's brows. She saw a chance to learn more about him. She took it.

"Was there someone like that for you?"

Almost definitely. A man as simmering as Nathan didn't wake up one day and discover he'd become sexy. That kind of charisma came from childhood. And people responded to charisma. No matter the shape or size or age. They just changed the manner of response. He probably didn't even know he had it.

He blinked three times. Rapidly. "What?"

She glanced down at her empty margarita glass leaned forward to refill it, smiling more comfortably now that the topic had moved on. "If there was ever a candidate for a *Graduate* moment, it's you. Was there some kind of older woman that excited you, Nathan Archer?"

His gaze darkened and his mouth formed a harsh, straight line. Tension radiated from him in angry ripples.

"No."

That one word was sharp and tight and sounded like the ugliest of curses. And just like that, all the joy sucked out of their beautiful, special meal.

And both of them knew it.

"I…" What could she say? She let her lips fall shut and shifted her eyes away from the sudden strain. And chivalry must have died because Nathan didn't swoop in and try to ease her discomfort. He just sat there, as awkward as she was.

When he did finally speak his voice wasn't seductive any more.

"Why don't you have a job, Tori?" he nearly sneered. "How do you make rent?"

If she'd thought he was asking because he was interested, she would have told him, even though it was a critically rude question to ask. But he wasn't. He was asking to strike back at her for whatever she'd said to offend. So Nathan had a mean streak. Good to know. But she'd learned a thing or two about independence since moving to New York, and about how the world worked. Men like him might run the world but *she* ran her part of it.

She took her napkin and dabbed carefully at her lips, then pushed her chair away from the rooftop table. "Goodnight Nathan. I'll email you the web files and you can finish the site at your own apartment."

Her legs took her nearly all the way to the door before she felt his warm hand on her shoulder. She shrugged it off.

"Tori, wait." He moved around in front of her.

She crossed her arms in front of her. "Get out of my way, Nathan."

"Tori. I'm sorry. That was a cheap shot."

He wasn't moving, though. She kept her muscles rigid. "If you want me to listen to you then I suggest you get out from between me and the only way off this roof."

He glanced behind him and cursed under his breath, then stepped back. "I'm not making this better, am I?"

She turned her eyes up to him, taking care to keep them neutral. Suddenly she regretted the jar-and-a-half of margarita. She'd rather do this with a full complement of faculties. "I understand privacy, Nathan, better than most people. But if there's something you don't want to talk about, just say so."

He blew his frustration out through clenched teeth. "I let my guard down. I wasn't prepared. You blindsided me."

"With a casual question about your childhood?"

He looked as confused as she felt. "Everyone has triggers, Tori. You just stumbled onto one of mine. A raw one."

"So you hit back?"

His face fell and the abject misery glowed as neon as the storefronts down on the street. It niggled at her conscience. "That was my poor attempt at changing the subject. But it was harsher than I'd meant. I'm really sorry, Tori."

She stared at him a moment longer. "I pay the rent from money I got when I sold our house in Oregon."

He held up a hand. "It's none of my business. You were right not to—"

"I have nothing to hide, Nathan." Not, strictly speaking, true, but that was an inner demon for another lifetime. "Rick left me his half of our grandmother's house in his will. I sold it to come here and the rent comes straight out of that bank account. I don't even see it."

His shoulders slumped as he nodded and he wedged his hands into his jeans pockets. An eternity passed silently and then Tori turned for the door. Just as she reached for the handle, he spoke. Flat. Strained.

"I grew up in a building…much like this one."

The surprise was enough to halt her fingers on the door handle. But she didn't turn.

He continued behind her. "I know you imagined me growing up in a brownstone with loving parents and a matched pair of retrievers but that's not how it was."

His tension brought her focus around to him.

"Money was a rare commodity in my world. It was just

my mother and me and she was always…occupied…with her work."

Tori frowned at that choice of phrase.

"So, no…my childhood really wasn't peppered with idyllic moments, and the sorts of people in my mother's industry were hardly the type to inspire thoughts of great romance in a young boy."

"What people?" The pain was so evident as it twisted his handsome face into a fierce scowl, but she needed to understand. Even if her heart beat hard enough to hurt. "What industry?"

He lifted bleak eyes. "She was in sales."

Something about the way he said it. Like it was a lie he'd been telling for so long it had started to sound like the truth. She had to push the words out of her tight throat as a whisper. "What did she sell?"

A moment ago her heart had hammered because of him. Now it pounded blood ruthlessly against the walls of her arteries *for* him. Every part of her wanted to spare him from the truth she could read between the pained lines of his face.

Don't say it. Don't say it…

He shrugged. "Whatever men were buying."

Years of controlled breathing in oxygen-deficient environments had trained her well. She swallowed the shocked gasp. "She was a prostitute."

"At least."

She let that sink in. Imagining what he'd seen. Empathy for the hurt little boy he must have been flowed through her. "I'm sure she was only doing it to—"

"Don't." His hand shot up, large and firm. "Do you think it hurts less thinking she was doing it to feed and clothe and educate me? That belief tore my soul to shards until I realized it wasn't true. I gave up defending her years ago."

The sounds of carousing down on 126th Street drifted up to them in the silence that followed and mingled with the dense cloud of pain suddenly hanging heavy on her rooftop.

What should you say to someone who'd just spilled their

soul at your feet? Exposed their deepest secrets. Should you thank them for their trust? Should you comfort them for their shame? Should you gloss over it and try to put things back to how they were five minutes before and wish you'd been a little more tolerant and a lot less reactive?

Tori stepped up to him and curled her fingers around his and did the only thing she would have wanted in his place.

She traded him.

"Rick died while he was climbing with me," she said, quietly. "I watched him fall."

CHAPTER SEVEN

THAT brought his eyes up sharply and drove the misery straight from them. They filled instead with clear, glinting compassion. "You saw your brother die?"

"I watched every last second until I lost sight of him." *As penance.*

"Christ, Tori…"

"I don't want your pity, Nathan. Any more than you want mine. But I wanted you to know that I do understand something about triggers. About the everyday little things that leap up and ambush you when you're not at all prepared." *You blindsided me.* "And how hard it can be to stay rational when those feelings swell up."

They stared at each other until she finally spoke again. "So, I believe you when you say you're sorry. And when you say you didn't mean to be harsh. But can I trust you not to do it again'?"

He was recovering his composure by the second. But he still frowned, not entirely back to cool, calm and collected Nathan. "You can trust me to not want to. And to do my very best not to let it happen again."

She stared at him, long and hard. Could she have offered more in his place?

Probably not.

"Good enough," she said, as a shudder rippled through her.

Nathan stripped off his coat and swung it around her bare

shoulders then held it together at her throat. The warmth soaked immediately into her frigid skin.

"You guys were climbing together?" he asked, carefully.

Of course he was going to ask. No one would walk away from a pronouncement like that. And she'd pressed *him* for details. But her instinctive defenses came straight into play and locked up her muscles.

"We broke our own rule."

"You were climbing alone." She nodded. As usual his quick mind took him straight to the important part. He freed a hand to rub up and down her arm. "You had to deal with it alone. That must have been hell."

No one had ever asked her this. Amongst the many, many questions about Rick's death at the inquiry, about which peak they'd chosen and why, about how thoroughly they'd hammered in the cams, no one had asked her what it had felt like walking off that mountain without the brother she adored. The boy she'd shared a womb with.

She dropped her eyes. "I couldn't leave him at all for the first few hours. But I couldn't drag him out either, he was too big. And I had to get back into radio range." She straightened her shoulders and snuggled more deeply into the warmth of Nathan's jacket. "Leaving him behind was the hardest thing I've ever done."

Third-hardest. Lying back against the snow drift knowing that she lived when he'd died…

Infinitely worse.

And number one…

She shook her head and blinked back the tears that always came when she relived that day. The last thing she wanted to do was cry in front of Nathan. She cleared her thick throat.

He pulled her toward him and wrapped his arms around his own coat, speaking against the top of her hair. "Would Rick blame you?"

Would he? Given they'd both ended up in the same perilous situation? That it could just as easily have been her on the wrong side of the anchor. "No. He hated it when I pulled rank. He considered us equals."

"Then let yourself off the hook. You didn't cause his death."

Her gut flipped back on itself and then squeezed into a tiny fist. There's no way he could truly understand, any more than she could do more than graze the surface of empathy for a little boy growing up in Nathan's impossible situation.

But in a weird, hopelessly antisocial way, knowing he'd endured pain too actually helped her manage hers. Knowing he understood—the concept if not the detail. It made her feel closer to him—to any human being—than she'd been in years.

She pressed her forehead against his shoulder.

"Thank you for telling me," he murmured, still against her hair. "I know it can't have been easy."

She leaned into his hard body where her fists clenched the front of his coat shut. *Honey, you don't know the half of it.* Watching Rick fall was only part of her nightmare. But there were some things you never aired.

Ever.

"You're welcome," she mumbled into his broad shoulder, letting herself enjoy the gift of his heat.

"We make quite a pair, huh?" His chuckle was more about tension than humor.

A pair. It took that phrase to draw her attention finally to something startlingly obvious that she'd been missing. She was standing under the stars, wrapped up snugly in Nathan's coat, buried in his arms with her lips practically pressed against his shoulder. Pairs made her think of couples. And couples made her think of coupl*ing*. And coupling made her think of...

Desire pooled thick and low in her body as his scent worked its way right into the pores of her skin and brought her mind full circle.

...Nathan.

Wrapped in the arms of the sexiest man she knew. Close enough that she could feel his steady heartbeat. Close enough that she could feel the plane of a ridged pectoral muscle beneath her clenched fists through his light sweater. Close enough that she could die right now and happily spend eternity swilling in his scent.

Time to move.

But no sooner did her body warn her to withdraw thaw those strong arms tightened. Keeping her close. One hand slid around to her back and recommenced its hypnotic circling there. Tori fought the insane desire just to melt into him. To surrender... everything...for a moment and let someone else take all the weight.

For a few heavenly moments.

How long had it been since anyone had touched her, let alone a man? Let alone like this. She took her moments of bliss where she could find them.

She leaned more closely into his hard body and added a fistful of his sweater into her tight clutch to keep them close. Her eyes drifted shut. Somewhere a thousand miles off music tumbled out of a window, the ballad drifting up to them on the night air. He leaned a fraction to his left and she followed him, loath to lose his warmth and the connection so soon. Then he moved back slightly to the right, that magic hand going around and around against her spine the whole time. And she followed.

Step...after step. Swaying left then right.

The rocking motion soothed as much as it serrated her body against his in a delicious, subtle, unfamiliar friction.

"Tori..." he mumbled, after a lifetime of gentle movement "...are we dancing?"

She didn't lift her lashes. The real world wasn't welcome back just yet. She mumbled, "No, we're shuffling."

She felt him smile against her forehead. "Okay, then."

They swayed in silence for the rest of the song. Nathan gathered her more firmly to him and Tori burrowed happily into his hold. She'd worked hard on her ability to push unwanted thoughts out of her head and she prayed thanks for it now, for the toasty, naive glow that could fill her soul while she kept the hard, real world carefully separate.

Their feet slowed to a halt and Nathan rubbed his face down hers, nudging it out and up, while his hands stayed tightly locked around her body. The seductive graze of his prickled jaw against hers, the blazing tangle of his breath and the hammer of his chest against hers...all whipped her heartbeat into riot and sent her senses skittering wildly around them like a mini dervish. A ton-weight pressed in on her chest.

Oh, God, he's going to kiss me...

And if he didn't, she was going to kiss him.

Or possibly die from oxygen deficiency.

She lifted her heavy lids and glanced at him. This close, his blue eyes were as clear and deep as any glacial lake but fringed by dark, soft lashes and blazing the icy fire of a question unasked. Somewhere in their depths a cautious uncertainty did a lazy backstroke but it was overwhelmed by the bubbling energy and focus of the last thing she'd ever expected to see from him.

Desire.

The moment their gazes met, all the reasons this was a bad idea—how unprofessional it was, why she didn't deserve a moment like this and why he was totally unsuitable and unsafe for her—dissolved just like her caution when she was facing a new mountain for the first time. Something other than sense was ruling play here, surging through her bloodstream and setting fire to every cell it passed. Bringing them scorching to vivid life.

Baying for more.

She let her mouth follow her eyes and turned her head naturally into the heat of his, dropping her lips slightly open.

His focus flicked down to them a bare moment before he closed the gap with a whispered groan.

The moment Tori's lips met Nathan's soft, warm ones, her body lurched with the involuntary gasp of air that rushed in. He captured her parted mouth with his again. He tasted of tangy citrus and chili and something rarer, something indefinable. Something she'd never experienced but wanted, in that moment, to keep forever. Her blood pounded everywhere it came close to the surface and robbed her of strength. Her mouth slid against his—tasting, exploring, feeding—and her hands curled more tightly into his sweater to keep him close. He shifted one hand lower, to press her hips into him and the other higher, tangling in her hair and taking the weight of her head as she let it fall back to give him more access.

"Tori…" he gasped, as they both sucked in a desperate breath. But she closed the gap again, nowhere near done with learning the shape of his lips, the taste of his mouth, and the slide of his teeth. He met her with interest, tangling tongues the moment she invited him in and sending her mind spinning off with sensation.

She curled one arm around his bent neck, pulling him closer, and his hand abandoned her nape in favor of a slow, sensual slide down her shoulder around to her side and under his own coat that heated her like a sauna all of a sudden. He burrowed under her thin cotton blouse and curved big fingers around her waist, his skin blazing hot against hers.

"So soft… So tiny…" he murmured against her mouth.

Funny, exactly the opposite of what she'd just been thinking. *So hard. So male.* The sort of man to make a tomboy feel like a princess. Alone together on this towering rooftop, under the magical stars. Where anything goes…

That thought brought her crashing back into focus. Back to the place where she didn't deserve the pleasure that was threatening to make her sigh. Back to the reality of who she was and who he was. And the fact they'd both got way too carried away with a margarita-fuelled candlelight dinner under the handful of stars that the lights of Manhattan allowed.

She gently pulled back out of his grasp. He let her go reluctantly, those big man hands trailing across her midriff as she stepped clear of him on unsteady legs.

Her chest heaved as hard as his as she breathed out a wobbly exclamation. "Wow."

He shook his disheveled hair. "You sure don't kiss like a novice, Tori."

Given she could count the number of men she'd kissed on one hand—fingers, not thumb—it definitely wasn't from practice. She took a shaky breath and smiled, filled for the first time with some ancient goddess magic that made her feel invincible. And woman. And utterly, utterly sensual.

"Natural aptitude?"

His laugh was as rocky as the geysers at Yellowstone, releasing the tension built up inside on a hiss. What did other people do in situations like this? When you'd just been crawling inside the skin of someone you were supposed to be working with? When you barely knew each other?

"Nathan, I—"

"Please don't say you're sorry, Tori. Let's just call it a great way to end a truly enjoyable evening."

"The evening's over?" Was that her voice sounding so thin? So disappointed?

"I...think it has to be. That conversation was only going one place and I'm not about to take you there."

Conversation? Well, they *were* using their mouths.

She probably should have been all uptight about the implication of Nathan's words. But she was too muddled to do anything but take him perfectly literally. "Why not?"

"Trust me. You deserve better."

"Than what? Dirty rooftop sex. Or dirty rooftop sex with you, specifically?"

He reached out and readjusted his coat more firmly around her shoulders, avoiding the question and accidentally brushing one still tingling breast as he slipped a button through its eyelet. It screamed at her to argue the point.

"When you have sex for the first time Tori, it should be memorable for all the right reasons."

Will you be there, Nathan? But she couldn't ask that. Her courage only went so far.

He smoothed the sleeves of the coat down her arms and the move struck her as just a little bit too patronizing. It plucked away more of the golden strands that had lain so heavily over her usual defenses. Her eyes narrowed. "Shouldn't that be my decision?"

He stared at her and ran well-manicured fingers through his own hair to restore some order. "Tell you what, Tori. Tomorrow morning when you no longer have a belly full of Mexican food and margarita and lust, if you still think this is a good idea you just give me a call and I'll happily oblige. But tonight…it's goodnight."

Oblige. Like it would be some kind of civic duty. Part of his community service. Anger bubbled up. "What makes you think I don't have plans tomorrow?"

Wow, did rampant sexual frustration make everyone this irritable?

But it seemed to be catching. "You haven't had a single plan since I met you," he gritted.

That was too close to the truth, and she felt the boiling of sudden shame. To a man like him, staying at home a lot probably did seem like loser territory. Let alone all the time. She used the moments it took to shrug off his coat to master her brewing pique, and then folded the jacket carefully before handing it back to him.

She met his frown and threw him her best couldn't-care-less smile. "Don't wait by the phone, Nathan. If it rings it won't be me."

CHAPTER EIGHT

THE phone did ring the following workday—many times—and it was never Tori.

Nathan stared up gridlocked Columbus Avenue toward Morningside. Again.

She'd said she wouldn't call. She would have come to her senses five minutes after coming down from that rooftop—from the amazing natural high of their kissing. Women like Viktoria Morfitt didn't belong with men like him. No matter how much tequila they'd ingested. She came from a good, wholesome family and he...just didn't.

But she'd know that now. After his extraordinary Dr. Phil full-confession moment by the stairs.

What the hell had he been thinking? No one but his most trusted circle knew about his mother. Dean and his parents, his school counselor who'd endorsed him for early admission, the financial aid registrar.

Okay so a few people knew. But he'd never imagined Tori would be one of them. And at his own admission. Desperate times, desperate measures—the way she'd stalked, so stiff-backed from the table. It had just tumbled from his lips rather than lose her and the beautiful evening she'd gone to such trouble to create. He would have said just about anything in that moment to keep her with him.

And then she'd trumped it. Well and truly.

She was there when her brother died. The *only* person there.

What kind of courage did it take to go for help and hold it all together until rescue arrived? Half a day on a mountain with a corpse that, just hours before, was the person you'd loved and teased and spent a life with.

Unimaginable.

But she'd endured it. Her eccentricities made a little bit more sense of that now. Something like that was bound to mess with your head. Change your priorities and the way you approached life. Even her folks had opted out and hit the road. Maybe this crazy existence she was living was the Tori equivalent of turning nomad.

Between the origami laundry, the tutoring, the crazy-dog minding, the photographs and the falcons—and there was undoubtedly a stack of things she was doing that he wasn't aware of—it was just as well Tori didn't have a job to be going to. She'd never have the time. She hadn't liked it when he rattled her about having no plans, but facts were facts. She was always home when he called, she was always home when he came for community service or when he dropped by with camera parts or televisions. As if she truly had nowhere else to be.

He frowned. Nor, apparently, did he.

An honest-to-goodness, New-York's-richest-list bachelor, struggling to find something better to do with his time than visit a beat-up century-old building uptown.

It wasn't until that moment—until he started counting up the visits—that he realized how much time he was spending at Tori's or on the phone to Tori. Or hunting down the perfect replacement apartment for Tori. Or thinking about Tori. Very little of it could be chalked up to a court order. There was something about her. Something unusually comfortable about being with her. Amazing when you consider how very *un*comfortable he was in that building. Yet here he was trying to come up with a good reason to go back, even now.

He glanced at his desk. And here he was finalizing the documents that would tumble the building to the ground. Even as he'd sat on the roof of it and eaten Mexican and kissed one of its inhabitants.

Guilt chewed like a dog on the rawhide of his conscience, but then reason kicked in. It was fine; Dean's team had already located alternative lease accommodation for twenty-eight of the thirty-five tenants—dog-friendly ones, kid-friendly ones, nana-friendly ones—and the remaining nine weren't far off being finalized. All within a twenty-block radius of the existing building or the tenants' workplaces. All with longish leases to give them time to make their own alternative arrangements. To see them right. He had something special in mind for Tori. Bigger and more comfortable than her modest little Morningside rental.

The phone rang and he reached for it absently. "Archer."

"I'm calling to apologise."

He dropped into his chair and then stood again—ridiculously—at the sound of Tori's breathless voice. For one crazy moment he thought she might be taking him up on his offer, tacky and ill-conceived as it had been. The absolute last thing he wanted to do was complicate things further by getting physical. Even if it was also the thing he wanted most.

But if he wanted to touch her, he'd have to tell her what was going on. About the demolition.

"Apologise for what?"

"I was supremely ungrateful last night. I never thanked you for all the work you did on the website. I was just looking at it again on my desktop. It really is amazing."

Apology accepted. As if he wouldn't. "Just a bit more to do and it will be ready to go."

"Thank you, Nathan."

God, he loved the way she said his name. That gentle west-coast accent, the breathlessness like light fingers trailing down his spine or the touch of her lips.

"And I wanted to make good on my part of the trade, at last," she went on.

Uh-oh…

"So I thought I could throw a small open house to celebrate the peregrine website going live. Give you a chance to meet some of your tenants. Give me a chance to get them excited about Wilma and Fred."

From her point of view it was a good idea to get the other tenants invested in her falcons. But it was a spectacularly bad one from his, for so many reasons. He still wasn't in a crashing hurry to meet anyone else from the building—anyone who might recognize him, or might see Darlene in Nathan's own dark coloring and do the math. Or simply recognize his surname. He had no idea how many of them had known his mother by anything other than her working name.

And somehow he thought it might be easier for them as tenants not to have met the man who was about to rehome them. To have shared coffee and cake with them, unawares. That felt more than a little wrong.

Like keeping the truth from Tori was starting to.

"So I was wondering if you could give me a realistic time frame on go-live day?"

Realistically? Today, if he pulled his finger out and got working on it instead of sitting around mooching about her. But the moment the website went live he'd have no more falcon project to work on and no more reason to see Tori.

And he really wanted to see her face when he showed her the new apartment. Personally. Frame by beautiful frame.

"Uh, how does Friday sound?"

"Friday would be great. That gives me a few days to plan. Will I—" she cleared her throat and spoke in a rush of words "—will you be coming around before then?"

"I have the code on my flash drive, so I can finish it here if you like. And I can do all the uploading and testing remotely." He paused, wondering if he was laying it on too thick when he really only wanted to know one thing. "I wasn't sure I'd be welcome."

Her sigh breathed down the phone. "I'm so sorry for

being snappish, Nathan. You didn't deserve that. We're both consenting adults. And it was just a kiss."

"Right..."

She didn't sound any more convinced about that than he did, but her remorse seemed entirely genuine. And, who knows, if she was as inexperienced as she made out then an unplanned, hot-and-heavy make-out session might have thrown her equilibrium. It threw his and he was much more used to casual contact. He specialized in casual. "Tensions were high. I imagine we both said more than we meant to."

"I guess it wasn't the usual after-dinner conversation," she murmured.

Hardly.

Dead brother. Hooker mother. *Another mint?*

"Tell you what. I'll finish the site from here and bring it round to you tomorrow evening. Will you be home?" It was almost pointless asking, but assuming—with her—would be relationship suicide.

He frowned. Relationship? Was that what they had? He didn't really do relationships, not with women. He saved those for the diminishing circle of friends he trusted. Relationships required emotional investment. Sex required nothing but time.

Why did he even care what she thought of him? But his body's response to the soft, low smile in her voice as she said, "Yes, I'll be home," made him realize he was starting to care. Inexplicably. And very much.

And that really wasn't a good idea.

She might be the virgin in a technical sense, but when it came to genuine, loving relationships she was miles ahead of him. She'd had a brother she'd loved with everything in her. Loving parents. Grandparents.

He simply had no point of reference at all.

When it came to love *he* was the virgin.

He shoved his hands deep into his trouser pockets. This really couldn't be about what he wanted. If it was he'd just call

Simon around to the front, get him to drop him at Morningside and not collect him until morning.

As he had so many times in so many other buildings in the city.

But Tori was different. He was drawn to her in a way he could barely understand.

Deep inside. Where he never, ever went.

Time to set up some boundaries.

"They have eggs!"

Tori launched herself at Nathan the moment he stepped through her door, her excitement driving away the residual discomfort at what a social klutz she had been two nights ago. Sure, it had been a while between kisses—a long while—but that was hardly Nathan's fault, hopefully he'd forgive her ridiculous overreaction. Her embarrassing and far too revealing *over-participation* in the kiss.

Or not, she realized, as he gently but firmly peeled her arms off him and set her away, keeping his focus safely elsewhere. A part of her wanted to shrivel at the careful neutrality of his expression, but the thrill surging like champagne bubbles through her blood couldn't care less about her blushes, and so she snagged his hand and dragged him to the television where the webcam showed a fabulous center-of-screen view of Wilma happily spread low in the nest box, patiently guarding something.

That got his attention. "Have you seen the eggs?" he asked.

"Nope. But she wouldn't be brooding if they weren't there." A strange, almost forgotten lightness filled her. It had been a long time between lightnesses, too. She turned her face up to him. "They've bred, Nathan!"

He wasn't looking at the screen anymore; his eyes were fixed firmly on her. And they were dark with something she thought was confusion. Or surprise. Or both. "You're radiant."

Heat raced into her cheeks. She'd made an effort to dress for him this time. Nothing flash, just her best, butt-hugging jeans and a simple shirt in the most flattering color she owned. She knew she had no real right to be this happy, but Nathan just noticing when she looked good added to her already erupting excitement about the falcons. "I'm sure it's not *that* unusual. I can be happy."

The expression settled into a frown. "It's good to see."

But then his focus flicked back to Wilma who looked comically uncertain about what her instincts were making her do. The she-falcon glanced anxiously around her, as if expecting more. Or some help. Tori hugged her arms around herself and worked hard not to bounce up and down.

Babies. Not the first she'd seen, but definitely the first she'd gone all squishy over.

"How long before the eggs hatch?" Beside her, Nathan's voice was measured but pleasingly rumbly.

"About a month."

"Then what happens?"

"Then Wilma and Fred raise the ones that survive. Teach them how to fly, hunt. How to be independent."

"How long does that take—until they're independent?"

Was he worried he wouldn't be around to see it? "About six weeks. You can watch it all on the webcam, Nathan."

Something finally dented the natural high she'd been on since switching on the webcam and seeing Wilma on the nest. Heck, since she'd drowned in Nathan's kiss on the rooftop. How sad that he wouldn't be here to see the hatching in person. That they'd go their separate ways any day now.

Sad for him.

Sadder for her.

Her heart squeezed hard. "We have to get this live as soon as possible," she mumbled, thrown by the sudden, intense ache. "People will want to see this part. How much time do you have this afternoon?"

His enigmatic eyes came back to hers, distracted by a visible uncertainty but then clearing as he seemed to make a decision. Their warmth reached out to her. "As much as you need."

Tuesday—Nathan had to be busy with work stuff today. No wonder he was distracted. The time he was giving her was so generous.

She took a deep breath.

"Well then, let's get to work."

They spent the whole afternoon and most of the night editing footage from the moment the webcam was powered up, hunting in fast forward for the best bits of footage and making a "What You Missed" archive for the website: Wilma and Fred checking out the box, visiting and revisiting, a short, solitary, X-rated Wilma and Fred, and then, finally, Mom on the nest and Dad hovering anxiously by, alert for interlopers.

If Tori had stuck her head out that bathroom window they would have been off, never to return. No question.

Wilma had laid during the night so it was almost impossible to see how many eggs there were, but peregrines usually produced three or four with the hope that at least one would survive to juvenile status. She'd have to feed eventually so perhaps there'd be a brief moment when Fred took over when Tori could catch a glimpse of how many eggs they'd made together. Would there be a Pebbles and BamBam, too?

She sighed. *Ah, reproduction, such a wonderful thing.*

And not just because she couldn't get her mind off the human equivalent lately; it was such a disturbingly short mental journey from Nathan to babies.

They worked through dinner, sharing ideas, compromising on differences, anticipating each other's thoughts, and celebrating the amazing footage and photos that the site brought together. Tori caught herself resting her gaze more on Nathan than the screen several times and had to force her focus back to proofreading the text content or making a decision on footage, only to catch herself doing it again a few minutes later.

He compelled her gaze toward him exactly the way her

climbing tools sometimes stuck to the natural magnetism of certain rock faces.

His own fault for being so good to look at. He was tall and built for endurance, where her climbing friends had been solid and built for bursts of massive full-body power, but she would have picked Nathan anyway. His brilliant mind would have ensnared her even amongst all their outdoorsy muscle. But the thickening stubble of beard he hadn't shaved off since Sunday night grew hard along his strong cheekbones and highlighted their strength. And she was way too aware of how his lips had felt on hers to worry whether they might be, technically, a little on the thin side by Hollywood standards. And every time she had an idea that he didn't like and he slid those deep-blue eyes sexily sideways at her in doubt...she just melted that little bit more.

She stared at him now, while his attention was thoroughly focused on the computer screen.

It couldn't hurt just to look, surely. To speculate.

All the excitement she felt now about the peregrine eggs only simmered in amongst the residual tingles from spending the last two nights reliving the feel of his mouth on hers. The strength of his arms pinning her to him. The feel of his hard planes under her hands. And creating endless, breathless scenarios about what would have happened if she hadn't pulled away from him back on the rooftop. If she'd heeded the raw, base call of a virile male. If she'd let the hungry ancient goddess in her respond.

Knowing how much she needed that.

Believing how little she deserved it.

"Coffee?"

She was on her feet and moving towards the kitchen before he could answer. She gulped down a glass of cold water and willed away the pheromones she could practically smell churning around her. They weren't helping her keep her mind on the job and the last thing she wanted was to be sitting so close to Nathan while practically radiating "take-me-now" vibes.

Rick had lost the chance of finding the right person for him; reaching out and grabbing what Nathan offered just didn't sit right with her.

Not that Nate had really offered anything. Nothing serious, anyway. Sex…if she wanted it. His offer to *oblige* might have been flippantly delivered, but Tori had the feeling that if she took him up on it he'd be as good as his word. And hopefully every bit as good as her fantasies. But that's it. A Manhattan-born captain of industry just didn't do more than slum it with maladjusted girls from Morningside.

Cinderella never would have actually ended up with the prince.

But she'd have had fun trying.

Tori dug down deep into her conscience to see how it felt about that? About a strictly physical experience. Exploring these feelings she'd pretty much given up on ever having. Not romance, not love—definitely not happy ever after—those were totally out of bounds. Just happy ever…now. A little more light-ness now that she'd been reminded of how good it felt. She held her breath better to hear her conscience's verdict.

Silence. Just the relentless thump of her tortured pulse. And that was as good as a yes.

She lifted her head and blazed molten fire at the broad back of the man in her living room. The reality of what to do next was almost crippling. She'd never seduced anyone in her life. Of those few paltry kisses she'd had, she'd only instigated one and that was stolen from a very unwilling Michael Toledo in fourth grade and it hadn't really ended all that well. He'd cried and she'd spent the afternoon in the Assistant Principal's office sharpening pencils.

The idea of walking up to Nathan and grabbing his square chin the way she'd done with Michael's round, pudgy one…

Not an option.

But neither was backing away from this decision now that she'd made it. Now that her conscience had, amazingly, ap-proved. It was far too rare a gift to give back.

"Have you got something stronger than coffee in that kitchen, Tori?" he asked, lightly, back over his shoulder.

If I had, I'd be drinking it right now. Heat simmered up from under her shirt as her whole body got in on the act of wanting him.

"Uh...no. Why?"

He turned and smiled one of his most knock out smiles. "Because unless there's anything new you've thought of, then we are officially done."

That stopped her cold. Every part of her.

The heat...

Her pulse...

Her tight breath.

Like the water sucking out to sea in advance of a tidal surge. If they truly were done, he had no good reason to be here anymore. The wave crashed back in over all the flipping fish of her emotions, carrying blind panic at the thought she wouldn't see him again.

Her voice shook as she risked speech. "The website's finished?"

"Yep. It'll take about three minutes to upload all the files and then your falcons are out there for the world to see."

Excitement and terror scrabbled and clawed for dominance. She'd been looking forward to this moment since Nathan had first put the idea of a webcam into her head. But for it to come now—just when she'd decided to throw herself at his feet...

Three minutes. That wasn't a lot of time for finesse.

She crossed out of the kitchen and moved towards him with purpose. "I've changed my mind."

He frowned at her. "You don't want to go live?"

Why hadn't she worn something more alluring than jeans and a T-shirt? Or brushed her teeth before answering the door? "I do want to go live. I've changed my mind about..." *Oh, God.* Her heart pounded hard enough to hear in her voice. "...about our conversation on Sunday night."

A cautious suspicion blinked to life in his eyes. "Which one?"

"The one in which you said you'd sleep with me if I still wanted to in the morning."

All six-foot-three of crafted muscle stiffened instantly. "Ah, Tori…"

She stepped up closer to him, hard against him and did her best to saturate her voice with confidence. "I still want to."

He slid his hands up her arms, but not to bring her closer. He forced an inch of sanity between them. "No, you don't. You're just excited the project's finished."

She used her upper-body strength to resist his gentle pressure. "I am excited that the website's finished, but not that our time together will be finished."

And there it was. Couldn't be plainer than that.

Take me, I'm yours.

He groaned and his tongue stole out to wet suddenly dry lips. Tori's eyes locked on it the way Fred and Wilma tracked pigeons. "Tori… You have terrible timing."

"Why?"

He looked around for inspiration. "It's 2:00 a.m. We've worked into the night."

Desperate measures. Nathan might be in denial, but she knew exactly what she wanted—for the first time in years. She slid one hand boldly under his shirt and rested it right over the hard warmth of his heart. It thumped powerfully against her fingers and he flinched backward on another deep groan.

She smiled to see him so affected. "I may not have been born in New York, but I'm pretty sure even here 2:00 a.m. is a perfectly good time for…"

The actual words evaporated.

"Sex?" His expression softened and he cupped his hands around hers through his fine shirt "You can't even say it comfortably—how were you planning on doing it?"

Heat roared up her neck. "I was hoping there wouldn't be

a whole lot of talking about it. I certainly wasn't expecting to have to beg."

She glanced away, but his silence brought her eyes back to him. "You wouldn't need to beg, Tori. I meant what I said the other night." His eyes flicked to the bedroom. "I would like nothing more than to carry you in there right now."

"Then *oblige* me." She threw the word intentionally back at him, her chest heaving.

He winced. "It wouldn't be fair on you, Tori. I can't offer you more than a good time."

"Okay." That tied in nicely with her own needs, anyway.

"It's not okay. You deserve someone who can care for you. Who can give you...more."

"I'm not asking for more."

He stroked her cheek with one finger. "You should be. You're worth someone's whole heart."

Rejection flamed wildly beneath her blood, whipping it into a bubbling frenzy. "Apparently not yours."

His lips tightened. "I should go."

If he went he wouldn't be back. She scrabbled for inspiration as he started to push away. "I'm asking you to be with me, Nathan. To teach me."

He swore under his breath and lifted pained blue eyes back to her. She wedged herself bodily into the chink she could suddenly see in his armor. He wanted to do this. He *did* want it. "Are you seriously going to walk away and leave me wondering?"

His gaze narrowed. "Wondering what?"

"How we'd be together."

His nostrils flared and his lips pressed together against something he wanted to say. His voice vibrated with tension when he said instead "You'll meet someone else." But he flinched slightly as he said those words and Tori's chin—and confidence—lifted.

She tossed her hair back. "You'd prefer to outsource this?"

Deep heat blazed dark and raw in his eyes, turning them

indigo. *No.* Everything in him said it. But outwardly he just repeated "I should go."

He swung around and checked the files had finished uploading, grabbed his coat and turned for the door. "Goodbye, Tori. I'll call in a few days and see how the site's going."

No!

Him leaving now was not an option. Not when she knew full well she'd never see him again. Not when she knew he wanted her as much as she wanted him.

"Nathan—"

He was out in the hall before she could pull enough salient words together. She shot out after him. "I'll ride down with you."

He didn't exactly protest, but he strode down the hall and into the stairwell without a word. His whole body was rigid as his long legs carried him down the stairs. She kept up easily, and her light jog matched her fevered thoughts perfectly. Neither of them spoke as they emerged onto the eighth floor. She noticed his glance didn't flick toward the empty 8B the way it usually did, then he palmed the elevator button.

The elevator car was still sitting at the top of its range and when the doors opened, she slipped in behind him and then stood in the same stony silence as him and stared at the faded light countdown that marked their interminable descent.

Confusion and mortification swirled in her addled mind.

He was really going to walk away from this! From her. Despite wanting her as much as she wanted him. The incredible buoyancy she'd been increasingly feeling since he'd turned up on her doorstep, court order in hand, came into crashing context.

He made her feel good. *He* brought lightness back into her world. *He* had her springing out of bed in the morning rather than crawling.

Nathan.

Not just any guy. And not just because he was good-looking. And not just because he was charming.

Because she was falling for him.

And as the momentousness of that sank like a stone into the pit of her stomach, Tori knew she was finished begging. Because him saying no now would mean so much more than him saying no five minutes ago, before she realized her heart was involved—the heart that was hammering hard enough to burst right open. But she couldn't just let him walk. Even if he was only in this for the short term.

She couldn't keep him forever—fine—but couldn't she have him for just a bit longer?

The elevator lurched to a halt on the ground floor and the old door started to groan open. *Only seconds now*...Nathan reached across to slide back the ornate outer door opening into the building's entry foyer. The move brought him closer to her for a bare moment and she swayed toward him instinctively. But then she squared her shoulders, lifted her eyes and spoke quietly past her wildly thumping pulse.

Not a plea, just a fact.

"Last chance, Nathan."

The corner of his eye twitched and his jaw tightened, but otherwise he kept his focus fixed on the door to the street—his escape—then stepped past her out the elevator door, and into the silent lobby...

...and was gone.

The acid of rejection burned high in her throat as the doors retracted agonizingly slowly across the elevator opening. Old, familiar pain burbled up from the place she'd worked so hard to bind it.

She should have known. Her conscience had set her up so thoroughly for this lesson in payback. It had seen what she, clearly, had not. That despite the dubious romance of a tequila-fuelled kiss, Nathan really wasn't all that interested in more from her. Not even casually. No matter what he said.

She kept her focus forward, her chin high until the moment the doors obscured her from his view should he look back.

But the second she couldn't see him—nor he, her—she

released the pain in a choked moan. She'd survived much worse, she knew she would survive this. But in that very moment it was impossible to imagine how.

Suddenly the door's slide yanked to a halt, and Tori lifted her face as it hauled open with more gusto than it had ever displayed, and Nathan surged back into the elevator. He swept her up in his tide and pushed her back against the rear of the tiny box, his mouth crushing down on hers while she was still sucking in an elated breath.

"This doesn't mean I care for you." He ground out the words against her lips.

Triumph exploded in every cell of her body. Her arms hooked instantly around his strong neck, her hands plunging their way deep into his dark hair, and she breathed a response in the half heartbeat he took to get a better angle on her mouth. "I don't want you to care for me."

God help her, it was the truth. And also the worst of lies.

Recognizing the truth was so exquisitely painful it was hard to separate it from the elation still surging through her blood. She didn't deserve someone like Nathan in her life forever. The only thing letting her have this moment for herself was the fact that there was no chance of it ending well for her beyond the priceless opportunity to feel this glorious man naked up against her. To steal something to remember him by. To remember lightness by—for when it was gone again.

He'd been crystal-clear. For now, not forever.

No wonder her conscience had been fine with it. It saw what a dead end lay ahead. It had nothing to lose.

Nathan groaned against her mouth and shuffled her sideways so that he could punch the up button on the elevator. She lurched against him as it began its creaking ascent, but he held on to her, sharing air, tangling tongues, grinding into her, their body temperatures rising with the elevator. Tori grew lightheaded from oxygen depletion and plain old sagging relief and she clung to him desperately.

There was a feverish quality to Nathan's kisses that hadn't

been there on the rooftop. An urgency that perfectly matched her own. He leaned her against the left side of the elevator and then a moment later pulled her back up into the centre, before shifting to the right. Every time they moved a different part of her throbbed with need, but no part of her was going to get satisfaction.

He was as restless as his hands...and as unsettled as she was beginning to feel. She tore her mouth free and gasped "What's wrong?"

His gaze ricocheted around the tiny space, hyper. "Nothing."

Tori frowned. She could be self-conscious, she could worry that he'd changed his mind or that she'd done something wrong. But something about the wild passion on his face as he'd forced his way back into her elevator forced the doubt to heel. This wasn't about her. And the fact it was about him worried her even more.

That was pain she could see in the shadows at the back of his eyes.

The elevator continued its torturous ascent, grumbling unhappily. She pulled her fingers out of his hair and slid them to either side of his flushed face, forcing him to look at her, and held his eyes steadily.

If he changed his mind now her life would be over, but at least she would know.

She stroked his jaw with her thumb. "Tell me."

Heat pumped off him and the wildness of his eyes took a moment to ease. Emotion flickered across his face until it finally resolved, taking the frown lines with it.

"Nothing's wrong." He took a deep breath and drank her in. Really looked at her. "Just a memory." A tiny smile broke free and he stooped to kiss her gently. "Something that doesn't belong here anymore."

He kissed her again—a different kind of kiss to his first ones, to the rooftop. It was a kiss full of light. Full of relief. She stretched up and kissed him back, taking care to strip it of any clue about how deeply her heart was involved. It was still a good kiss. Actually it was a fantastic kiss.

Which only made her wonder what it would be like to kiss him with love between them. Instead of...

Whatever it was they had.

The elevator hit the end of its reach and Tori led the way out to the stairwell, her heart hammering relentlessly against her ribs.

He must have picked up on her tension because he said, "You're sure?"

She stopped and looked back at him in the entry to the dim stairwell. One strong arm stretched up the door frame, hovering on the cusp between common sense and no return, equally willing to go with either. His concerned frown only drew her more to him.

"You thought I wouldn't be?" she murmured.

"You know what this is—between us?"

She thought about that long and hard. "I have no idea what this is. But I don't require promises, Nathan. Only honesty. I'm in no position to be asking for forever."

This might be as close to forever as she came.

She held out her hand towards him, steadier and more confident than she felt, and he pushed himself away from the door frame and was with her in a few easy steps, his eyes holding hers. His fingers dwarfed hers, stroking softly across her skin, and then folding through her own to form a sensual lifeline.

She led the way up two flights of stairs toward her bedroom—the one room he'd not been into—and gripped that human lifeline as tightly as any mountain rigging.

CHAPTER NINE

RIGHT up until the moment the cool of her bed linen kissed her naked back, Tori might have chickened out. But the moment she'd felt the touch of the safest *place* in the world within the safest *part* of her world in the arms of the safest *man* in her world, she knew this was one hundred-percent right. It wasn't forever—they both knew that—but it had been coming since the first moment she saw him.

Nathan's lips hadn't left hers since the two of them crashed through her new door, twisted up in each other's arms, stumbling in their rush to get each other naked. To know each other. To love each other.

Just for one night.

Now, his skin still radiated a blazing heat, lying half-sprawled on top of her, one sweaty leg thrown over her two, simmering blue holding her enraptured while her strained chest rose and fell heavily from the gymnastics of the past hour.

Of all the things she had secretly hoped to discover about making love for the first time—all the things she *did* discover—finding out she almost wasn't fit enough was not on her expected list.

"My chest is about to explode," she gasped. "You'd think being climbing-fit would have helped. How do normal people cope?"

Nathan chuckled close to her ear as his fingers traced lazily over the ridges of her brow, her nose, her lips. She bit gently at the fingers and heard the controlled heaving of his own lungs between his words. "I'm not sure most 'normal' people would have put quite that much effort into it."

Tori's flushed skin couldn't accommodate any more blood, so her blush had no purpose. "Really? Was I too…?"

Vigorous? Enthusiastic? *Trying too hard?*

Nathan's lips split wide in a dirty grin. "You were amazing." Then the smile sobered just slightly and he dragged his thumb over her bottom lip. "You *are* amazing."

Oh…

Moments like that made it hard to forget this was a one-off.

Moments like the one when he'd turned her blazing gaze to his and held it. When he'd gently stroked away the sneak of moisture that had escaped her eye after it all got too overwhelming. When he'd pulled her into his shoulder and murmured words of reassurance as she'd fragmented into a million shards of the sweetest diamond dust.

He hadn't made love to her like a man who didn't care.

And she hadn't responded like a woman who didn't want to be cared for.

Whoops on both their parts.

Not that there was any question about *whether* she cared. She wouldn't have risked—trusted—just anyone. Only Nathan. Arrogant, brave, wounded Nathan. But would she ever lie in her big bed again and not think of the wasted size of it? Would she ever touch her lips and not taste him there? Would she ever be the same? There were some consequences that a condom couldn't prevent.

The emotional ones.

Maybe she shouldn't have given in to her baser instincts and ripped open Pandora's box knowing she would never let herself keep what she found inside.

Not that he was offering. At all.

Even now.

Her eyes slid sideways again and collided with his electric-blue one. "Thank you, Nathan."

"This wasn't charity, Tori." His large hand slid around to tangle in her damp hair. "I've wanted to get you naked since the day you ratted me out to the cops."

She smiled. Was that only three weeks ago? "I'm still grateful. I'll always remember this."

When you're gone.

Nathan wiggled in harder against her and buried his lips somewhere near her ear. She was just as happy not to see that thought echoed back to her in his gaze. Her lashes drifted shut as his lips traced the outline of one lobe and she groaned her appreciation. As tired as she was it was a strange kind of exhaustion. The kind that could leave you ready for a repeat almost immediately. Not a bad system, really.

"There's still the launch party, remember?" he murmured, hot and damp against her ear.

Her eyes flew open. She spoke to the ceiling, virtually holding her breath. "You're going to come?"

"I figure I owe it to Wilma and Fred for invading their privacy so thoroughly yesterday."

Thoughts of the brief, frantic bird-sex they'd caught on the camera brought a smile to her lips. "Maybe they returned the favor just now."

He lifted his dark shaggy head and turned towards the window. Neither of them had bothered with the curtains so the whole bedroom stood exposed to the darkened ledge outside. The bed shook as Nathan laughed, deep and sexy.

It felt way too good to lie naked in his arms joking around. Dangerously comfortable.

Dangerously addictive.

She forced her thoughts onto something else. "I'm not sure how many people I should invite. It's not that big an apartment."

Beside her Nathan stilled. She could practically hear him thinking. Finally he spoke. "You'd like a bigger place?"

"Not especially, though it would be handy at a time like this."
Not that throwing a party happened more than once every...
five years. In fact, this would be her first.

Actually, a crazy dream of renting the apartment next door
with its park-facing aspect and opening it up into one big apartment had occurred to her last year. Not that it was available,
and not that she could afford it if it was.

Nathan rolled onto his back, dragging the light covers up and
over both of them. He turned toward her on the pillow. "If you
had a blank check, what improvements would you make?"

She frowned at him. "Is all post-coital conversation this
suburban?"

He leaned over and kissed her—roughly, soundly. Fabulously.
"I'm recharging. Humor me."

Tori's heart squeezed. After what they'd just done together
how could a simple kiss still steal her breath? Yet it did.

"Ah, blank check...okay," she said as soon as she was able.
"I guess I wouldn't mind making it a bit bigger. And actual park
views instead of the glimpse I get right now. But I wouldn't
want anything flash."

"Why not?"

Because there was something suitably monastic about living
a simple life. Denying herself comforts. "I don't need it."

"You don't need a tantalizing Mexican spread on a rooftop
either but you enjoyed it."

She had—a slip on her part. Maybe she'd become all-round
too indulgent since meeting Nathan Archer.

He took her silence as reluctance and nudged her with
his foot. "If you won't take pleasures, then what about
conveniences?"

He really wanted to play this game. Okay. She turned to face
him. "I guess a built-in laundry would be convenient. It would
save me having to go to the basement."

"Balcony?"

She expelled a frustrated outburst on a small puff. "If we're
going to totally redesign the building, sure!"

"Not here then. Anywhere. Anywhere in Manhattan."

She sat up straighter and threw him her best probing look. "Are you trying to seduce me with imagined spoils? Because… you know…I'm already naked, you really don't have to try that hard."

His smile turned sideways to fit her mouth better and he kissed her to silence. "Come on, Tori," he said when they finally came up for air. "Play the game. Anywhere at all on Manhattan."

Her eyes explored the room as though she'd find inspiration there. "Okay…if imaginary money truly is no object then let's talk park frontage."

"Central Park?"

Her laugh was immediate. "Don't be ridiculous. They don't make blank checks with enough space for all those zeroes. A more modest park will be just fine."

"That's what you'd like? A mid-sized place with a heap of facilities facing a park in a nice neighborhood?"

She sat up carefully, wondering how she could cut out the chit-chat and get back to the physical intimacy. Their best-before clock was ticking. She rolled fully over and met his eyes. "Yes, Nathan. That is my fantasy apartment."

And fantasy it would remain because not only did she have extremely limited income but, out here in the real world, moving was not even on her radar. She was more than happy where she was. Comfortably settled.

Entrenched.

In fact, the thought of shifting away from all the people she'd filled her life with, and her apartment with its soft colors and mismatched furnishings made her stomach positively lurch. "Where is all this going?"

"I'm just—" his expression grew cautious "—getting to know you better."

She shifted to her side and tucked the covers in more firmly around her. "Why? You'll be gone in a few days."

Somehow, through all the thick shields she usually kept

around her heart, she knew that his next words would really matter. Her heart set up an insistent thumping.

A scowl marred those beautiful eyes and he looked as though he was on the verge of saying something difficult. But then the moment passed, and he shifted more comfortably in the bed and when he lifted his face again his eyes glittered with speculation. "Got something other than conversation in mind for the few hours until breakfast?"

If she hadn't spent the past five years keeping her own secrets she wouldn't have so easily spotted his. But there it was, laid out on the bed in front of them, metaphorically shrouded so that she couldn't quite make out its shape. Not that she had any real desire to find out. Look what had happened last time he'd shared something with her. And she only had one secret left to trade him….

"We could sleep," she said lightly, knowing full-well that wasn't an option. If they only had one night she wasn't wasting a second of it on oblivion.

He gave her that smile again. The one that turned her insides to mush. The one that made her forget anything but him. "Is that what you'd like to do?" he murmured as he stirred against her.

She stretched out along his length. "Nope."

"What would you like to do?"

Be yours forever.

The force of her mind's whisper slammed the breath clean out of her and robbed her of speech. They didn't have forever. They had until morning. Until the launch party…max. She knew that.

She *knew* that.

Why was her subconscious taunting her with thoughts of forever—with what she hadn't earned? Was it still playing cruel games? Or, worse, had she done the unthinkable and fallen harder than she realized?

"Tori?" He sat up more fully as she sagged back against the pillows. "Are you okay?"

Her heart pounded. "I'm…um…" What could she say?
I think I love you, Nathan.
Surprise!
Instead, she did what she'd been doing so well for the past five years: she pushed the emotion deep down inside and slid the I'm-okay mask firmly into place. "I just realized we don't have any more protection."

Nathan's gaze instantly heated up and he lowered his smiling lips closer to hers, which seemed to tremble and swell in anticipation. "Well, then we'll just have to get creative." She wriggled down lower in the bed and willed a smile to her waiting lips. He swiped his mouth back and forth across hers and his hand slid resolutely down to hook under her knee. "Lucky you're athletic."

It took only a cluster of rapid heartbeats for his talented lips and hands to gather her fully back into his command, to finely tune her body back with his. Tori's chest made the transition from tight pain to lancing desire immediately, her tattoo-heart switching rhythm easily. It was far too possible to let herself sink into the swell of rising passion rather than face the reality of what her subconscious had just tossed up.

Love.

The one thing she absolutely, categorically could not have with him. Or anyone.

Love was something you earned.

CHAPTER TEN

"TAKE it easy, Tori, they'll come."

She knew by Nathan's narrowed gaze that she was completely failing to mask her nerves as she wiped down the coffee and dining tables for the third time. It would have been the tenth if not for his solid, reassuring presence that grounded her. As much as was possible.

It didn't matter that she knew everyone invited to the webcam launch tonight. It didn't matter that she liked everyone invited. This was the first time she'd brought her neighbors together in one place in the entire time she'd been resident in this building, and she was insanely, inexplicably nervous. She wasn't stressing that her guests weren't coming…

She was stressing that they *were*.

Ironic. The high school senior voted Medford's most likely to have a beer with a President, and she was nervous about serving her neighbors a bunch of finger food.

She balled the sponge into her tight fist and returned it to the immaculate kitchen, then mentally reviewed everything that was laid out on the counter. Again. Not surprisingly, it was all exactly the same as the last time she'd counted it.

"Tori…" Warm arms slipped around her and drew her into rock-solid strength, gently halting her frantic cleaning. "It's going to be fine. Everything looks great and we've catered for a football team."

We've…plural.

Double tension scored her subconscious. It was bad enough having a party—she had no one but herself to blame for that—but the end of the party technically signaled the end of something else. There was no good reason for Nathan to return after the last party guest walked through of her shiny new door. The gathering had bought her a few extra days—of the most blinding, pleasurable intimacy imaginable—but nothing more. Nothing else had changed.

There had been no talk of anything more. Despite Nathan's occasional slips into plural.

She had enough self-awareness to realise that the falcons weren't the whole reason she was throwing this ridiculous party. She wanted Nathan to meet her neighbors. To get to know them. She wanted them to get to know him, to like him. This motley group of New Yorkers was her de facto family and, on some deeply buried level, she wanted their approval.

Even though it was completely and utterly pointless.

"I don't know why I'm so nervous," she said, snuggling in more tightly against his strength and pressing her cheek over his heart so she could hear its reassuring beat.

He gathered her in and touched quiet lips to her hair. Was he counting down the kisses to their last one the way she was? The way she had been since their first one? "You're launching a webcam. It's a big deal."

She tipped her head back to look at him—her favorite angle, up along that tanned, rough throat and jaw—and frowned. "No it's not. These are my neighbors. This should be nothing."

His eyes clouded. "Is it because I'm here?"

"I don't think so. I want them to meet you."

His lips tightened. "You do?"

"Well... You know. Without you there would be no webcam project."

She wasn't fooling him any more than she fooled herself. Not only was she apparently too chicken to have her neighbors over for snacks, but she was too afraid to let him see how she felt about him.

Coward.

Then again, courage was something she'd said farewell to five years ago.

Behind them a sharp rap heralded the exact moment the clock switched over to six o'clock. Trust someone to be uber-prompt. She stiffened her back, pulled away from Nathan and turned for the door.

Game on.

Angel the actress was unfashionably on time, standing in the hall with a bottle in her hand and a curious smile on her face, but others weren't far behind. Tracey and Neville Radcliffe, then Mr. Broswolowski, the deCostas. Her neighbors from either side. Tony Diamond from the end of the hall—the only real magician she'd ever known—turned up a bit late, but he'd taken the time to escort Nancy Smith down from her top-floor apartment.

They and a handful of other neighbors were mingling fabulously and exclaiming how odd that they'd not had more parties like this—the high-rise equivalent of a street party—while Tori faked endless tasks in the kitchen as her heart hammered and her mouth ran clean out of saliva. It wasn't quite as awful as she'd worked herself up to believe, but it wasn't entirely comfortable either. Very crowded. Very oxygen-depleted. Even with the safety windows slid open. More than ever, she longed for the vast, open spaces and arctic winds of the high mountain ranges.

She closed her eyes and tried to remember what that had felt like buffeting against her skin.

"Tori?"

Nathan swung past her servery for the seventh time, bending to see under the overhead cupboards and snaring her gaze. He'd been his typical charming self, winning over her neighbors, circulating, working the room. Tori envied him the apparent ease with which he could speak with interest to anyone about anything and have them eating out of his hand. Angel Santos was just about ready to have his children and she didn't even know he was rich as sin.

Tori had told them he was a friend and they'd been working on a project together, but that was it. It was Nathan's call whether he wanted to out himself as their landlord. Or her lover. So far he'd chosen neither.

Though glancing at him across the room, seeing his smile and secretly knowing what that mouth had done for her just hours earlier was the only thing that effectively distracted her from her annoying anxiety. And judging by the twist of his lips, he remembered too.

Were all sexually active people this smug?

"Everyone's getting restless," he said now. "Could be time for the falcons?"

"Really? Now?" As excited as she was to be launching the website, the idea of standing in front of people and speaking formally suddenly brought a hint of bile to her mouth. She frowned, remembering how many presentations she'd done to climbing groups back in Oregon. How effortless they'd been. Talking about things she was passionate about had never been an issue. "Can't you chat to them a bit longer?"

Nathan's brows dropped. "These are *your* friends, Tori. I'm doing my best—" and it wasn't until that moment that she realized how strained he actually looked "—but it's not me they came to see."

He moved around into the kitchen, positioned himself against the counter in such a way that his body shielded her from the view of her guests as he said gently. "You've climbed mountains, Tori. Talking about these birds should be nothing."

Should be. "Then why isn't it?" Her pulse chattered rapidly.

She was hiding in her own kitchen. She'd left Nathan holding the bag for entertaining her friends. She would have happily crawled back into bed right now until every last one of them left.

Oh, that was not good.

Her head came up. She glanced at the people milling around her tiny living room. She tuned in to the hammering of her heart. Then she looked at Nathan—his handsome face filled with patience and rather a lot of confusion.

She could do this.

She sucked in a deep breath, lowered the bowl she'd been filling with yet more unnecessary snacks and turned to her living room.

"Okay. Let's start."

And if he noticed *her* unintentional plural, he didn't say a word.

The room came buzzing alive as Tori spoke to them about the peregrine webcam project and how, despite other parts of Manhattan having them, theirs would be Morningside's first wildlife webcam. Her use of *theirs* had to be intentional and Nate watched her enthusiasm wash over every one of her guests like a seductive wave, despite her stumbling nerves at the start. In return, their growing excitement cross-infected her and she grew louder and more confident as she got closer to the moment of switching on the webcam monitor.

Her eyes glittered, her smile beamed. This was more the Tori he'd expected tonight. This was the Tori he'd selfishly lost himself in the past few nights. Radiant, courageous, wild Tori.

Timid kitchen Tori was not a side of her he'd ever expected to see. It threw him, though he knew how much she liked to work within her comfort zone. It just reinforced how little he really knew about her. How not-real this whole *thing* between them was. And it really shouldn't matter because in a few hours their *thing* would be over. The project was finished.

Neither of them had spoken of more.

Coming here tonight had been a risk. His heart had been in his throat since that first knock on the door. Wondering if he'd be recognized. Wondering if he'd bump into someone he used to see taking out the trash a lifetime ago. Could he rely on the vast physical changes between seventeen-year-old Nate and the man he was now? Getting into discussions about the bad old days was really not his idea of a good time.

But as more guests arrived and minutes turned into hours and no one said a word or even looked askance at him—beyond the obvious speculation in most expressions as to what his relationship with Tori was really all about—he'd realized that no one *did* remember him. And the only one he recognized for certain was Miss Smith, who remembered nothing at all most of the time.

"Here they are, Wilma and Fred." Tori activated the plasma with a theatrical flourish and every person in the room craned forward to see it. The screen glowed to life and caught Wilma in the middle of her regular bath, that talon-like beak rifling through slick brown feathers, completely unaware that she was being watched. Thirty days on eggs. Thirty days barely leaving that ramshackle nest.

That took a special kind of bird.

Or person. The thought flitted across his mind that Tori would have that kind of focus. Especially if it involved thirty days indoors. She did love her apartment.

He frowned. She really did.

She pulled up the website on the monitor and talked everyone through the various parts of it, showing them her photography, the live webcam box, the species information. The links to New York's other urban raptor sites.

Marco deCosta was the first to jump on the computer mouse and start effortlessly navigating his way around the detailed site—it was a healthy reminder that the sorts of tools Sanmore had grown great on were just commonplace for kids now. Marco's parents followed and then, one by one, everyone else began to explore.

Tori chatted to Tracey and Neville Radcliffe—the owners of that mad mini-horse, Gretel—and her origami-laundry friend, the theatre producer. She showed them through her photo album of raptor images. They hung on her words as though they'd never seen or heard about Tori's background at all.

Maybe they hadn't. The way he'd had to pry it from her determined lips...

Yet her neighbors had become so fundamental to her life here in Morningside. Like a regular mini ecosystem with every person depending on every other for some aspect of day-to-day life. Most aspects, in Tori's case. She'd be lost without her portfolio of trades. Life would certainly cost her a whole lot more.

And, once again, his chest tightened at the very real necessity of moving everyone out of the building. Of splitting up friendships. Of displacing Tori.

He'd opened his mouth any number of times over the past few days to tell her what he had planned. But every time he'd even looked as though he might be working up to some serious conversation, Tori cut him off, distracted him with a question, an activity, a kiss. Almost as if she didn't want to get deep and meaningful with him.

At least not emotionally.

The more time he spent with her the more he realized how much structure her days had. Not that his corporate days had any less, and not that she wasn't willing to throw it all to the wind in order to spend hours with him under the sheets. It was just...rigid—compared to how he imagined her earlier years must have been as a nature-loving, mountaineering tomboy.

But then she'd lost her brother and had stopped doing all the things she loved. Maybe it had changed her. Which didn't mean she wasn't capable of changing back. She just needed the right incentive. And less structure.

He maneuvered himself through the throng and closer to her side and took a risk—did something unexpected. Scandalously unscheduled. He slid his hand around her waist and onto her hip and whispered in her ear, "Anything you need from me?"

Her startled look back over her shoulder pleased him and worried him in the same moment. He loved that he could get her pupils flaring like that just with a touch, but the immediate way she stepped clear of his hold—smiling beautifully the whole time so nothing looked amiss to her speculative neighbors—and firmly put him at a distance…she did it all too naturally and he noticed it way too much.

…for a guy who didn't plan on being here past morning.

His stomach rolled. It was Friday. His time with Tori was up.

Tick-tock, tick-tock…

That bothered him a heck of a lot more than it should. The last thing he wanted to do on their last night together was spend it talking business. Talking about the demolition. He'd tell her personally, but not here.

Not tonight.

It took another hour to get the last of them out the door. The magician had left early to head off to a gig somewhere, forgetting that he'd escorted Nancy down. That meant she was the last person left sitting on Tori's sofa, an embroidered cushion clutched in her parchment hands.

"I'm missing *Ellen*," she whispered as Nate sank down next to her.

She'd been a ferocious television addict when he was a boy. Watching seventies reruns on the box while he did his homework at her dining table. Not interfering, not parenting, just being a friend. He slid his hand over her bird-like one and years of gratitude leached through that one touch. And he remembered that, for all his childhood challenges, there was light too. And lemonade.

"The party's over, Miss Smith," he said softly. "Would you like to go home now?"

He glanced over his shoulder, saw that Tori was busy saying farewells to Mr. Broswolowski at the door and turned quickly back to Nancy. "It's not much of a thank-you for everything you did for me, I realise." Having this conversation was no risk. It was like speaking into a vacuum. "But I've chosen your new home carefully." And though she didn't yet know it, he'd committed to paying her way until the end.

That was something he could do for her. To approximate how much she'd done for him.

"Everything rolls to its appointed end."

He stared at her. That was what her muddled mind chose to hold onto—*William Bryant?*

"I still have that volume," she said, quietly, and her eyes lifted to his. Decisively. His pulse thundered and his breath sucked out of his lungs. Her lips split into a gentle smile. "You always did enjoy it particularly."

Every bit of saliva decamped from his mouth. "You remember me?"

She turned those vacant eyes on him and they did seem a little less...absent. "It takes me a bit more time these days..." She squeezed his hand. "But yes. Welcome home, Nathan."

Blood rushed in torrents past his ears, almost drowning her out.

"I'm pleased you did so well in life," she said. "I so wanted that for you."

His throat tightened, which didn't make swallowing what little moisture he'd managed to generate any easier. He practically croaked his response. "Thank you, Miss Smith. For everything."

She looked back down at the cushion in her hands, lifted her face again and looked around. "Whose house is this?"

What? "This is Tori's apartment."

"Tori?"

A sinking feeling hit him. "You came to her party."

Her smile was beatific. "I love parties." And then she started to hum an old waltz tune, smiling to herself. Lost in memory.

Lost—again—to him.

He slid his other hand over hers and blinked back emotion. He'd never let himself ask as a boy. A point of pride. But he could ask it now. "Miss Smith, may I come up?"

She turned her radiant, vacant, aged face up to his. "Oh, yes!"

It took him an age to get her up two flights of stairs and settled back into her own apartment. She barely even seemed to know she'd been out. But she knew her household routines and she slipped straight back into them in a way that made him feel more comfortable about leaving her alone. She made a cup of tea, swapped her good shoes for slippers, turned on *Ellen* and promptly began watching as though he'd ceased to exist.

She had as much daily structure as Tori and had obviously grown extra reliant on it. Clearly, in her own environment, she was infinitely more in control of her faculties.

And he was about to tear her out of that. Guilt nagged, despite all the nursing care he'd bought her for the rest of her waking days. And, inexplicably, his mind went straight back to Tori. To the other woman who loved things just the way they were.

Even when she didn't.

He took the stairs in pairs in his haste to get back to her. It was going to be tough for him to come up with any decent reason to keep seeing her now that the webcam and the launch party were over. They both knew this was temporary, they'd both enjoyed it enough to stretch it out all week. Whatever move he made now was either going to send the wrong message, or bring an end to their short relationship.

Neither of which he wanted.

What he wanted to do was send the *right* message and have her give him the *right* answer.

Stay.

But he wouldn't. He might have failed—abysmally—in his attempts not to let himself care for her, but the one thing he did have from growing up almost completely responsible for himself was killer self-discipline. He'd give her a final night she'd never forget, tell her about the redevelopment and the new place he'd found her, make sure she knew what an amazing woman she was and then kiss her one last time.

Before leaving her apartment forever, honoring the commitment he'd made himself.

Viktoria Morfitt could do so much better than a workaholic with a shame-filled past and no interest in committing. But she wasn't going to find better while he was around taking up space.

"So the place survived the onslaught?" He made light as he came back through the door into the now-spotless apartment, critically aware that they only had a few more hours together. Though, as Tori turned to him with a blazing smile and moved with her catlike grace across the room, his whole body rebelled at the very thought. How could he be a man of steel resolve one moment and have it melt to a molten metal puddle the moment she locked him in her focus?

Just one more reason to get out now. While he still could.

"Nathan, thank you for all your help. I seriously don't think I could have got through without you."

"Sure you could. At worst you would have had to cut up your own carrot sticks."

She stopped before him, below him, and peered up through those enormous gray eyes. His heart started thumping.

"Let me be grateful, Nathan. You did help me." A shadow flitted across her face and was gone. "In ways I wasn't expecting. I don't understand why I was so nervous."

The heart-thumps turned into painful squeezes and he dug around for a way to keep things from getting any heavier. Ironic, given it had been her keeping things comfortably undemanding for the past few days, but if she asked him to stay forever right now he'd have a hard time saying no. Not that he thought for a moment she actually would ask.

His hands slid up her arms and around under her shoulder blades. "You want to show gratitude?"

A deep light flared in her gray depths. "Another massage?"

"No. No massage." At least not just yet. "But we will need to be lying down for it. If you're that grateful…"

She smiled and stretched her arms up around his neck. "Extremely grateful…"

And then her lips were on his and he forgot everything but the feel and taste of her.

CHAPTER ELEVEN

TORI woke to the sound of someone rummaging around in the kitchen—singing—and her sleep-addled mind immediately lurched into tightness. Into the past.

Rick!

But a bare moment afterwards, reality intruded as it did every morning and she remembered. Not Rick. Not anymore. But instead of the deep sorrow she had grown accustomed to carrying around for the first minutes of every day, a warm gooey honey washed over her instead.

Nathan.

That was his terrible singing coming from the kitchen. She lay back against the pillow and let the sadness leach away under the fresh breeze of her smile. There was something supremely endearing about a man who couldn't sing but didn't care who knew it. Nathan had the casual confidence only fortune and success could bring and, clearly, he had no need or value for perfect pitch.

Which was really just as well. She'd have to tell Pavarotti to tone it down before he scared Wilma right off her nest.

She pulled the sheet up under her arms and trailed it behind her out of bed and into the kitchen. She stood silently behind him and watched the way his powerful body moved through her kitchen. Decisively. With confidence. And he was only making breakfast.

No wonder he made love with such proficiency.

"It's Saturday, why are you dressed for work?"

Inane, yes, but even after three days she still wasn't used to morning-after conversation. In fact, she was thoroughly out of practice with conversation at any time of the day if you didn't count Gretel. And after what they'd shared last night, he was lucky she could even form sentences.

Nathan had made love to her as though she was made of blown glass. Slow, tender, beautiful. Long into the night. In a way that made it so hard to remember he was leaving.

But she suspected, because of that.

He spun around to face her and patted his coat pocket, the bulging one. "A CEO's diary does not discriminate."

He moved towards her, slid one hand behind her head and dragged his lips back and forth across hers, sending her pulse into riots and shooting spurs of desire straight to her core. If she'd expected regret she wasn't going to get any. He looked pretty darned pleased with himself. And painfully gorgeous.

"There's that smug expression I was telling you about," she said, sagging slightly against her pantry door.

The smile twisted into a full-blown grin. "Sorry, can't help it. You draped in a sheet standing in the kitchen like some kind of Greek goddess is going to take a little getting used to."

Going to? Those weren't the words of man who was packing his bags. The part of her that knew better did a little happy dance and it just felt so foreign. She stepped closer and pulled his phone out of his coat pocket and slid it behind her back. "So…does this mean you can hang around for a few more hours before yielding to your non-discriminatory diary?"

Lord, she didn't want him to go just yet.

He pulled her into the circle of his arms. "Do you want me to?"

She weighed her words. No point in denying everything she'd said and done last night. But old fears died hard… "I don't want you *not* to."

His eyes darkened and flicked over the place between her

breasts where one hand clutched the sheet to her. Then they lifted back to hers. "I have a couple of things I need to do."

"Is one of them kissing me?"

His gaze was shadowed. "Several of them involve kissing you. But also some work stuff." His eyes flicked away and returned. Then he reached around behind her and liberated his phone. "I also want to talk to you about something."

Oh. Her stomach dropped as she saw the fleeting doom in his expression. *This was it.* She took a mini breath. "Okay…?"

"Do you want to get dressed?"

Her heart constricted. She stepped back from him and pulled the sheet tighter around her body. "Do I need to get dressed?"

"If you want me to concentrate, yes."

Either that was a monumental save, just as her demons were surging to the fore, or it was the truth. "Okay. I'll be right back."

He called behind her, "I'll have coffee ready."

He did. And honeyed toast. It was all disturbingly domestic and more than a little alarming. Either he was going to tell her their time together was officially over—a proposition she'd been in serious denial about this week—or…

Nope. She had no idea what else it could be. The demons did exuberant laps in her mind as her pulse rate picked up pace to match them.

"So, I've been thinking about something you said the night we were first together…"

Heat immediately climbed. God, she'd said so many things. And groaned some. And cried some. And whimpered some. Most of them embarrassing.

She cleared her throat. "About?"

"About how you value honesty."

The demons retreated to hover nearby just in case they were needed on short notice, and they made room for a breath, albeit a tight one. "Okay. How about you just spit it out?"

"Delicately put." His smile completely disarmed her, as

usual. He leaned forward. "Okay, here's the thing. I may have found you a new apartment."

She stared at him. Of the million things he might have said to her just then… "I don't want a new apartment."

"It has everything on your list. Space, park view, trees, built-in facilities, in a good area, closer to me, actually…"

What list? "Nathan, I don't need a new apartment. Why would you look for one?"

His eyes grew cautious. "I'm not a terrible landlord, Tori. There's a reason Sanmore hasn't spent more on this building."

"*Asset strategy*, you said." And she hoped her snort told him exactly what she thought about his strategy.

"Right. But there's more to it." He studied her closely. "What would you say if I told you I was planning renovations?"

She sat up straight in her chair. "Renovations! Fantastic. We're so overdue for some work."

"Extensive renovations."

Her bubble burst. She frowned. "How extensive?"

"Very."

A nasty, twisty bite took hold deep inside and her stomach curled up to protect itself. "'Very' as in days of inconvenience?"

His eyes were as blank as she'd ever seen them, in awful contrast to the fiery passion of last night. "'Very' as in weeks, possibly…longer."

From nowhere, a deep panic started to take hold. Breathlessness. Dry mouth. Fast heart. Exactly the sort of thing she'd had when she first started climbing. She curled her rapidly cooling fingers into her palms. "Why are you telling me specifically?"

"Because we… Because I don't want it to be between us. Going forward."

The anxiety stirred her anger though she didn't quite understand why she was feeling either. Wasn't he just being honest with her? "I was under the impression there would be no going forward?"

His face was cautious. "Is that what you want? To end things?"

"It's what we agreed."

"I didn't have all the facts then."

"What facts?"

"I had no idea who you were. What we'd be like together." He cleared his throat. "How you'd make me feel."

She stared at him, crystallizing ice racing along her veins. "And now you do, you're keen to bundle me up and throw me into an apartment closer to you so you can reduce the mileage on your booty calls, is that it?"

His head jerked. "It's not like that. You know it's not."

"Then explain it to me, Nathan."

"I respect you, Tori."

"And?"

"And this is your home. I thought you'd want to know first. So you can plan."

She swallowed but there was nothing in her mouth to swallow "So this is more FYI than community consultation?"

"Tori…"

Her heart pounded. "The renovations are a done deal?"

"More or less."

"What about everyone else, Nathan? There's thirty-five households in this building. Where will they go for weeks on end?"

"I'm going to find each of them alternative accommodations. And pay their rent."

Her nostrils flared. "A good financial deal, but what about their day-to-day lives?"

"I've had my best people working on this. Finding good matches. A place close to his brother for Mr. Browoslowski. A small loft in SoHo for Angel. One block back from Riverside for the Radcliffes—awesome Great Dane country…"

Tori watched his lips moving but struggled to take in his words. The blood was rushing past her ears way too fast.

"A three-bed right over the road from Marco's school for the deCostas, a wonderful place with 24/7 medical care for Nancy—"

"You're putting her in a home?"

"It's not a home, Tori. It's an independent aged-care apartment. With daily medical assistance."

"No, *this* is her home, Nathan. Here. Where she's lived her whole life." Panic rushed up into her stomach and bubbled there.

"She's not safe here, Tori. How much longer before she *has* to move anyway?"

She ignored his logic. "And the deCostas' apartment?"

"I thought the proximity to Marco's school made it perfect."

"And how do you know where Marco goes to school? How do you know where the Radcliffes like to walk Gretel? How do you know where Mr. B's crazy brother lives?"

"Tori…"

She pressed her lips together. "Were you mining me for information every time we were together?"

"No, I wasn't. But I remembered things you told me. You *wanted* me to get to know my tenants."

"Not so you could throw them out on the street!"

His eyes glittered dangerously. "Do you *know* how much I'm spending specifically so that I *don't* leave them high and dry?"

Her whole body physically shook. "Don't throw your money at me, Nathan Archer. Don't come in here and exploit my party and my friends the way you've exploited me."

He hissed his frustration. "I did *not* exploit you or your party. I *carried* your party while you went all Greta Garbo on us. I just listened to—"

She shoved away from the table and to her feet, and marched resolutely away from him into the room where they'd spent so many extraordinary, precious hours together, slamming the door shut on so much more than the conversation and hauling the pillow that had so recently cushioned his head across her chest. Confusion and anger and seething anxiety all raged within her and overwhelmed her senses. She'd worked so hard to numb herself internally over the past five years. To survive what had happened in her family.

Her stomach lurched. What had she imagined would happen if she opened the door to more sensation? To love. To desire.

To trust.

How her subconscious must be cackling. It would have seen exactly where this was going to end. She'd broken the golden rule—she'd let Nathan close and tried to have something for herself. Maybe she should count herself lucky it was only her heart this time.

Last time she broke a golden rule, someone she loved died.

The doorknob started to turn and Tori squared her shoulders and took a deep, shaky breath. Nathan's beautiful dark head peered around the door. It killed her that her wounded heart still gave a pathetic little lurch at seeing him.

"Can I come in?"

She shuddered full-body. The ache intensified into a sharp blade that slipped neatly through the muscles between her ribs and poised over her heart. Three weeks ago he'd kicked the door in, desperate to save a stranger. Or had he just been in the building anyway, measuring up for all these renovations?

She pressed her lips together. "Suit yourself. It's your apartment."

How easily it came back to her: the careless shrug, the vacant stare. She hadn't used them since the days following Rick's fall. Her soul had been collapsing in on itself then, too.

His shoulders sagged. "Tori...I didn't use you to get information on your neighbors."

"So you say."

"Are you seriously thinking that an officer of the court

colluded to place me here so that I could get a handful of not terribly interesting facts about the tenants in the building?"

Tori fought the frown birthed by that irritating bit of common sense. But she couldn't hide it completely.

"Right." Nathan stepped toward her, nodding. "So none of this was planned."

"Then you're just an opportunist?"

"Absolutely, I built my business on capitalizing on opportunity. But I wanted to do the right thing by everyone."

"The right thing would be finding a different way to do your renovations. Floor by floor. Without disrupting everyone."

A dark shadow crossed his face. "It's not that simple."

Panic started to well. "Why can't it be? Why do you have to throw everyone's lives into turmoil?"

My life.

"This is a good outcome for the tenants. Six months free rent will set them up with a deposit on a better place, or a foundation to keep renting the places we've found them if they want to stay. Or time to find somewhere new if they don't."

"Do you imagine Nancy will think about it that way?"

"I don't expect Nancy to think about this at all."

"She's eighty years old, Nathan. This building is a part of her. Just because she's drifting off doesn't mean she doesn't know her essential surroundings. Or the people around her. She runs her life by the strict order in her apartment, her routines and patterns." Her pulse rate started to skyrocket and tiny pricks of light exploded behind her eyes. "Have you even considered that? I know she's a stranger to you, but she's like family to us."

His nostrils flared. "Yes, I've considered that. I'm getting just a little bit tired of you assuming I'm this corporate ogre come to sack the village before torching it. Every one of you is on a lease, Tori, including Nancy. A lease with an end date. By your own choosing."

She didn't want to hear his logic. "Where's your loyalty to

some of the people who've been on those leases for decades—?"
To the woman whose body you were sharing.

Frustration hissed from his lips. "I've rewarded their loyalty
tenfold. I sourced Nancy's new place personally and picked the
best medical care I could find."

Everything began to spin and Tori couldn't grab all of the
thoughts and images fast enough to force them into some kind
of sense. She shook her head. "Why?"

"Because I—" He pinched his lips shut and changed tack.
"Because she has no one else."

"What about the falcons? How do you think they're going
to manage raising their young with the sounds of jackhammers
pounding relentlessly behind them?"

"Seventy days, you said. To hatch, fledge and be independent. I've scheduled work to begin in seventy-five, so they
should have moved on by then."

Her pulse began to hammer and dark spots flashed briefly
across her eyes. She rubbed them and realized how damp her
hands were. *Seventy-five days.* She had to be out in ten weeks.
Hardly any time at all.

"You think they'll just fly away and come back next year?
It doesn't work that way."

"According to your own fact sheet it does. Over generations.
I can design the new building to be falcon-friendly. We'll have
to trust that they return eventually."

Everything started to close in.

"Eventually?"

"You told me they're unlikely to breed again until their offspring move out into their own breeding territory."

Him being right didn't help. And him having thought a lot
of things through carefully only boiled her blood more. She
waved her hand out the bedroom door in the direction of the
high tech monitoring gear. Her chest squeezed so hard it nearly
stole the breath she needed to accuse him. She forced the words
out.

"You knew the whole time you were installing everything,

designing the website, that it would barely get a few weeks of use? What a monumental waste of everyone's time."

His jaw clenched visibly. "It wasn't a waste. Look what it has achieved. The webcam wouldn't have had anything to show outside breeding season anyway. Just an empty box."

"Why didn't you just tell me about the renovations? We could have waited until after they were finished."

Nathan stared at her long and hard. "Because they won't be finished for some time."

Everything in her prickled at his tone. "How long?"

His eyes grew flinty. "Two years."

Her world lurched and tipped violently. *"Two years?* What the hell kind of renovations are you planning?"

"I wanted to talk to you about this, explain personally…"

"We're talking now. So explain."

His chest rose and fell on a controlled breath. Tori totally held hers. "I'm constructing a whole new building on this site."

Her blood froze over, her word barely more than a whisper. "What?"

"I'm demolishing this old building and erecting something new in its place. Something larger. More contemporary."

The knife poised between her ribs shifted trajectory and neatly pierced her lungs. All the air escaped in a pained whoosh. The room began to spin slowly. "No…"

"It's too young to have heritage status and too old to be economically maintained…."

His lips were moving but his voice warped in and out of focus in ears that thundered with sudden panic. *Demolition…* Her home. Her sanctuary.

"You can't…"

"It's all arranged." He frowned as he noticed her white-knuckled grip on the quilt. "Tori, are you okay?"

"You can't, Nathan. You can't." Her voice echoed in her head like a bad amusement ride. High-pitched. Discordant. But there was nothing she could do to stop it. "I can't."

"I found you a beautiful place, surrounded by trees. Right on the park. Only a few blocks from me. It's yours for a year. Longer if you want it. And if you want to come back here when the new building's up I can sort that, too."

His words washed in and out of her ears making little impact on her brain. *Coming back would require leaving.* The world dropped out from beneath her like the worst of free-falls. Except, abseiling down a rock face had never made her feel like this. She struggled valiantly to disguise how difficult it was to breathe. "I can't leave here, Nathan."

"Just come and check it out with me. I know you'll make it as nice as you've made this apartment. It has everything you spoke of that night."

She fisted his shirt and pulled herself closer to him, the fear clawing. "You're not hearing me. *I cannot leave here.*"

He stared at her, then looked around and then back at her with a deep, pained frown. "Tori, what's going on? It's just an apartment. It's not like you'll be homeless."

What *was* going on? Her whole body was reacting. Trembling. But she fought to hide it from him. He wouldn't understand how important this apartment was to her, how much she relied on routine to get her through each day since she'd lost Rick.

She barely understood it. Although she feared she was beginning to.

Nathan took a deep breath and watched her through narrowed eyes. "When was the last time you went outside?"

The ridiculous question distracted her. "With you. On the roof."

"I mean out on the street. When did you last go through the front door?"

She blinked. It was easy to recall those first days when she'd moved in, when everything was furnished, unpacked and in its place. Then there'd been a bunch of trips into the surrounding neighborhood to get her bearings. Then ever-decreasing errands the more she set up trades within the building for things she needed. She really scraped her memory…

Her heart thumped.

...and came up blank.

Her brows drew together. Suddenly she saw the past five years played back in fast forward. Every time she'd hedged. Every time she'd stalled. Every time she'd ordered in instead of dining out. Every single trade she'd offered the people in this building to ensure that the world came to her....

So that she didn't have to go out to it.

And it frightened the hell out of her. When had her entire life become a series of carefully controlled, deeply comforting routines? Her pulse started to beat at the fine skin containing it.

"I..." But she had no idea what to say next.

His eyes flooded with pity. "Have you tried to get help?"

Help? "For what?"

"Tori. You haven't been outside in...what...years?" He shifted closer to her. "You're agoraphobic."

Her laugh sounded brittle, even to her and her breath grew painfully tight. "Don't be ridiculous. I'm a mountain climber. How can I possibly fear open spaces? You've seen me on the roof. On the ledge. All that wide-open sky..."

Deny that, genius.

But he couldn't. "It's still not normal."

She pushed away, her breath still straining. "Normal? Are you really sure you're fit to preach about what's normal?"

His eyes narrowed dangerously. "Tori..."

But she was in pure survival mode and, just like last time, her body was making the calls on how best to get through this. She felt her lips curl up. "You've driven yourself into the ground trying to prove something to a mother who probably never even noticed. Did she even know how rich you were at the end there? Where you ended up?"

"Don't make this about me, Tori."

Every time he said her name it was like a warning. His tight tone said they were at DEFCON three.

And she ignored it completely.

"Why not? Isn't this exactly about you? Your desire to make more money? Your desire to prove yourself and beat your sucky childhood? To build something shiny and expensive? Did you get your revenge that way, Nathan, living the high life while she lived in squalor?"

"This has nothing to do with her."

"Oh, really? Did you buy your mother her own apartment with park views, then? Or do you save that sort of thing for the women you're sleeping with?"

He glared at her. "She always had a safe roof over her head, until the day she died. I bought out her lease. And then I bought the whole building."

What? She took three steadying breaths. "How many buildings do you own?"

His eyes glittered like dead sapphires. "Just the one."

And with those three little words everything came together. Apartment 8B. The notorious Domino. The way he'd subtly avoided meeting any of the building's old-timers. The way he was neglecting the building to rubble.

"*This* is the place where you were so unhappy?"

His silence was assent enough.

A deep nausea washed over her. "You bought the building you grew up in. And now you want to tear it down. Have you even been back into your family apartment since she died?

More silence.

She stared at him. "And that strikes you as normal, does it? Have *you* tried to get help?"

Throwing his words so brutally back at him only served to crank him up to DEFCON two. But his anger was underpinned by visible pain. "This is business."

"Oh, please! Anyone else would just move away and move on."

The way you did? her inner voice accused.

"Columbia is looking for new student housing in the area, Tori. I'll make a killing."

"Then why didn't you just sell out to them years ago?"

"I wish I had," he ground out. "Then I never would have had to—"

He cut himself off way too quickly to ignore and pressed his lips against whatever he'd been about to blurt. Hurt twisted in her chest. "Meet me?"

"I was going to say 'have this ridiculous conversation.'"

The ice in her veins solidified that little bit more. "You don't think it's significant that you've only bought one piece of real estate in your life and it's your childhood home? That you're demolishing it when you don't have to?"

"It's business, Tori. Risk is what I do. Sometimes I win, sometimes I lose, but my instincts are seldom wrong." His nostrils flared wildly. "And at least I'm out there, living my life amongst real people."

"And I'm living mine here," she said, her voice painfully tight. "Just differently to you."

Both their chests heaved. "It's not living, Tori. It's just existing."

Her throat ached from wanting to shout at him. And from the strain of not crying. "Huh. Funny, these past few days have felt pretty alive to me," she said thickly. She'd been gradually thawing out since the moment he'd first caught her up in his smoky gaze. His smile. His kisses.

He swore under his breath and grudgingly met her eyes. "They were. I haven't felt so...connected... Ever."

She was only a deep breath away from hysteria. "Me, too. Let's celebrate by popping a cork or ripping down a building."

His lips thinned. "Your sarcasm's not shoring it up any. It's only reinforcing that nothing good comes out of this building."

Tori stared at him. "So this *is* personal?"

His face took on a wild hue. "No. It's not. But I won't be sorry that the building and its misery are gone. A nice side benefit."

"Is that what I was this week?"

His face turned ashen. "No. You were not." He swallowed hard. "But even you have to admit your life here hasn't been a riot."

"Sorry to bust your theory but my life was perfectly crap before I moved in here, thank you very much."

His face shuttered over. "Your brother."

She pushed to her feet, past him out into the living room. "Einstein."

He pursued her out the door. "You're here because of him."

"I'm here because New York offered me a new life. A fresh start."

"No." The intent look in his eye was too all-seeing. "You're living in the most crowded and anonymous city in the country on the money Rick left you, sequestered in this tower like some kind of twisted fairy-tale princess, banished from the people and mountains you love, punishing yourself."

She spun on him, clutching the pillow close to her chest. "Punishing myself—for what?"

"For living. When he didn't."

Every molecule of oxygen sucked out of her body, rearranged itself in the atmosphere and then flooded back in on a rush of heat. She marched straight up to him and every step was on razor wire. Fear gripped her deep and low. "You have no idea what you're talking about."

He towered over her. "Really? Do you imagine I don't know a thing or two about guilt? I was the unplanned pregnancy that cramped my mother's style her whole life. I was the irritating expense as I outgrew uniform after uniform at school. I was the reason she had to drop a days worth of clients to clean the fetid apartment once in a while for Social Services to come around." He stabbed stiff fingers into his chest. "I grew up thinking my mother sold her body to anyone who had need of it so that *I* could eat a warm meal each day. And to top it all off I had to deal with the guilt of being so damned *relieved* when I finally realized she was doing it for money and not for me."

Tori flinched at the pain in his face and her whole body cried out in sympathy.

"So yes, Tori, I recognise survivor guilt when I see it because I survived my childhood and it took me a long time to let myself be proud of that." He stepped closer. "You lived when your brother died. And you think that deserves punishment. But you're wrong. Living is a gift, Tori, and finding the right person to live that life with is more extraordinary than anything."

Tears surged suddenly from nowhere and spilled uncontrolled onto her raging-hot cheeks. Nathan's lips squeezed tight against saying anything more and he stepped toward her.

She stumbled back—desperate not to hear the promise in his words, desperate not to tempt the hand of fate by embracing the tantalizing hint of happiness he offered—and consciously euthanized everything they had built between them.

"I killed my brother, Nathan." Her voice was hoarse and unnatural. "I killed Rick to save myself."

The only sound in the entire apartment was the tight wheeze of her own tortured throat. Nathan didn't even breathe. He just stared at her in horror.

Totally deserved.

Tori swiped at the tears spilling down her cheeks. "He was so much bigger than me, hanging over that abyss. His weight was dragging us both over. It took forever, slipping closer to the precipice. I scrabbled and clawed and tried to arrest my slide but I couldn't get purchase. Rick couldn't climb back up and I couldn't hold him forever." She heaved in a tight breath. "We both knew what had to happen, but his left hand was twisted up in the rigging—he couldn't reach his knife."

Her eyes dropped to shake the image burned into her retinas. "He was screaming at me to do it before he dragged me over, but I couldn't. I wanted to save him or die trying. Because I loved him more than the air we breathed." A shudder racked her body and the tears stopped flowing. They sucked back into her stinging orbits. A numb stillness settled over her instead. "But I got within a meter of the edge and, in that moment, right at the last moment I realized I was too afraid to fall. To die. So I did it. I held my breath, released my knife and cut the rope. And he fell."

Endless silence followed. And why not—there was nothing more to say. She'd said it all five years ago to the relentless line of strangers who investigated the accident. Nathan stepped towards her and she stepped back, crossing her arms in front of her.

His voice cracked when he finally spoke. "You had no choice. You would have both died."

She lifted anguished eyes to his. "I wish I had. Everything I've done since is just taking up air."

"No..."

"Maybe I am punishing myself. But Rick will never laugh or cry or be loved or watch sunsets or hold a sleeping child in his arms. Why should I get to?"

"So...what—you're just going to rot here in this apartment? Forsaking any goodness that might creep in under your defenses? Until you're old and senile and die alone in this apartment?"

Her chest squeezed hard and she thought immediately of Nancy. Was that why she felt so close to the older woman? Because she saw herself in Nancy? She straightened her back and the effort half killed her. Nathan was handing her the perfect excuse to end things between them. To do what she knew she had to. It would be better for him in the long term if she just unraveled the complicated tangle that had formed from her heart to his and tore it away.

She closed her eyes. In her mind she lifted a knife to the rigging of whatever it was that had brought she and Nathan together. Held them together now. "Yes." She took a long breath. "Starting with you."

He stared at her, his burning regard dark in bleached skin. But something about the raw pain she saw swilling in the twin depths made her pause her mind's knife. Offer him—

them both—one last chance. "Will you leave the building standing?"

His nostrils flared and his eyes blazed at her. "I can't, Tori. Not just because you can't go outside…"

Air sucked into her lungs of its own accord and it was strangely reinforcing. But it didn't do a thing to diminish the ache that filled her.

He wouldn't do it for her.

Because his own reasons were too strong.

Her heart cracked wider. "Then I don't want your new apartment. Or your charity."

She crossed to the refridgerator, snatched free the single sheet of paper stuck to its front and scribbled across it with her pen. His community order, fully signed off. She pushed it into his chest, and sliced the knife clean through the final golden filaments binding them together.

"And I don't want you to come near me ever again."

The ghosts of the building held their breaths.

Nathan stared at the order and then at her, deep and unreadable, although his chest pumped hard. "This is not really about the building, Tori." But then his lashes dropped and he twisted away and flicked a business card out onto the counter. "When you decide you need help—when you decide you need me—you know where I am."

She held herself perfectly rigid as he moved toward her front door. The door that had somehow come to symbolize her: as hollow and out of place as she always felt.

Except when she was with Nathan.

He stopped at the door and looked back at her, burning to say something. But he glanced down at the floor and then lifted carefully blank eyes back up to her and murmured a few words before disappearing out the door.

Tori waited until she heard the door latch quietly closed and then she took the pillow still smelling of him and hurled it, internalizing her scream so that it hurt more. So that the memory would be branded into her soul. So that she'd never again forget why she didn't let anyone in. Why she'd embraced this careful, controlled world where everything happened in the same way every time.

She and Nathan were not meant to be together. It was hard enough finding a perfect match for your outward qualities without also expecting your raging demons to get along. There was more than one way to be incompatible.

It had been a long time since her body had harbored intense pain—her routines and rules and cloistered ways had done their job in holding it at bay—but she felt it now, surging back in, raw and razored, at the thought of losing the man she'd only just found.

The man she hadn't even known she needed.

Her heart squeezed into a twisted pulp.

She stared around her now at the familiar sanctuary of her apartment. Her old furniture. Her familiar view. Her entire world. And she knew that, even if it *had* tiptoed up on her and taken over her life, this apartment was directly responsible for keeping her alive these past five years. For helping her breathe. For letting her heart beat. And it was going to be ripped into tiny pieces and hurled to the pavement at the hands of a man she'd given herself to, body and soul.

Nathan was going to rip her out of her safe life the way he'd come into it. In an explosion of timber shards.

*Forgive yourself...*he'd said right before he disappeared through her open doorway. But then he'd whispered the rest, and she'd almost not heard him over the roar of her frantic heartbeat past her eardrums. *Forgive yourself for choosing life that day...*

She folded her arms over her head and sank down onto the floor, releasing the pain on a stream of hot, blinding tears.

...but not for wasting it.

CHAPTER TWELVE

"YOU'D better get up here, Nathan. There's a woman hanging from your building and there are an awful lot of people starting to gather."

The moment Nate retrieved Dean's voice-mail message he knew exactly who the woman was and what she had done. He slid over to his desktop and fired up Sanmore's latest internet browser. He hadn't visited the webcam in a couple of weeks—every time he did it only reminded him of Tori's warm little apartment, of the wild, beautiful birds, and the wild, beautiful woman who cared for them. It reminded him of what he no longer had a right to dream of at night. But he still kept the link in his favorites folder. And he still hovered the mouse over it from time to time. The only thing that stopped him from clicking it was that he felt vaguely like a stalker.

She'd made it perfectly clear she wanted nothing more to do with him and he'd always been a man of sterling self-discipline. To the point of pain.

But better him in pain than her.

The website loaded and he paused for a nanosecond to look at some new imagery on the homepage—two robust, browning chicks that had been tiny balls of fluff the last time he'd checked.

His eyes flicked to the visitor-counter and widened, seeing a number in five figures. Low five figures, but still...That was a lot of people checking out Morningside's raptors in just a few weeks.

In the top corner, something about the thumbnail for the webcam didn't look right. As if it was blocked by something. He activated the cam and held his breath while it loaded.

"Oh, you are kidding me..."

There *was* something blocking the camera's view of Wilma and the chicks. A piece of card, propped up by a soda can, and kind of off center as though the wind—or an inquisitive falcon—had knocked it askew. It had a bold message in Tori's handwriting scrawled in thick, black ink.

Help save Morningside's falcons.
Help save their building.
Add your voice to the protest.
4:00 p.m., June 23

And that would be today. Nate's lashes drifted shut.

But then he couldn't help smiling. A normal person would have added a tastefully bordered HTML message to the home-page with five minutes' work. But Tori did nothing the normal way and her personalized message achieved two things. It added some raw urgency to her plea, which site fans would imme-diately respond to, and it blocked the birds from the view of those ten thousand plus visitors, effectively doing exactly what demolishing the building was going to do. Make them disap-pear. Which the site users wouldn't like. Maybe enough to get off their butts and travel up to Morningside for the protest that started—he looked at his watch—ten minutes ago.

Tori was an accidental genius.

And a total thorn in his side. She haunted him at night. She troubled him during the day. He caught himself making busi-ness decisions he thought she, rather than his shareholders, might approve of, and he spent way too long each day obsess-ing on which tenants had begun to move out and waiting to see her name show up on the report. So far most of the neighbors he knew had shifted to their new accommodations, even Mr. Broswolowski, whom he'd figured would have stuck in there with Tori. But he'd personally signed off on Mr B's relocation expense just two days ago so—other than Miss Smith who was scheduled for the end of next week—Tori was all out of friends in that big building.

Who was looking after her now?

The tenants' deadline was up in just a week. But if she was planning eleventh-hour protest rallies then she wasn't going anywhere soon. That meant she was holding out for the bailiffs. Or she was still in denial.

He groaned.

She didn't have a textbook phobia—that would be too simple and Tori was everything but simple. She had developed her own special blend of dysfunction; one that made her overly reliant on her ordered, predictable world, to counteract the damage she'd done by choosing life that day on the mountain. He'd looked into it to understand. To see if it truly was a big enough deal to throw away everything they'd shared. Apparently it was.

And accepting that was one of the hardest things he'd done. Forcing Tori back into the world would only hurt her more. Between them, they had two lifetimes of damage conspiring to keep them apart. And it wasn't often he met someone who trumped him in the screwy stakes.

He asked himself, again, what he'd been secretly asking himself for weeks—what she'd asked him.

Was she right? *Was* he demolishing Morningside for the wrong reasons? He had a written expression of interest from Columbia University's legal department telling him otherwise but he *could* have sold them the building right away. Let them do all the dirty-work with the tenants.

His heart heaved.

Let them throw Tori's world into disarray.

He missed her. Even the screwy parts. He missed the way she teased him mercilessly and laughed at him if he tried to talk up his achievements. He missed her warm body against his at

night and the incredible rightness of being joined with her. He
missed the wonders that he got to teach her and the amazing
wilderness stories she got to teach him. He missed turning up
on her doorstep at 4:00 p.m. sharp, knowing the day was just
getting going.

But he didn't miss hurting her. Or forcing her to look at
things she wasn't ready to face.

His gut lurched. He'd hated that.

He'd had a full private session with the psych that he'd lined
up for Tori ready for the day she called him to ask for help—
not that she ever would call, and the psych knew that even if it
had taken Nate a while to catch on. He'd told Nate that forcing
Tori back into the world was the fastest way to ensure she never
healed. And given she'd thrown him out of her life for good,
helping her more gently wasn't really an option. He could only
hope that the looming eviction deadline would trigger some
kind of change. But he'd expected it to be in the form of sticking an experimental toe out the front door.

Not arranging a rally for a thousand wildlife fanatics.

He could only imagine how intensely uncomfortable the very
idea would have made her. Which said a lot about how desperate
she must be feeling. And desperate people did desperate things.
Like making a nestful of birds seem in more danger than they
actually were.

Help save Morningside's Falcons.

Might as well have said *Please help me.*

He winced and snatched up his desk phone. "Karin, can you
get the car out the front? I'm going uptown. And then get on to
Tony d'Angelo at the NYFD…"

When he arrived, Simon had to let him out up the block because 126th Street was gridlocked thanks to the mix of people
spilling out of the laneway behind his building. Young hippie
types, older retired types, backpack-wearing corduroy types.
Mothers with children. Hundreds of people. Traffic was still

getting through, but it was car by car and walking pace to make sure no one got hurt. On foot was definitely faster.

Nate rounded the corner just as he had that first day and elbowed his way through the milling crowd, dodging the odd placard before it took his eye out. He glanced upward immediately.

And then his stomach flipped.

Dean wasn't kidding when he'd said *hanging from your building*. Tori dangled from the bedroom ledge one floor up from hers, fully rigged out in climbing gear, with a brightly decorated bedsheet saying Save Morningside's Falcons furled out below her. It took him only a blink to realize that she couldn't have opened 11B's bedroom window, so she must have climbed down the outside of the building to get to the ledge.

Crazy fool woman!

He looked around. The crowd was looking uncertain. Like a mob who'd forgotten why they were at a lynching. A bad feeling settled in his stomach.

"What's going on?" he asked a woman standing nearby. "Why isn't she doing anything?"

The woman shrugged. "Everyone was cheering as she shimmied down the building and unfurled the banner—" his stomach dropped clean away at that image "—but then she kind of just...stopped. We're waiting for something to happen."

"You care what happens to these birds?"

"Well, sure. There's not a lot of community spirit around these days. And *she* cares. Look at that. Who does that?"

His gaze followed the woman's finger upward again. There was definitely something spectacular and inspiring about a woman clinging like a backward starfish to the outside of a building. But then he narrowed his eyes and looked at Tori's posture.

Really looked.

She kind of just...stopped.

Nate sucked in a breath. Not stopped. *Froze.*

He sprinted for the building, fighting his way through more

and more people who were arriving and packing into the small space below until he got around to the fire exit at the base of the stairwell. He pulled his keys out and sorted through them until he found the one he needed and then flung the doors wide before running inside. The elevator would take a lifetime to get up there and Tori might not have that long. So he stuck to the stairs, not even counting the floors as his long legs ate them up.

By the fifth floor they protested and by six they shook with a hot burn. But the image of Tori hanging, terrified, from the building filled his mind and drove him onward. He visualized a scenario in which he got up there and she yelled at him for interfering. Called the cops on him. Slid her hands onto those beautiful hips and glared impatiently because she was actually *perfectly fine*, just…taking a breather.

He'd take that. He'd love that. Because it would mean she was okay. It would mean she was coping.

But deep down inside he knew she wasn't. She hadn't been coping for a really long time but she'd had everyone fooled. Her parents. Her neighbors. Him.

Herself.

Sometimes even the unrescuable needed rescuing.

As he passed the seventh-floor landing, his lungs pure agony, Nate realized that he wasn't going to be able to pull Tori up from the ledge outside 11B's sealed bedroom pane and there was no way he'd fit through her bathroom window. The only way he was getting her down *was* down and the only apartment that would put him close enough for that was his own.

His mother's.

His throat threatened to close right over and end it all here on the steps. He pushed through the landing doors and took a sharp left. The whole floor was ominously quiet, with most of the building now vacant. It practically echoed with the sound of his racing feet.

He didn't waste time searching for that little bronze key, hurling himself instead at the locked door. His whole left side

screamed on impact but the door creaked and shuddered. He
backed up and slammed again and the lock burst from its frame,
throwing him hard into the middle of what his mother used to
call the "receiving" room.

There was only one thing he'd received there and that was
an awful, early education.

The apartment was musty with age and dank with mildew
but otherwise empty of anything that would have identified
it as his. He'd donated the entire contents to Goodwill when
his mother had died and had called professional cleaners in
to scrub any echoes of their life from the nicotine-stained
walls. But memories still reached out and snatched at him as
he pushed himself to his feet and ran through to the bathroom.
The window resisted at first but he forced it open and stretched
through it.

"Tori!"

He couldn't see her but he heard her tentative response, tight
and small. "Nathan?"

Everything in him threatened to go wobbly at the sound of
her fear. But he forced himself to stay strong until she was safe
again.

"Tori, can you get back up?"

"I…I can't. I can't move…."

She sounded so much more than scared. Angry. Incredulous.
Distressed. Heartbroken.

He craned his neck around to the left and saw an old lump
of concrete sitting on the ledge. Dangerous, but maybe the only
way. He took a deep breath. "Tori, I need you to turn completely
away from the building. Can you do that? Face the Hudson."

He listened for her response but only heard a mewling sound
that could have been "yes" or could have been the falcon chicks
two storys up expressing their displeasure at the disturbances
going on all around them. He slid back through the window,
then wiggled an arm through ahead of him, just long enough
to reach the concrete lump. He grabbed it and brought it back
through into the bathroom. Then he sprinted through the old

kitchen, stripping off his tie and shirt as he went, and wrapping them thickly around his right hand and forearm before fitting the stone back into his swaddled fist.

His hands shook so badly he nearly couldn't tie off the swaddling. *Tori...*

In the master bedroom he yanked back the old curtains and a decade of mildew and dust exploded into the air. Nate fixed his eyes on the view outside, determined not to visualize what this room had once looked like or what had gone on here. He saw Tori's shoulder down at ledge level and the head she'd screened with her arms to shield it.

He lifted the rock and slammed it against the edge of the glass farthest from her.

The window cracked on first impact and smashed outward on the second. Glass fragments went everywhere and he hoped he'd managed to control the spray so it fell on the ledge and not on the protesters below. Tori turned toward him, wide-eyed and pale.

And wildly, patently, relieved.

His determination doubled. He used his wrapped fist to punch out the entire left hand pane of the bedroom window and then sweep the worst of the glass into the corner of the ledge. Then he unraveled it and threw the shirt aside and boosted himself out the window before he thought too much about the danger of what he was about to do.

Or how high he was.

Eight storeys seemed to swim in and out of focus below him. One minute the people below were just a bright sea of color and the next he was making out the tiniest and most inconsequential details. An overly large nose. A Lakers cap. And all of them with one expression in common—wide-eyed, excited disbelief that *someone else* was now climbing out onto the building's exterior. A half-naked man.

So much better than video games!

Nate dragged his focus back to the woman he loved and tried not to think about how far away the hard ground was and what it might do if he was to suddenly rush toward it. Or if she was...

Because he did love her. And it took a ridiculous incident to make him acknowledge it. He'd been half in love with her when he'd first kissed her in that elevator. And then their week together as lovers had sealed the deal. He'd loved her then but not been able to admit it.

Any more than he was prepared to admit she was right about this building.

Because he feared he'd be as bad at love as his mother and as just blind to his own failings.

"Tori..."

"Nathan, be careful!" Her eyes were as wide as those of the people in the crowd below.

He slid down into sitting position and hung his legs over the edge, close to where she hung suspended and the world lurched sickeningly. "I could say the same thing. What are you doing?"

"I'm trying to save the building!"

Even speaking made his chest ache. Five kinds of fear congealed in his lungs. "By fixing yourself to the outside of it? You think you wouldn't just be a convenient target for the wrecking ball?"

Slipping straight back into their usual, bantering dynamic helped take his mind off the fact that his entire future hung suspended in space and so, practically, did he. Joking seemed to help Tori, too. She loosened up just a bit.

"I used 11B's bedroom ledge to come down from so I didn't disturb the birds. I just wanted to hang the banner but then I looked around. At all the people. And I just... Everything just..." Her face folded.

He reached forward with his legs and hooked them around the taut rigging that held her weight, and she lifted her arms and grabbed his ankles immediately.

His smile was half grimace. "You've done this before."

Her voice tightened through clenched teeth. "This isn't the first time I've gotten into a tricky spot while climbing."

He swore and didn't bother to disguise it. "I kid you not—when I get you in you are never leaving the house again."

The irony of that made them both laugh, tight and strained. Nate locked his abs, tilted back onto his coccyx and contracted his legs back toward his body. The first little bit wasn't a problem because the rigging offered no resistance, but as he pulled, even Tori's slight weight dragged him forward a bit and he had to grip the concrete with what little nails he had. She turned in his grasp until she was facing him. The deathly pale bleach of her skin sunk home.

He had a sudden and crystal-clear vision of her, tear-streaked, exhausted and scrabbling inexorably down a mountain face, trying desperately to hold onto her brother while her heart ripped apart. He knew how he would feel if he dropped her now.

His life would be over.

A deep and abiding purpose flooded through him. He was going to build her a new life. "Hold on, baby. I've got you."

She locked her eyes on his, pale and frantic. "If you slide, you let me go."

He pulled harder and grimaced past the pain. "Not going to happen."

Her breathing was fast and urgent. "I'm rigged, Nathan. You're not. If you start to go you just let me go. I cannot lose you."

Lose you.

Not "lose you *like this*".

Absurdly, given the peril that they both faced and despite the deathly drop below him, his heart lifted. "You belong in my arms, Tori. We're not stopping until you're back there." He wriggled into a surer position. Every part of him protested. "The longer you talk the weaker I'm getting. Now shut up and start climbing."

She was still too low for the ledge, but she wasn't too low to climb his legs. She gasped a few instructions on how he could best brace himself and then she twisted the rigging in her fist and used it to take the bulk of her weight while her other hand clasped hard around his thigh for purchase.

She pulled. He braced. Then he tightened his legs under her armpits so she could release the rigging and reach for a higher point. She did, hooking her free hand onto his belt. It was worth every one of the designer zeroes it had cost as it helped pull Tori up and half across his lap.

So close.

He let go of one of his brace points and wrapped his arm around her torso and then used every fiber in every thread of every muscle in his body to pull them both back into a prone position on the filthy, pigeon-poop-covered ledge.

It might as well have been a down comforter.

He circled his screaming arms around her and pulled her hard up against him, the rigging protesting at the stretch, shards of broken glass slicing into his unprotected back.

Tori scrabbled to release the clips that kept her from Nathan and when the tethers swung free there was a joyful cheer from the crowd below. She flung her arms around him, reveling in the feel of his hard, shirtless body against hers, and she twisted her legs sideways so that one hundred percent of both of them was supported by flat concrete ledge. No chance of him sliding off.

No chance that she'd kill another man that she loved.

She buried her face into the sweat-covered curve of Nathan's neck and inhaled the heated scent raging off him. Every part of her started to shake and he absorbed her tremors straight into his skin. It didn't matter that the last time she'd seen him she'd thrown him out of her apartment. Her life. That she'd confessed her greatest shame to him and he'd accused her of wasting the life she'd chosen that day on the mountain face. That he'd lied to her about where he'd grown up. And that he was going to destroy her home.

All that mattered was that Nathan was here. In her arms.

And his heart was beating sure and hard and eternal against hers. For whatever minutes they had together.

She'd take it.

Eventually he spoke, his voice cracked and gravelly against her ear. "Are you hurt?"

Only inside. From so much. She shook her head.

"I need you safely inside, Tori. Can you stand?"

Her eyes dropped to his biceps. "My muscles aren't the ones twitching with exhaustion. Can *you* stand?" His color hadn't come back yet.

"Don't worry about me," he said. "You first."

She scrabbled over him, knowing he wasn't moving until she did. And more than anything in this world she wanted carpet under his feet. And, for the first time ever, under her own. She practically tumbled into the empty apartment and then rolled away from the window to make room for Nathan.

Through the window that was so much like her own, she watched him pull himself into sitting position on the ledge and sucked in a pained breath as she saw the shards of bloody glass sticking out of his back like some kind of masochistic body art. She glanced around and saw his torn-off shirt on the floor. She had it ready when he finally slid through the shattered window and landed with a thump next to her on the floor.

He looked baffled by his own weakness.

"Fatigue," she croaked. "And shock. Give yourself a minute for the adrenaline hit to pass." But then she lunged toward him and snagged his shoulder just as he might have leaned back against the musty apartment wall. Against the forest of broken glass peppering his skin. "You're going to hurt any moment, too."

She saw the moment he did. As the pain of thirty slices registered on his handsome face. The face she'd believed she'd never see again.

Compassion washed through her. She crawled around behind him and sat, spread-eagled, with her thighs either side of his hips to keep him from slumping backward. Worrying about him kept her from thinking about herself. About what had just happened. Just like getting Rick help gave her something to focus on when he died.

To hold herself together.

"Hold still." She picked at the larger pieces of glass, wincing as Nathan flinched. The easing of the blood confirmed they weren't as deep as she'd feared.

His voice was strained and low as he said, "Don't ever do that to me again."

"I have to get the worst pieces out—"

"I'm talking about the stunt you just pulled. I'm talking about looking up from a crowd full of strangers and seeing you hanging there, petrified, and at risk of falling."

Petrified. She had been, too. Completely overcome with an emotion that just froze every living part of her. Until she'd heard his voice... Her body shuddered with remembered relief. She picked more glass out and softly stroked every spot where she hurt him before moving on to the next. Then she paused.

"I don't know why..." She frowned at the unmistakable breathlessness of anxiety rising in her chest. Climbing was all she'd had left of her old life. "Do I not even have that now? I can't even climb a building without freaking out?"

He reached his right arm around behind him and curled his hand around her hip, holding her tightly against him. "I don't care. I'm just glad you're okay."

The awkward, tender touch broke her in a hundred places and gave her the strength to whisper something she'd realized as soon as she turned out there on the building face and saw all those people below her. All that vast, unfamiliar city stretching out beyond her. What he'd been trying to say the last time they spoke.

When she'd said such awful things to him to distract her from the truth of his words.

"I'm not okay, Nathan." Her eyes stung from so much more than the summer glare coming in the window. Her body heaved with a sob bursting to express itself. "I haven't been okay for five years."

He twisted around to see her but the pain of his shrapnel back stopped him with a jerk. Instead, he brought his left arm up over those powerful shoulders and snaked it around her neck and pulled her hard against his damaged flesh as though he just didn't care. Tori pressed her face against the hard angle of his jaw and did her best not to injure him further.

They both needed the contact before all else.

"I was terrified I was going to fall," she whispered against his ear.

He pressed his face back into hers. "There are much worse things than falling."

God, how true that was.

He turned toward her, bringing his lips mere millimeters from hers. But it wasn't their lips that met, it was their gaze. His breath was warm and comforting so close to her as he spoke. "Fear is good, Tori. It's normal. It means you have something to lose. Not fearing means not caring."

She frowned. How long had it been since she stopped caring about life?

"I tried to come to you."

His eyes darted towards her. "When?"

"About two days after you left. I wanted to show you I could. Show myself. But I didn't get past the sidewalk." She pressed her lips together to stop them trembling. "That was when I knew it had gone far enough. Knowing how I felt about you and still I couldn't…."

Her eyes misted over and tears choked her. She rested her chin on his shoulder, glad she couldn't see his reaction to her inadvertent declaration. "What's happening to me, Nathan? I'm normally the master of my fear."

"You haven't been mastering fear, you've been minimizing it. Avoiding it, by controlling your environment so tightly."

Her heart protested with a violent lurch. She traced her fingers carefully across his back and resumed picking at the glass, the hypnotic actions clearing her clouded, cluttered mind and forcing her chest to ease. Nathan settled back against her fingers and let her do it, giving her the breathing space she needed.

Was that what she'd been doing—avoiding her fears rather than facing them? She'd told herself she wanted to be safe... But maybe it was more that she wanted to be *Safe*—uppercase. She'd built herself a complicated world that meant she never had to jeopardize her boundaries, meet strangers, risk loss. A world that had seemed complete and varied and even rich until she shoved it up against the world of someone like Nathan and realized how homogenized and...beige...hers had become.

Worse, browned with stale air.

"I don't want to be Nancy. I don't want to live a life without risk. Why would I do that to myself?"

He spoke again, soft and close. "Two people died on that mountain, Tori. Except one of you kept breathing."

Everything in the room stopped. Pulse. Noise. The tiny particles of dust that danced like fairies in the shafts of light streaming in the window. Was that what she'd done five years ago? Stopped living? Was she truly the walking dead? In a rush of awareness she realized that was exactly how she'd been feeling for...a long time. Despite the neighbor friends. Despite the keeping busy. Despite the secret dreams of "one day."

Until a knight in such thick shining armor had barged his way into her familiar apartment and her safe, ordered life all those weeks ago.

Her breath resumed and the dust-fairies fluttered downwards. She pulled the final glass shard from his shoulder blade, kissed the vacant spot it left and then left her lips pressed to his flesh and murmured, "I feel alive right now."

Anyone else would have heard it as a come-on. But not Nathan. Because they were too similar. He knew her heart was suddenly beating as hard and as enthusiastically and as *vitally* as his. He knew her fear was still pulsing through her system, waking every long-dormant cell in her body with the clanging of bells. He knew how her flesh sang when it came anywhere near his.

Because he was part of her, too.

"It's what we do to each other," he said. "We bring life."

She wiped away the final trickle of blood and tossed the last glass shard to the tiny pile a few feet away from them. Then she pressed herself fully against his back as if to stem the claret floodtide. She slid her hands around under his arms and flattened them against his hot steel chest and let his strength soak into her.

"How do you know me so well?" she whispered.

He took an age to answer. "Because I am you."

She sat up straighter and he twisted around, bringing her half around onto his lap. "What do you mean?"

"Look around us, Tori. Where are we?"

It was only then she stopped to wonder about the empty apartment they were in. There was no way that the fastidious Barney would have let his apartment get like this, even before moving out last week. Which meant they were two floors down and not one. Which meant this was—

She sucked in a breath. "Your mother's apartment."

"I haven't set foot in here in sixteen years."

She glanced around. "Looks like no one has."

Sealed up as tight as his wounded heart. Tori sucked back an ache. It would have been bad enough hearing the raw pain in his voice without also seeing it tarnish those compassionate, brilliant eyes. "And you never came back here? Except to buy the building?"

His lips pressed extra-thin. "Even then I did it through a proxy. I had no interest in setting foot in this place. Ever."

Tori's stomach squeezed for him. "You planned to demolish it even then?"

"No. At first just owning it was enough. It was a statement I thought I was making for other people. For her, maybe. But I think I was really convincing myself of something."

Tori slid her hand up to cup his cheek. "Of what?"

Two pained creases appeared between his brow. "That I'd made it. I'd survived."

She stroked him carefully. "Those memories are part of who you are."

"Not the best part."

She winced at the self-loathing in his expression. "No. But they forged the best part. You can't deny them any more than I can pretend Rick's death never happened."

Much as she'd been trying. No photos. No family. Avoiding. *Oh.*

And just like that, the light streaming in the window might as well have shifted and fallen directly on them because the truth blazed golden and obvious down on the two of them, curled around each other on the filthy apartment floor.

They'd both enshrined their memories to protect themselves. She'd chosen to sequester herself away from hers. Nathan had entombed his whole childhood in this room.

"Were there no good times at all, Nathan?" Had he slid the stone shut on everything that happened?

Pain sliced across his face, more serious than the superficial wounds on his back. Those would heal. He looked around and shook his head. "It's hard to remember a single one. Not in here."

"Would you have felt differently about what she did for a living if she'd not been such a miserable parent?"

His eyes grew round with pain and then incredulity. "I just can't even conceive of her as a better mother."

She turned her hand and ran the backs of her fingers over his jaw. "What if she was disappointed in herself? That she wasn't a stronger person?"

"Then her whole life must have been a disappointment."

Tori frowned. "Imagine living with that. Knowing it was true." Nathan stared at her. She held his gaze. "I know something about self-loathing, Nathan. After a while it's hard to imagine you have any worth at all. It becomes possible to justify anything."

Look what she herself had justified.

His pain—old and entrenched—swamped her. "Hating her hurts you."

"I hate what she did."

Tori took a breath. "I think you hate what she didn't do."

"What's that?"

Gently, gently. "Put you first."

His eyes spat pain. "Isn't that what mothers are supposed to do?"

She thought of her own. The grieving woman she'd carefully partitioned out of her life rather than let comfort her. The woman who'd lost two children that day.

"Yes, it is. But when you're fighting for your psychological life there's not a lot of room for anyone else." Unless they force their way in. She curled her free hand around his as a silent thank you. "A lot of years can go by in the void, Nathan. It's a miserable, lonely place."

He stared at her, a deep frown cutting between blue, blue eyes. "Is that how you've felt? Are you lonely, Tori?"

No, I'm fine. The words instantly sprang to her lips. Because she was so used to saying them. Telling others. Telling herself. Ad nauseam.

Until she believed it.

But she looked back at the past few weeks and how she'd obsessed about saving this building. For Nancy, for the birds. How she'd stumbled back inside from that curb and let the fear cripple her into inactivity until the very last minute when desperation drove her to stage today's protest. How she'd forced Nathan from her mind but couldn't evict him from her heart. How she'd convinced herself he'd betrayed her and that it was no more than she deserved.

Was she lonely? She lifted her gaze. "Not right now."

"I missed you," he said, simply.

"I felt close to you, knowing you'd grown up in this building.

You were everywhere I looked. Forcing yourself into my consciousness. No matter how hard I tried to shove you down."

His lips twisted for the first time since he'd come smashing back into her life. The way he'd entered it originally. "That's me. Pushy. I'm sure you'll grow to hate it."

"I'm sure I'll grow to love it." Then, as his pupils flared, she raced on before the heat stained her cheeks. "It's not like you're exactly getting a prize in exchange."

"In exchange? I thought you didn't want me anywhere near you in the future."

"I was angry. And frightened. I overreacted."

"I'm demolishing your building."

"I know. And the thought makes me sick. Literally." As it had done many times over the past few weeks when the anxiety had just got too overwhelming. She pressed her lips to his knuckles. "But that in itself tells me something. A building should not have that kind of power over me." She held his focus. "Or over you."

His chest heaved.

"It's an inanimate object, Nathan. As much a victim of your childhood as you are. It's not responsible for what happened to you, though you've been punishing it all this time. Maybe forgiving the building is one step closer to forgiving the woman who lived here?"

Blue eyes glittered dangerously. Then they jerked around the room and came back to hers, conflicted. "You want to stay that much?"

With everything in me. But that in itself was not reason enough. Not anymore. She shuddered and sat up straighter. "I want this for you. I want to see you exorcise the bad memories and replace them with good ones, rather than just create a shrine to your unhappiness. No matter what glittering building you erect in its place."

His nostrils flared. But then the icy confusion bled out of his gaze and left a wounded blue in their place. "The building's rapidly running out of people to make memories with. What are you suggesting?"

She tossed her head back. "Renovate it. Reinvent it if you want. Then invite everyone back and give it back its soul."

"What about you?" *Oh, so careful.* "How would you feel about all the disruption?"

She took a massively deep breath. "I won't be here."

His voice tightened. "You're going to take the new apartment?"

She shook her head. The very thought made her stomach roil. "No. I'm not that brave. Not yet at least." He looked as confused as she was uncomfortable. It had been a long time since she'd taken any kind of risk at all. Talk about starting with a doozy! She filled her lungs with the warm New York air streaming in the window. "I'm coming with you. To your place. Until mine is fit for habitation again. I think I'll be able to manage that as long as you're there. If that's okay with you."

She fortified her heart and waited for the awkward silence. The stuttered denial. The astonished laugh. But all she got was...

"Are you serious?"

A barb of pure pain sliced low across her soul. Humiliation hovered just at the periphery of her mind, gleefully rubbing its hands together. Tori from yesterday would have cringed and accepted whatever knock was her due. Tori today shook her hair back out of her face and held his eyes. "Deadly. But if you're not interested—"

His hand shot out and stopped her from scrabbling to her feet. He stared at her, incredulous. "I meant, do you seriously think I'm letting you out of my sight once I've had you for my own? There's no way you're moving back in here."

For my own. Her heart set up a relentless thrumming.

"I like Morningside. And old habits die slowly." Surely he'd understand how difficult this was going to be at first. There was a time that a move would have excited her, not filled her with dread.

He read very clearly between the lines. "Then I'll come back with you."

Hope welled unfamiliar and rusty in her chest. "You hate this building."

"I'd have a different...lens now."

What was he saying? The hammering intensified. "You'd go insane in my tiny apartment."

Inspiration blazed bright in his eyes. "I'm not thinking about your apartment. I'm thinking about a super-apartment up on twelve. We can merge the west end of the building. Give you those park views you wanted."

"Not Nancy's place?"

Nathan frowned. "Nancy Smith was the closest thing to parenting I got, growing up. Maybe it's time I tried to be a better son to her." He smiled. "That's if you don't mind us looking out for her."

Tori kneeled up and clasped his hands. "She can stay?"

"Until she wants otherwise. She might have to move into your place while the renovations on her floor are happening. Do you think she'll manage?"

"The question is, will you manage? Can you do this?"

"*We* can do this. Together. It's not going to be easy for either of us but a demon shared is a demon halved, right?"

Old anxieties surged forth. "What if we get it wrong?"

"Would you rather not try?"

She stared deep into those eyes and borrowed his courage. "No. I'm through hiding."

He pulled her forward into his arms and she braced her hands against his scorching chest as his lips branded hers. Her already swimming head spun at the first touch of lips she'd thought never to taste again.

"But for the record..." he said, as they surfaced for air. "We're not getting it wrong. This is about as right as I can imagine. I love you, Tori. In my own messed-up, dysfunctional way. I love your honesty and your vibrancy and, beneath it all, your courage."

The slope of a vast uncharted rock face loomed before her. One part of her shied away from the unfamiliarity of it all. But an older part—a braver part—remembered how it used to feel to discover new mountains. Her pulse pounded and her blood filled with bubbles of joy. "It takes one to love one. And I do love you. So much."

"Enough to commit to a future together?"

"What exactly are we committing to?"

"Each other."

The hands that squeezed hard around her heart protecting it, unfolded like a lotus, letting the muscle leap and surge back to full blood flow. "Forever?"

"Hey, if I'm ripping down walls for you, I need a long-term commitment."

"Is this a proposal?"

"This is a job offer. I'm going to need someone to manage the building and tenants for me. Someone I can trust not to let the place rot."

She pretended to think about it longer than the nanosecond it really took. The opportunity to have purpose again... "That sounds like a reasonable trade." Her eyebrows shot up. "Oh, my God...I just realised. The boy who started the whole trading thing—was that you?"

His smile broke her heart. "When you have nothing you tend to get creative."

"You're preaching to the choir."

"Viktoria Morfitt, your days of having nothing are gone. If nothing else, you will always have me."

She took a deep breath. "Again...is this a proposal".

Please. Say yes.

"This is a promise. When I propose I'm going to do it properly with a ring and champagne. Not on a manky carpet surrounded by broken glass with an angry mob waiting down below—"

"Oh!" Tori pushed out of his hold and surged to her feet. Her surprisingly steady, optimistic feet. "The protest!"

She raced to the window and used the curtain to shield herself from injury as she boosted back out onto the ledge. She pulled herself carefully to her feet but smiled back at Nathan as she felt his strong hands curl around the waistband of her climbing pants tethering her to him more surely than any metal fixing.

They'd lost some of the crowd but the majority was still there. They all snapped their faces skyward as she reappeared on the ledge her hands raised and their chants of "Save the falcons, save the building," petered out expectantly.

Tori took a deep breath and yelled down to them. "The building stays. The falcons stay."

A surge of energy burst up from below as the crowd roared with elation. Tori almost stumbled at the wave of positivity that buffeted her like a rising thermal current, but Nathan's hands kept her secure. As she knew they always would.

She turned back to look at him, at that gorgeous, twisted smile he got when he was feeling particularly pleased with himself. But this time she understood. She felt it, too.

As the sounds of wild cheering rippled through the streets, two brown shapes exploded from above into the sky, disturbed from their happy nest. Wilma and Fred soared upward, then turned and dive-bombed down a few floors before wheeling right and coming back up past Tori.

As though they were waiting for something.

And then it happened. Two more shapes, smaller, slower, infinitely less proficient, joined their parents on the warm, summer air and the four of them twisted and soared and wheeled toward the Hudson and the rich pickings of the pigeon-rich bridges.

Tori leaned back into the strength of Nathan's grasp and let her imagination take her. It was as though the falcons departed with the demons that had haunted his building—their lives— leaving it clean and pure and ready for a new beginning.

LET'S TALK

Romance

For exclusive extracts, competitions
and special offers, find us online:

- facebook.com/millsandboon
- @MillsandBoon
- @MillsandBoonUK

Get in touch on 01413 063232

MILLS & BOON

THE HEART OF ROMANCE

A ROMANCE FOR EVERY KIND OF READER

MODERN

Prepare to be swept off your feet by sophisticated, sexy and seductive heroes, in some of the world's most glamourous and romantic locations, where power and passion collide.
8 stories per month.

HISTORICAL

Escape with historical heroes from time gone by. Whether your passion is for wicked Regency Rakes, muscled Vikings or rugged Highlanders, awaken the romance of the past.
6 stories per month.

MEDICAL

Set your pulse racing with dedicated, delectable doctors in the high-pressure world of medicine, where emotions run high and passion, comfort and love are the best medicine.
6 stories per month.

True Love

Celebrate true love with tender stories of heartfelt romance, from the rush of falling in love to the joy a new baby can bring, and a focus on the emotional heart of a relationship.
8 stories per month.

Desire

Indulge in secrets and scandal, intense drama and plenty of sizzling hot action with powerful and passionate heroes who have it all: wealth, status, good looks…everything but the right woman.
6 stories per month.

HEROES

Experience all the excitement of a gripping thriller, with an intense romance at its heart. Resourceful, true-to-life women and strong, fearless men face danger and desire - a killer combination!
8 stories per month.

DARE

Sensual love stories featuring smart, sassy heroines you'd want as a best friend, and compelling intense heroes who are worthy of them.
4 stories per month.